"The mo
the book
talent."

Madel

"Like all the best speculative fiction set in the future, *Windswept* is also about the way we live now, and Adam Rakunas tackles what matters most with a metric tonne of humor and heart. A promising, thrilling debut."

Robert Levy, author of The Glittering World

"Lush and exotic, Rakunas's *Windswept* is like the booze that powers his world: a delightful cask aged añejo rum that keeps revealing greater complexity and depth the more time you spend with it. I didn't realize I had been lacking rum-running space opera in my life, but after *Windswept*, I definitely have a thirst for more."

Mark Teppo, author of Earth Thirst and co-author of The Mongoliad

"Adam Rakunas is one funny SOB, and now everyone's going to know it. *Windswept* is a zippy, zany ride, with more fast turns than a Wild Mouse rollercoaster. There's more witty banter and laughs per page than anything I've read in years, making this, my friends, the rarest kind of science-fiction-comedy novel: one that's actually funny. Buckle the hell up."

Daryl Gregory, award-winning author of We Are All Completely Fine

"*Windswept* is a classic noir story shot full of space-rum and rocketed into the future."

Seattle Review of Books

ADAM RAKUNAS

LIKE A BOSS

An Occupied Space novel

ANGRY
ROBOT

ANGRY ROBOT
An imprint of Watkins Media Ltd

Lace Market House,
54-56 High Pavement,
Nottingham,
NG1 1HW
UK

www.angryrobotbooks.com
twitter.com/angryrobotbooks
Strike!

An Angry Robot paperback original 2016

Cover by Kim Sokol
Set in Meridien and Video Tech by Epub Services

Distributed in the United States by Penguin Random House, Inc., New York.

ISBN 978 0 85766 481 5
Ebook ISBN 978 0 85766 482 2

Printed in the United States of America

9 8 7 6 5 4 3 2 1

What the woman who labors wants is the right to live, not simply exist – the right to life as the rich woman has the right to life, and the sun and music and art. You have nothing that the humblest worker has not a right to have also. The worker must have bread, but she must have roses, too. Help, you women of privilege, give her the ballot to fight with.

– Rose Schneiderman, at the
1912 Lawrence textile strike

ONE

I was sitting at my usual spot at Big Lily's when I got a call. The words THE REAL JOB floated in front of my eyes, and I groaned. That this happened on my one day off from the water works meant one thing: something had gone wrong at the Old Windswept Distillery. *My* distillery. I took the call. "What's up?"

"Bearings," said Marolo, my foreman.

I took a sip of heavy mint. "Well, I'm looking out toward the lifter, so I guess it's due west."

"Ha. And ha," said Marolo. "You know which ones I mean."

"I wish I didn't." I got up from my stool and wandered to the lanai. The summer sun sat high in the sky, baking all of Brushhead. The rooftops gleamed, all the photovoltaic paint soaking up photons and sending electricity into bakeries, forges, machinist shops, recording studios, and all the other tiny businesses that kept the neighborhood chugging along. The city's gentle hills rolled down to the ocean, and I ticked off the names of the other Wards: Chavoen, Faoshue, Beukes Point. The sun was too high to reflect off the ocean, but in a few hours the water would turn into liquid gold.

It was a gorgeous sight, but it was nothing compared to the smells.

The afternoon scents of Santee City swept up from the ocean: goat curry and pineapple empanadas and boiling sugar from the six hundred distilleries that dotted the city below. I took in a snootful of air as the wind wafted over the buildings. There were plenty of bad bits: heated rust, acetone from an etching shop, the unique odor of baking, fermented garbage. But every time the breeze shifted, it picked up something new and wonderful: the linseed varnish from Lu Nguyen's violin shop, sweat from America Matisse's dojo on Leaping Frog Street, the smell of crushed cane from a hundred backyard presses. All of it swirled in the salt air, making that heady mix that knocked the first colonists off their feet and gave them second thoughts about remaining a part of the Body Corporate. Windswept, the lot of us.

I should have been enjoying this, but no, THE REAL JOB now had my undivided attention. "Didn't we just clean the press last week?"

"Indeed we did, and now we'll have to do it again."

"Then get to doing."

"It's a little more complicated than that."

I sipped my tea. "I seem to recall paying you an exorbitant sum so I didn't have to worry about complications."

"And yet here we are."

I sighed. "What exactly is the problem, Marolo?"

"I think it's best for you to come out here and see it."

"Jesus, really? This is the first night in months I get to enjoy my cushy life as a distiller! I was going to get dinner, go to Novice Theater to see this monologist perform, pick up strange and exotic men–"

He laughed. "Since when do you go to *monologues*?"

"Where else do you think I find the strange and exotic men?"

The sound in my head turned to rattling. Marolo must have been shifting the old hard line phone from one ear to the other. Oh, my kingdom for a planet full of paied-up people, just to make the business calls go faster. "I am sorry to call you, Padma, but I really think it would be a good idea to come down tonight. Especially if you want this batch to get pressed on time."

That got my attention. "We're ahead of schedule."

"We are *now*. But we won't be for long."

A prickle of ice scritched across the back of my brain. Anything that got in the way of production of Old Windswept Rum was enough to let The Fear stir inside my head. I took a breath and tamped it back. *Not today, asshole.* "Why not?"

"Come and see."

"What, it's too late in the day to use your words?"

He sighed. "Look, this is one of those things that's above my pay grade. You're the owner."

Arg. *You're the owner* was the time-honored euphemism for *your employees are pissed*. Of course Marolo couldn't talk over the phone, not when the people who worked for me were gathered around, listening to his end of the conversation. Or both ends. That was the thing with hard lines; they could be easily spliced. With a pai call, no one could listen in unless they were great at decryption, breaking the law, or both.

I blinked up the time: three forty-six in the afternoon. The distillery was too far for a bike ride, but I could catch the Red Bus in twenty minutes and still make it there and back in time for Six O'Clock. "Okay. I'll catch the next bus and be there in an hour. Can you hold everything together that long?"

Marolo chuckled. "That I can manage."

I killed the call. So, there was a crisis important enough

for me to haul off to the far northern edge of Santee City, but not so important that I could take the time to use public transportation. What the hell was going on?

Whatever it is, you'll probably make it worse, hissed The Fear.

I took one more hit of the afternoon air, deep enough to banish The Fear to its hidey hole in the back of my brain, and returned to the bar. Big Lily had just set down a plate of steaming kumara cakes, which she picked back up when she saw the look on my face. "I'll pack these to go." She got a tiffin-box from under the bar and upended the plate.

"Thanks." I drained my mug. "This is not how today was supposed to work."

"Trouble down at the mill?"

I snatched one of the cakes out of the tiffin-box before she could close it. It singed my fingers, which meant it was at the right temperature. "I'm not so naive to think that life was going to be peaches and curry after I retired, but it would be nice if I could just *enjoy* owning the distillery, you know?"

Big Lily gave me a raised eyebrow. "You have a funny definition of 'retired.'"

I split the kumara cake in two, and its sweet purple insides dribbled onto the bartop. I scooped them up and popped them in my mouth. Heaven. "At least I'm not sitting around listening to people complain about their jobs all day."

"I fail to see how cleaning the mains counts as not working."

I contemplated another kumara cake. I went for it. "Until I can convince someone to give me a giant pile of money or a better gig, cleaning the mains is all I can do."

She shook her head. "I still think you should have fought that judgment. Leaving you on the hook for the lifter reconstruction was wrong."

"I couldn't afford to fight," I said. "That, and most of the lawyers in town didn't want to do business with the woman who blew up the lifter."

"What about the donations?"

"Poured them all into the distillery," I said. "I needed the funds to keep the place running."

"You know, you could always sell out."

I put a hand on my chest. "What? And give up my sole source of economic empowerment?"

"Then you could leverage that place, scale up production, be the biggest rum producer on Santee."

I sighed. "And if I thought it would make a dent in my debt, I would. But it can't, so I won't." That, and the fact that I *needed* the Old Windswept Rum Distillery to be run exactly as it was.

But I couldn't tell that to Big Lily. Or anyone.

Big Lily snapped the lid on the tiffin-box. "Just think about it, okay? I'd hate to see you spend the rest of your life slaving away in Bloombeck's old Slot. Getting out of that job is worth another appeal."

"Thanks." I blinked in payment for my tab. Big Lily didn't try to rebuff me, though it would have been nice if she had. A night on the town wouldn't have sunk me too much, but I could feel the pressure of bills piling up, payroll especially. Today's issue would probably demand a little more of that cash.

I stepped out onto Mercer Boulevard. The place felt dead, but I knew every bistro, bar, and bouncehouse was gearing up for the evening crowd. Tuk-tuk drivers hunched in the front seats of their rides, slurping noodles and trading gossip. The smells of onions, ginger, and lime drifted out of Aunty Gee's Grill, and the plumeria at the corner laundry house gave one last burst of scent in the warm afternoon light. In three hours, this place would be packed with people reuniting after their shifts, looking to see their children, their lovers, their debtors. My neighborhood would jump back to life, and I would be counting down the minutes until Six O'Clock.

Oh, Six O'Clock. Quitting time for some people, the start of a shift for others, and the only thing that had kept my brain from falling apart for the past fourteen years. I had lost track of how many meetings, riots, and dinner dates I had had to cancel in order to make Six O'Clock. Most of my friends just accepted it, though a few made a point of mocking me, saying I was leading a double life as a crime-fighter and/or Ghost Agent for the Big Three. I wondered how disappointed they would be if they found out what I really did at Six O'Clock: I sat down and sipped a finger of Old Windswept Single Batch Rum.

Of course, it wasn't just about the rum. Fourteen years ago, I was a bright-eyed member of the Body Corporate, ready to join the WalWa drones in Colonial Management. The lengthy transit to Santee Anchorage in a semi-comatose state had screwed up my brain functions in a way that gave birth to waking nightmares and that nasty, brain-sapping mental monster I called The Fear. When I had had enough and Breached, Doctor Ropata was the first person I talked to. Non-Corporates didn't have access to the vast array of pharmaceutical solutions that were available to everyone in Thronehill, so he made do with a local solution: Old Windswept. The rum had some mild psychoactives that, when combined with the ritual he designed, helped kickstart my stalled-out prefrontal cortex. I had to draw the blinds closed, light a candle, and picture the vastness of the universe and my little place in it.

Whether he was speaking from experience or bullshit, it didn't matter. The ritual (and the rum) worked, keeping my brain functioning and The Fear at bay. I had to admit it worked even better now that I owned the Old Windswept

Distillery and didn't have to worry about the supply of rum running out.

Of course, it would have been nice to figure out just why that transit had damaged my brain, whether it was the hibernant the techs had poured into my sleeping bag or the length of the trip or, hell, even the bag itself. It also would have been nice if it rained almond bialys instead of water. I had long learned to accept that Old Windswept was the way to remain a functioning (and occasionally happy) human being. Granted, if I ever met the WalWa Travel Comfort Systems scientists who designed and built the outfit I'd used, I probably wouldn't hesitate to punch them in the neck.

I popped open the tiffin-box and took a bite of a kumara cake. It was crisp on the outside and molten gooey goodness on the inside. Every bite was a wonder, and I laughed at the thought of where I'd be if I hadn't walked out of that WalWa office fourteen years ago. All that triple-scrubbed air inside the Colonial Management Complex at Thronehill would never smell as good as this, not even on Employee Appreciation Day when Human Resources would pump artificial flavored spearmint and mild stimulants into the HVAC system. Even on my worst, lowest day, when I was cleaning out the worst, lowest intakes in the water treatment plant, I knew I would never return to that life. Nothing could drag me back. Not after everything I'd built and bought and outright stolen.

I rounded the corner onto Beda Street, where the Red Line bus stop squatted between a strip club and a library. The bus system had started a year ago. A few Breaches had come shimmying down the cable in a loaded cargo can, hiding among the flatpacked buses. Rather than give the parts back, the Union confiscated and built them out. Hacking the control software turned out to be a pain, leading to the occasional bus stopping dead in its tracks. Still, it meant more people could get to and from the kampong, and it was cheaper for me than hiring a tuk-tuk, even though Jilly's company still cut me the Friends And Family rate.

The Red Line went all the way from Brushhead to Tanque, the Ward on the far edge of town where the late Estella Tonggow had set up the Old Windswept Distillery. She had been able to cruise there and back in an armored limousine. I had to settle for the bus. Though, as I approached the stop, I might not have been able to settle even for that.

The stop was little more than a caneplas box surrounding a pair of benches. Three sunburned people in ragged clothes snoozed on the benches, their bags at their feet. A scrawled sign glued to the side of the shelter said NO SERVICE TODAY DUE TO. The rest of the sign had been torn away, and the greasy fingerprints on the paper left the reasons to my imagination. I blinked up the Public and saw no notices about a system stoppage. "Excuse me," I said to the people, "what's up with the bus?"

One of them, a woman with a massive salt-and-pepper plait, opened her eyes and said, "What? You never ride a bus before?"

I took a step back. Her eyes were hard and cold, like a shark on the hunt. I peeled the sign off the shelter and held it up. "I don't think any of us are taking this bus."

She squinted at the sign and groaned. "Aw, spit. That must have happened after we got here."

"How long ago was that?"

Now she squinted at me. "What's it to you?"

I gave her a side-eyed look. Not everyone in Santee City was a friendly, happy, we're-all-in-it-together type. But this fast pivot toward aggression felt off. She didn't look or smell drunk, but I felt my guts shrivel the way they always did before Last Call. I held up my hands and gave her a gentle smile with no teeth. "Just wondering. I need this bus to get to work."

She dialed back the squint a little. "Yeah. Us, too." She nudged the other two people awake. "Hey. Our ride's not coming."

"Fuggoff," said one of them, a man whose face was more beard than skin.

The woman with the plait walloped him upside the head. "Don't talk to me that way, jackass."

The third, another woman whose hair was short and slicked back, shoved both of them. "All of you shut up. I'm tryna sleep before our ride gets here."

"It's not *coming*," said Plait Woman. I blinked her face into the Public so I could get her name, but she didn't register. None of them did. That was weird as hell. They all had Union fists under their old Indenture tattoos. These people didn't just fall out of orbit into the middle of Brushhead.

"It will," said Short And Slicked. "Just wait."

"We've been waiting all *day*," said Beard Face.

"Then you can wait some more. Shut it."

"But they said we were gonna start working this morning 'cause they had a deadline–"

The look that Short And Slicked threw at Beard Face was so sharp that *I* felt it. He shut up and looked at the ragged bag at his feet. I glanced at it and saw the seven-pointed star stenciled on its surface. I looked behind the bus shelter; squeezed between the library and the strip joint was a police sub-station, closed for the day. All of it clicked together: the star was the symbol for Maersk Island, Santee Anchorage's prison. The substation was closed because releases were filed in the morning. These three hadn't been able to summon a tuk-tuk because their pais had restricted access. I couldn't blink up their profiles on the Public because they hadn't earned them back. They were parolees.

"I heard nothing," I said.

"There was nothing to hear," said Plait Woman. "We're just waiting for a ride."

"You want me to call you one?" I said.

She waved me off. "We got it covered."

I nodded. Eighteen months ago, finding them housing and jobs and counseling would have been my concern. It didn't happen often during my time as Ward Chair, but it was always tough. Parolees were kept on short leashes until enough people began to vouch for their behavior, and that meant sticking them in the worst of the non-Slot jobs. People got sent to Maersk for crimes against other people: assault, rape, murder. I've been all over this planet, but I've never had reason to visit Maersk. Not even when Evanrute Saarien was sent there.

I clenched my jaw. I hadn't given Saarien a moment's thought until now. He'd been a Ward Chair from Sou's Reach, home of the first cane refinery in the city. While some people would have seen that as an opportunity to be a good steward to a historic facility, Saarien turned it into the base for destroying the entire trans-stellar economy. He blew smoke up the Executive Committee's ass, telling them he was using his Ward's maintenance funds to build a community of artisans to boost the local economy. They were so taken with the weavers and glassblowers, they failed to notice him building an underground refinery to grow and process new strains of sugarcane that would have poisoned *all* the cane in Occupied Space. If he had succeeded, billions of people would have died from the ensuing upheaval. The son of a bitch had tried to burn me alive, and I sometimes wish I'd left him to die in the firestorm he'd intended for me. Instead, he was rotting away on Maersk, serving fifty years for fraud, embezzlement, conspiracy, kidnapping, attempted murder (including mine), and generally being an asshole. I entertained the notion of asking these three parolees if they had seen him, but the discussion probably wouldn't end well. What would be the point in reminding them they'd been in prison?

A few moments later, a beat-up covered lorry pulled up to the bus stop, and the passenger-side window rolled down. "Get in," said a girl's voice. The parolees gathered their gear and hopped into the back. The girl leaned toward the side window to get a better look at them, then at me. Her eyes went wide, and so did mine. She was one of my employees, a Freeborn kid named Ly Huang. I didn't mind my people moonlighting, so long as they did it when they weren't supposed to be on my clock. "Oy!" I yelled, stepping toward the lorry.

Ly Huang's face disappeared from the mirror, and the lorry rumbled away in a cloud of cane diesel exhaust. I blinked in pictures of the lorry's tailgate, only to see that it didn't have a license tag. The parolees all looked at me from the back, hunger in their eyes. What the hell had that kid gotten mixed up in? Is this what Marolo couldn't tell me over the phone? Sweet and Merciful Buddha, this was not how being a member of the landed gentry was supposed to go.

I made a note to yell at Marolo about this withheld information and blinked up the time: three fifty-nine. I was going to have to spring for a tuk-tuk. I blinked a text to the We Laugh At Physics Travel Corporation, the company my protégé Jilly ran. She had put aside her dreams of becoming an airship pilot as the planetary economy slowed. Santee Anchorage still sent more industrial molasses up the cable than any system within a six-jump radius, but the demand for everything else we made had dwindled. It made more sense for a young woman Jilly's age to keep schlepping people around on the surface than via the air.

She'd done really well for herself since her days as a cab driver, even joining the Union and earning a fist on her cheek. But she could never get a pai, not unless we convinced the right people with the right tech and the right skills to hop down to our dirtball. In the meantime, though, she carried a battered handheld that I could text at a moment's notice. Now was one of those moments. *Need pickup to avoid horrible catastrophe*, I texted.

On it, Boss, she texted back. The kid had gotten really good at texting. She could type with her thumbs almost as fast as I could with my eye movements.

Two minutes later, a candy apple red tuk-tuk screeched to a halt in front of the bus stop. A young woman with biceps the size of ripe coconuts huddled behind the wheel. "The boss sends her regards," she said as I hopped in behind her.

"What, she couldn't get drive herself?"

The driver turned and laughed over her shoulder. "Not unless there's a race for beer money."

"Sometimes I wish that kid had stuck with flight school," I said.

"I don't," said the big woman. "Jilly's pay rates are great, and she lets us take our tuk-tuks home."

"Is that an issue?"

"When you've got tuk-tuks getting boosted from every depot in the city, it sure is."

"Well, that's a damn shame," I said. "There was a time when no one screwed with the Drivers' Committee. Not unless they wanted to get their own teeth fed to them."

"We'll find the thieves, don't you worry," said the woman, and I felt sorry for whoever was going to be on the business end of her fists. She wore a tailored blouse that managed to make her look businesslike and even more physically impressive than if she'd worn a tank top. Her arms and shoulders bulged as she fiddled with the tuk-tuk's console. She had either spent her life slinging bundles of cane or winning prize fights. Maybe both. "What's your name?"

"Sirikit."

I held out my hand. "Padma Mehta. You know where we're going?"

Sirikit nodded as she crushed my hand. "The Old Windswept Distillery, right?"

"You got it."

"I'll have you there in twenty minutes."

"But it's a forty minute drive to Tanque."

Sirikit flexed her neck as she turned toward the steering wheel. "Not the way *I* drive." She punched the stereo to life, and Balinese opera blasted out from the speakers. I had just enough time to buckle in before we took off like enthusiastic bullets.

TWO

Nineteen minutes and forty-two seconds later (I had blinked up a timer, because watching it kept my mind off the terror of Sirikit cutting around cargo lorries and land trains at ridiculously unsafe speeds), the tuk-tuk came to a gentle halt in front of the two simple pourform buildings that housed the Old Windswept Distillery. Estella Tonggow, the late founder, had been a brilliant chemist and designer. And, as I dug deeper into the books, I learned she had also found new and interesting ways to redefine "frugal." While other distillers built fancy facilities with verandas and swooping lines, Tonggow had spent the bare minimum on two squat blocks that required no maintenance and could withstand force ten winds. The place was as ugly as a swamp hog's backside, but it was what happened inside that counted.

Marolo stood outside the entrance, his face streaked with grease. He held up a caneplas box that rattled as he shook it. I could tell that he wanted to talk about the box and its contents, but it could wait. "Shouldn't Ly Huang be here?"

He gave me a crooked smile. "Ah. I'm glad you decided to dispense with the small talk and get right to work."

"I'd like *her* to get right to work. Why did I see her driving a lorry when she should be helping crush cane?"

"We'll get to that." He tipped the box toward me. "These bearings are shot."

I peered at the two dozen metal balls inside the box, all bouncing off each other as he shook it. "We just replaced these! Hell, *I* just replaced them."

"They're defective," he said. "They worked for about a hundred hours, and then they started pitting."

I picked up a bearing and cursed. What should have been a perfect sphere looked like it had been nicked and scratched with forty-grit sandpaper. I sucked on my teeth to calm myself, because I knew there was no point in getting angry at Marolo.

"You need me to stick around?" asked Sirikit from the driver's seat.

"Please." I turned back to Marolo and held up the bearing. "These were rated for ten thousand hours, if I recall."

"Fifteen thousand, actually," said Marolo. "I made sure we saved the boxes. And the receipts. On paper."

"Paper?" I shook my head. "Whatever happened to using a tablet?"

"You know anyone on this rock making replacement tablet parts?" He shook the box. "These were relatively cheap. Getting circuitry to fix a busted tablet would cost more than you pay me in a year."

"I pay you a lot."

"That you do," said Marolo. "But unless you know of someone growing computer hardware on Santee, I'll stick to paper. I can always get more of it."

I dropped the ruined ball bearing back into the box. "When can we get more of these?"

"We have them. Like I said, they were cheap."

I sighed. "Then why in hell did you haul me all the way out here? Is it so I can fire Ly Huang? You know you have the power to do that without my say-so."

"Ly Huang's absence is one of the many things I wanted to talk with you about, starting with the way this place runs," said Marolo. He put the box on the ground. "Those bearings are just the icing on the ridiculous cake."

"I told you this was going to be a weird gig."

"Yeah, but not that it was going to be like this!" said Marolo, pointing back at the distillery. "You have machinery that dates back to the Information Age! You're using parts that break down when there are upgrades that will last until the heat death of the universe! You've got people beating cane with cricket bats!"

I shrugged. "It's the way Madame Tonggow did it."

He threw his hands into the air. "And there it is. The one thing that everyone says when I question why they're doing the stupid thing that they're doing. 'Estella Tonggow always did it this way, so that's why we keep doing it.' Why, Padma? For God's sake, why do you keep invoking that woman like she's the Creator?"

"Because she *is*," I said. "She made this distillery and this rum, and whatever she did we are going to keep on doing because it *works*."

"But even she must have improvised or changed or–"

I held up a hand to Marolo's chest. "I don't care. If we want to keep making Old Windswept Rum, that means we make it her way. We don't have the room to experiment, especially since neither of us are chemists like she was."

"We can find chemists."

"And they are welcome to monkey around with their own formulas in their own labs. But not here." In the back of my head, The Fear uncoiled itself, its frozen breath sending shivers down my spine. *Maybe you should tell him why?*

Marolo actually took a step back. I cleared my throat.

"Look, I appreciate you looking out for this place. I know it all seems weird–"

"Because it *is*–"

"But it's only been eighteen months since I've taken over. Madame Tonggow had thirty years of experience running the distillery, and that was after another thirty years of playing with MacDonald Heavy's chemistry sets." I laughed. "All my time at the plant didn't set me up for the intricacies of her operation. That's why I hired *you*."

He made a face. "I thought it was because the previous foreman had quit on you."

"So we had some personal friction." I put an arm around his shoulder and guided him up to the press house. "That always happens when an outfit changes hands. And, hey, hasn't this gig been better than schlepping cane out of the kampong?"

He nodded. "It's certainly weirder."

"No arguments there."

Marolo stopped at the door to the press house and opened it for me. There was no need for a lock because there was nothing inside worth stealing. Everything was third-hand and held together with baling wire and foul language. The giant rollers on the cane press were scarred and scratched and completely worthless even for scrap. The still itself, a conglomeration of funnels, coils, pots and pans, all made from copper or coral steel or, in the case of the second condenser, palm fronds, wouldn't have gotten more than a couple of yuan because there would have been no way to take it out the door except in tiny pieces.

I took a whiff of the air inside: machine oil, damp metal, and the bright green scent of crushed cane juice. Bits of bagasse littered the floor, and the giant rollers glinted in the afternoon light. "These still need a wiping," I said, walking up to the rollers as The Fear hissed about how good it would feel to stick my head between them and see how quickly they'd crush me. The Fear, in addition to being a bully, was also stupid as hell, seeing how it would go along with my brain. Yet another thing to bring up to a shrink.

"I know, but that's somebody else's job."

I turned around and gave him a look. "Spoken like a Union diehard."

He chuckled without mirth. "You take that back."

"I will if you tell me why the rollers aren't clean."

Marolo grimaced. "I had someone who was doing that, but then she up and left."

"Who?"

He cleared his throat.

"I don't get it," I said. "Ly Huang's been here almost as long as you have, and I thought she liked it. Hell, she's one of the few people who doesn't wince when I sing with whatever bollypop comes over the wireless. If anything, she sings louder than me."

"You haven't been here in a while," he said, grabbing a couple of towels from a work bench and tossing me one. "Two weeks ago, she showed up long enough to clear out her locker and tell me to take my job and shove it."

"What?"

He nodded. "Caught me off guard, too. She told me off, then she walked away."

"Except I saw her *today*, in Brushhead, driving a lorry."

He gave me a look. "You sure it was her?"

"She took off as soon as she saw I saw her. It was her."

I got to work wiping down the rollers with Marolo. While some distilleries contracted out their pressings, Tonggow had insisted on keeping the whole process in-house. She even owned the land where the cane was grown, saying the terroir was vital. The fact that the faces of the rollers were scratched and dented was also vital. Everything, as far as I was concerned, was vital, because it continued to work for me. I tested every new batch, which was an odd experience. For years, I'd hoarded bottles of Old Windswept, never cracking a new one until I'd drained the previous. Now I got to dip into the supply whenever I wanted. The Fear hated that. I loved it.

But leaving cane juice on the press, that was a no-no. The rollers' beat-up surface meant that all kinds of lovely bacteria would grow if left alone. Every day, the press had to be wiped down, then sanitized with vinegar (not bleach, because, again, *Tonggow*) to make sure nothing contaminated the freshly squeezed cane juice. Marolo and I knocked it out within fifteen minutes. "Did Ly Huang say anything before she left?"

Marolo grunted. "Other than that I was a sellout, giving up my natural born rights to keep a rotten system going."

"Since when was she into labor theory?"

He shook his head. "You know how these kids are. One day, they're plugging away, happy as clams. The next, they're railing about worker exploitation."

"Yeah, I'm sure it happens all the time."

The rollers cleaned, we wheeled over an ancient hydraulic jack to the press's left side. I coiled chain around the axle, and we took turns loosening the seven-centimeter bolts that kept the rotor housing in place. We always did the left side first because it was what Tonggow did. Also, it always stuck more, so doing the right side would feel easy.

I finished the last bolt and handed it to Marolo. He handed me a packet of new ball bearings, and I slipped them into place. "So, we're only going to get a hundred hours out of these?"

"If we're lucky," he said. "I'm no engineer, but even I can tell inferior materials when I see them. All this equipment that Tonggow insisted on using, it's all crap."

I made sure the bearings were set, then refit the housing. I had to give it an extra tap with the butt of the wrench. "But it's *cheap* crap."

"Which you will not be able to afford in a few years."

I gave him a sideways glare. "Worrying about the books is *my* problem."

"Well, it's everyone's when we depend on the paycheck." He had rinsed and dried the bolts, making sure to wipe some palm oil on the threads. "You know, I talked with the old-timers, the ones who've stayed on. They said that Tonggow was rich as hell, that she blew all kinds of cash."

"That she did." The bolts were numbered, so I put number one into place and started cranking. "But her fortune is still tied up in probate, and it isn't connected to the distillery. I don't have that kind of money, and I don't think I ever will."

"Maybe if you found that missing case of Ten-Year."

"Oh, God. I've told you: there's no such thing. We don't age our rum that long anymore."

"But we should," said Marolo. "I've always got people telling me they'd pay top yuan for a shot."

"Then they can buy a barrel of our Classic and let it sit for a decade. They want Tonggow's mystique, and we don't have that any more. We've just got the old standby, and that brings in enough money to keep us all happy."

"But what will you do if that runs out?"

"Work, just like I always have." I put in bolt number two and took a breath before tightening it. This one always threatened to go out of alignment and strip its threads.

Marolo cleared his throat. "And, um, what about us?"

Ah. I gave number two a crank and rested the wrench against my leg. "I told you when you came on board there were no guarantees. The chances are still really good that I'll bring this whole distillery down in flames. I might even do it literally, since Old Windswept is one hundred and fifty proof."

"Please don't joke about that," said Marolo, handing me bolt number three. "I did enough slash-and-burn drills when I was a kid." He snorted. "Dig, cover, hold, my ass."

"I don't think we have to worry about that, seeing how Tonggow made everything out of metal and pourform." I cranked in the bolt and reached for number four. "Are you really that worried, Marolo? Am I mismanaging this place?"

"I didn't say that."

"But you've sure implied it."

He quirked his mouth and held up bolt number five. "I know you are incredibly busy back in Brushhead. I just want to make sure you're aware of everything that's going on here."

"Like the fact that you and I are the only ones here on a Thursday afternoon?"

"Ah. So you *are* aware."

I cranked in the last two bolts. "Ly Huang's not the only one who's left, is she?"

"Well, she's the only one I can't get a hold of."

"Where is everyone else, then?"

Marolo looked away as we lowered the roller back in place. "I think everyone else has quit without quitting."

I stopped the jack in mid-crank. "I've heard of a lot of passive-aggressive labor moves in my time, but this sounds new."

"Nobody wants to come in because they're convinced you're going to lay them off."

"Well, people do tend to lose their jobs when they don't perform them."

Marolo took a breath, then caught himself before he could speak. Two years I'd worked with him, and he was never one to beat around the bush. It was one of his better qualities, and certainly one I wanted in the person in charge of maintaining production of the one thing that kept me sane. Whatever he had to say, it was going to be big, and probably a bit weird.

"This is a hard thing for all of us," he said. "You know how rare it is for us Freeborn to leave the kampong and work in the city. It just doesn't feel right, the way all you Union people stare off into space when you're typing with your eyes."

"You know, there are Freeborn in the Union," I said. "The Prez, for instance."

"But she's rare," said Marolo. "Besides, she actually likes being a manager."

"And you don't?"

"I run a small distillery," he said. "She's gotta run a government. That means more people, more money, more headaches." He made a face. "Not that I wouldn't mind us getting our act together. I don't know how you Union people do it."

"Probably because we don't resort to blowing stuff up."

"Hey, it was never proven that the Freeborn Organizing Committee had *anything* to do with those bombings."

I held up my hands in surrender. "I know. I know. Besides, that was all before my time. I was still an Indenture when all that went down."

Marolo gave a *harrumph*. "That sounds like a lot of other people I know. It was either before their time or beneath their interest."

"You think I don't care about working conditions for Freeborn people?"

"I think you may not know the whole story."

I leaned on the jack. "I have plenty of time, apparently."

He waved a hand. "No, forget it. It *is* history now. And it's just as well the FOC burned out. That would have meant turning this place into more of a city."

I resisted the temptation to tell him that Tanque, the Ward we were in, barely qualified as "city." We were kilometers away from the edges of Santee City, more in the kampong, really. The only things that kept us connected were the single-lane road made of crushed palm crab shells and the line of ramshackle network towers that ran alongside said road. But, when you've spent your entire life surrounded by sugarcane and people without computers in their eyeballs, your perspective would be different, too.

"I hope you guys don't all think I'm some lunatic who's going to destroy your lives," I said. "I've never made anyone sign long-term contracts or anything that ties them to working here. And what about Martha? I got her that gig over at Bill Beaulieu's when she wanted to be closer to her dad."

"This is all true," said Marolo. "But the city's not the kampong, Padma. It moves faster, it's not dependent on rainfall or cane rats or fungus."

"So, it's different from what you know."

"Exactly!" he said, beaming.

I climbed down from the ladder and put a hand on his shoulder. "And it is different for everyone else who comes here. It's a shock for someone who Breaches, no matter where they lived before. Hell, I've been here fourteen years, and I get thrown every now and then."

"What, you?"

"Yes, me," I said. "There are little things, like using tiffin-boxes instead of food wrappers or shortages of staples like coffee or curried ketchup. The big things, too. I was born in a hospital that looked like a greenhouse. My pediatrician was a palm tree."

He rolled his eyes. "See, that's not fair, trying to make me feel like a hick."

"I'm serious!" I said. "My pediatrician was terrified of getting germs from his patients, so he used an animatronic palm tree to talk with us. He'd operate it by remote control from a bunker. Sweet guy, always gentle with the exams. That would never happen here. It wouldn't be a thought for anyone." I squeezed his shoulder. "I know this sounds cliché, but all of us, Union and Freeborn, we're all trying to live our lives and not get too screwed by the Big Three."

He nodded. "That's a great line."

"Isn't it? And so's this: are you going to do this zen quitting on me, too? Or are you going to help me figure out how to get everyone back?"

"That's easy," he said. "Everyone just needs to see you here more often."

I took a step back. "Really? That's it? Everyone went home because they think I'm some absentee employer? The city's only a forty-minute ride away!"

"But it's still the city. They want to know you'll work out here, with them."

I sighed. "Okay. What the hell. I don't have that much of a life, I might as well spend the little I've got out here."

Marolo smiled. "Also, everyone would like you to talk with that guy from the Co-Op."

I froze. "*What* guy from the Co-Op?"

Marolo waved his hand over his chin. "You know. The one with the funky beard. The kind that looks like he's got a crab hanging from his lower lip."

I didn't have to blink through my buffer to know who he meant. "Vikram Ramaddy? What's he been doing here?"

"Trying to get the Co-Op to buy you out."

The wrench slipped out of my grip and clattered on the pourform floor. "He... what?"

Marolo's face crumpled. "Oh. You mean, you haven't talked with him?"

I took a deep breath to keep myself from screaming. "No," I said, my voice level as the ocean on a windless day. "I don't believe I have. Though I'm sure as hell about to. Probably with a cricket bat." I let out that breath, drew in a longer, deeper one. "Did he make an offer to you?"

"Not as such," said Marolo, taking a step back from me.

I gave him a glare. "Marolo, did the vice-chair of the Santee Anchorage Distillers Co-Operative give you an offer on this place? Or is this some new kind of zen aggression?"

"It's nothing like that," said Marolo. "He just came here yesterday, took a look around, made sure our payments were up-to-date, asked what I thought about the cane harvest–"

"Wait." I held up my hands. "What *about* the harvest?"

Marolo waved his hands like he was shooing a fly. "Other producers are having problems getting the cane they were contracted. But that's because they're idiots who work with idiot growers. Remember that guy in Bangsar? The one who flooded his fields with raw sewage because he thought it would help the soil?"

"The guy who lost a foot to sepsis, yeah. What about him?"

"Those are the growers Vikram's dealing with, and it doesn't affect us, because we grow our own." He let out a slow breath, his body curling around his midsection. He gave me a smile. "That, by the way, is one of the things I'm glad I don't have to worry about. Nothing's threatening our supply of cane."

"No, but Vikram Ramaddy is threatening my calm and placid mind. What did he *say*?"

Marolo cleared his throat, and some of the tension returned to his spine. "He was worried about the future of this distillery because of certain rumors he'd been hearing. Rumors about people not showing up to work, about slowed production, about…" His eyes flicked at me, then looked as far away as possible.

I put my hands behind my back and rocked back and forth on my feet, my work boots squeaking against the floor. "About?"

He opened his mouth, closed it, then blurted, "About the state of your mental health. He was worried that all of this work, here and in the plant, it was all too much pressure, and he wasn't sure you'd be able to meet your obligations to the Co-Op. And if that happened, if I saw any signs that you were going to crack, then he and the other owners would be happy to make sure we all kept our jobs and kept this place running by making a takeover offer under Article Thirty-Three."

I stopped rocking. "Article Thirty-Three?"

"You know it, right?"

"I have the entire Co-Op Charter memorized, and I am intimately familiar with Article Thirty-Three." I bent down and picked up the wrench, put it back into the toolbox.

Marolo exhaled and relaxed. "I really thought you'd be more upset."

"Oh, I am," I said, looking at all the other wrenches and screwdrivers and spanners in the box and wondering how I could use each of them to murder the other members of the Co-Op. "However, I am a professional, so I'm not going to let my anger take charge of my actions. Not until I'm sure I can legally punch that crab-bearded motherfucker into the middle of the ocean."

Marolo nodded. "That sounds more like you."

"He actually invoked Article Thirty-Three?"

Marolo gave a half-shrug. "Well, like I said, it wasn't an official *offer*, but it sure sounded like he was dancing around the subject."

I growled. "See, *this* is the reason why it would be worth

you having some kind of recording device on your person at all times. So you can stop people from sneaky underhanded moves and force them to pull blatant underhanded moves."

Marolo shrugged. "I did tell him thanks but no thanks."

"Doesn't matter," I said, looking around the distillery. "He smells blood in the water, and he's not going to stop until the Co-Op gobbles this place up."

"But they can't do that, right? Not yet?"

"We are *fine*, finance-wise. I can show you the numbers."

He held up his hands. "I know them. You sing them to me every payday."

"Then I'll have to sing louder, because you're the only one who's heard." I opened my arms wide and did a slow circle. "What do you see?"

Marolo beetled his brows. "An empty distillery?"

"And why is it empty?"

He scrunched his forehead a bit, then opened his eyes wide. "Oh, Lord. Everyone has panicked, and that will mean nothing gets done, so of *course* the place will go under." He looked at the toolbox. "Now *I* want to hit him. What should I use?"

"You leave that up to me."

"Not on your life." He picked up a torque wrench. "He wants to come in here and screw up the best job I've ever had? Not without a fight."

"Which, like I said, you will leave up to *me*." I held out my hand. After hesitating a moment, he gave me the wrench. "I'm the owner. I'm in the Co-Op. They want to try and screw us with rules and procedure? We'll use 'em right back."

"You got a lawyer?"

For a brief moment, I thought about Banks and wondered where his skinny ass had gone to. By now, the ship he'd boarded would be near the Red Line, ready to jump off into the Great Beyond. I didn't expect to hear from him ever again, but, right now, it would have been nice to ping him a message and bully him into helping me.

"I used to," I said. "But I think I can handle it." I patted the torque wrench. "Especially if I've got *this*."

THREE

After telling Sirikit to drive much, much slower, we eased to a stop in front of the head office of the Santee Anchorage Rum Producers' Co-Operative, way the hell northwest in Xochimilco Grove. This was where the sidewalk ended and the kampong began. The Co-Op office, an architectural student's fever dream of warped glass, reclaimed hull plates, and ironpalm deckwork, huddled at the end of Chung Kuong Street. Behind it spread the kampong, the great fields of sugarcane that rolled beyond the western horizon. The only thing I could hear (after Sirikit killed the stereo) was the rustle of millions of hectares of cane, their leaves shaking in the evening breeze.

Sirikit sniffed. "I thought it would smell more like rum."

"Not here," I said, hopping out of the tuk-tuk. "This place is nothing but business." I pointed at the buildings that lined the street. "Everything here used to support the distilleries, back when there were only a few of them. Sand would get hauled up to that plant" – I nodded at one squat square coated with soot – "and melted into glass for the bottling plant *there*" – I turned to a triangular building made entirely of blue-green glass – "before getting labelled *there*." Now I looked right at the site of the Co-Op.

"Not anymore?"

"Too many distilleries now," I said. "Not enough room. Also, some members like to control every aspect of their operation, but they stick with the Co-Op."

"Why?"

I shook my head. "Damned if I know. You need anything?"

Sirikit scratched her neck. "I'd kill for some omusubi right now."

I handed her a hundred yuan note. "Two streets south, three streets west. Find the place with the blue maneki-neko on the door. Ask for Ian or Keiko, and they'll hook you up."

She grinned. "You expect me to spend this whole blue boy?"

"Depends on how hungry you are. Come back in twenty minutes, please."

Sirikit zipped away for food while I stood in front of the Co-Op. I tapped the torque wrench against my thigh, wondering how I would have to play this.

Swing first, ask questions later, hissed The Fear.

"Shut *up*," I murmured, blinking up the time. Four fifty-eight. Oy.

I'd been here every two weeks ever since I first showed up with the deed to the distillery, and every time I'd wanted to claw my eyes out. It wasn't the members (most of whom were lovely) or the building itself (which had a really nice view from the second story that made me feel like I was on a boat on the edge of a great green ocean). No, it was the meetings.

One insomniac night, when I'd had way too much coffee and not nearly enough sex, I tried to bore myself to sleep by recounting how many meetings I'd attended over my entire career, starting from when I was still an Indenture in the glorious Life Corporate. I could access footage from my pai, of course, but I thought the best way to bring my brain back into neutral was to drag the recollections out of my memory. From university to business school to my WalWa gig to becoming Ward Chair, I had probably attended three thousand, two hundred ninety-four meetings. None of them, not even the times when I had to negotiate between the teams that controlled the soap supply and the ones who mucked out the water plant's shit tanks, were as interminable as the ones I had attended at the Co-Op.

I had hoped that everyone would be as passionate and mysterious as Estella Tonggow, but they all turned out to be penny-pinching parliamentary procedural nerds. They made motions and counter motions just to discuss where to order pastries, and that was only after the Pastry Subcommittee had determined that it was financially feasible to even *have* pastries at the Co-Op's monthly meetings. Members spent more time jockeying for assignments to study groups than they did discussing the actual running of the Co-Op upon which our incomes (and my sanity) depended. What should have taken thirty minutes at the most would stretch on for hours until, out of desperation, I'd make a motion to run through the real meaty items on the agenda. It usually worked, but I had to threaten whoever sat next to me to second the motion or else.

Now, I'd always had the feeling that there was a second, deeper group that kept things humming along, one that met somewhere tucked away from eavesdropping and the Co-Op's lengthy by-laws. Tonggow would never confirm, and everyone else would always deny, that this was true, but the fact that the six hundred distilleries scattered across the planet had managed to keep the Co-Op functioning and profitable told me that *someone* had a steady hand on the tiller and another on a cricket bat. I only had to look and wait and I would get a sign. Maybe Vikram Ramaddy's visit to my distillery (*my* distillery, dammit) was the opening move I'd needed.

I gave the torque wrench another tap on my leg. Going in swinging was not the right move, as good as it might have felt. I had friends and allies here, people who'd lent me time and expertise when they hadn't had to. They probably would abandon me if I walked in and smashed everything in my path. I wouldn't blame them; violence had threatened to tear the Co-Op apart before, and it was no longer tolerated. Mutual benefits meant mutual profits, and that meant everyone had to behave themselves or face expulsion.

But that didn't mean I had to play the helpless sucker. If someone with Vikram's mojo was trying to undermine me that meant I had to let him know I wouldn't be intimidated. I leaned to my right and put the wrench through the hammer loop in my cargo trousers. It hung there, just out of immediate reach, but close enough for anyone to see. As far as I knew, implied violence was still okay under the by-laws.

A young woman in a business suit came out of the building, her face lit with a smile as she flipped through a sheaf of papers. She stopped short of bumping into me, and the smile vanished when she saw the Don't-Mess-With-Me look on my face. "Don't worry," I said. "I'm a Co-Op member."

She smiled again, and there was something about her perfect skin and perfect teeth that screamed *Life Corporate*. She had no tattoo on her cheek, however. Otherwise, she could have been me, if I'd have Breached right after business school. "In that case, can I interest you in contributing to the Co-Op Mutual Fund? It's a way to share our success with the rest of the planet."

"Maybe another time," I said, jiggling my leg. The wrench clanked, and her eyes drifted down to it. She nodded and hustled away as fast as her pumps could carry her.

I entered the building, the battered steel doors whispering behind me. The interior offices were built around a central atrium filled with all the varieties of heirloom cane, the kind that made rum instead of industrial fuel. A white kid in his twenties sat behind a desk made of burnished metal, its top covered by cheap brochures hawking Co-Op rums and the Co-Op Mutual, a scheme that got suckers to invest in the Co-Op without having any voting rights.

The kid's un-inked face stared down at a terminal. Soon, Freeborn like him were going to outnumber Breaches like me, and I had no idea what would happen. Now, however, I had age, authority, and a very heavy wrench.

I tapped on the desk, and the kid looked up and gave me a smile so sweet my pancreas freaked out. "Good evening, Ms Mehta! How may I help you?" The name plate in front of him said TODD.

"Is Vikram in?"

Todd's smile flickered. I didn't wait for a response. Around the table, through the atrium, and up the stairs I went, the kid's feeble pleadings following me. Vikram had the third-best office in the building, the one with an eastern-facing window looking out over the city and the water beyond. The Co-Op Chair, Elisheba McInnerny, got the best office, the one opposite Vikram's; its windows emptied onto the kampong so the room would fill every morning with the deep green of the cane. The second-best office, the one in between both, went to the member with the best production that month. Tonggow had never won that space, and I hadn't felt the need to compete for it either.

I blinked my pai into recording and gave Vikram the

courtesy of knocking twice before opening his door. He stood at the eastern window, his back to me. In his left hand he held a crumpled piece of paper. In the other was a bottle with a few centiliters of golden rum swirling around the bottom. He didn't flinch when I barked his name. He just turned to me, and I shuddered. Deep bags hung under his red, puffy eyes. His Indenture tattoo, a galleon's steering wheel, stood out on his blotchy skin. Snot dribbled out of his nostrils down into his mustache, where the sunset-orange dye he so loved on his facial hair had run like mascara from hell. The stuff leaked down his chin and neck, staining his otherwise bright white shirt.

Vikram burst into tears. "Oh, Padma! Thank God you're here! We are *so* fucked!"

I took a moment to drink this in. Also, to make sure I hadn't been hit on the head.

No, I was not hallucinating. Vikram Ramaddy, his lower face and shirtfront painted bright orange, stood in front of his window. He cried, but it was the desperate crying of someone who had just been told that the little tummy bug he'd been diagnosed with was actually untreatable cancer that had also spread to his balls. It was the crying of someone at the end of his tether. Seeing how Vikram was the most uptight human I'd ever met, he had to have been in a seriously bad way to fall apart like this.

I did not smile. "Vikram, what is going on?"

"The end of days, that's what." He nodded and swigged from the bottle. "Oh, God, we're done. We're *so* done." He swayed his way to his desk, knocking over papers as he flopped down on the top like it was a bed. "How could this happen? What are we gonna *do*?"

I had prepared myself for a confrontation filled with shouts and recriminations and me taking the wrench to some of Vikram's furniture. But I had no idea how to deal with a blubbering man leaking orange snot all over his paperwork. I've had people fall apart on me before, that wasn't new. But I hadn't wanted to kick their asses beforehand.

I cleared my throat and crouched in front of the desk, keeping my head level with his. "Vikram? Are you there?"

He held up his left hand, the crumpled paper flapping like a flag of surrender. He didn't say anything. He just waved his arm back and forth until I plucked the paper from his grip. I held it with two fingers, careful not to touch the orange spatters on both sides. It looked like Jackson Pollack had redacted it.

The paper was a summary of heirloom cane yields for the past month. The last time I had seen numbers this low was eighteen months ago, after we'd burned out the last of the crops infected with Vytai Bloombeck's mutant black stripe. A quarter of the planet's cane had to be burned to cinders, and it had set back the Co-Op for months. Everyone tied in with the cane industry (ninety-nine percent of the planet) had made sure to mention their losses whenever they talked to me. And while they never used words like, "And I blame *you* for bringing all this misery and strife on my head by blowing up the lifter and screwing me," their tone and faces said plenty. I looked again and realized the yields were even lower. "Is this right?"

Vikram poured the rum into his upturned face, turning his desk into an orange toxic waste dump. "Paper doesn't lie. Except when it does. But this doesn't, because I have checked." He slid off the desktop, his butt hitting the floor, until all I could see was his head. His beard and mustache were now black with flecks of gray. He looked like an ancient head on display in a museum, the kind left over from a civilization that had committed suicide. "We are *fucked*."

"Is there a new infection? Something screwing with the

crops?"

"That." He pointed at me. "Something is indeed screwing with our crops, our cane, our livelihoods. And it starts with Wal and ends in Wa."

I forced my hands to relax. It was reflex to make fists when I heard the name of my former employer. "What do they have to do with us?"

"Everything," said Vikram, the despair in his voice boiling into white-hot rage. It wasn't a pretty sight, but it also wasn't enough to scare me. I had twenty centimeters and ten kilos on him, alcohol-fueled fury or no. My understanding of Vikram's personal history was that he had come to drinking after a lifetime of abstention. Whether he was a teetotaler because of his beliefs (the orange beard being a mark of a Muslim who had done the hajj to any of the approved Meccalites) or because of his time at a starship's helm, I didn't know. We hadn't talked much, which was partly my fault. I thought if I talked about anything personal, it might lead him or anyone else in the Co-Op to understand the truth of why owning Old Windswept was so important to me. Now, however, was not the time to start sharing.

Vikram jabbed a finger toward the window. "Those goatfuckers in Thronehill have refused to re-certify our cane for export."

"What, again?"

"Yes, again." He turned back to his desk and leaned on it, knuckles down. "And not just the industrial muck we send up the cable. Now they're not going to let us export our rum, even if it was bottled before the lifter blew up."

"That's bullshit!" I pounded his desk, the blood pounding in my head.

"Indeed it is!" he cried, pounding his desk, too. "Which is why you need to give us *your* cane."

The blood stopped pounding. "Excuse me?"

He pointed at me. "Yes. *You* had to keep doing things the way Stella did. Making your own deals with your own producers, paying above the Co-Op's rates, getting your *own* certification... what's the point of being *in* the Co-Op if you're not going to look out for its interests?" His face softened. "Why are *you* here?"

"You mean, right now, or in a general, existential sense?"

He shook his head, then slid out of sight. I heard more weeping.

I walked around the desk and dragged Vikram out. I turned him on his side and held him in place. He protested, but it was token resistance. The rum and his despair had done their work. "Vikram, did you try and push an Article Thirty-Three on my foreman?"

He laughed. "You would have been compensated. Two and a half million, easily, just from the cane alone. Throw in the actual product, and three is a fair offer."

"Why would you try to buy my perfectly profitable distillery?"

He moaned. "Because we're fucked."

I flipped him on his back. "I think you need to explain that. Right now."

He flailed his head from side to side. "I feel sick."

"Vikram, I'm recording this. You can either explain it to me or in front of the entire Co-Op."

"They won't care," said Vikram, turning his head away from me. "They want your cane because all of ours isn't coming in."

I grabbed his cheeks and squeezed his head into place. "You just said the problem is with WalWa."

"It is," he said through squished cheeks. "Part of it."

"Tell me what's going on. All of it. Right now."

He laughed, the sound tight in his mouth. "No one wants to work for us anymore."

I let go of his face. "What, at the distilleries?"

He shook his head. "In the fields. There's no cane coming in because the farms are being abandoned. Haven't you heard?"

I sat in his chair. "I spend ten hours a day in a hole in the ground, Vikram. I'm lucky to know what week it is. How long has this been going on?"

"Three months." He curled up into a ball and rocked onto his side. "No one's cutting cane. No one's setting it out to cure. No one's bringing it to the presses. Millions of hectares are just growing wild, and no one's around to take care of them."

"How do you know?"

Vikram rose to face me. "Because I've been out there! I spent the past week touring cane farms, and all of them are abandoned. And I'm not talking about the little ones. I mean outfits like Royo's and Shar's. Big producers." He waved a hand in the air. "All empty. Like the people were plucked into the sky."

"And you haven't asked around?"

"Who?" He sank back to the carpet. "Who is there to ask? We went to the police, and they said there's been no crime, no reports of missing persons, nothing they can do. It's a big planet. People move around all the time." He moaned. "I just wish they all hadn't moved at once."

"So you thought the best way to fix this was to scare my employees into leaving, all so my distillery could fall apart and you could snap it up?"

"It sounded better when we planned it out." Vikram started to turn green. I nudged a waste basket near his face.

"You could have *asked*," I said. "That's what adults do when they're in business together."

Vikram pulled himself up the basket, clutching it like a life preserver. "And would you have given it all up? Because that's what we need, Padma. If the Co-Op's going to keep producing enough rum to meet our obligations, we need eight hundred thousand kilotons of certified cane by next month."

I did some quick mental math. "Vikram, that's more cane than I grow in a *year*. What the hell is going on?"

"We have obligations."

"You said that. I have the feeling they're not orders for rum."

He made a face like he'd just swallowed a whole, live, and very pissed-off frog. "People want to start cashing in their Mutual certificates. We need to back them up. The only way to do that is to sell more rum, so we need more cane."

I laughed. "Well, you'll just have to tell them to wait, 'cause it's not going to happen now."

"See? See?" He sneered as he got to his swaying feet. "That's the same kind of attitude Tonggow would have given us. She may have been a member, but it was more in name than in practice. She always kept to herself, always donated the minimum."

"Some members haven't ponied up at *all*," I said, blinking up the Co-Op's records. "You've got some who are years behind on dues."

"And now they'll be even farther because *you* won't help them!" His sneer melted, and he leaned over the waste basket and started vomiting.

I wrinkled my nose and went to the window for air. "You know, Vikram, I get why the Co-Op exists. We do all need each other. But there are some people who seem to think that the members work to keep the Co-Op going, and not the other way around."

He dry-heaved, then spat into the bin. "You don't get to lecture me."

"Oh, yes, I do, because I have video of you talking about

a conspiracy to screw me out of my hard-won business. And it's the kind of video that can knock this place to its foundation."

"You wouldn't."

I put my hands on my hips. "Do you think I'm an idiot, Vikram? Do you think I'm just going to roll over and show you my belly because you've got a nice office? Have you not heard my theme song?"

He gagged again. "I *hate* that song."

"And I can have the entire Brushhead Memorial Band here in ten minutes to play it live if you don't shape up."

Vikram wiped his face. The orange transferred back to his lips and mustache. "What do you want?"

I patted his chair. "I want you to sit down, drink some water, and sober up. Then I want you to tell me every single producer that's not producing anymore."

"Why you?"

"Who else?" I laughed. "I can't stand you assholes, but we're still in the Co-Op together. That seal means I get a good price on my rum, and that means I can pay my people, so they're happy to stick around and make more rum that I can sell with the Co-Op seal. That's how business is supposed to work."

He snorted. "You and I know that's bullshit. Business is about grabbing as much as you can for yourself before the other guy can."

I slapped him on the head. "Which of us went to b-school, and which of us piloted starship tugs?"

It took Vikram another half hour of retching and rehydrating until he started to feel better. He kept babbling the names of abandoned farms, and I kept blinking up the locations and marking them on the map. I had to give him credit: at least he'd schlepped out there for himself instead of getting an underling to go in his place. It all added up to a big, frightening picture: farm workers, whether they were Freeborn or Breaches, were disappearing, which left the Co-Op with a dwindling supply of crushable cane. And what little cane was left wasn't going up the cable, thanks to WalWa's dickishness.

I kept watching the time: Six O'Clock loomed closer. I held up my hands. "I think I have enough to go on."

Vikram stopped in mid-heave. "What do you mean?"

"I mean I'm going to solve this problem for you. I'm going to get people back into the fields, get the cane harvest in, and this will all go away."

"It will?"

I nodded. "Provided you do something for me."

Vikram let go of the waste basket and clutched at my calves. "Anything, Padma. Oh, anything."

I stepped out of his grip. "The first thing is that you're going to round up everyone who tried to bully me into giving you my cane. And you will tell them that, when this is over, they are all paying my share into the Co-Op for the rest of my natural life."

Vikram gawped. I took a step toward the door. Vikram leaped to his feet, then fell over. "All right! All right." His lips were mooshed to the floor, so it sounded like a walrus barking instead of someone giving in.

"The second thing is that you'll resign as Vice Chair."

"But my pension!"

"Oh, intercourse your pension," I said. "You wanted to play hardball, this is what happens when you lose."

"No," he said. "I refuse."

"Then enjoy it when you're impeached." I didn't bother to wait for his reply; I knew he'd give in after he'd had time to vomit some more. I gave the kid at the desk a nod as I strode for the door to find my driver and a quick bite.

The red tuk-tuk sat in front of Hareta Hi, the omusubi-ya

I always went to after Co-Op meetings. It was a tiny shop, barely three meters wide and twice as deep, with most of the space taken up by the counter and the rice cooker. Keiko Nakashima, the owner, was working tonight, and her face brightened when I ducked in the door. "Your friend here has become a fan."

Sirikit sat at the counter, leaving a sliver of room for me. She held a triangular rice ball wrapped in nori, her eyes closed, her mouth chewing away like a rock crusher during construction season. "These are so *good*," she said. "How have I never had them before?"

"You got me," I said, squeezing into a seat. "Didn't you have rice on the kampong?"

"Yeah, but it got mixed with peas and goat and curry." Sirikit's eyes opened wide and locked on Keiko. "Please tell me you've got curry, because that would be the greatest thing ever."

Keiko smiled and started rolling another omusubi. "I think I can make that happen. You want one, too, Padma?"

"Hell, yes. How's business?"

Keiko held a wad of rice in her palm. She scooped a spoonful of orange-brown curry into the middle, then started pressing the rice with her hands. "Been busier. Just as well, seeing how Sammy quit."

"Your niece?"

Keiko nodded, her face darkening. "Two weeks ago, she shows up late to her shift, announces she's learned a better way to live her life, and that she needs her salary right then and there."

I thought back to Sammy: a funny, bookish eighteen year-old who studied polymers. She was the picture definition of punctual, even for her seven a.m. classes at Santee Open School. "What did you do?"

Keiko snorted as she handed an omusubi to Sirikit. "I

told her to get to work. She cleaned out the cashbox, called me a parasite enabler, and marched out."

"Holy shit."

"You got that right."

Sirikit made all kinds of happy moaning noises as she ate. "How could she leave this? It's so *good*."

"No idea," said Keiko. She stopped in mid-scoop, her hand shaking. "I don't think it was drugs or drink or hormones. Sammy had a steady girlfriend, and she was doing all kinds of great research at Open School. It was so *sudden*, so unlike her."

Sirikit gulped some tea. "You know, same thing happened in my family. I live in the city, but my folks are still in Lualua, you know? Couple days ago, Mom comes to the shop and tells me my youngest brother had up and left. Grabbed everything valuable he could, said we were foreclosing on our legacies as Freeborn, and marched out into the cane. No one's seen him since."

Huh. First Ly Huang quits in a huff of misapplied Marxism, then Sammy, and now Sirikit's brother. There was no way this was coincidence. But how were they connected, except they were all young, Freeborn, and pissed off? I thought about Evanrute Saarien, how he'd grabbed workers to staff his secret and highly illegal cane refinery and left cloned bodies behind to cover his tracks. He was still in prison, wasn't he? Would I have to start checking morgues?

"Well, *I've* sure seen Sammy," said Keiko, going back to making the omusubi. "Two days ago, Magdalena, a girlfriend who runs a veggie shop, she calls me, says Sammy had just boosted a case of carrots. Instead of siccing the cops on Sammy, Magdalena tails Sammy to this run-down spot on Hudson and Hawkes. Sammy goes in with the veggies, and these two giant people at the door stop Magdalena from going in. They said only those wanting salvation can enter.

Magdalena just wanted her carrots."

The hairs on the back of my neck prickled. Saarien used former Big Three security goons as his heavies. "Have you gone to this place, Keiko?"

She nodded. "I got the same treatment: two big people at the door, bit about salvation. All these other people keep coming in and out, and I can hear a lot inside: people laughing, someone preaching. It was weird." She made a sour face. "I kept bugging the big guys, and then someone comes out, this white guy I'd never seen before."

I swallowed. "Freeborn?"

Keiko shook her head. "His skin was terrible, but I could make out some ink. He gives me a smile, and asks if I'd come to be saved. I told him I'd come to get my niece. He just smiles, says there are no nieces here, just brothers and sisters in the struggle to liberate their souls, and he leaves."

My spine turned to ice. The Struggle. Saarien wouldn't shut *up* about The Struggle between the Union and the Big Three. "You get a good look at this guy? The smiler?"

Keiko shrugged. "Mid-forties. Looked beat up. Wore a suit that was too big for him."

Oh, no. No no no no no. "What color was the suit?"

Keiko didn't look up. "White. Sparkling clean, too. I don't know how he did it." She handed me the omusubi.

"Make it to go," I said, getting up. "And give me the address."

Fucking hell. Evanrute Saarien was out of prison.

FOUR

It was five after five when Sirikit screeched in front of 1801 Hawks Street. I used to come to Hawks Street all the time, back when my dentist had an office on the corner of Hudson Drive. She retired two years ago, right around the time Evanrute Saarien was being sentenced. My teeth hurt. I had been grinding them the entire drive over.

There was nothing that made me think Saarien had magically appeared at this blank storefront on Hawks Street. He had pulled double duty as the Ward Chair of Sou's Reach and the manager of the old cane refinery that squatted in the middle of the neighborhood. Both the Ward and the refinery had fallen apart under his watch, thanks to his neglect and embezzlement. He should have been rotting behind bars until we both were old and decrepit.

1801 Hawks looked like someone had taken care of it, at least from the outside. There was no sign in front, just a stenciled picture of a Union fist holding a star going supernova. The walls were scrubbed clean of dirt and graffiti, and the double doors swung open easily for the few people who came in and out. Even the former goons stationed at the doors wore clean clothes. I noted they wore glass pins with the same fist-and-nova as the sign in front. Saarien had had a thing for glasswork back at Sou's Reach.

I had blinked up Saarien's record and found that he didn't exist anymore. There was a data footprint that began the day he arrived on Santee Anchorage and ended when was remanded into custody on Maersk. No mentions of release or parole. He just vanished, leaving behind a lot of pissed off people and a giant black mark on his Union profile.

Was it really him? Or did someone just copy his act and open a storefront church? It happened a lot on Santee; revivalist fevers would sweep the planet, burn bright for a few months, then fade when the congregations would either mellow out or realize they'd been taken in by a con man. At first, I would laugh at the suckers, but then The Fear would remind me that some people needed a little extra to get through the day. Whether it was the belief in the Virgin Buddha or Vishnu Christ or the Great And Unfeeling Void, I had no use for religion, but I understood the need. The universe was a big, scary place, and knowing that something bigger and scarier was looking out for you (or out to get you) gave people a sense of order and peace.

Evanrute Saarien had believed in The Struggle with the ferocity of a religious fundamentalist. Or, at least, he'd convinced everyone that he did. I took no small amount of satisfaction in seeing Saarien taken apart one piece at a time during testimony. All the talk about how he was leading the Union in the epic fight against the Big Three, about how he worked to help us maintain our basic human dignity, all while he was fleecing his Ward and trying to burn down the entire world… it was a sweet sight when he blubbered to the judge and threw himself at the mercy of the court. Fifty years was too good for him.

I looked at Sirikit, munching on an omusubi. "I have a favor to ask. Will you come in there with me?"

She swallowed. "You scared of something?"

I nodded at the blank door flanked by two beefy men with barrel chests and no necks. "I think the guy in there is someone who tried to kill me."

"Over what?"

I sighed. "Money. Turf. The purity of my commitment to the Universal Freelancer's Union."

"And how do you feel about that?"

I laughed. "I'm sorry?"

Sirikit pursed her lips, then gave me a polite nod. "How did that make you feel?"

I laughed again until she put a hand on mine. Her face softened, and she said, "I'm not just a tuk-tuk driver. I'm putting myself through school to be a post-traumatic stress counselor. Do you want to talk about what happened to you?"

For a brief moment, I thought about opening my mouth and just spilling *everything*: how my transit had screwed with my brain, how Old Windswept kept it working. And not just that: I wanted to tell her about the frustrations with my jobs, my astonishment at how Saarien went from being a mere pain in my backside to trying to burn me alive, the way the Co-Op and the Union and the Big Three and every institution I knew tried to suck all the life out of me and her and everyone else.

I looked at Sirikit and said, "Not yet. But thank you."

She nodded and patted my hand. "Whenever you're ready. Words matter."

Then I saw him.

In the evening hustle, I spotted another pair of former goons, each of them two meters tall and a hundred kilos heavy. Between them marched a man in an immaculate white suit that hung from his shoulders. All of them had the same glass pins as the goons at the door.

The man in the middle looked like a skinnier, balder, blotchier version of Evanrute Saarien. It sure as hell looked like someone aping his style. How had he kept those suits so clean when he worked in a cane refinery? During the trial, I kept hoping someone would ask him that, but I supposed it wasn't relevant to the crimes he'd been accused of committing.

"Is that him?" asked Sirikit.

I leaned forward in my seat, holding my hands together. His walk was stiff, as if his joints were full of glue. This was a man who used to glide into Union meetings like a champion ballroom dancer. The guy on the sidewalk looked like he was scared someone would leap out and take his lunch money.

But there was the suit. There was the smile.

I nodded. "Yeah."

"What do you want to do?"

Saarien stopped at the door. The two goons standing guard reached down and grabbed him. They crushed him in their massive arms. I felt my knuckles pop at the sight: *Holy crap, they're killing him...*

Then they let him go, and they all laughed. The goons weren't assaulting Saarien; they were *hugging* him.

Well.

I sat back, all the tension draining from my body. "Ten minutes ago, I would have said I wanted you to punch his light out. Now? I have no idea."

"Whatever you do, just keep calm."

I nodded, more to myself than to her. "Right." I got out of the tuk-tuk and marched across the street before Sirikit could respond. "Hey!" I yelled as loud as I could. "HEY!"

The four goons and Saarien turned. The goons all tensed and turned toward me, their hands clenched into fists. Two of them pulled billy clubs from thin air. I didn't care. I felt a hot rush come up from my chest, as if someone had lit a fire in my lungs. I wanted to burn the goons down. I wanted to burn Saarien down. I wanted to burn his crappy storefront church down.

Fear flickered across Saarien's face as the goons with clubs shoved him behind their giant backs. "Can we help you?" one of them asked.

I pointed at them. "You can step out of my way. I have to talk to *him*."

Sirikit ran to my side. I had no doubt of how she'd do in a fight against four goons. But I also knew that starting a fight was a good way to lose track of what had happened to Keiko's niece. I cleared my throat and thought about what to say. "I need to talk to Evanrute Saarien. He knows who I am."

The goons froze, then looked at each other. I considered using command presence on them to get them to freeze when a pair of beat-up hands appeared on their shoulders and nudged them aside like curtains. Evanrute Saarien stood before us, his eyes watering. "Sister Padma? Is that you?"

I nodded. I felt bile at the back of my throat, but I nodded and gave him a tight smile.

He took a few careful steps toward us, and I had to work to keep my face from crinkling in shock. Saarien's cheek bones jutted out from a hollow face. Liver spots dotted his thinning pate. He looked like he'd aged thirty years. Maybe Maersk had been harder than I'd realized.

He held out a hand, wrinkled like a crow's foot. I punched him in the nose.

It was a perfect punch, a right hook that caught him square in the middle of his face. His smile didn't have time to fade as his eyes rolled into the back of his head. His body tilted on his heels. I didn't wait for him to hit the ground. I jumped on Saarien, and all the air whuffed out of his lungs as his back met the pavement and my knees hit his waist.

I hit him, and I hit him, and I would have hit him again and again if it weren't for the fact that The Fear filled my skull in a way it hadn't since I first woke up from hibernation. I couldn't make out the words, but I understood the tone. It was an animal sound, high and shrill and furious. The Fear wanted me to hit Evanrute Saarien until I had pulped his face. I let Sirikit pull me off him, my fist still cocked.

The goons helped him up. His left eye had started swelling shut, and blood streamed from his nose. He leaned forward and spat a red gob on the sidewalk, still careful to keep his impossibly white suit clean. One of the goons handed him a handkerchief, which he pressed to his nose. He looked at me with his other eye and said, his voice wavering, "I'm sorry. I deserved that and more."

I didn't say anything. Sirikit's hands gripped my upper arms with enough force to keep me from leaping forward for a second go-round.

Saarien tried to smile around the handkerchief. His teeth were ruined, and not from my punches. They were stained, and one of his upper incisors was gone. "Actually, I'd hoped we could meet. I have a lot of apologizing and explaining to do."

"I don't think I want to hear it."

"I know," he said. "I wouldn't expect you to." He hawked a little more blood on the ground and fingered the glass pin on his lapel. "This must all seem strange."

"You have no idea."

"Oh, but I do!" He waved a hand toward the storefront. "I have been humbled, Sister Padma."

"Don't call me that."

"Of course, of course!" He gave me another gap-tooth grin. "I forget, I'm not in the Union anymore, even though we're all united together in the Struggle." Jesus, he was still speaking like those words were capitalized. *The Struggle*.

Saarien beckoned us to follow. "Services are going to start soon. There's refreshments, though no rum, I'm afraid." My face must have twitched, because he laughed and said, "But we're not teetotalers! Oh, no. We just don't have the budget right now."

"If I let you go, are you going to hit him again?" whispered Sirikit.

"I make no guarantees," I said. Oh, for a sidekick with a pai, just so we could text.

The goons crowded in front of Saarien, but he waved them off. "Won't you let me show you around? Just a brief tour. There's so much I have to do to atone, and this is part of it."

I looked back at Sirikit, who gave me a stern eye. "You start swinging again, I'm not going to stick around."

"Okay," I said, and she let go. I flexed my fists and willed them to relax. "Okay, Saarien. Let's see what you've got."

He coughed, and the blood flowed from his nose again. He clamped the handkerchief to his face and led me toward the door. "I've wanted to talk with you, but I was sure you wouldn't want anything to do with me. I'm very thankful that you've come here."

I nodded, making my mouth turn into a convincing smile. I didn't want to smile. I wanted to grab him by the lapels of his baggy suit and demand that he tell me why he wasn't rotting in prison. I wanted to kick this man in the head and yell at him for trying to immolate me and Banks and Wash before bringing down all of Occupied Space. My stomach roiled, and The Fear raked across the back of my brain. It didn't say anything. It didn't have to.

I thought about Sunny and Ly Huang. Both of them were serious about their studies and their work. They were bright, happy kids who were charting their futures. If they had pitched their plans to walk into whatever Saarien had cooked up, then they were in danger. He could talk about atonement all he wanted; deep in my guts I knew he was a con artist and a liar. However he had gotten out of prison, I would make sure he went straight back in.

I cleared my throat. "This is very difficult for me, as I'm sure you can tell."

He nodded. "I can only imagine. I was terrible to you. I tried to *kill* you. I can never expect you to forgive me for that, but I'm thankful I didn't succeed. You're a good person, Padma. You've given so much to this city, to the Union, and I don't think you've ever been properly rewarded."

I shrugged. "I never expected a reward."

"But you *deserve* one," he said. "Everyone here does for living our lives. Every day when we're not living under the Big Three's control is a victory. Every day we help each other is a good one."

Still sounds like a con, hissed The Fear. For once, I agreed with it.

Saarien pushed open the doors. "Come inside, and maybe we can start righting those wrongs. Come and see what the Temple of the New Holy Light is all about." He walked into the building, the goons holding the doors for us. I took a step, then froze. I didn't want to go in there. I didn't want to do anything but get back to my flat for Six O'Clock.

But I had made promises to Marolo and Keiko and Vikram, though, hell, I could have blown off Vikram and not felt bad about it. But Keiko, she was a friend, and Marolo had always been good to me. Their families were in trouble, and I said I would help. If the kids weren't inside right now, they would be eventually. I had to make sure they were okay. I gave Sirikit a nod, and we entered the building.

It was boring.

There was a single room, twenty meters square, with dingy beige walls and sputtering LEDs overhead. Six benches made from castoff crates and ship parts faced a battered podium. At the far wall was a makeshift altar with a picture of the Working Christ, a carved Buddha, and an icon of Ganesha. Cheap incense smoldered in the offering bowls. It looked like Saarien was pandenominational; I wondered what kinds of theological hoops he jumped through to make this all work.

On either side of the door were two long tables. Two women sorted clothes on one table, and two men sorted jars of jam and preserved fish on another. Someone had written TAKE WHAT YOU NEED, GIVE WHAT YOU CAN on the wall above the tables. Two electric hot plates sat on the floor, and giant kettles of green soup simmered inside.

And the people. They all looked ragged and hungry and *tired*. The last time I had seen a room full of people so exhausted was ten years ago during Contract Time. WalWa's initial offer to the Union was an insult, and they answered our counter by having their ships empty their sewage systems into Santee's atmosphere. Whether they were coming from a position of perceived strength or they just wanted to be dicks, I have no idea. What I do know is the entire planet went on strike for half a year, and it damn near wiped us out.

With no cane going up the lifter, we had no hard currency or Big Three items coming down, which meant that stuff started falling apart fast. Every machine more advanced than a bicycle was shut down to save on wear and tear, and a lot of people walked just to save their bicycle chains from strain. WalWa threw kites into the air above Thronehill, and they became giant screens that broadcast images from the Life Corporate every hour of every day. They'd turn on fans and waft the scents of machine oil and hand sanitizer

over their wall to break our resolve. We answered back
with slingshots and fresh bread (though the bread started
to run low toward the end; people were too tired to work
the ricewheat harvest). When WalWa finally caved and the
strike ended, everyone slept for a month.

All the people in this room looked like they wanted to
sleep for a year. "Where did they all come from?" I asked
Saarien.

He sighed, his skinny shoulders rising and falling beneath
his massive suit. "From the kampong, and from the alleys
of the city. They're the people who've fallen through the
cracks."

"There are no cracks," I said. "Everyone on this planet
gets food, shelter, medical care."

"But some *don't*," said Saarien. He pointed at a couple
in their fifties cradling bowls on their laps. "Maurice there,
he's a Shareholder who used to have his own welding shop.
His pai malfunctioned after the last firmware update, and
he kept losing texts from clients. They got so frustrated
they stopped going to him for work, and his reputation
took a hit. He lost the shop, and then his husband Diem got
meningitis, which screwed up *his* pai. They got booted from
their flat 'cause their landlord wanted an excuse to tear it
down and rebuild, and they can't keep their appointments
with lawyers or doctors. They'd given up when I found
them."

He nodded at a young woman unwrapping a coil of wire.
"Su Yin came from the kampong to go to the Open School.
She got her tablet stolen her first day in the city, before she
could even get herself on the Public. It's a four-month wait
to get on the rolls through paper channels because no one
in the Union wants to deal with finding the forms. She's
ashamed to go home because she thinks it would mean
admitting defeat. She slept in our doorway."

Saarien led us around the room, talking about the people who sat on the benches and made the soup and mended the clothes for giveaway. The more he talked, the more I remembered all the Ward Chair meetings where he would wheedle and cajole and outright lie to get more and more money for the greasy spit of a neighborhood that he was supposed to look out for. He had turned it into the base for upending the entire transstellar economy, all while letting the refinery he was supposed to manage slip into ruin. Every time someone talked about the casualty numbers out of Sou's Reach, Saarien would just smile and say they would be remembered as valued martyrs to The Struggle. Then he would move on to bilking more cash out of the Union.

But this man here, if he didn't genuinely care about the people under this roof, then he was putting on the greatest dramatic performance in human history. People smiled at him. His eyes got moist as he hugged them and fed them and helped change a diaper.

My brain did a backflip at that: *Evanrute Saarien just changed a diaper.*

His suit remained spotless.

"How did this all happen?" I said. We sat at the front of the building, bowls of stuff resembling lentil soup on our laps.

He smiled, a bit of tomato wedged in the gap between his teeth. "It was in prison. Have you ever been to Maersk?"

"I've tried to avoid it."

He shook his head. "That's how I felt when the airship dropped me off. The criminals who get sent there are the worst of the worst, the ones who had no business being a part of society. I was sure I would get murdered within two minutes of landing."

Saarien put down his bowl of soup. "But it wasn't like that. If anything, it's harder. The guards and the prisoners have to work together to grow crops, to keep the water flowing, to make the place thrive. Three hundred people on a patch of land that's only five hundred hectares, and if you don't get with the program, you don't eat. There's no black market, no underground trading, because everyone's busy repairing fishing nets or manning fishing nets or gutting fish." He shook his head. "I'm not a fan of fish anymore."

I ground my jaw to keep me from yelling, *Why aren't you still there?*

He put his hands in his lap. "Everyone talks, too. We talk while we work, we talk at meals, we talk during sessions. We have plenty of time to reflect and think about what we did. I thought it was all bullshit until my second year."

I shifted in my seat. "What happened?"

He gave me a small smile. "I realized that *I* was all bullshit. Everything I'd done, it was all for my own purposes, starting with me becoming a recruiter for WalWa. I just saw people as units to process and take advantage of. I was so disconnected from humanity, even after I Breached, and I couldn't let go of that. It took going to prison and losing all my power to remind me that I was a person, and I had to rely on other people, and to do that I had to *earn* their respect."

This all sounded like a great line. I nodded, waiting for him to show me a sign that it was all nothing but a line. "Is that how you got out so early?"

His eyes grew sad. "I didn't want to go."

"What?"

He nodded. "There was a structure and a peace that came from living and working there. And the fact that all of us had to talk and *listen*, that made it clear that I'd lived my life the wrong way. I did all the talking, but I never listened. I never thought about what *I* had to do to make others' lives better. I was elected to leave early and bring that attitude back here." He held out his hands. "I'm starting at the bottom with this."

"With a church?"

"Faith without works is dead," said Saarien. "I still have faith in The Struggle, but I know it has to start in here." He pounded the center of his chest like he was hammering nails. "I found something I can't put into words, but I can put it into action." He blinked, like he'd just been poked in the ribs. "Speaking of action, it's time for the five-thirty service. Can you stay?"

NO, I wanted to scream at the tops of my lungs, not with Six O'Clock looming. No way in hell. But I hadn't seen Sammy yet, and I had to get something to bring back to Keiko. I looked at Sirikit. "Can you get me to Samarkand Road before six?"

She furrowed her brows. "We can stay ten minutes."

I turned to Saarien. "I have an appointment, but I can stick around."

He smiled, showing me that gap. I wondered: had someone knocked his tooth out? Had he just let himself go until he found whatever it was he was about to preach? I could figure that out later, right after I found out about the missing kids.

Saarien walked to the front of the room and clapped his hands. "Has everyone gotten enough to eat?" There were calls of varying enthusiasm. Maurice and Diem, the couple he'd pointed out, took extra helpings of soup and sat down in front. People appeared from back rooms and from the front doors. Within a few minutes, thirty people had filled the benches. A third of them had ink. None of them were Sammy or Ly Huang.

He stood in front of the altar, took a breath, and, for a moment, I saw the same Evanrute Saarien who had tried to kill me: the rolled-back shoulders, the slick smile, the *suit*.

Then he exhaled, and all that confidence drained out of his body. He deflated into the smaller, sadder version that had ushered me in here.

"Friends," he said, his voice just strong enough to still the crowd. "It's been a tremendous week for our flock. We've gotten new donations of jellied eel from Beckton's, and I understand our PV Committee will be installing some new cells this week on the Wisniewski's house." A young couple with a baby waved at everyone.

"Yes, a good week." He nodded to himself, let his eyes drift toward the back walls. "And there's always more we can do. There's more we *must* do, and not just here in the city, but for our brothers and sisters in the kampong. They're the ones whose toil lets everyone live. The more cane they cut, the more money flows back to us." He focused his gaze on a Freeborn woman in the front row. "Though we know that's not quite true, right?"

Everyone nodded. The murmuring took on a hotter tone. I could feel it right away: these hungry people were *angry*. I made a mental note to feed all this footage to every Ward chair and remind them they were falling down on the job.

"No, it's not true. If it were, we wouldn't be here. We'd be in our flats, at our jobs, maybe knocking back a few fingers of the Co-Op's finest." The anger grew sharper, not only on Saarien's face, but on everyone else's.

Saarien held out his hands to still the crowd. "But what can we do? What *should* we do?"

"Protest!" yelled the mother.

"March!" yelled Maurice the welder.

"Fight back!" yelled a man with a beard down to his navel.

More words floated around, until a girl from the back called out "STRIKE!" Saarien pointed at her, his face lit up like a Diwali firework display. He nodded, and then that smile returned, the one that said everything Saarien had told me was, indeed, bullshit. He was back in the game.

Sirikit leaned over. "We have to go if you want to make your six o'clock."

I looked at Saarien, getting ramped up about The Struggle, about how the cane workers did the most important work but got the least in cash. He was rebuilding, and he would try and kill me again. I could feel it.

But I could also feel The Fear scrabbling around my brain. I got up and hustled to Sirikit's tuk-tuk.

FIVE

"You want me to stick around?" Sirikit asked as we pulled up to Number 42 Samarkand Road. "I have the feeling you'll have more places to go."

"Not tonight." I hopped out, and shadows from the koa tree in front of my building wrapped around me. Three of the Patil kids stuck their torsos out of their window, right next to mine. They waved and sang until their father, Swaroop, called them to stay away from the fire escape and come to the dinner table. I smelled roasted kumara and fishcakes and heard arguments and prayers. I walked to the empty front stoop and patted the spot where the late Mrs Karpinski used to sit and smoke. God, I missed bullshitting with her. I blinked up the time: five fifty-five. "But tomorrow, probably, yeah. Around four-ish. And tell Jilly she needs to get out of the office."

Sirikit honked the horn. "I'll send the boss your regards." She zipped off into traffic, and I ran five flights up to my flat.

Once inside, I didn't waste any time. I locked the door and went to the kitchen. The bottle of Old Windswept sat in the back of the cupboard, hiding behind the spices. I could have left a case of it lying around, but, you know, old habits.

I walked around the flat, closing all the blackout curtains but for the one covering the window facing the ocean. I set the bottle on my dining table and pulled a hurricane candle and a matchbook from underneath. I blinked up the time: five fifty-nine. I closed the last curtain, giving a nod to the mourners filing out of Longxia Cemetery a block away and cursing my landlady for saying the flat had a "territorial view" instead of "a living room overlooking a bloody graveyard." I lit the candle.

And there I sat: bottle, candle, the dancing flame. My little room, now bathed in the warm glow. Me, sitting in this chair, at this table, in this flat, in this neighborhood, in this city, on this planet, in this system, in this cluster, in this galaxy, in this universe. I let myself drift outside my tiny frame of reference, let my mind float farther and farther back until I was lost in the great sea of stars. I had no idea how many of them were full of life or strife, how many were being born or dying. I knew I had a place somewhere in all of that, and I had a short span to make it count. I had this time, this place, and this one sip of Old Windswept.

I unscrewed the bottlecap and took that tiny sip. The warm line of rum ran down my throat into my belly, and I imagined that heat shooting up my spine into my brain. All those spots that got screwed up by my transit, all those neurons fried by the hibernant or business school or bad luck, none of that mattered for this moment. Here and now, I was whole and healthy, and fuck you, The Fear.

"That looked delicious."

I jumped out of my chair. Rum sloshed out of the bottle as I held it in front of me. A woman sat in my overstuffed chair, her hands on the armrests. I did a quick look behind me to make sure no one else was hiding in my flat. I moved to the nearest curtain and threw it open. When I saw who was in the chair, the bottle dropped, along with my jaw.

Leticia Arbusto Smythe, the President of the Santee Anchorage Chapter of the Universal Freelancers' Union, gave me a polite smile, her un-inked cheeks glowing. She uncrossed her legs, her cargo trousers rustling and clinking. She had her electric green hair tied up, a sign that this was a business call. That still didn't stop me from saying, "What the fuck are you doing in my flat, Letty?"

She reached into her jacket and produced a cigar. "Your landlady let me in."

"I'll have to file a complaint with the Housing Committee, then. No one's supposed to come in here without my say-so."

Letty shrugged as she fiddled with a matchbox.

"Or smoke."

She glared at me. I shrugged. "It's in the lease."

Letty *hmm*ed, then tucked the cigar back in her jacket. She nodded at the bottle on the floor. "You gonna waste that?"

I looked down. Old Windswept came in triangular bottles of sea-green glass. This one was open. Once upon a time, I would have dived for the floor to keep any of the rum from spilling, but I had learned that, once you owned your own distillery, that kind of thing just wasn't *done*. I picked up the bottle and put it away.

"Not even a finger for the Prez?" said Letty from her chair. *My* chair.

"I'm always happy to serve my guests," I said, closing the cabinet. "My *invited* guests."

She laughed. "Oh, come *on*, Padma. You still owe me a drink."

"Since when?"

"Since that night you dragged me to karaoke."

"First of all, that was nine years ago. Second, *you* dragged *me* to that crappy little bar. And third, you didn't even *sing*."

She shrugged. "I don't like the way my voice sounds."

"You give weekly speeches on the Public."

"That's *speaking*. Singing is another beast. Besides, this was the only way we could talk without all the eyes and ears of the world watching us."

I tapped my temple. "We both have video cameras in our heads."

"But they don't work when I have this." She held up the matchbox.

I blinked back my pai's buffer and got static. I put my hands on my hips. "Letty, are you jamming me? In my own home?"

"I am indeed." She pocketed the jammer. "Because the Union needs you, Padma, but no one can know about it."

I walked to the door. "Thank you for visiting, I'll be sure to take this into consideration come election time." With a flourish, I opened the door and bowed low. "Now go home."

A woman in a deck jacket and work boots swung around from the door posts. Before I could react, she got between me and the door. I didn't even have time to yell as she closed the door with a solid click. She put her back to the door and faced me, and I had the damnedest feeling of déjà vu.

The woman looked my age, though her skin was so smooth that there was no way she'd spent any time in the sun. She had a LiaoCon Security Services tattoo on her cheek: a deep green dagger with a red merlion coiled around the blade. The inklines were crisp, like she'd only gotten it a month ago. She squared her shoulders at me, and her eyes said she would break me in half if I made a wrong move. There was no way she was a rookie.

I threw up my hands. "This is some shameful shit, Letty. Breaking into my place, having your little thug keeping me from bouncing your ass on the street. You really want me to go to everyone else on the Executive Committee? Don't you think Ly An Nogales would love to hear about you getting all power-grabby?"

Letty tented her fingers and rested her elbows on her knees. She looked like an illustration from one of my B-school manuals about executive poise. "I think Ly An would do the same if she faced the same situation."

"Which is what?"

She smiled. "Pour me a drink, and I'll tell you."

I jerked a thumb at the woman guarding my door. "Tell your attack poodle to wait outside. She doesn't look housetrained."

The woman's eyes narrowed. She made a sound like a jet engine starting up as she uncrossed her arms.

"No, it's okay," said Letty, holding up a hand. "Thank you, Jennifer. Please wait outside."

Jennifer's upper lip twitched into a microsneer as she slipped out the door. I threw the deadbolt. "Where did you find *her*?"

"Same place I find everyone else who's useful: a bar."

I got a bottle of Beaulieu's Blend out for Letty. Endless supply of Old Windswept aside, I wasn't about to share my best with her, not after this crap. "Well, she certainly has a great tableside manner."

Letty moved over to my little table and blew out the candle. "She just came down the cable earlier this year. Interesting story: she was in personal security for some ag executive, and her boss wanted her to go out and rough up some tenant farmers. She punched out her boss, freaked out, and stowed away on the first outbound ship she could find." She shook her head. "Four years later, she slips down the cable, and Little Charlemagne put her to work as a bouncer."

I put the bottle and two glasses on the table. "Is that why his place started getting good reviews? I know it wasn't for his food. He burns water."

"She certainly changed the ambiance," said Letty, eyeing the two fingers I poured in her glass. "Once she rousted out the troublemakers and bullies, it became a more pleasant place to hang out."

"Yeah, but pity wherever the troublemakers and bullies landed." I held up my glass, and we clinked them. "To personal security; would that we all could have some."

Letty snorted and took a deep sip. I just mouthed my rum; it was too close to Six O'Clock to put other forms of alcohol into my system.

She held the glass up to the evening light and swirled the rum. "You know, Padma, whenever the Executive Committee is kibitzing amongst ourselves, this comes up a lot. You and this hour of the day. Back when we were both Ward Chairs, I remember you kicking up a fuss because Ted Fantodji wanted to have a meeting at six. It almost came to blows."

I shrugged. "It just wasn't a good time." I was glad the jammer was there; it saved me the embarrassment of reviewing the memory, filed away on the Public for all to see.

"But it's *never* been a good time." She tapped her temple. "I checked. You are always *here* at six o'clock, but for a few occasions like hurricanes and dealing with Ghosts." She took another sip. "Why the ritual, Padma?"

I made myself laugh. "I have no idea what you're talking about."

Letty put down her glass. "My mom was a canon. I grew up surrounded by bread and wine and all the stuff that transforms it. I *know* ritual when I see it, Padma."

"Is that why you came here? You got a bet with the rest of the Executive Committee about how I spend my time? Joke's on you; I've actually been running a pit fighting ring."

She tapped the glass. "That's why I like you. Even when you're neck-deep in bullshit, you make with the funny."

I poured her another finger. "Madame President, why did you break into my home?"

"Because I have something that needs fixing, and you're the only one who can fix it."

Now I laughed for real. "If I had a hundred yuan for every time someone's used that line on me, I could buy *two* distilleries."

Letty shot the rum and hissed in a breath. When she exhaled, she leveled her eyes and said, "Evanrute Saarien is going to destroy the world."

I took her glass and mine and brought them back into the kitchen. Deep in my gut, I could feel the acid roiling. There were only so many times you got to speak truth to power, and I had to make sure my next words were cool and clear. As much as I wanted to yell at her, I had to keep myself together.

I placed my hands on either side of the sink and leaned down, as if the cool of the glass tile could keep me from boiling over. "Evanrute Saarien got that way because *you* let him."

Letty shook as if I'd slapped her. "*What*?"

I kept pushing down on the counter, willing the tiles to snap under my weight. "I warned you and everyone else up and down the food chain that Saarien was, at best, full of shit whenever he talked about The Struggle." Letty quirked her mouth; anyone who'd been around Saarien had gotten their fill of his rhetoric. "You had every opportunity to stop him, to cut his funding, to get him tossed from Sou's Reach. I told you and I told you and you *never listened to me*."

I pushed back from the counter. "It took him trying to burn me and Wash and Banks alive before you all realized that you'd created a monster. He was ready to destroy *billions* of people, including our Union brethren *right here*, and you *let him happen*. Why in hell should I do anything to help *you* when you wouldn't listen to me when we could have done something?" I shook my head. "He's out of jail forty-eight years early and starting his empire of bullshit all over again. What the *hell*, Letty?"

To her credit, Letty didn't interrupt. She didn't flinch. She held her hands in her lap, calm and collected. When I'd blown myself out, she gave me a nod, like she was asking if she could have the floor. I held out a hand: *by all means*. She looked me in the eye and said, "You are absolutely right. About everything."

I blinked. "Now I wish you didn't have that jammer."

"I'll be happy to say that again on the Public when this is all over." She put the matchbox on the table. "You were at his church this afternoon. What did you see?"

I told her about the food and clothes, about the busted people sitting around. "He's right, isn't he? About the people slipping through the cracks."

Letty nodded. "We've had a breakdown in social services over the past nine months."

"How?"

"Because there is no longer enough money to convince everyone to keep working," said Letty. "We need two point eight million yuan to keep everyone paid for a week, bennies and all. Right now we're getting nothing."

"Why?"

"Because of Vytai Bloombeck's black stripe."

I blanched out of reflex. Bloombeck had been a constant pain in my ass ever since I came to Santee Anchorage. When I was a fresh Breach, the only place I could afford was a shared hutong flat with Bloombeck and five others. He was always wheedling us to go in on his small-time scams: pretending to get in tuk-tuk accidents, renting out neighbors' laundry, rolling drunks for pocket money. His biggest con turned out to be his last one: in return for helping him buy a plot of land, he sold me the name of a ship with people who wanted to Breach, and they all turned out to be a Ghost Squad. Then Bloombeck turned out to be a genius-level gengineer with a grudge as big as his stench. I often wondered what the last year and a half would have been like if the Ghosts hadn't killed him. He'd probably still make my pai freak out and jab me in the eye. "What about it?"

"After the black stripe infected our cane, we had to torch a quarter of our fields to make sure it didn't spread. The Big Three weren't happy about that."

"Who cares what they think?"

"We do, because they have since decided we aren't a reliable supplier."

"We make enough for four other worlds. And that's in an off year."

"We do, but we don't get paid like we used to."

"But the Contract—"

"Got negated when the black stripe ripped through our fields." Letty ground her teeth. "Those rates and goods we got from the Big Three were dependent on us raising healthy cane. We fought to make sure that we didn't have to rely on Big Three pesticides or herbicides, that we could grow cane *our* way. It's labor intensive, but we have plenty of labor to draw from. When Bloombeck's black stripe got out, we voided our part of the Contract. The Big Three cut us off, and rightly so."

I glowered. "I never thought I'd hear you take the Big Three's side."

Letty made me a face. "Spare me the purity bullshit. We need the Big Three's tech and their money to live the way we want. Or do you want us driven back to the Steam Age? You know what kinds of horrible diseases people died from then? Remember when cancer was still fatal?"

"No."

"No, because we live in a time and place where medicine has eradicated all that." She straightened up in her chair. "You and I and everyone on this planet will live a good long time, provided we don't starve. People need to eat, and we need to pay people to grow food, and that money comes from the Big Three because it's the only currency they'll accept. And we get that money by selling our cane, which we are not providing enough of. It's circular and ugly, but it's the system we have, and it means none of us are Indentured to the Big Three anymore."

I touched the ink on my cheek. "Us?"

Letty shook her head. "You really gonna give me shit because I've never had needles jab my face?"

"Maybe a little."

"You know, the fanatics in the Freeborn Organizing Committee thought that was a sure sign of dehumanization. Getting stamped like cattle."

"Do you?"

She snorted. "I always thought the FOC were loons. And worthless, too. All that babbling about changing the world, and all they did was blow up a post office and make the rest of us look like terrorists. No, I'm Union, Padma. I know the weird balance we have with the Big Three. We may depend on their cash, but they don't directly control us. If some mid-level director in Thronehill issues a memo saying everyone has to start buying twice as much Tasty Choice Caffeine Lubricant, we don't have to follow along."

"Especially since Tasty Choice tastes like crap."

"*Exactly*." Letty let a smile slip. "I know our relationship with the Big Three isn't perfect, but it means we get to live our lives."

"Except when it doesn't."

She sighed. "And now is one of those times."

"Why hasn't WalWa certified the cane for export, Letty?"

"Because that magical pool of labor that allows us to grow cane by hand is vanishing. WalWa knows it. People are leaving the kampong, and the fields are going fallow. That's why I need your help."

"To do what?"

"To stop Evanrute Saarien."

"No."

I said it before my brain could scream *Wait until you hear the terms!* I reminded my brain there were no terms in the world big enough to deal with him ever again—

"I'll forgive your debt."

My brain said *Oh, yeah?*, and I leaned forward. "I beg your pardon?"

Letty spread her hands on her lap, as if she were laying out a complicated hand of cards. "You are on the hook for blowing up the lifter. You will be in debt for the rest of your life, and the only position open to you is one where you put on a leaky environment suit and wade through filth for ten hours a day. Do you really want to do that for the next eighty years?"

I shrugged, trying to stay cool. The first rule of negotiation was to be able to walk away at any time, no matter how incredibly good the deal was. "I could always get another job."

"Not if I have anything to do with it."

I narrowed my eyes. "Madame President, are you threatening to infringe on my right to be professionally mobile?"

Letty smiled. "I've always thought that threats happen before the action. Once the action's been taken, words don't matter as much."

I let my head bob just a tiny bit, enough to acknowledge:

touché. "Well, there's always the possibility that Old Windswept becomes the hot ticket item among the Body Corporate. I've been sending samples to Thronehill and getting some orders."

She laughed. "Your rum may be good, but I doubt it's one-trillion-yuan good."

"Buy a case. You can find out for yourself."

"I could buy a million cases, and you'd still be in debt for what you did."

"What I did saved Occupied Space's population from getting thrown back into the Stone Age."

Letty rolled her eyes. "Please. Late Information Age at the worst."

"Cancer would still have gone back to being fatal. Same difference."

A flash of anger broke through Letty's calm facade. "Are you really that proud? You'd rather spend the rest of your life in the bottom of the plant than do this for me?"

"You want to strong-arm Saarien?" I went to the door and flung it open. The woman with the perfect skin spun around, her hands up and ready to hit. I pointed at her. "Get her to go down to his crappy little church. Have *her* break his thumbs. I don't do anyone's dirty work, no matter what they're offering."

Letty sighed. She picked up the jammer and fiddled with it as she peeled herself off the chair. "I really like this piece," she said, nodding to the chair.

"Yours isn't comfy enough?"

She shrugged. "Every time I'm in my chair, people yell at me to make their lives better. Gets unpleasant after a while."

"Then you should try another gig. I know one in the plant that can be filled immediately. You'd be great at it, seeing how well you shovel shit."

Letty didn't look at me as she breezed past. "That church

isn't the only one that Saarien has. You think a man as ambitious as Evanrute Saarien would limit himself to Hawks Street?" She shook her head, her smile growing bigger and meaner.

"So he's franchising."

Letty stopped at the threshold. When she turned to look at me, the smile she had made me think of every trophy fisherman I'd seen when they'd hooked a big one. Sweet Working Christ, this woman was *good* at pushing buttons. If I weren't so pissed at her, I would have asked for her to teach a master class at manipulation. "Ask around. You think you're the only employer losing people?" She shrugged.

I shrugged back. "There's nothing in the Charter stopping him."

"No, but what he's doing is going to tear the Charter into tiny, tiny pieces," she said. "You were there. You heard his sermon."

"I heard *part* of it."

"You heard the bit about the strike."

"How do you know?"

She pursed her lips, and her eyes flicked away. She clenched the jammer. I tensed. "Are you… are you hacking into my feed?"

She said nothing.

I shook my head. "Well, I never thought I'd see the day when the Prez herself became Big Brother." I pointed out into the hall. "You'd better hope that jammer works, or I will bring you down so fast you'll get the bends."

Letty's smile was gone now. "Padma, I'm asking you to do this because you are the perfect candidate for this gig. You're stuck in the worst job in Brushhead, and you have a history with him. He's acting contrite as hell, so he might be willing to bring you in."

"Why would he do that?"

"To prove he's changed. I don't know what's motivating him to start this strike, but I can see that he's going after it with the same fervor he had when he was in the Union. He only got out three months ago, and he's already got eight hundred people following him. It's just a matter of time before he's back to his old tricks."

"Then talk to the Parole Committee," I said. "If you can screw up my life so easily, putting him back in prison should be a cinch."

"It doesn't work like that," she said. "I can't override that decision. Checks and balances."

"Oh, so you can violate my buffers, keep me in my job, and break into my home, but you can't do anything to him? You need to find some better checks."

"*Or* you could take me up on my offer." She tapped on the doorframe. "I know you pay a ridiculously low rent for this place. I'm pretty sure if your landlady filed a complaint with the Housing Committee that she'd be able to charge market rates."

I ground my teeth. "I think it's really cute how you're being so tough with me but you couldn't have been like that with Saarien. Did I say 'cute'? I meant 'go fuck yourself.'"

Letty's bodyguard took a step toward me. Letty just turned her head, and the bodyguard froze, her fist raised to her chest. "There's no need for violence," said Letty. "We're all going to use our words."

"I just did," I said. "I can use them again. Go fuck yourself, Letty."

She smiled and turned to her bodyguard. "See, this is why it's a good thing she's Union and not still with the Big Three. She doesn't let up, even when she knows she's wrong. A steel will, this one has." She looked back at me. "The Union will forgive your debt in its entirety if you can stop Saarien from starting his strike. I don't care how you do it, as long as it doesn't end up with him in the hospital or dead."

I snorted. "You've got muscle, and you're afraid to use it? Maybe you're not cut out for office after all."

She shook her head. "Muscle is just another tool in the box. I don't want to break Saarien. I just want him stopped. I want any talk of a strike stopped."

"So we can't even use our words now?"

"A word like 'strike' can hurt a whole lot of people," she said. "It starts out as a whisper. Then it turns into talk. Then it's shouted by people throwing rocks. If there's no cane harvested, we don't get money. We don't get money, people start to starve. And then it gets *really* ugly."

"Then maybe you can loosen up the purse strings."

"You think I don't want to?" The smile faded, and Letty held up her hands, like she wanted to grab my shirt front. "You know how many times I've gone over our budget, Padma? Should I cancel preschool or elder care? Should I shut down the court system or food distribution?"

I narrowed my eyes. "Is it that bad?"

"You think I'd be doing this if it were good? Padma, I am *begging* you to help me. Just a week of work, and I'll cancel the debt."

"Turn off the jammer and say that again."

Letty shook her hand. "I can't let anyone else know about this."

I shrugged. "Then I can't take this deal." I closed the door.

"Wait!" Letty shoved her boot in the doorway.

I sighed and opened up. "How do I know you'll follow through on your part of the bargain? I don't work for handshakes. You put something on the Public or it's no go."

"If I talk about this, it's going to backfire," said Letty. "If Saarien thinks you're working for me, then you won't get far. And if anyone else on the Executive Council knows, they won't let me forgive the debt." She grabbed my arm. "I *need* you, Padma. This planet, this Union, we *all* need you." Her look softened. "Can't the Sky Queen of Justice help?"

I rolled my eyes. "I should say no just for you invoking that song."

"But you'll do it?"

I took in a breath. On the one hand, I didn't like the idea of sneaking around and doing Letty's dirty work. I never had, especially when I was a Ward Chair. She liked cutting all sorts of behind-the-back deals that usually messed with my headcount or funding. And the fact that she'd let Saarien walk all over us made me want to reject her on principle.

On the other hand, I had a trillion-yuan debt to pay. I didn't plan on having kids, but I could see Letty having me cloned so my duplicates would have to work it off.

I gave her a very slow nod. "Okay. Say I agree to this. What guarantee do I have that you'll follow through?"

"You'll just have to trust me."

"You broke into my *house*, Letty. I'd say trust is in short supply."

She scratched her neck. "Okay. I'll remove fifty thousand from your debt. Right now."

"I thought you said there wasn't any money."

Letty shrugged. "There's money, and there's discretionary funds. I've been saving for emergencies. I can move numbers around, and fifty K are gone from your total. I know it's not much, and it'll take a week or so to clear, but I hope you'll take it as a sign of my sincerity."

I narrowed my eyes. "I don't like it."

"You don't have to. You just have to do the job." Letty held out her hand.

And, like a fool, I shook it.

SIX

My first boss when I joined the Union was a foul-mouthed former data analyst for MacDonald Heavy named Hieu Vanavutu. The day I signed up to be an organizer, he sat me down and told me that the only thing that mattered in this job was planning. Forget all that bullshit about issues and personal leverage and knowing who was having sex with whom. A good plan of attack could make or break a labor action. And that meant sifting through data until your eyes hurt and your brain demanded alcohol and sex.

So, I sat back in my overstuffed chair (after I gave it a quick wipe-down; God only knew what horrible political diseases Letty had brought in with her) and poked around on the Public for any mention of Saarien's churches. Well, first I blinked up my debt balance. Sure enough, a pending credit for fifty thousand yuan had appeared. Granted, she could revoke it if I pissed her off, but, for now, Letty had followed through. That meant I had to do the same.

What I found made my guts shrivel. In the past three months, Saarien had set up twenty-two churches. Most were scattered around the city, with one lone outpost in the kampong. He had certainly been busy since his release. Now

I had to figure out who he was pulling back into his orbit.

I blinked up who had been inside the churches, just to see how many Union people had fallen under his spell. A few hundred, it turned out. They came from all kinds of jobs: a few doctors, some engineers, a lot of mid-level hands-on types. There was no pattern that I could make out right away, but there were a dozen people whom I had met face-to-face. That would be as good a place to start as any. If I had to stop Saarien, that would mean doing good old fashioned organizing work, and that meant bullshit sessions and beers. I would have to see how far Saarien's influence had reached out to the wider community. I would have to find out how many people were that upset with the way the Union was acting. And I'd have to make sure I had enough cash available if I went to a Freeborn-run bar.

The sun had set when I stepped out of my building onto Samarkand Road. I had split so much time between the plant and the distillery that I hadn't been able to enjoy my neighborhood at the end of the day, my favorite time. Most of the workers had clocked out, and the swing shift was wrapping up their dinners. That meant the air was alive with a symphony of smells: kimchi and fufu and tri-tip, grilling and baking and steaming, vinegar and sugar and fire. The thrum of cane diesel motors from tuk-tuks and lorries bounced off the row houses, their rumbling accompanied by the ringing of thousands of bicycle bells and the calls to prayer at the Emerald Masjid and Our Lady Of The Big Shoulders Cathedral. Brushhead was a mess, and Santee was a bigger mess, and I loved every inch of it. I loved the chaos. I loved the attempts at order. I loved living here, and I was pissed that it would take dealing with Evanrute Saarien again to keep this place going.

Unless he was right. Was he right? There was no way that dicktree was right.

Aw, dammit, I had to see if he was right.

I blinked my pai into hidden mode as I walked down Samarkand to Koothrapalli Avenue, Brushhead's main drag. I could have called Sirikit to take me around, but I had to move under my own power tonight. I grabbed a bike from a share rack and hopped into traffic. I hadn't had a chance to do this in sixteen months, just ride and take in everything zipping past me. The neighborhood sat in a sweet spot for me: lively enough that it didn't feel like the sterile graveyard that was Thronehill, but slow enough that I didn't get dizzy keeping up with the crowds.

Part of me wanted to do nothing but cruise for the rest of the night and see what was happening. That was the one part of being Ward Chair that I'd enjoyed: just seeing what was going on. I could just walk up to a group of people and ask: what's up tonight? And they'd direct me to hear a new band or check out a new machinist's shop or try someone's taco stand. And, inevitably, I'd start hearing about what was going wrong with their lives: the bass player didn't like the mandolin player, or the price of palm oil had gone up, or the permits for the taco stand were slow to come through. It would be my job to listen and take notes and do something about it, even if that something was to shake my head and say *Well, if you don't agree on how to arrange your songs, you should probably look for a new band*. There would be drama and accusations and grumbling about what the hell good was the Union anyway, but they would still come to me for solutions. It never ended. I missed it, and I was glad it was someone else's job now.

Most of the people on my list had also hidden themselves. I'd have to track them down the old-fashioned way: grabbing people they knew and telling them I wanted a meeting. But, for tonight, there were some Union people I could find. Plus, I really wanted to corner Ly Huang myself and find out what her deal was. I sent out texts to twenty people: *If you see this woman, tell me and I will buy you beer and burritos for a week.* I attached a picture of Ly Huang, one where she was working the cane press, laughing at a joke Marolo had told her.

In the meantime, I would start with the first person on my list of Saarien's congregants: Serena Llorens. A lifetime ago, she had been a shift supervisor at the cane refinery at Sou's Reach. It had been her job to keep that horrible place running, which had been a neat trick considering how Saarien had funneled all of its upkeep money into his various plans to Immanetize the Labor Eschaton. She had testified about being told to falsify safety records, to skimp on routine maintenance, and to stay quiet if she'd wanted to keep her job. She'd moved to another refinery on the Greenbelt, one that wasn't a deathtrap. We'd talked a bit after the trial, and she had even apologized for the way Sou's Reach had been such a mess.

My pai highlighted my route as I rode down towards the coast. The smell of decomposing seaweed hit me like a fist wrapped in kelp. The Greenbelt got its name long ago, back when the city was trying to become a place to live instead of a place to survive. Some of the first Breaches had moved here to get away from Thronehill. They would drag bundles of seaweed into carefully laid-out plots in order to fertilize the soil. Some of the choicest produce came from the Greenbelt, and I made a point of coming down here when strawberry season started. It made up for the fact that the neighborhood smelled like a baked tide pool. The cane refinery squatting on the shoreline was new, so its air scrubbers kept the odors of solvents and burned sugar inside.

Serena's pai placed her in a pub at Yusunori and Lowland, a place I'd never been to, called the Mermaid's Kick. I dropped my bike in a share stand and watched the clientele: they were all clean and wore nice clothes, like they'd scrubbed up before coming here. The sign was a picture of a mermaid with cornrows, bulging biceps, and clenched fists. She used her tail to knock a shark unconscious. Maybe it would be my kind of place.

The minute I walked through the door, I realized it would not. The lights were bright and harsh, the colors were muted pastels, and the people inside were punching at speed bags or doing yoga. A sign behind the bar boasted eight kinds of fruit juices and two raw vegetable entrees. It wasn't a pub; it was a fitness studio that had gutted and taken over a pub, the same way a parasitic wasp lays its eggs inside a caterpillar and eats the host body from the inside out. The whole place felt like it had been lifted out of Thronehill, down to the mind-breaking abstract pattern in the carpet.

I crouched down. Holy crap, the carpet *was* from Thronehill. Of all the things to remember from my time working in the Colonial Directorate, this ugly swirl of brown and purple had burned itself into my damaged brain. What's more, it looked new, like it had just come down the cable from an off-world WalWa factory.

I looked closer at the customers and saw they were all doing horrible impressions of people who worked for the Big Three. Their hair was slick and sculptured. Their clothes were tailored to be stiff and uncomfortable. Everyone clenched their glasses at chest-level, like we were taught to do in B-school, and everyone looked into each other's eyes with unblinking stares. I saw all kinds of Indenture markings: Medical Research, Nuclear Engineering, Heavy Entertainment. All of these people were acting as if they were still living the Life Corporate.

"Can we interface in a meaningful professional

interaction?" said a woman at my shoulder. It had been fourteen years since someone had said that in earnest, and I shuddered at the sound of that greeting.

She had a funny mark underneath her tattoo (a merlion wrapped around a planet: LiaoCon Colonial Preparation), and I blinked her face into the Public to find her profile. Ernestine Andrada, a Union liaison for the refinery at Beukes Point. She had Breached six years ago. I realized the blotch on her cheek was her Union fist covered by foundation.

"Fuck, no," I said, and I pushed my way towards Serena's dot.

She was in the next room, where she stood in front of a seated group of people, all wearing workout gear. Serena wore a sweat-stained red gi, and she exchanged a series of furious punches with a gray-haired man half her size. The man swept her leg, and she hit the floor, only to bounce back with the kind of speed that would have made Michelle Yeoh rise from her grave on Dead Earth and cheer. She knocked her sparring partner to the ground and rammed her fist toward his face, stopping just short of his nose. Her face was beet red and shining as she stepped back so the man could get to his feet. They bowed, and he sat back down.

I glanced at the wall: there was a schedule of classes posted. Tonight's was *SELF-ESTEEM THROUGH SELF-DEFENSE*. Jesus, even the names were straight out of the Life Corporate. What was going on here?

"I don't expect you to be able to do *that* right away," said Serena, and the people laughed. "But if you continue with your practice, you'll be faster, stronger, and better equipped to take on your daily challenges. And we all want to be prepared for anything that might happen, right?"

"YES, SIFU!" the class responded in unison.

She bowed, and they bowed, and everyone went for fruit smoothies.

I blinked up my buffer from Saarien's trial. The woman on the stand was definitely not the woman toweling herself off at the front of the room. Two years ago, Serena Llorens looked exhausted and ill, like she was going to throw up and pass out. Now, her skin flushed from an evening of beating up people, she looked like she could knock out the world with one punch.

"You here for the next class?" she said. "You're going to have to put on appropriate clothing…" She stopped and blinked.

I held up my hands. "Please don't hit me."

She focused back on me. "Why would I?"

"I have no idea," I said. "But that seems like a good thing to say in a place like this." The walls were decorated with WalWa motivational art: nude people climbing mountains, lines of happy customers buying NutriFood, executives trading grooming tips and social diseases. "Though, I have to admit, I'm not sure what *kind* of place it is."

Serena licked her lips and nodded at the art. "Nostalgia. Or something like it."

"For the Life Corporate?"

She tossed the towel into a battered bag. "You ever miss it?"

"Hell, no."

Serene shook her head. "That was a pretty quick answer."

"Because it's the truth. Working for WalWa was a disaster. I gave everything to climb the ladder, and it almost killed me."

"How?"

The Fear stirred. "That's none of your business."

"Then what is? What are you doing here, Padma?"

"I should ask you the same question." I tapped a poster, an image of a multi-ethnic crowd, all of them smiling, their teeth identical. "I realize we don't know each other, but after all that time basking in Evanrute Saarien's bullshit, you really want to tell me you're longing for the days before you Breached?"

"The one has little to do with the other," said Serena. She picked up the bag. "You want a beverage?"

"No, I want a *drink*."

She snorted. "With an attitude like that, you *should* have some juice. My treat."

I followed her out of the room as eager students in jodhpurs and riding boots entered. I gawped at them; where in the world could they have found equestrian outfits? What kind of weird hell had I entered?

At the bar, Serena got two glasses and filled them from the taps. She gave me one. It smelled like lawn trimmings. "To nutritional optimization," she said. When I realized it was a toast, I clinked glasses and slugged it in one go. Serena laughed. "It's better if you sip."

"What was it?" I put the glass back and tried to swallow the taste away.

"Sea grapes, collards, and ong choy. All locally grown."

"Well, I can sure taste it."

She took a sip. "You must think we're all mad. To be here."

I looked around the room and remembered the hundreds of conferences, mixers, and think-alongs I had attended during my illustrious Indenture. "There was a time when stuff like this was my life. Nineteen hours Standard Time, we would clock out and socialize with our colleagues, try out the latest improved intoxicants, attempt the latest sexual positions, work for another couple of hours in our housing, then collapse and do it all over again. I thought that was all there was until I Breached. Then I learned that you can leave work, hang out with *friends*, drink stuff that people had made with care, fall in love, try and build a future on our own."

She smiled. "I remember feeling like that, too."

"But you don't anymore?"

Serena took a long pull on her juice, then gritted her teeth like she'd just drank primer. "I know why you're here, Padma, and it's not like you think."

"What isn't?"

She put down her glass. "I don't want to go back to Thronehill. Not now, not ever. You know why I Breached? Because everyone in my department was offered promotions if they went and got brain surgery. It was an experiment to see if LiaoCon could squeeze a little more productivity out of us. Everyone would get implants to regulate adenosine and melatonin, all to keep people awake as long as possible. Do it for eighteen weeks, measure the results, bam, instant raise in pay and benefits."

"Did you do it?"

She bit her lip. "No. But I *wanted* to. I wanted that promotion so bad I was willing to let someone cut into my skull and keep me awake for eighteen weeks. I put in for a transfer to a new colony, just so I'd have the opportunity to jump ship. Took me a while to get here, and I would never go back."

She swallowed and looked at the executive cosplay. "But my life had an *order* back then. You get that, right?"

I nodded. "But it also didn't have freedom."

She snorted. "Freedom is an illusion. Come here, and you're free to starve. Free to get left outside in a hurricane. Even the people doing the worst Corporate work had a guaranteed income and bennies. Not here."

"It *is* guaranteed."

"Then where is it?" She pointed at the people in the crowd. "Everyone here has been passed over for promotion, or they've been bumped from their housing, or they've just been screwed in some way because someone higher up in the Union could do so. And I'm not just talking about people in Contract Slots. Everyone here is a Shareholder, but their Share income is drying up. They can't live on it anymore, and there isn't enough work to make ends meet."

"So they dress up and come here?"

"How is that different from going to a bar and getting loaded? People are hurting, and they need something to take away the pain. If it's not rum or chiba, why not pretend you're back in a time and place where everything made sense?"

"Because…" I looked at the people in their business suits, talking like they were making billion-yuan deals. "Because it's just so fucked up."

Serena laughed. "Our lives are fucked up. And they're only going to get worse."

"Why's that?"

She shook her head. "You wouldn't know, what with your distillery and all. You're part of the problem."

"Because I make rum?"

"Because you consume cane. You need it just like the Big Three, just like everyone." She bit her lip. "I've spent my entire adult life processing that stuff. We grow it, and we burn it, and we grow more, because it's the way we've always done things. We don't try and harness the sun or the wind or the tides, not when we can just grow our own hydrocarbons."

"And what's wrong with that?"

"Because it still takes *people* to make it happen, and…" She sighed. "I saw how the Big Three were grinding people up. I Breached, and now I see that the Union is doing the same. There's a lot of anger out there, in the city and in the kampong. You need to get ready for what's coming."

I nodded to her makeshift dojo. "That's why you're teaching that class?"

She nodded and smiled. "That, and it's cheaper than therapy."

"Sounds like you've got it dialed in." I thought about ordering another drink, then remembered where I was. "What I don't get is why you go to Saarien's church."

She scrunched her face up. "I don't know what you're talking about."

"On Lu Yua Street, about six blocks from here. You've visited three times a week for the past six weeks."

She stiffened. "Are you tracking me?"

"I'm tracking a bunch of stuff, because none of it makes any sense. Why would someone like you fall back into his orbit after what he did?"

She shook her head, hard and fast. "You don't know me." She went for the door.

I waited until she had left before bolting after her. She walked up the Belt, her head down and her steps quick. "Serena!" I yelled, then ran. She didn't stop or turn around, not until I put a hand on her shoulder. She grabbed my wrist and spun me around, smashing my face into a café's window. I glanced down at a couple, cups halfway to their open mouths. I tried to smile, but it probably looked like a grimace as she drove her elbow into my back.

Serena put her mouth next to my ear. "You don't touch me, you understand?" she hissed.

"Okay," I said.

"You have no idea what I've been through."

"You're right."

"And I don't need your pity."

She gave my arm an extra crank, and I yelped, "Okay!" She eased up enough for me to peel my face off the window. I backed away, my hands up. Her entire body coiled, ready to lash out, ready to *hurt*. "I don't want to cause trouble, okay, Serena? I just... I want to know *why*."

Her eyes were fixed on my feet, so I took another step back. If she bolted, I would have to let her go. But I didn't know how to keep her here, keep her talking. All I could do was bullshit. "I went to his place on Hawks today."

She looked up. "Then why did you come to me?"

"I didn't *stay* there," I said. "I just heard that he was out of prison and had started a church. I had to see for myself. He tried to kill me, remember? Remember the trial?"

Serena nodded, and she straightened her shoulders a little. "I don't know how he got out early, either. I wanted him to rot." She shook her head. "It was so hard running that refinery, to keep scrimping for parts and expertise. People got hurt all the time, and it was on *me*. You know what that's like, to have everyone think you're incompetent when the problems start from above you?"

I nod. "I work in the lowest part of the water plant. I know."

She nodded, her face still taut. "I went to Lu Yua 'cause I wanted to punch his lights out. I wanted him to tell me *why* he built that secret refinery."

"Did he?"

Her eyes softened. "He did. He said he was an asshole and that he was wrong and that I should have been given everything I needed to be successful. I didn't believe him, and I *told* him so."

I nodded. "I didn't either."

"He said he didn't expect me to believe him, but he wanted to make amends. He had to *show* me that he was sorry, that he'd changed. He asked me to spend the day with him bringing food and clothes and meds to people who needed them." She laughed. "I said he was full of shit, but I went. Just curious, I guess. We went all over the city, finding people hiding in tenements and hovels. And I kept running them through the Public and seeing that they were supposed to get all kinds of help but weren't." She shook her head. "Our system has broken down, Padma. It's just like the old refinery, teetering along, ready to collapse."

Serena looked me dead in the eye. "So, yeah, I go to his church, because I'm actually *fixing* things. The Union's supposed to take care of its members, whether they're working Slots or they're living off pensions. Everyone's supposed to have a floor to hold them up, but it's punched full of holes. I don't know who's letting this happen, if it's the Executive Committee or the Prez or what. What I *do* know is that Evanrute Saarien is committed to helping out everyone who's getting left behind."

"But you trust him?"

She shook her head. "I probably never will. But I trust the work that he's doing. I can see it right in my own neighborhood. I know three different people on disability who aren't getting their pensions, and that means they go hungry. Saarien's church has kept them fed. I trust that's going to make their lives better. Even though things are going to get worse first."

A chill ran up my spine. "Is that why you're teaching people how to punch each other out?"

"I'm showing people how to take care of themselves."

"By beating up their neighbors?"

"What neighbors?" Serena pointed at the couple in the café, who were staring at us with worry in their eyes. "Do you know everyone in your building? Do you know everyone on your block?"

"You just talked about people in your neighborhood."

"But I don't *know* them. This city's changing so fast that no one knows who's who any more. People come in from the kampong, they leave for other parts of the planet, they don't stick around long. No one wants to put down roots. They just want to get by until they can move onto something bigger."

I felt this horrible tension gripping my chest, like everything she said was squeezing my heart. "Serena, aren't you still Union? Don't you still have a voice? Why aren't you and everyone in that... place all up in arms and pounding on your Ward Chair's front door?"

"Because our Ward Chair was the guy I sparred with tonight. He's with us, too." She slung her bag over her shoulder, a clear sign: *I'm through talking with you.* "There's a storm coming, Padma. You'd better take cover now."

I watched her go up the Greenbelt. Overhead, the night sky was perfectly clear.

SEVEN

I walked into the first bar I could find, made sure it was *actually* a bar, then ordered a beer. I took a few sips, glad that it was hefeweizen and not wheat juice. How many of those awful mixers had I gone to when I was still an Indenture? All those suits, all that barely veiled backstabbing, all those lists of approved intoxicants. I shuddered at the thought of the crowd at the Mermaid's Kick, all pretending they were still living the Life Corporate.

I couldn't just sit here. I knew that. Serena hadn't used the word *strike*, but everything in her speech and body language screamed it. The way she railed against the Union not keeping its promises, the frustration of nothing getting fixed, that bit about how *things were going to get worse first*. That was the talk that got people building barricades and hiding caches of rocks and diesel bombs. How many other people who weren't mixed up in Saarien's churches felt the same way? How many of them were learning how to beat the crap out of each other?

I finished half the beer and blinked up a map of all the Temples of the New Holy Light. There was the one on Lu Yua Street, of course, but Serena had probably gone there and gotten my face blacklisted. I still didn't get what had brought her into that place, but it didn't matter. She was there, as were a lot of other people. If they were all as angry and ready to strike as Serena, there could be a strike in the next few days, never mind weeks. If I couldn't understand why this was happening, maybe I could short circuit it.

I blinked texts to my little surveillance network to see if any of them had leads on Ly Huang. Odd Dupree, an old colleague from the plant, thought he did, though his pai and his brain were acting up a lot, thanks to his Indenture time as a pharmacological test subject. He sent me a fuzzy picture of a woman who looked a lot like Ly Huang. She was walking past a glowing sign written in Cyrillic. The picture didn't have a landstamp, but my pai could locate the sign: a Serbian bakery in Globus Heights. I groaned at the thought of riding another five klicks uphill, but a lead was a lead. I texted Odd to trail her as best he could, then grabbed a bike and took off. I hoped I could get there faster than Serena could send word that I was out and digging around. I blinked my pai into hiding as I passed a flashing Public terminal. Word-of-mouth still traveled faster than texts, but what the hell.

Thirty minutes later, I clunked the bike into a rack and slid out of the saddle. Odd gangled at a table outside Lepa's Bakery. "You want some proja?" he said, holding up a plate of cornbread as I collapsed into the seat opposite him. "You look like you need some carbs."

It took everything I had not to dive face first into the plate and gorge. I tore off a hunk and chewed, taking the minimal amount of time to swallow before taking the next bite. After I had demolished the entire piece, I ordered two more, along with some cheese spread. Odd smiled. "I started coming here a year ago. It's a great spot. Plus it's close to church."

I stopped chewing and looked at Odd. "I didn't know you

were a churchgoer, Odd."

He nodded, his floppy hair bouncing. "Glenn and I started coming here a few months ago. I think. I'm still kind of fuzzy on keeping time, but it's getting better." He rubbed his beard, the whiskers covering most of his old Indenture tattoo.

"You're looking a lot more relaxed."

He nodded and grinned. "It's being a part of something bigger than me. I like that."

"What about the Union?"

Odd made a face. "Well, that was nice at first. You know, when I Breached."

"I remember, Odd. I signed you up."

His face brightened. "You sure did! You helped me find a flat and get treatment for my condition."

I nodded, thinking back to those early weeks when Odd had waded out of the ocean. He'd been a pharmaceutical test subject for LiaoCon, and the decades of getting pumped full of drugs had done a number on his brain. He would have seizures, memory loss, the whole kit.

He pursed his lips. "But you also got me that horrible job."

"Which I also got you out of."

He nodded. "Yeah, but that took, what, eight years?"

I held out my hands in supplication. "Odd, if I had any control over how many people Breached, do you think I would have let you stew there for so long?"

He waved his hand, dismissing the thought. "No, of course not." But then the thought came back, because he furrowed his eyebrows. "But, still, I felt kinda forgotten. At church, it's not like that. We're actually doing *something*."

"Like what?"

He ticked off his fingers. "Preschool. Meal delivery for shut-ins. Extensive medical background interviews."

"What?"

He nodded. "We're building a database of all the conditions all of us Breaches have as a result of our Indentures. There's a lot of messed up people here, Padma. Genetic disorders, physical handicaps, all kinds of mental trauma. You know anyone with that?"

The Fear laughed. *I know someone who fits that description.* Good Lord, it was only eight in the evening; how could The Fear come out to play so soon?

I put my hands flat on the table. "If I knew anyone with those problems, I'd tell them to talk with their Ward Chair, like I used to do with you."

"But did you all the time?" Odd's face crumpled. "Even before all this business with the lifter and your distillery, I always felt like you spent more time at Big Lily's than you did going around and talking with people."

"That's bullshit, Odd, and you know it!"

He leaned back, and I cursed under my breath. "I'm sorry," I said. "I know I can get a little heated–"

Odd put his hands on mine. "I think you need to come to church with me."

"I'd rather you tell me about the woman I asked you to find."

He smiled. "Come with me and you'll see."

The church was a block away, halfway down a dead-end alley off Lutyen Avenue. There were no guards outside, and the doors were wide open. Light and music bounced around the alley walls, the sounds of fifty people singing their hearts out (*I had a job once cutting cane, worked all day through blood and pain*) and clapping their hands off. "I don't think this is the place for me," I said.

Odd nodded. "I'll save a seat for you." He ducked under the doorway, into the blast of heat and music.

I peeked around the corner and saw a room similar to

the one on Hawks. There was the table with food, there was
another with clothes, and there was an altar. Fifty ragged,
happy people smiled as they swayed to the accordion and
euphonium duo playing up front. I got a lump in my throat
from the sound of the squeeze-box, but the player was a
little old lady, not Washington Lee. Saarien wasn't here in
person, but he was on a battered two-meter-wide screen
hanging from a corner. He clapped along with the music.
Maybe every service was networked through worship. I
made sure to keep out of sight of any cameras or eyeballs.

When the song came to its thunderous conclusion,
Saarien spread his arms wide. "Has everyone had enough
to eat? Is there anyone who wants to bear witness before
we close out?"

A sunburned woman stepped up to Saarien. She had a
salt-and-pepper plait that went down to the small of her
back. She turned to face the camera, her dark, shark eyes
glinting in the light. It was the woman who'd hopped into
Ly Huang's lorry. The light glinted off her glass supernova
fist pin as she introduced herself as Saraphina Moss, fresh
out of jail. She rambled about how she had found meaning
in her life after joining the Temple, how she was a criminal
but was paying her debt to society. I didn't hear her words.
I just looked at those eyes and wondered how I could make
a point to stay as far away from them as possible.

Saarien thanked the woman. "Peace and joy to you!"

"AND ALSO TO YOU!" roared the congregants.

"Lift up your hearts!"

Everyone held up their hands. "WE LIFT THEM UP
TOGETHER!"

"Lift up your fists!"

Everyone clenched their hands into fists. "WE LIFT
THEM UP TOGETHER!"

"Now let us all go in peace, to love and serve one another."

The congregation hugged each other as the screen flicked off. I scanned their faces until I saw Ly Huang. She stood next to the euphonium player. Ly Huang had always looked relaxed at work. Here, she seemed ready to fall asleep. Her eyelids were heavy, and she kept swaying even though the music had stopped. Was Saarien drugging the food? Where could he have even gotten drugs?

People filed out, some of them giving me stoned nods, others hurrying off into the night. After a few minutes, Odd beckoned to me from the soup table. I squared my shoulders and marched in, keeping watch on Ly Huang from the corner of my eye. "You hungry?" said Odd, handing me a bowl.

"No, thank you. I had enough proja." I eyed the soup, wishing my pai had a working chromatograph. Saarien was no chemist, but he certainly knew a lot from his time at the refinery. If he could pull Serena back into his orbit, who else had he got his claws into?

"It was good, wasn't it?"

"Delicious. What was the deal with the fists, Odd?"

He smiled. "It's a reminder that we're all in this together."

"Really?" I touched the fist tattooed on my cheek, right below my old Colonial Directorate ink. "See, I thought the fist symbolized how we would all come to each other's defense if the Big Three tried to screw us."

Odd looked at me, his eyes so clear and calm that it scared me. "Then what do we do when the Union screws us, Padma? An attack on one is an attack on all."

I leaned over the table to put my face close to his. "Is that what Saarien's telling you? That the Union, the group that's protected us, is *attacking* us?"

"What else do you call it?" His smile faded. "You don't think it's a form of violence, what's going on? People getting booted from their homes, getting left behind? That's against the First Clause, as far as I'm concerned."

"No, it's exactly what Saarien used to do when he was still a Ward Chair," I said. "Every chance he got, he would moan about how hard things were in Sou's Reach, and that he needed extra funds to feed orphans and re-educate single fathers. And do you remember what he did with all that money?"

A woman cleared her throat behind me. "Is there a problem?"

I looked over my shoulder. Ly Huang stood there with two goonish-looking people. She wore a supernova fist pin, this one made from stainless steel. Her look grew harsher when she recognized me. "You have some nerve coming here, Padma."

I turned around, keeping some space between my butt and the soup table. "Really."

She nodded. "All this time, I thought you were a good boss. But now I know you're just another parasite, sucking value and life away from me."

"Ah. That's why you walked off your job without telling Marolo or me?"

She spat on the ground. "My *job* was a joke. Pressing cane for pennies."

"You made forty yuan an hour when other distillers pay twenty. You got a month of paid vacation, medical, dental, education grants, and a better pension than the Union pays."

The two goons looked at each other. One of them, a woman with a shaved head, leaned over to Ly Huang and said, "Really? That's a sweet deal."

"It was garbage, is what it was," said Ly Huang, her voice harsh. "It was wage slavery."

"No, it was *work*." I pointed at the tattoo on my cheek. "*This* was a hell of a lot closer to slavery than you or any other Freeborn will ever know."

"And there it is," said Ly Huang, fire in her eyes. "The superiority of the Breach comes out."

"All right." I stepped to Ly Huang and put my nose a few centimeters from hers. "You want to play Who's More Morally Superior? Put on your big girl pants and get ready, kid, because I've been *winning* this game since before you were a fetus." I cocked my head. "How are your parents, by the way? They're still getting the remittances from your paycheck, right? The one that's helped them buy a more efficient digester and those new PVs? Your mom wrote me a letter thanking me for your pay. She can get those lung meds again."

Ly Huang spat. "You think you can buy my parents off? Bu wouldn't *need* those meds if she hadn't been breathing in smoke from slash-and-burns her whole life."

I shook my head, my eyes locked on hers. "I like your mother a lot, but you can't pin it on me or the Union if she worked *illegal* farms."

"She did what she had to do! She had to keep us alive!"

"By not coming into the city? By not finding a better gig?"

"What better gig?"

I shrugged. "Maybe one working on a distillery? You know, like the one *you* have?"

The other goon, a man with scars on his forehead, leaned over Ly Huang's shoulder and gave me a smile. "Excuse me. Do you have any openings?"

Ly Huang spun around and shot him a look so sharp it cut. The goon shrank back.

"Looks like you've got some pull around here," I said to Ly Huang.

"What do you care? Exploiter."

I kept my eyes from rolling. "If you want to call someone

names, Ly Huang, it helps to use the right ones. I may be a lot of things, but I have never exploited you or any of your co-workers. I'm always a phone call away if you need to talk to me, but you haven't said *boo* for the past year. If you and everyone else is scared the distillery's going under, don't be. You can come back to work right now, and we can let this all go."

"Wait, more of you left?" said the goon with the shaved head.

I nodded. "I had a crew of twelve yesterday, but everyone's walked off. You any good with tools?"

"Heck, yeah!" said the goon, her face brightening up. "I had a Class Two Mechanist's rating!"

"What's your name?"

She grinned. "Gwendolyn Barker."

"I'm Kazys Ming!" said the other goon. "I'm really good with words."

"I could always use marketing people." I walked around Ly Huang and held out a hand. "Can you start today?"

"No, they can't!" Ly Huang's voice shifted, her tone that of an angry dog owner. The goons, their brains programmed to respond to command presence, shrank back. Oh, those poor bastards.

Ly Huang took a sharp breath, her face screwed up in rage. "My eyes have been opened to what you and every other Union stooge has done to all of us. You make promises, you seduce us with so-called 'living wages,' all to distract us from the fact that *we* are the true owners of this and every other world. You were exploited by the Big Three, and then you come here and exploit us. It's in your nature, and you can never change."

"I'm not a scorpion, and you're not a frog," I said. "Everyone has to work to make a living."

She sneered as she shook her head. "That's easy for you

to say when you own the places we work. If you don't make enough profit, you just close things down. People lose their jobs, they go hungry, they get desperate."

"Or they go find some way to make a living. Are you trying to tell me that there aren't enough jobs on this planet?"

"Only if you work the cane fields," said Ly Huang. "If you want to spend your life cutting and stacking, sure. But if you want something better, you have to fight for it. That's what Reverend Saarien is showing us: how to fight."

"*Reverend*?"

She nodded. "He's been ordained in the eyes of the universe. He knows the way to liberation, and he's going to teach us. We are history's select. What we will start today is going to spread to Occupied Space until everyone is truly free!" She looked at the goons. "You keep her here. I have work to do."

The two goons gave each other pained looks. "Do we have to?"

"YES."

Ly Huang barked the word so loud it made all of us shake. The goons nodded, then swooped to me before I could move. They formed a human wall and pushed me into the table so hard it hit the wall. Hot soup spilled on the floor and splashed through my trousers. The goons' massive bulk blocked out any forward escape. Both of them stared down at me, their faces turned to stone masks, though the one with the scars gave me a brief look that said, *Sorry, it's corporate programming. What can I do?*

"Ly Huang," I called over the wall of goons. "I know Saarien's talking about a cane strike. You know that's going to screw things up for a whole lot of people, right?"

I could hear Ly Huang clear her throat. "When anything happens to disturb profits, what do the capitalists do? They go on strike, don't they? They withdraw their finances from that particular mill. They close it down because there are no profits to be made there. They don't care what becomes of the working class. But the working class, on the other hand, has always been taught to take care of the capitalist's interest in the property."

I ground my teeth. "Ly Huang, you may have had a tough life on the kampong, but you do not get to quote Big Bill Haywood back at me. Not until you've gone through half the shit *I* did to make sure that people like you could get things like schools, money, and healthcare."

She laughed. "Oh, right. I forgot. You and all the other big Union heroes got your heads caved in when you squared off against the Big Three. You did your marches, sang your songs, inked your faces to show everyone what you did to protect the workers of Occupied Space."

"Just because you weren't there doesn't mean it didn't happen," I said.

"None of that has made my life better. It hasn't made my mom's lungs any better. It hasn't kept people from begging in the streets for scraps."

"And if you start this strike, it's going to get worse. Please trust me on this."

"Why should I do that?"

"Because I've been through two strikes, and Saarien hasn't. He stayed holed up in Sou's Reach. Once you start a strike, things get ugly fast. The food's going to run out, and then the rum's going to run out, and then everyone will be at each other's throats. There's still time to talk and cool things down."

I heard quick steps as Ly Huang walked back. She climbed onto the goons' backs and looked down at me. "Actually, the word went out ten minutes ago. The bit about raising our fists? That was the signal. Strike Committees everywhere are seizing control and telling the people the truth. Your Union has failed again, and, when we're done and get what we want, you're going to wish you'd turned things over to us earlier." She hopped off the goons and left.

A few moments later, Odd poked his head around the male goon's biceps. "You sure you don't want soup?"

I struggled against the goons, but they held their ground, which held me in place. "Odd, can you help me? Can you get your... friends to let me go?"

"Sorry, Padma, but I never studied command presence." His eyes unfocused for a moment. "Hey, did you go to B-School? Didn't you study it?"

"Yes, but I can't really do it when I'm being crushed!"

"Oh. Yeah. That's probably tough." Odd sat down on the table and picked up a bowl of soup. He knocked his spoon around for a moment. "She is right, you know."

I stopped wriggling. "What?"

Odd nodded to himself as he spooned soup and watched it fall back into the bowl. "You are an exploiter. Not that you're a bad person! But you do use people. And you're not really nice about it."

I jumped at him, but the goons pushed back. My ass had now fallen asleep from getting shoved into the table's edge.

Odd held out his hands. "Plus you're really thin-skinned."

I gave one more shove against the goons. "You really think that?"

"Yep." Odd put the soup down and got up. "When I worked at the plant, I saw how you'd blow people off. They'd come to you for help, and you'd tell them you were busy but that you'd look into their problems. You never did. Everyone talked about it. People were glad when you took Bloombeck's old Slot. Said you deserved it."

The Fear chuckled. I kept my mouth shut.

"Now, I didn't agree with that," said Odd.

"You just said I was an exploiter."

"Oh, I'm on board with that. But the part about working Bloombeck's Slot? I respected you for that. Felt to me like you were doing penance. I've tried telling that to the others, but they just said it was high time you wallowed in shit like the rest of us."

"Real short-term memories there."

"I know, right?" Odd laughed. "And *I'm* the one with the neuron damage!"

I sighed. "For what it's worth, Odd, they're right. I did blow off people. I was so close to getting my payout, I lost track of my job. But that doesn't excuse what's about to happen."

"I think it's already happened, right?"

"Work with me, Odd. There is always time to get everyone talking. If the cane stops, so does the money. The money stops, it's going to get bad fast."

Odd pursed his lips. "Okay. I think you're right. Let's get you out of there."

I struggled against the goons. "I still can't get enough breath."

He nodded. "That's gonna be a problem. I was always impressed with the way you could change your voice when you were talking to goons. I remember that one time at Big Lily's how you did the command presence thing on this one guy, and he had to stand on one foot for an hour. That was funny. Kinda cruel, but funny."

The two goons stirred. Their eyes flicked toward each other. "Is that true?" rumbled Gwendolyn. Oh, shit, had they learned how to break their programming? Or were they just pissed off? They both pressed in closer. One of them poked me in the diaphragm.

I gasped and nodded.

Gwendolyn stepped back enough to allow my lungs to

reinflate. I fell to my knees, gasping. She took a knee and put her face in front of mine. "You know, we can't help how we are. All us goons. The Big Three modify our bodies when we go into Security Services. They change the cell structures of our muscles and bones, and we can't shrink back. My bones are so dense I need to eat coral just for the calcium. Did you know that?"

My head spun. "I did not."

"We need supplements that can't be made here," she said. "We have to scrounge to find what we need just to stay healthy, and the Temple provides that."

The other goon, Kazys, crouched down next to his partner. "We're not mindless, you know. I write monologues. About humanity's relationship with nature. I was going to perform tonight at the Novice Theater Group, but I had to come here to work."

"That was you?"

He perked up. "You heard of me?"

"I heard you're *good*," I gasped.

"Thank you."

"You're welcome."

"My point," said Gwendolyn, "is that we were supposed to be welcomed as members of the Union, but we're not. We're thought of as less than human, as these mindless machines that respond to people's voices." She touched my ink. "I'm sure the Big Three hurt you somehow. I can promise they hurt us, too. It would be nice if someone acknowledged that."

I looked at these two people and thought of the times I've faced off with lines of WalWa goons. They wore armor that made them look like metal rhinos, all sliding plates and sharp points. They didn't need weapons; one punch would be enough to break ribs and burst organs. Every time some former goon would come into Brushhead looking for work,

I would always send them to the shipbreaking yards or the heavy industrial parts of town. I had no need for brute force in my plant.

I nodded. "I'm sorry. You're right. I certainly did not think you or anyone like you were capable of getting hurt. That was wrong of me."

Gwendolyn. "I accept your apology."

"Now, may I please go and stop this strike?"

"No," said Kazys. "We've got orders to keep you here for the next forty-eight hours. Also, if you try command presence on us, I'm going to put my hand over your mouth." He held up his hand; it was big enough to cover my entire face.

"Okay," I said. I sat on the floor. "Can I get some of that soup now?"

Odd poured me a bowl. I threw it in the air. Both goons looked up, their mouths wide open. That gave me enough time to roll to my right and vault for the door. I slammed into it, and the door swung into an alley full of angry, chanting people. Some of them gave me hard stares. I didn't take time to explain. The goons fought each other to get out the door. I climbed up and over the crowd, apologizing as I stepped on shoulders and heads all the way out of the alley.

When I got to the intersection of Lutyen and Kamakiri, a blast of arena-concert sound hit me. The street was wall-to-wall bodies, all of them holding signs and chanting "OUR WORK, OUR PAY! OUR PAIN, OUR CANE!" I saw Freeborn, Union, old, young, the whole city, the whole *planet* moving like the tide up the street. I scanned feeds on the Public and saw the same scene everywhere. Human cordons stopped the cane trucks and the airships. Crowds flooded the lifter control room and the cargo depots. The planet had stopped working.

Strike.

EIGHT

It took me two hours to return to Brushhead. I had to go on foot. The streets were jammed so tight with people that bicycles couldn't even get about. I tried to take alleys and side streets, but they were also packed. Every time I blinked up a map, it looked like a rash. Everyone was out of their houses, out of their jobs, out of their churches, and into the streets. They were also moving opposite of where I wanted to go, which meant a lot of pushing and shoving and yelling at people to just *stop* for a minute and let me through, dammit.

So, I wasn't really in the mood for any more bullshit when I entered my flat and found, yet again, Letty Smythe sitting in my chair. Jennifer the bodyguard stood at Letty's shoulder. Letty had helped herself to the Beaulieu's Blend (not, I noted, the Old Windswept; she may have had no problems breaking and entering into my home, but at least she respected me enough to keep away from the good booze). "This," she said, holding her glass aloft, "is indeed a remarkable fuck-up."

"Don't you have a job to do, or an office to do it in?"

Letty shook her head and knocked back the rum. She

slammed the glass on the table and reached for the bottle. It took her a few tries to get a grip, and even more to get the rum into the glass. "I'll clean the table," she said as she reached for the glass. "Later. You know."

I shook my head and sat down. "Letty, I know I'm not privy to what goes on in our Union's upper echelons, but, outside, it looks to me like the entire city is marching."

She drank and nodded. "Excellent observation."

"I was under the impression that Saarien's movement was much, much smaller."

Letty nodded. "Did I say that? I'm not quite sure."

"Maybe if you hadn't jammed my pai, we could go back over my buffer and confirm that."

She snorted. "You're still hung up on that? By the way, you look like hell."

I put the bottle on the kitchen counter. "I'm going to take a shower. When I'm done, I expect you both to be out of here. And you can threaten me all you want, Letty. I'm too tired to care right now."

I plodded into the bathroom and turned on the taps in the shower. A spurt of water shot out of the showerhead, followed by a few more convulsions. The plumbing groaned like a giant having an orgasm, and the water stopped. I twisted the taps, then tried the sink: nothing. I marched into the kitchen and turned on the faucet. It spat water, coughed, and did nothing more.

Letty had retrieved the bottle and settled back in the chair. "Trouble?"

"Did you do this?"

"Oh, no. That would be the strike."

"Even at the water works?"

"Everywhere!" Letty waved her hands, and rum spilled out of her overfilled glass. "The entire planet has stopped, all thanks to Evanrute Saarien and his magical marching millions. They're probably gonna burn stuff down, starting with my office."

"Your office is made of solid pourform."

"You know, that's what all my advisors have said. They also told me that this unrest was limited to isolated pockets of Freeborn. Yet, there are many, many of our Union brethren in the streets, all of 'em chanting for a strike." She shrugged. "I'm sure those fuckers will figure some way to burn the Union Hall to the ground. They've probably got some magical Greek Fire shit ready to roll as soon as I show up."

"All the more reason for you not to be here. I happen to like my flat in its non-burned state."

"But don't you see that this is *both* our problems now?"

"Uh-uh. I'm not the Prez. I'm just a rank-and-file bozo. This is all on you. Not my circus, not my monkeys." I opened the door and waved my hand into the hall with a flourish. "Thanks for visiting."

"I will cancel your debt *now*. Right here." Letty pounded the table, sending her glass bouncing to the floor. It shattered, and Jennifer dove to cover her. "What was that?" Letty said underneath her human shield.

"Go home, Letty. We both know that you can't make any deals when you're drunk."

"The hell I can't!" Letty shoved and slapped at Jennifer until her bodyguard moved aside. Letty wobbled to her feet and emptied her pockets on the table. Out came two multi-tools, a mini-torch, keys, breath mints, and six matchboxes. She made a show of opening the boxes and showing me their sparkling electronic innards before smashing them to pieces with her fist. Then she scooped them into a little pile and lit the torch.

I took a step forward. "Hey, don't–"

Whoosh. The cardboard caught, and the stench of burning

cane plastic and solder filled my flat. "Don't worry, I got it," Letty said as a bright spot of fire rose in the middle of my dining room table. She sprinkled the mints on top of the electronic funeral pyre, and the sugar burned a neon green.

And that's when the rum ignited.

Letty yelped as the cone of blue flame spread over the tabletop. The rum had seeped into the table's seams, down its legs, onto the floor. Within moments, a full-blown fire had broken out in my living room. I ran for the sink to get a glass of water, but only got a cough of air. I reached for the fire extinguisher next to my stove, but it was too late: Letty had grabbed the bottle of Beaulieu's and poured it on the fire, forgetting that 140-proof rum has a tendency to burn when it touches an open flame. The ensuing fireball rolled up and out, catching the curtains and spreading to the ceiling.

"OUT!" Jennifer threw Letty over her shoulder and ran for the door. I pulled the pin on the fire extinguisher and sprayed down the table. The foam crackled as it hit the flames, but it wasn't enough. The fire jumped to the highback chair. It rolled into my bedroom. I dropped the now-empty extinguisher and bolted for the door.

I hacked the rising smoke out of my lungs. All around me, people burst from their apartments holding spouses, children, aquariums. Swaroop Patil's children clustered around his knees; I picked up the two closest to me and shouted for everyone to follow me out. When Swaroop didn't move, I kicked him in the ass. He started and began cussing me out as I ran down the hallway to the fire door.

Down the rickety fire escape and onto the street we went. The building's muster point was at the koa tree out front, and all our neighbors had gathered round in a sooty huddle. By the time we reached the tree, Swaroop had cooled down, though the fire hadn't. Flames gushed from every window on every story. I handed Rohit and Aman back to Swaroop and blinked up a schematic of the building. Everyone trackable had gotten out. I sent texts to everyone who lived at 42 Samarkand, just to be sure.

The clang of bells cut through the noise of the crowd. A truck – not a fire truck, but a regular old MacDonald Heavy Hanuman Cargo Truck – nosed its way through the rubberneckers. A dozen people hopped out, all of them carrying axes and fire extinguishers. They wore heavy coats and work boots, the kind of gear you'd see on an airship ground crew. "Is everyone out?" asked one of them, a Freeborn man with tight cornrows and the most impressive mustache I had ever seen outside of a military history book.

"I think so," I said.

He grunted. "Well, did you check?"

I gave him a look. "I'm sorry. I was helping my neighbor with his kids as we fled for our lives. Who the hell are you, anyway? Where's the fire department?"

"We *are* the fire department," he said. "At least, until the pros can get here. The marchers have cut off access from the station, and we were nearby."

I gave their tools – machetes and rakes – the once-over. "You guys are cane cutters?"

The man grinned, his mustache making his smile look even wider. "Best in the biz. We can clear a hectare, do a controlled burn, and have everything stacked, all before the dinner bell. We been busy doing mop-up burns for the black stripe, and we were nearby for a–"

A window blew out on the top floor, and a sooty face looked down. "HELP!"

It was Agamjot Patil, Swaroop's youngest. Oh, crap, she must have gotten lost on the way out. I sized up Mustache Man; he was too short. Another cutter was more my size. "Give me your coat!"

"What?"

I grabbed at his coat and started peeling it off. "This is my building, and you don't know the way up there." I threw on the coat and checked its pockets. Cane crews had to carry breathing gear and portable heat shelters in case they got caught in the middle of a burn (even though burns were illegal and inefficient as hell, the regulations for their gear had stuck around). I pulled the respirator mask from one pocket and snapped it over my face. I pulled the shelter – a folded-up foil balloon – out of the coat's other pocket. Mustache Man looked at me. "What are you waiting for?" I grabbed his fire extinguisher and ran to the front steps. Two blasts of foam in the door, the balloon over my head and shoulders, and I went in.

The mask wasn't tight enough to stop the smoke from seeping in. The stench of burning fabric and smoldering caneplas burned the inside of my nose. I wanted to push the mask into my face, but one hand was keeping the shelter up while the other spurted at the flames. I heard the other cutters behind me, all of them coughing and joking about the heat. I turned and lifted the shelter high enough to make eye contact. Mustache Man and seven others stood there. "Stick close! Stairs are to the left!"

I led them up the stairs, wondering what the hell I was doing. Leading crowds out of burning buildings was one thing, but leading wannabe volunteer firefighters *in*? Maybe I'd get some kind of special solidarity award to decorate my tombstone.

The heat grew more intense the higher we climbed. The shelter was meant to be sealed, so using it as a cape only prevented me from getting burned. Sweat slicked off my forehead, leaking into the mask's poor seal. By the time we got to the fourth floor, my eyes burned more from perspiration than smoke. The extinguishers helped push back the fire, but it couldn't save the structure. Holes had opened up in the floor and ceiling as the wood turned to cinders, and the floor began to make scary noises with every step. I hoped *we* wouldn't need rescue ourselves.

I counted off the doors; Agamjot had appeared in Millicent Cadwallader's window, sixth from the stairs. I pointed at the door, and we took turns smashing it with our almost-empty extinguishers. Finally, the door gave, and we burst into the smoke-filled flat. Agamjot lay beneath the window, one arm hanging outside. "Look in the other flats for anyone else!" I yelled above the roar of the fire.

I rushed into the room and slapped my respirator on Agamjot's sooty face. She still had a pulse, and she stirred as the first puffs of clean air hit her lungs. "Good girl," I said, wrapping the shelter around us.

There was a crash, and I turned to see the ceiling collapse behind me. A shower of sparks rushed into the flat, pyro pixie dust riding an updraft toward my face. With a great *crack*, another beam smashed to the floor. A wall of burning timber cut me off from the cutters.

I picked up Agamjot and cradled her so the respirator would stay on. We'd have to go out the window and use the fire escape. No one liked using the fire escape. The kids wouldn't even climb on it. But it would have to do.

As I looked out the window and tried to figure out how to get us both down, something heavy hit the floor. "You're not supposed to be here."

I looked over my shoulder. Jennifer stood in the middle of the living room, sparks drifting down on her from a hole in the ceiling. Her clothes were singed, and her face was sooty, and she looked *pissed*. She pocketed a tiny rebreather and closed the gap between us in three fast strides. I had enough time to throw my body over Agamjot before Jennifer brought an elbow down in the middle of my back.

My arms gave out, and the kid fell to the ground. I lost my grip on the shelter, and it slid off me to cover Agamjot. At least, I think it did. It was hard to tell after the follow-up kick I got to the side of my head.

I flopped next to Millicent's coffee table. The table was solid glass, and it had this collection of polished glass bricks on top. Each brick held a sea shell in its center. Making those knick-knacks was Millicent's hobby, and I never noticed before how pretty they were. Above me, I saw Jennifer, her face backlit by the burning ceiling overhead. She looked at me the way someone would look at a cockroach, and she lifted a boot. I held up a hand. "Wait," I gasped.

She paused and cocked her head. "Why should I?"

My head lolled in Agamjot's direction, and Jennifer's eyes followed. The transformation on her face was remarkable. The cool rage melted, and she froze. "You gotta help me get her out," I croaked.

Jennifer blinked as if I'd slapped her. "I don't have to do anything you tell me."

"Then just be decent and help me help this kid."

She sneered and flicked away a falling ember. I glanced up; through the holes in the ceiling, I could see a sagging beam in the floor above. It had a giant crack in its middle, and it looked ready to come apart. I couldn't outfight her, but there was no way she could win against a collapsing roof.

"We don't have time for this," I said. "What's she paying you?"

That got a laugh. "Are you serious? I know how broke you are."

"I own a distillery."

"I hate rum."

"I'm not asking you for a drink, I'm telling you I can pay more than whatever Letty's paying you!"

Jennifer's amused look faded. "You can't buy your way out of everything. Definitely not this." A half dozen pinpoint embers dropped on her head. The beam and everything it held up groaned.

"No," I said, hauling myself upright. "But I can buy time."

She narrowed her eyes. A shower of sparks fell on her, and she looked up long enough for me to grab a glass brick and hurl it at her face. The brick hit her in the chest, but it gave me enough of an opening to scoop up Agamjot and leap for the fire escape. Out of the corner of my eye, I saw Jennifer pivot to grab me. Her nails raked through the jacket, so sharp they cut through to my skin. I didn't care because I was too busy pushing aside the flower pots filled with petunias and cannabis.

Jennifer roared, and I clung to the fire escape as the ceiling came down on her. The rest of the building began to collapse in on itself, and the coral steel platform creaked away. I tried to climb down, but ironwork trellis moved too fast for me to do anything else but hang on to Agamjot. The fire escape smashed into the koa tree, and the branches jabbed at us as we came to a gentle halt. I looked down at my neighbors, who looked back at me.

Rohit Patil called up, "You put your foot on that branch to climb down!" He waved in the direction of my left foot. Below was a well-worn spot in the bark. I clambered to the ground, where Mustache Man and his crew had gathered with everyone else. I handed Agamjot to her father. She was still out, but breathing.

A small explosion blew out the windows on the second floor, and the whole building rumbled. I grabbed Mustache Man by the shoulder. "Can you and your crew make sure this fire doesn't spread?"

He whisked ashes out of his facial hair and grinned. "Like I said, we're the best in the biz."

I rolled my eyes. "Don't bullshit me, man. Can you keep this under control?"

He nodded. "We'll need help."

"You'll get it." I climbed into the lowest branches of the tree and yelled, "LISTEN UP!"

The crowd stopped talking.

I pointed at Mustache Man. "This right here is…' I leaned over and hissed, "What's your name?"

"Onanefe."

I nodded, then looked back at the crowd. "Onanefe and his crew are going to keep this blaze under control until the pros get here. He'll need your help. Our building's a goner, but that doesn't mean anyone else has to lose their home tonight. Can I count on you?"

Silence.

"Oh, come *on*, people," I said. "I know I've been busy, but are you really gonna tell me that you're not going to work together to keep the rest of this block from going up in smoke?"

"Who put you in charge?" said Millicent, clutching the lone surviving pot of sativa close to her chest.

"No one," I said. "I have absolutely no authority here. I'm just a regular schmoe like the rest of you. But I'm still a schmoe who believes in this." I pointed at the fist on my left cheek. "I still believe in working together to fight anything that threatens us. And right now, this fire is threatening our block, and maybe our neighborhood. Onanefe and his crew work in the cane fields. They know how to shut down fires. Their livelihoods depend on that. And I *think*, Millie, that they might be the most qualified people here to fix our common problem. Don't you?"

Millicent sniffed and cradled the plant. "I was just checking."

"I thank you for that," I said, hoping it didn't sound too

sarcastic. "Does anyone else have any further objections?"

The people looked at each other and shrugged.

"Good. Shall we?"

Onanefe and his crew divided the crowd up into teams and directed them to work.

An ambulance finally made an appearance. Its bubble lights splashed color across everyone's faces. I ran to the driver's side and banged on the window. "Look, you gotta call Search and Rescue or someone. There's a woman trapped in there–"

The driver looked up. It was the woman I'd seen earlier today at the Co-Op, the one who'd asked me about the Mutual Fund. Her face was cold and hard, and I realized she was the spitting image of Jennifer.

I took a step back, right into someone that felt as solid as a brick wall. I turned. It was Jennifer, her clothes torn and burnt and her face screwed up in a look that said she was going to kick my spine out the top of my head. "Get in," she said, pointing to the back. I was too stunned to protest.

The ambo's back doors opened, and, this time, I let out a yelp. Letty sat on the bench, an O2 mask to her face. She took a deep breath and offered me the mask. "Need a hit?"

The recently on-fire Jennifer pushed me into the back and pulled the doors shut behind her. She sat down next to me and clamped a hand around my upper arm. With a *whoop-whoop*, the ambo reversed and eased its way onto Samarkand Road. The back bay of the ambo opened up into the driver's seat, so I could see out the windshield. We edged through the crowd, the younger Jennifer pulling her hat down lower on her face. "Do I get to know what's going on?" Letty just chuckled. I tried blinking up video, but, of course, I got an eyeful of static. All three of them probably had scramblers.

The Jennifer driving the ambo stepped on the gas. We

peeled through the few boulevards free of marchers until we were on the bumpy road to the kampong. I lost track of time, what with the terrible road conditions and the human vise grip on my arm. We eased to a halt, and the older Jennifer let go. I gasped at the ice-fire that zipped up and down my arm. She had left marks in my skin. She might have even left fingerprints.

The older Jennifer wiped the soot off her face with a towel. She tossed aside the dirty cloth, and her skin *glowed*, like she had swallowed a searchlight.

Letty took one last puff of O2. "They make 'em a lot tougher than when you were an Indenture."

I eyed Jennifer and realized she had no pores. Her skin was a smooth, continuous surface, as if she'd been glazed and fired like a ceramic statue.

Letty smiled. "Carbon silicates in her skin, five times the hemoglobin, funky muscle fibers. She could tear an entire goon squad apart before you could blink."

"And it looks like she comes in pairs."

The older Jennifer nodded. "Triplets, actually."

"So is the third the maiden or the crone?"

The Jennifer nearest me narrowed her eyes. "She's none of your business."

"Let's talk," said Letty. She climbed past me and opened the doors.

The smell of caramelized sugar and burnt ironpalm barrels hit me, and I didn't have to climb out to see we were parked in front of the Old Windswept Distillery. I eyeballed Letty. "What, you weren't satisfied with torching my house? You gonna do the same to my distillery, too?"

Letty grunted as she climbed out. "Seeing how there's no fire response out here, that would be pointless. Besides, I like your rum. You coming?" The Jennifer in the EMT outfit appeared at her side, and the Jennifer in the ambo gave me a jab with her finger.

I sat back and crossed my arms. "I'm not going anywhere with you until you tell me what the fuck is going on. Starting with why she" – I pointed at the Jennifer who'd tried to kill me – "tried to kill me."

"Nonsense," said Letty. "She wouldn't do that."

"Are you gaslighting me, Letty? It's bad enough you're packing scramblers. Now you're going to tell me that your bodyguard didn't try to kill me?"

Letty gave the older Jennifer a glare. "We've talked. Things got a little more heated than they were supposed to."

"Not the best choice of words, considering you *burned my building down*."

"Oh, please." Letty dug around in her pockets until she found her stogie and a matchbox. She took out an actual match and lit her cigar. A few toxic puffs later, she smiled. "Your whole block is a dump. Once this all blows over, it's going to get rebuilt."

"What whole thing? You mean this strike?" I vaulted out of the ambulance, clearing the distance between us in a few steps. Both Jennifers leaped to Letty, their hands loose at their sides. I didn't care. I got in Letty's face. "Did you let this whole thing happen on *purpose*?"

She took a puff on her cigar and blew the smoke out the side of her mouth. "You are sharp, Padma. I shouldn't have let you take that crap job. You'd be a lot better off working for me."

"Thanks, but I'm not a fan of arson." I sniffed at Letty. "I don't smell any alcohol. Were you even drunk?"

She smiled, took another puff.

I looked at the two Jennifers and wondered if I could take a swing before they could react. Their slate-gray eyes turned to me, their neck muscles flexing. They could probably knock my head off my shoulders before I twitched. If Letty could set my building on fire, then she could easily have these two kill me and make my body disappear. Hell, I was still sure she *did* try to have me killed. For now, I would have to use my words.

"I have no idea how to help you here, Letty. I really don't. I went to another one of Saarien's churches, and – oh, that's right. You've already seen everywhere I've been and reviewed everything I said. Why rehash it for you?"

Letty ground the cigar out on the sole of her boot and put it back in her coat pocket. "But I don't know what you're thinking, Padma. It's not enough to know where you've been. I don't know what your gut is telling you about the strike."

"That it's stupid and wrongheaded and that you should end it right away."

"How do you suggest I do that?"

"Give the strikers what they want."

"Which is?"

"What, you don't know?"

She shook her head. "I have yet to get a list of formal demands from anyone. All I've seen is the city flooded with angry Freeborn and a whole lot of Union people walking alongside them."

"Then maybe you can hack into all those pais and find out for yourself."

"I can't."

"Bullshit."

She shrugged and showed me her open hands. "It's the truth, Padma. Hacking into your pai was a one-time trick. I start getting into everyone's heads, I'm going to leave fingerprints, and then it's all over for me."

"Ah. So it's perfectly acceptable for you to violate only *my* head. Got it."

Letty bit her lip. "You think this is easy for me? You think

I *like* having to go to these measures? We are up against the wall, Padma. Not just the Executive Committee, but *everyone* on this planet, Union and Freeborn alike." She looked away, her mouth turning into a sour frown. "I told you about the Big Three cutting back on the amount of cane they're going to buy from us, right?"

"You have, though I don't see why you haven't told everyone else about it."

"Because I didn't want a full-blown panic."

"Instead you've got a full-blown strike. Great move."

"And we can still stop it!" Letty put her hands on my shoulders.

I tensed, ready to pop her one if she tried to hug me. I was so not in the mood for a hug from this woman. "You keep saying *we*, but I really think you mean *you*. As in *me*."

"Because you can still move around in all the circles that matter. I can't go out into the streets without worrying about getting assaulted."

"You're the President of the Union!" I flicked her hands off me. "It's your *job* to talk to everyone, especially when they're unhappy and pissed off. That's why we elected you."

She smiled. "Good to know I had your vote."

"You're not getting it again," I said, walking toward my distillery.

"Come on, Padma! What about our deal?"

"It went up in smoke with my building."

"I don't remember those terms."

"Well, gee, Letty, maybe if you hadn't insisted on all this cloak-and-dagger bullshit, we could have come to actual terms. I should have sussed this before. You're using me as a proxy, even though I've been out of any serious Union work for almost two years. You talked about the strike as if it were something on the horizon when it was ready to explode *today*. Not even Saarien could motivate that many people to march on short notice. He's been out for three months, and that tells me he's been *building* his movement for three months. And there is no way someone in your position couldn't have seen this coming. You're too wired in, Letty."

She shrugged. "Even I can get things wrong."

"Not like this. You got me wrapped up in this for some reason. You burned my building down for some reason. And you know what? I have no desire to figure those reasons out. I've got rum to make." I walked up the crushed shell path to the press house.

As I approached the front door, Letty called out: "What are you going to do when you run out of cane, Padma?"

I gave her the finger before slamming the door behind me. My office chair had never felt more comfortable.

NINE

It was still dark when I woke up, and I didn't bother to blink up the time. The camp bed squeaked, and I shivered as I wrapped the blanket tighter around me. My office was the designated hurricane shelter for the distillery, which meant all the survival gear lived in my desk. I figured it had nothing to do with how Old Windswept was made, so I had splurged for good stuff. Even though it was great not having to worry about making Six O'Clock, a week of living on canned food and sleeping on a bed made of pipes and canvas had taken its toll. I wanted to do *something*.

I was still half-asleep when the idea hit me: I should fire up the whole operation and make a batch of rum all on my own. I got as far as loading cane onto the press when I realized I was working with the wrong batch. Tonggow had created a complicated curing process, with some stalks sitting in sunlight while others hid in the shadows. I had loaded the sunlight bundles first instead of the shady ones. *There's a lot of biochemistry involved*, she had told me, and, no matter how many times I watched the footage I'd shot of our talks, I could never get a handle on just *why* she had done these things. I only know that she had, so I had to, too.

I got the sunshine cane out of the press, wiped the whole thing down, then lay the shady cane in a neat row before the rollers. I would have to stop the press after each rolling in order to feed the cane back in. *Thirty times through gets you what you need,* Tonggow had said. With a crew of five, this was an easy task. With just me, it would suck. The controls for the press were hard-wired, but at least the cord was long enough that I could walk all the way around the press without getting tangled. I clicked the green START button, then ran around to catch the cane as it tumbled through the rollers. Cane juice gushed out of the rollers into the tray that sloped into a funnel.

A click of the red STOP button, and then I brought the cane back to where it had started. I could do this, I told myself as I fed the cane back into the press. Marolo and Ly Huang and everyone else wanted to walk away? Letty wanted me to stop the strike? Forget them. I could make Old Windswept on my own until menopause and senility and everything else came for me. Besides, I had stashed rum all over the planet. Not even the Big Three with their Ghost Squads could find all of them.

The cane weighed no more than a couple of kilos, but the whole process – load cane, press green button, grab cane, press red button, repeat – made my brain itch. Also, only a trickle came out after the first few passes. By the twenty-third run, my forearms were scratched raw and my back muscles burned. I watched a few lone drops slide down the funnel. Seven more times, and then do the whole thing all over again with the sunshine batch? No.

I found a clean cup and dipped it into the collection bucket. The cane juice was an emerald green, murky and sweet-smelling. Marolo had taught me to squirt a little lime into my juice to give it kick. Of course, he had taken all the limes home with him. I took a sip, let the sugary rush run up and down the sides of my tongue. I looked at the massive stacks of cane, enough to create fifty thousand liters of juice to be fermented and fed into the distillation tower. I glanced at the bucket; there was maybe half a liter in there, less the portion in my cup.

So, no, I couldn't make Old Windswept on my own, not unless I wanted to spend the rest of my life strapped to the press. Even if I went down to microbatching, I wouldn't make enough rum to last me the rest of my life, however long that might be. I was in great health, even taking into account my time knee-deep in sewage, but I knew entropy would catch up with me in a few decades. I would need all of the medicines that came from the Big Three's pharma mines at one point or another, and none of that would be buyable with the planet's economy at a standstill.

How could this have happened? I wished I had someone to help put this together, Wash or Soni or Big Lily, someone to give a fresh set of eyes and ears to all of these mismatched puzzle pieces. Saarien got out of prison three months ago and put together this movement. But the cracks had to have been there longer before he could wedge himself in. When I was still Ward Chair, we'd have issues with social funding, sure, but we made it work. Other Wards would pitch in, knowing I'd return the favor. We talked. We fixed it.

Something had happened in the past sixteen months to cause this fissure in my city. Whether it was fallout from the Ghost Squad's soiree or something from the Executive Committee, I wasn't sure. Any other time, I would have left it up to someone else, some young up-and-coming in the Union to call for committees and find facts and do all that crap. Now, I didn't have the luxury of making this Someone Else's Job. If I wanted to get my crew back here and get the cane back into the refineries and get all those angry people happy, I'd have to do it myself.

And that meant getting back to the city. The crew had taken their bicycles with them, and the distillery was three klicks past the end of the Red Bus. I pinged Jilly, but I only got a message: SORRY, BUT WE'RE ALL ON STRIKE. It took me a moment to realize it came from the Public's sysadmins. They had walked off the job, too. Terrific. I'd have to walk until I could hitch a ride into town.

I slugged down the last of the cane juice and cleaned up. My former employees had taken their shares of the hurricane food home with them, so the only thing left for breakfast were the stale date bars in the survival gear. I pocketed the bars and slurped the last drops of the cane juice. Those calories would have to last me until I could finagle my way into a meal. Some enterprising cook would have set up shop at the Red Bus stop. Strikes were a great time for entrepreneurs, provided they dealt in food, booze, or weapons. The faster I figured this all out, the better my chances of stymying the arms merchants. I locked up the distillery and headed down the road. The sun poked over the horizon.

The first two kilometers, I had the road all to myself. My only neighbors were Mueller Ngapoi, a Freeborn goat farmer, and Theo Papadopolis, a former MacDonald Heavy advertising executive who spent all his time making wind-powered sculptures that looked like goats. The two herds would mingle, usually with comic results. The windbeasts would butt into the ewes, and the rams would attempt to mate with the windbeasts. Every spring, there would be a fresh round of bleating goats and splintering wood. Mueller and Theo would both come to the distillery, complain about each other, then walk away with a case of rum apiece (sold to them at cost, of course. Good discounts make good neighbors).

This morning, the goats were tucked away in the barn,

and the windbeasts roamed the paddocks. They clacked and clattered as the wind pushed against the sails on their spines. Their caneplas cloven hooves picked and dug at the dirt, churning the goatshit in with the grass. For all their complaints, Mueller's and Theo's herds got along quite well. I was pretty sure Mueller's goats were so healthy and strong because the windbeasts made the paddocks produce such rich grass. Neither would admit it, though, not even after they had downed a few cups of Old Windswept. Even my rum couldn't overcome a hundred years of Union and Freeborn animosity.

As the crushed palm crab shells that lined the roadbed turned into actual pourform, I heard people coming out of the dawn fields. They spoke in low tones, the kind of hushed conversations people had as they were walking up on the way to work. I heard the giggles of children, the moaning of old people. The road was crowded by the time the egg-yolk sun had made a full appearance. I had the feeling none of this would be over or easy.

I smiled at a young mother walking next to me. She wore battered work clothes and had a baby strapped to her chest, her deck jacket acting as a blanket. She was Freeborn, and she made a lot of nervous glances at my cheek. "Busy day," I said.

"Mm-hm," she said, keeping a hand on top of the kid's head.

"I haven't seen it like this since the last City Cup."

"I don't really follow footie," she said.

"I don't blame you," I said. "Last year's match was a complete mess. Still, gotta go where the customers go, you know? Rum doesn't pour itself."

She gave me a side-wise glare. "You a distiller?"

"I am indeed." I held out a hand. "Padma Mehta."

Her look softened as she took my hand; her fingertips

were rough, despite a thin layer of lotion. "Meiumi Greene. With an 'e' at the end."

"I don't think I've met any Freeborn with a last name."

Meiumi laughed. "My wife's idea. She's Union."

"You both work in the city?"

She nodded. "I'm a welder on a digester farm. Faye – also with an 'e' – she's a safety inspector at a refinery."

"Hard work."

The baby stirred, and Meiumi cooed. "It is. But we're building a future for this little stinker, so it's worth it. Most of the time."

I nodded. "I never did those gigs, but I know the feeling."

We walked in silence for a moment. The wind rustled the ricewheat fields on either side of the road, and the crowd's volume grew with the daylight. "Are you both on strike?" I asked.

Meiumi's face grew hard before she relaxed and looked at me. She couldn't have been more than twenty-five, but she now looked fifty. "I didn't want to. Neither of us did. But we've had day care cut over the past year. It used to be I could drop off Lucius and know he'd be in good hands until Faye picked him up. We were subsidized, but that dried up earlier this week. The money was just gone. Now we can't find anyone else to watch him because all of our sitters had to find better-paying jobs. I tried leaving Lucius with my gran, but then her meds allowance got cut, too, and her vertigo came back. Now I have to find someone to watch over *her*, too."

"But why go into the city?"

"To let the Prez know that I'm not going to stand for this. That, and I've got to pay my respects. Uncle Gorsky died last week, and I couldn't get to the funeral."

"I'm sorry to hear that. About all of it."

She shrugged. "Uncle was old, so it was a matter of

time. And, unless you're in charge of the Social Services Committee, the rest isn't your problem."

No, I wanted to tell her, *it* was.

Lucius the baby had woken up by the time we got to the terminal. The queue for the Red Bus, the line that went direct to the city center, snaked around and back on itself, an ouroborus of anxious people. Hawkers selling condoms and beignets worked the line, and a few people wearing the stainless steel supernova fist of Saarien's church asked, *Do you need medical help? Do you require succor?* I bought a coconut and a bag of bao and offered some to Meiumi. She demurred. "Sorry, but I really shouldn't."

"Because I'm an evil distiller?"

A few people in the queue turned to me. One woman shot me a death glare.

Meiumi nodded. "I know your name, Ms Mehta–"

"Padma."

She smiled, flustered at my interruption. "Okay. Padma. Like I said, I know your name, and you've got a good rep. But you're kind of the problem."

"Because I make rum?"

She looked both ways, then leaned close, her voice a harsh whisper. "You need to be real careful here. A lot of people, they work the cane fields, and they're not too crazy about distillers *or* Union. There's a lot of bad blood out here, you know?"

I shook my head. "I don't think I do. But I have the feeling I should."

Meiumi stroked Lucius's hair. "I got family who've been screwed on paychecks or lost bennies. Everyone's used to the price of cane rising and falling, but ever since the black stripe, it's gotten bad. And there's a lot of people who are still pissed at that guy, the one with the church. He *stole* people out of the kampong."

"He stole Union people, too."

"I know." She nodded. The queue shuffled forward. "But we have Union people out here who are promising the world and delivering nothing. I mean, I came to the city, learned a trade, so it doesn't affect me directly. But my family who are still here? They're hurting, and they want to see the Union hurt back. They're all coming into town to bring everything to a standstill, starting by leaving the cane fields."

"You know there are Union people on strike, too."

"I know, I know, it's…" She quirked her mouth, her words trying to come out. "It's like there's this one level of Union people, people like Faye and everyone on her crew. They all work, they pay dues, they give back what they take. And then there's this level *above*, the ones who run the Committees, and they just *take*. No giving." Her green eyes drilled into me. "I don't know what kind you are, but, if you're in the Co-Op, it's like you're on the same level as the higher-ups. You're standing on everyone's backs."

I must have looked horrified, because she brightened up. "But not you! I mean, probably not you. I really like your theme song, and you don't sound like that."

"Thanks." I bit into my bao. It tasted like bagasse pulp.

One Red Bus after another lined up at the terminal's entrance, each one filling within minutes before chugging off for town. All of them had STRIKE EXPRESS – NO LOCAL STOPS on their front signs. It took an hour before the queue worked its way to the loading bay. Meiumi offered me the seat next to her. I knew at any point I could have gotten word to Jilly and gotten a lift, but now, no. I had to go into town with everyone else and find out just what was pissing them off.

And I heard plenty of it.

"You know how much I used to get paid an hour?" This

from an old guy sitting in front of us. A snow-white braid ran down his back. He had two anchors inked below his Union fist. "Sixty-five yuan, fifty hours a week, guaranteed."

"Yeah, but that's before the work dried up," said a woman across from him. Her betel-nut-stained lips were as red as her sunburnt face. Her coat was dusted with flour. "There was a time when everyone had work in the off-season, before the harvest. Now?" She shook her head. "No one can afford my buns."

"I still can, darlin'," said her seatmate, a wizened old man with a diving regulator strapped around his neck. She smacked the man, and the whole bus erupted with laughter.

"Things have gotten worse, all right," said Two Anchors – I hated not being able to blink up his Public profile and get his actual name. "Sexually harassing someone."

"We're married!" said Regulator Neck.

"Not if you keep embarrassing me in public," said Flour Coat.

"Well, it's not like you let me embarrass you in *private*."

This time, she belted him so hard he wept. Everyone else did too, but only because they were laughing so hard.

"Look, I get what you're saying," said Regulator Neck. "Everything's been sliding downhill ever since the lifter blew up."

"No, it's been bad since *before*," said Flour Coat. "When we first met, there was so much traffic coming into Santee it blocked out the stars at night. You remember that?"

The older people all nodded to each other. I remembered it, too. Fourteen years ago, Santee had ships lining up ten deep in orbit. Constellations would form around the anchor, the sun glinting off their hulls as they dropped their empty fuel tanks or took on new ones, freshly loaded from the ocean. I would lie in bed at night, watching the shipping queues, wondering which ones had crews I could convince to Breach. Year by year, the traffic decreased. Now, I didn't even bother looking up, not even when I spent nights at the distillery.

Regulator Neck went *pfft*. "You can't blame everything on the Big Three *or* on the Union *or* on us."

"Who said I'm blaming it on us?" said a Freeborn man behind us. He clutched a tool bag to his chest.

"*I* did," said Regulator Neck, jabbing himself with his thumb. "Every time the Contract comes up, we get an offer to join with the Union. We always say no."

"That's because we're *not* Union," said Flour Coat.

"Yeah, but we're also not Big Three," said Regulator Neck. "We all get screwed by them. Shouldn't we wise up and work together?"

"What, like those terrorists from the FOC?" said Tool Bag.

"They weren't terrorists!" said Flour Coat.

"Really? Then what do you call the people who blew up that post office?"

"Assholes," said Flour Coat. Everyone grumbled assent.

"I didn't like the violence," said Regulator Neck, "but the people in the FOC were right. We had to get a seat at the table."

"And lose our independence?" Tool Bag snorted. "No way."

"What independence is that?" said Two Anchors. "You're just as dependent on the Big Three as *we* are. Or are you gonna tell me you don't work in the city supporting some Contract gig?"

"Why, you got a problem with that?" said Tool Bag. "I gotta make a living."

"We all do," said Two Anchors. "But you Freeborn talking about independence is like a piglet complaining it has to go to some other sow's teat."

There was silence. "That makes no sense," said Regulator Neck.

"I know," said Two Anchors, pinching the bridge of his nose. "I haven't had any coffee this morning."

"If we wanted to, we Freeborn could completely cut ourselves off from you Inks," said Flour Coat. "*We* can always grow our own food, make our own goods, live our own lives."

"That why you make pastries ten hours a day in a Shareholder bakery?" said Regulator Neck.

Flour Coat smacked him again. "I swear, if I could afford a lawyer, I would divorce your ass in a heartbeat."

"Thirty years you been saying that, and yet you keep coming back." Regulator Neck made a kissy face. "You know I'm the only one who's got what you need."

"I can always find another plumber."

The whole bus howled. Regulator Neck threw his hands in the air and slid out of his seat. The only empty seat he could find was at the back of the bus.

Two Anchors chuckled. "Still, he's got a point. All of us work for the Big Three one way or the other."

Flour Coat made a face. "How you figure?"

"Who buys your pastries?"

She shrugged. "Just people. Anyone."

"And where do they get the money to buy their pastries?"

"From their jobs."

"And every job here centers around cane. You're growing it, you're cutting it, you're turning it into molasses, and all of it goes up the lifter."

"Not *all* of it," said Tool Bag.

"Okay," said Two Anchors. "We keep some to power things. But my point is that almost everyone is supporting or supported by cane. Occupied Space runs on burning cane. Freeborn people grow it, Union people process it, Big Three people consume it. We get Big Three money, and it comes trickling down into our pockets so people can buy your pastries."

My stomach rumbled. As good as the bao had been, I would have loved an almond bialy and a coffee.

Flour Coat sniffed. "Well, I can always quit. Start my own shop. I don't have to depend on someone filling a Slot for me."

"Then why don't you?"

"'Cause the money's too *good*."

"Or it was," said Tool Bag.

"Yeah," said Two Anchors. "No doubt there."

The Red Bus slowed as it approached North Terminal. The traffic was thick: Blues from San Monique, Greens from Hawthorne, Yellows from way the hell on the other side of the island. There were no police to direct traffic, just a lot of honking and jostling for position at the loading bays. Our bus hissed to a stop and the driver said, "You got five minutes to unload."

"Or what?" I asked.

She looked up at the mirror and caught my eye. "Or you'll be stuck in a bus. I'm taking this to the depot, and then I'm marching with everyone else."

As we disembarked, people handed out signs saying STRIKE and NEW DEAL NOW. Some of them had steel Temple pins, and a few had added the supernova to their Union ink on their cheeks. I caught sight of Meiumi and her son before they were swept into the mass of bodies. Meiumi Greene. With an 'e'. I hoped she would be okay.

I grabbed the first bike I could and rode straight to Brushhead, taking every side street and back alley that wasn't filled with people. By the time I got to Budvar, I had to ditch the bike and walk. People jammed the streets, all of them bright and bubbly. Every café, bar, and strip club was open and full. I took off my coat and tied it around my waist, the heat of the morning and the crowd baking through my clothes. I saw strikers walk off the street and hand their signs to people blinking their way out of coffee shops. The slogans were all generic: SOLIDARITY and UNFAIR and STRIKE. None of the signs had demands. None of the people talked about demands. What the hell kind of strike was this?

Two hours and a twenty-yuan egg sandwich later, I arrived at the remains of my home. The building was now a charred shell. The roof and top two floors had collapsed. Blackened beams and studs leaned against each other. It looked like the skeleton of a whale that had fallen from the sky and auto-ignited on impact. Long tracks of dirt snaked up to the foundations.

Onanefe and his crew sat around their Hanuman, all of them sooty and bleary-eyed. They held bowls of noodles, but none of them ate. They just stared into the distance. I picked my way over the burnt remains of the building's rose garden. "You guys okay?"

Onanefe groaned as he slid off the hood of the truck. "You missed a hell of a good time."

"I was detained."

"For a week?"

I shrugged. "Entropy happens. I see you saved the day here."

Onanefe stretched, his neck popping as he twisted it from side to side. "I don't think we ever worked like that. Cutting cane's going to be a vacation."

"Anyone else get hurt?"

He shook his head and brushed his mustache. Parts of it had singed away. "There were fires all over the neighborhood. Been busy for days." He pointed at the building next to mine. "We had to work like hell making sure the fire didn't spread. It just got hotter after you left, so we started a bucket brigade and brought dirt up top to tamp things down. It's gonna take a while for the neighborhood garden to bounce back."

"I think everyone will forgive you." I held out a hand. "I never had a chance to introduce myself. Padma Mehta."

His eyebrows shot up. For a moment, I thought he was going to start singing my theme song. Then his eyebrows came down, along with his expression. "You owe me fifty thousand yuan."

"You're kidding."

He crossed his arms over his chest. The rest of the crew rose to their feet and huddled around him. "We never kid about wages. You own the Old Windswept distillery, yes?"

"Yes."

He nodded. "We own a plot out in Erendiz Flats. We raised heirloom cane, supplied a lot of distillers. I grew good stuff."

I nodded to myself. "Okay. Where do I come into the picture?"

"About a year and a half ago, I got a massive order from Estella Tonggow. My entire stock for a year, exclusive. It was COD, which I *never* do, but Madame Tonggow's reputation was impeccable. I signed, I delivered, and I never got the money."

"Why?"

"Because she was dead."

"Wait." I tried to blink up all of my contracts from the distillery, but the Public just gave me the finger. "Dammit, I can't connect right now. Look, I hope you can understand why this is a bit of a shock to me, right?"

He shrugged. "Whether it's a shock or not makes no nevermind. What matters is that we get paid."

"Then why didn't you bring this to me?"

"I did," said Onanefe. "Every month, I'd send letters by courier to your office. You want to tell me you've never seen them? I got the receipts in my kit bag."

"Yes, because I *haven't*," I said. "My manager deals with all that."

"And she wouldn't think to say, 'Hey, boss, you owe this guy fifty large'?"

"No, *he* sure as hell would. But since *he* hasn't, that means I either have to fire him or–"

"You need to pay up!" yelled one of the cutters.

"We *counted* on that money!" yelled another.

"I need to pay for my husband's meds!"

"I need to pay for fixing our compost digester!"

"I need to pay for my daughter's gamelon lessons!"

The others looked at the last guy. "What?" he said. "Flora loves playing, and *I* don't know how to teach her!"

Onanefe put his hands on his hips and squared off toward me. "That money was going to make a big difference in all our lives, Ms Mehta. But when we didn't get paid, we had to hustle and start working other fields to cover our collective nut."

"What do you want me to do about it, then?" I turned out my pockets, and held up the contents: fluff, a ticket stub from the Red Bus, and three two-yuan coins. "This is all I've got."

Onanefe glanced at the detritus and sniffed. "What about the distillery?"

A chill raced up my neck. "What *about* it?"

He shrugged, and the edges of his mustache lifted up as he smiled. "Maybe we should look into garnishing your profits until we're paid. I'm pretty sure the Strike Committee would be happy to add that to their list of demands."

"Is there an actual list?" I said. "I'd love to see it."

"You come with us, we'll show it to you," said Onanefe.

"Maybe you should bring a copy here," I said, letting my weight sink into my shoes. I had no idea if these guys were going to try and take me, but it didn't hurt to be prepared.

Onanefe held up his hands. "Hey, hey. Don't get the wrong idea. We're pissed, but we're not like that."

"Good to know."

He laughed and slapped one of his crew on the shoulder. "You believe this? Lady, we just busted our picks to *save* this neighborhood, and we don't even live here. You know, this is just like you Inks, thinking all us Freeborn are a bunch of savages."

"I think you're a bunch of people who are tired, angry, and outnumber me," I said, not relaxing. "You'll pardon me for being cautious."

Onanefe's face became a grim mask as he shook his head. "And people wonder why Freeborn don't join up around Contract time. Okay, Ms Mehta, you win. I'll get someone to find a printer and show you the invoices–"

And that's when someone stabbed me in the shoulder.

TEN

Later, I would rewind my pai's internal buffer and study the moment: Onanefe turning away, his crew looking at me in disgust, and that one guy stepping out of the crowd with a steak knife in his raised hand. I had never seen him before, a clean-cut Freeborn man in a yellow linen shirt and cargo pants. There was nothing about him that said I should have worried. Nothing except the knife, of course. He pushed aside one of the cutters and brought it down into my left shoulder.

In the moment itself, though, all I got was his scream, followed by blinding pain up and down my arm and back and, really, my entire body. I went down, and he came with me, his beet-red face in mine. "PARASITE! TRAITOR!" he roared, and then he disappeared as the cutters lifted him up and away.

I didn't scream. It hurt too much to scream. I gave the knife one look – blood gushing out a hole in my shirt, the knife blade shining in the mid-morning sun – then turned away. I focused on breathing and not going into shock. Going into shock meant losing control, and that meant someone else could take another stab at me.

Someone put a kerchief on the wound. Calls went out for a doctor. I wondered who would show up. We had a fire and got cane cutters. Maybe this time I'd get a butcher. I felt the sudden craving for a tri-tip sandwich, then my head spun at the thought of doing anything other than not bleeding to death.

One of the cutters came back with two people holding kit bags and t-shirts from Santee General Hospital. They assessed my arm for a moment before one of them, a woman with a caduceus tattoo, said, "Seriously? You brought us here for this?"

That stopped the nausea. "What? Knife!"

"*Pfft.*" Medical Lady took a multi-tool from her pocket and opened the scissors. Three quick cuts, and she pulled my shirt off my shoulder. I looked at the wound just as she pulled a can from her bag and sprayed pink gel all over my shoulder.

"What's thaAAAAAAAAA–!"

She slid the knife out of my shoulder. I didn't feel it. I couldn't feel anything, really. That still didn't stop my brain from screaming *Holy shit, she just pulled a knife out of your body!*

"It'll hurt like hell once the gel wears off, but you'll be okay," she said, dropping the knife into a caneplas bag.

"Thank you for not going on strike," I said.

She made a face. "I'm marching like everyone else."

"Yeah, but you still patched me up."

"And you can expect one hell of a bill once the Public starts working again." She blinked in my face.

"So it's not just me? I haven't been able to get on the Public all day."

"The word is that everyone in IT is striking," said Medical Man. "They shut down the servers because no one would be around to babysit them."

Medical Lady snorted. "Just as well. My pai hasn't been able to upload any patient data for months. Incompatible model with the latest patches. How the hell does anyone expect to get continued care?"

"Well, I'm good for it," I said as they packed their bags. "Paying you, I mean."

Medical Man shrugged. "That's what the Medical Committee told us before they started holding up our reimbursements. You know how much CauterIce costs? That's, like, sixty yuan alone on your shoulder."

I looked at the pink goo. It had hardened and begun to flake away. The cut now looked like I'd just scraped my shoulder on a nail, not had a knife plunged into it.

"We've been dealing with dehydration all week," said the woman. I really wished I could blink up her name, just so I wouldn't have to keep thinking of her as *Medical Lady*. "At least salts are cheap. But if we start getting more knifings, we're gonna be out of supplies pretty soon."

"Is Santee General running that low?" I asked.

Medical Lady snorted. "Everyone's running low. Haven't you heard? Or have you been in a hole in the ground?"

I thought to tell her that, no, my distillery was actually quite comfortable, but held my tongue.

She shouldered her pack. "Before the strike started, we had enough to get us through the month. But that was a month of regular life. Things get uglier with strikes."

"Then who's supposed to be in charge of getting you what you need?"

Medical Man snorted. "The Medical Committee. But they have no money." He nodded to me. "Don't work that shoulder for a few days. The muscle needs time to knit itself back together." They pushed their way back into the crowd.

Onanefe gave me a hand up. "That was a bit of good luck, finding the medicos."

"They're always handy to have around when some nut wants to stab you." I gave my shoulder a tiny roll. The

CauterIce had left my entire arm numb, so I felt nothing. I peeled off the bloodied remains of my shirt and buttoned up my jacket. I'd have to find a cooler replacement layer soon, or I'd turn into one of those dehydration victims Medical Lady talked about. "Where is he?"

Onanefe gestured toward the back of the cutters' truck. "We got him here. Luccio used to farm pigs, so he's got the guy trussed up nice. What do you want to do with him?"

"Talk with him. From a safe distance."

My assailant lay in the truck bed, hog-tied on his belly, his head facing outward. His face was screwed up in a frown, and his eyes kept flickering from side-to-side.

I squatted in front of him. "Hi, there. People usually have a few drinks with me before they try and stab me. You want something?"

His lip quivered, and he looked me in the eye. "I wanted you out of my way."

"I don't even know you," I said.

"You are in my way!" he shouted, jerking against the knots on his wrists and ankles. He flopped toward me, his teeth bared. "You are in my way!"

I slapped him.

He stopped moving and stared at me. "You *hit* me," he said, all the fire out of his voice.

"And you *stabbed* me," I said. "If you're going to get worked up over a little slap, then you're more messed up than I thought."

"There's nothing wrong with *me*," he said. "I'm doing the people's work. I'm one of history's select."

I smiled, making my face as bright and open and gullible-looking as possible. "Selected by who?"

He grinned, showing me perfect teeth. "Wouldn't you like to know?"

"I sure would, seeing how it might keep you from getting

tossed into the clink."

He barked a laugh. "Who's going to do it? The police? They're with us. Besides, when they find out what I was doing, they'll let me go. I'm a hero, me."

"For stabbing innocent women?"

"You were in my way," he said. "No one is innocent if they're in my way. I am the fist of righteousness."

"Even if that fist has a knife?"

He blew his tongue at me, and I walked back to Onanefe at the front of the truck. "Does anyone know this guy?"

They all shook their heads. "City's getting super crowded with marchers," said Onanefe. "I hear there are people sailing in."

"From where?"

He shrugged. "Everywhere. It's a planet-wide strike, you know? All those farms have a couple of dozen people, and there are, what, ten thousand farms across Santee?"

"So he could be from anywhere. Terrific."

Onanefe rubbed his mustache. "I have the feeling he's local. Ish. His accent isn't sing-songy enough to come from the Western Chains, too harsh to come from the South Archipelago, and too flat to come from the North. His clothes are from a Big Three catalogue, not homespun. He's seen a lot of sun, but his skin's in pretty good condition. No scars, no ink. All of that tells me he's a Freeborn kid from Santee City or its immediate surroundings."

"You can tell all that from his voice, clothes, and skin?"

He nodded, then his face broke into a grin. "That, plus he dropped a wallet stuffed with receipts from a bakery in Globus Heights." He pulled a battered leather wallet from his trousers and held it up. Dozens of bagasse-paper slips stuck out of its folds, little flags flapping in the breeze.

I rolled my eyes. "And here I thought you were going to crack this case wide open just through observation."

He shrugged. "So I read a few detective novels. You get a lot of downtime in this line of work."

"Did that wallet tell you this guy's name?"

"It did not. Just that the dude loved him some proja."

I took the wallet and sighed. "Well, it's a start... Did you say proja?"

He nodded. "I'm not a fan, myself. A little too sweet. I like my cornbread crumbly."

I looked at the receipts. They were all from Lepa's Bakery, where I had just met Odd Dupree before he took me to Saarien's church. I rewound my buffer and saw it again: the knife, the anger, the screams of *PARASITE!* I rewound to just a few moments ago: *I'm one of history's select.* I rewound even farther: Ly Huang's smug face as she said, *We are history's select.*

"Son of a bitch," I said. I banged the hood of the truck. "SON OF A BITCH!"

"Hey, mind the wheels, please," said Onanefe. "This truck is our calling card."

"Sorry," I said through gritted teeth. "I think I know where this schmuck came from."

"Yeah?"

"You know the Temple of the New Holy Light?"

Onanefe nodded. "I'm familiar with it."

"The guy who runs it, the one who called for this strike? He tried to kill me once."

Onanefe's eyebrows shot up. "The skinny white guy? Bad teeth? Wears a white suit?"

I cocked my head. "You been there?"

He shook his head. "A couple of cousins got caught up two months ago. They were spongers, so I figured anything to get them out of the house, you know? That Temple's been trying to scoop as many people as they could into their flock." He sucked his teeth and spat. "I had to tell my cousins to stay in the city before they pulled their families' work crews apart. What is it with bums and religion?"

"That's what I'm going to find out," I said, wiping sweat off my forehead. "Right after I get a new shirt."

"I saw a place on Saroyan that's still open," said one of the cutters.

"What about Stabbing Boy?" said Onanefe. "You want we should find a cop?"

I winked at him. "That'll do."

I walked down Samarkand and got as far as the corner when I heard a scuffle of feet behind me. I turned, and Onanefe and the rest of the cutters bumped into each other as they came to a halt. All of them carried leather satchels, as if they were going to work.

"Help you guys with something?" I said.

"We're going with," said Onanefe. "If you don't mind." The cutters all nodded.

"I think I do," I said, taking a few steps.

The cutters followed suit. "It's just there's this little matter of the fifty thousand yuan," said Onanefe.

"Which I'm not about to discuss without a change of clothes and a consult with my site manager," I said. "What, you think I'm going to disappear?"

The cutters all looked at each other, then nodded.

I rolled my eyes. "Where can I *go*? Up the cable? If there's a planet-wide strike, it's probably going to extend to everyone working in orbit. Besides, it's creepy as hell to have you all following me. Knock it off."

"But–"

"No." I didn't yell it, but I put as much force into that word as I could as I held up a single finger. "You got a business problem with me? Okay. Then we will deal with this like business people."

"But–"

I put my finger on Onanefe's chest. He froze, and I pushed until he stepped back in the middle of his crew. "If I actually owe you money, I will make it right. But that doesn't mean you get to tail me, hoping I'm going to drop fifty K on the sidewalk for you to scoop up. You're freaking me out, and that makes me want to call a cop, not my manager."

"Cops are on strike," said one cutter. Onanefe shot him a withering look, and the man shrunk behind his comrades.

"I'm sure they are," I said. "But they'll look out for someone from their neighborhood who's got a dozen guys following her around." Or for someone who could call the police chief's direct line, busted Public or no.

Onanefe worked his jaw for a moment, then pulled his crew into a huddle. They conferred in low whispers, punctuated by the occasional punch to the shoulder. They stood up, and Onanefe said, "How do you feel about me going with you?"

"Still creepy as hell."

"I would like to point out that someone tried to stab you."

"What, you want to be my bodyguard?"

He smiled. "Why not? I have a vested interest in keeping you free from harm."

On the one hand, it still bugged me that these guys felt the need to stick with me. Then my shoulder twinged, like my whole arm had been jabbed with tiny, tiny needles. The CauterIce must have begun to wear off. It had been a long time since someone had tried to take me on at close range. The fact that I hadn't seen it coming bugged me even more.

"Here's the deal," I said, putting my hands on my hips and regretting it (*oy*, my shoulder). "First, the minute I feel like you're occupying too much of my space, you go. No questions asked."

He crossed his arms over his chest and swayed, like the

movement helped him weigh his options. He shrugged and nodded. "Done."

"Second, if someone tries to take a swing at me, you do not step in."

He snorted. "What, you want me to just stand by and let you get knifed again?"

"No, but I would rather you not get knifed on my account."

He swiped at his mustache with his thumb. "Okay. But I'm not going to let you get yourself croaked. Dealing with probate's a bear."

"I appreciate your concern."

"Anything else?"

"Keep up." I turned and walked down Samarkand.

Onanefe ran after me. "You always this quick?"

"Death threats are a great motivator." I looked up at the sun, now working its way toward the middle of the sky. "Besides, this coat is hot as hell."

We pushed our way through the mass of marchers working its way down Koothrapalli. The commercial enthusiasm I'd seen earlier had not touched this block. Only a konbini and a bar were open. Every other business had closed up, their storefronts covered by makeshift barricades. The ribs of airship canopies held battered deckplates over windows and doors, and worried shopkeepers cradled cricket bats and pipe wrenches as they eyed the mass of people. I couldn't remember the last time there had been any looting, not even during the messy weeks that led up to Contract Time. My neighbors looked at me like I was a barbarian raider, not as someone who bought eggs and face cream from their stores.

Saroyan Street was on the other side of Koothrapalli, and the open clothing store had marked everything up two hundred percent. I was out of cash, so Onanefe had to float me enough to buy a second-hand t-shirt covered in pinhole burns. "Factory seconds," said the woman behind the counter, a cigarette smoldering between her lips. The shirt itched, but I figured the holes would help with ventilation. I made a mental note to bring the owner in front of the Commerce Committee for price-gouging, assuming there would still be a Commerce Committee.

It was a long, long walk to Globus Heights. With no cash or Public connection to my bank account, I couldn't buy any of the food offered by the conspicuously non-striking vendors we saw. Onanefe, however, kept recognizing people along the way and cadged a sandwich here, some guava there, drinks of water everywhere. By the time we got to Lepa's Bakery, I was full, hydrated, and had to pee.

I assumed the woman standing in front of the bakery was Lepa herself; with no Public access, every face in the city now belonged to a complete stranger. Her hair was held close to her skull in a hairnet, and her lipstick was a bright orange. She held a rolling pin in her hand, and she had a rolling pin tattooed on her cheek. I walked up to her, my knees tumbling together to keep my screaming bladder from emptying. "Bathroom's for customers only," she said before I could even ask.

I gritted my teeth. "Then I'll take some proja."

"That'll be forty yuan."

"Can you take an IOU? I'm good for it."

She cocked an eyebrow. "'I'm good for it' usually means 'I don't have cash.'"

"The Public's down, and I had to shell out all my money for this shirt."

"My money, technically," said Onanefe.

Her other eyebrow went up. "You got ripped off."

"I got this," said Onanefe, holding up a ten-yuan note.

Lepa's orange mouth curled into a sneer. "What do you

expect to buy with that?"

"A bathroom break for my friend."

Lepa snorted. "You have any idea what my water bill has been for the past week? What toilet paper costs?"

"Look, forget it," I said, stepping between the two. "I'll cop a squat in an alley."

Onanefe held up his hands. "Whoa, whoa, whoa! Where's your dignity?"

"Dignity probably costs more than either of us have right now."

Onanefe pulled more bills out of his pocket, muttering under his breath. He held up the wad of cash in Lepa's face. "Is that enough for her?"

I batted his hand. "I do not need you covering for me, okay?"

"What, you're worried about adding more to your tab?"

I fought back my rising gorge. "You know, a few hours ago, I was prepared to give you a fair shake. I'd get my manager, talk this out, make sure we were square. But now? Now you're pissing me off. Now you make me want to get *lawyers*."

"Oh, look at Ms Distiller. How's the weather up on your high horse?"

"At least I can climb up on a high horse myself, without some asshat pretending to help me."

"Jesus." Lepa snatched some bills from Onanefe's hand. "I haven't seen drama like that since Shakespeare in the Bay." She unlocked the door. "You can do better than this, honey."

"I'm sure we all can." I hustled inside to the toilet, thankful it was also unlocked.

When I returned to the sidewalk, Onanefe sat at a table with Lepa. They stirred tiny cups of espresso. "You want one?" he asked.

"It would be on the house," said Lepa, clinking her spoon on her saucer. "Your friend told me about your building. My condolences."

"Thank you, but I've had enough caffeine for the day." I thought ahead to Six O'Clock, about drinking my rum and going right to sleep. Then I remembered my flat, my bed, and that bottle of Old Windswept were all gone. Prickles of icy panic ran over the back of my skull, and The Fear stirred. I cleared my throat to cover me shaking my head, trying to rattle The Fear back to sleep. I had backups. I had plans. If I could manage to make Six O'Clock work in the middle of a Force Eleven storm (take *that*, Hurricane Bessie), I could make it work now. "My friend happen to tell you why we're here?"

She nodded. "If the guy who attacked you hung around here, I'm happy to help you find him. I don't need that kind of reputation. You got a picture?"

"You okay with a local connection?"

Her mouth made a thin, orange line. "Looks like I'll have to be."

I blinked up the footage from my buffer and sent it direct to Lepa's pai. She blinked, then sneered. "*This* guy. He made a giant order last month, enough pita and knedle for a hundred people, deliverable today. Me and my husband have been working our tails off, and then he shows up this morning and gives us some song and dance about not having cash, and, what with the Public down – *tsch*."

"Did he say what this was for?"

Lepa shook her head. "He only said it was for a social function. I wasn't going to let him have anything, but then he yells and these two giants come in the door."

"Giants?" I said. "Like, goon giant?"

She touched the tip of her nose. "Just like that. If he hadn't surrounded himself with those goons, I'd have given him a bash."

"I think I can take care of that for you," I said. "He leave an address?"

Lepa tapped her temple. "I always keep receipts up here. He's around the corner off Lutyen–"

I didn't wait to hear the rest of it. I just saw red. I got up, excused myself, and marched up the street to Saarien's church. Onanefe kept pace, making sure not to get in my way. "I hope you're not going to go in there swinging."

I cracked my knuckles. "Don't worry. I'll be good and calm before I tear that white-suited sonuvabitch a new one."

"What if he isn't *there*?" said Onanefe.

"Then we'll see how fast word gets to him," I said. "If the Public's down, he's got to have some way to communicate with his followers."

"I really wish you'd have let me bring my crew."

"What, you don't think I can handle this?"

He ruffled his mustache. "I just don't like goons, you know?"

"Join the club."

The alley off Lutyen was packed. Tired teenagers slumped in the shrinking shadows, and kids painted the walls with smiley faces and STRIKE. Some people drank tea from battered caneplas cups, their eyes unfocused and bloodshot. It was a majority Freeborn crowd, and everyone handing out instruction sheets and directing groups in and out of the Temple were also Freeborn. One kid who looked no older than twelve juggled three different clipboards. "BUDVAR!" she yelled, and one of the teenagers heaved herself out of a crouch, took a sheet of paper from Clipboard Girl, and ran off into the street. A woman in her thirties hovered nearby, adding or taking away paper from the clipboards.

I nudged my way to the door, Onanefe sticking close to

me. Ahead of us stood a group of exhausted women holding babies and bundles of clothes. In front of me was an old lady with a monstrous stack of cloth diapers. "May I help you with that?" I asked, not waiting for an answer. I swept the diapers out of the old lady's hands, and she turned. Her ink, an IF/THEN logic gate, crinkled above a sweet and confused smile. I kept my head down as Clipboard Girl directed us inside. "And don't mess up the stacks!" she yelled.

The Temple was a beehive. I could hear nothing but the buzz of people talking about food runs, people talking about repairing PV cells, people talking about the best way to keep the Brapati Causeway blocked to motor traffic. The tables that had been covered with food and clothes were now empty except for a man sitting on one, cradling a baby. Everyone had sagging eyes and downturned mouths. The last strike, those looks hadn't appeared until the second month. I remembered spending every waking hour making sure people had their needs met and their gripes heard. Maybe Saarien hadn't planned this very well, and the whole thing would collapse on its own. Maybe the best thing to do would be to go back to the distillery and ride it out.

Someone *shhsh*ed, and the screen in the corner flicked on. There was Saarien, his eye a little swollen but still smiling. "Friends," he said, holding up his hands. "This has been a glorious first week. Our labor action has already unified the planet into a harmonious accord–"

I stopped listening to the words and paid attention to the sound. I could hear Saarien's voice echo in the room. At first I thought it was the screen's high volume bouncing around but then I heard it: a faint version of Saarien from inside the room that spoke before the screen. He was broadcasting from here. I scooted through the crowd as Saarien's voice rose and fell. The people clapped and hooted, and I lost the trail. I looked at the screen: behind Saarien was a wall covered in STRIKE graffiti. He squinted into the camera. A shadow flickered across his face.

"He's outside," I hissed to Onanefe, and pushed back to the door.

ELEVEN

Saarien stood at the end of the alley, the wall making a perfect backdrop. The two goons I'd met before, Gwendolyn and Kazys, held the crowd back but for a few kids gathered at Saarien's sides. I squeezed my way to the front row and glared hard. Saarien's eyes flickered over to me, and he paused in his speech. I couldn't tell what flashed across his face. Fear? Relief? Anger? He finished his remarks with the bit about lifting fists, and I could hear a roar ripple out of the alley onto Lutyen and beyond.

Saarien walked right up to me. "If you're going to hit me again, please don't hit me in the face."

"I'm not going to hit you again. Though I hope you don't give me a reason to."

He nodded. "I heard what happened. I'm so glad you're all right."

"I'll bet." The goons formed a cordon around us, pushing him way too close to me. "I don't have time to waste, Rutey. Who is this guy?" I touched his temple, and he opened a connection to my photo.

He blanched. "Oh, no. Are you sure?"

"You want me to send you footage of him stabbing me?

Who is he?"

"Octavian Noon. One of the more fervent members of the congregation." He rubbed the back of his head, and his hair pooched up to the sky. "Some of these kids, they get caught up in talk about The Struggle, and next thing you know they're grabbing weapons and going out into the streets—"

"Did you send him for me, Rutey?"

Saarien shook like I'd slapped him. "What? No! No, Padma, I would *never* do anything like that! This whole strike is supposed to be non-violent!"

The look of panic on Saarien's face wasn't that of a guilty man. It reminded me of the dozens of people I'd met over the years who had built up angry anti-Big Three movements, only to have them all fall apart before their moments of glory had arrived. Saarien wasn't afraid he'd been caught red-handed; he was upset that one of his overzealous followers had struck without his say-so.

But I didn't have to let him know that.

I shook my head. "You know I can go to Soni Baghram and have you chucked back in the clink, right?"

"But I'm out. I was *released*."

"That doesn't mean you're immune from going back on *new* charges, like conspiracy to commit murder. Soni *hates* conspiracy, and this looks like a textbook example. We got a firebrand preacher, we got a lunatic follower, and we got video footage of said follower using said preacher's words right after I get a knife sunk into my shoulder. Just one note from me, and you're done. All this is done. Soni would cross a picket line for me. You think she'd stay behind it for you?"

Saarien held up his hands. "No, of course not. Please, Padma, don't, we're working so hard for *everyone*, even you. I should have kept Octavian on a short leash, should have kept him from taking things so far. You understand that, right? Getting caught up in the heat of the movement?"

"I never felt the need to shank someone from the Big Three."

"No, but you probably wanted to crack a few skulls, right?" Flop sweat rolled down Saarien's temples. He leaned in close. "Please, Padma, it is getting tense out here. I'm hearing about people coming close to fighting, trying to settle old scores. If word gets out that someone made an attempt on your life, it could set off riots."

"Over little old me?"

"Over a symbol of the Union's triumph over the Big Three." He swallowed and made a face like he'd just eaten bitter medicine. "People are itching for an excuse to start swinging. It's harder to hold this coalition together than I thought, and if people hear that a Freeborn man tried to stab a beloved Union member, that would be enough."

I smiled. "*Beloved*? I need to update my theme song."

Saarien clasped his hands together. "Please let me handle this. Can you trust me to keep everything under control?"

I let my upper lip curl into a sneer. "That's a hell of a thing to ask."

"I know, I know." His hands shook as he pressed them tighter. "Our city, our *world*, it needs this to work. *I* need this to work. Don't make it for nothing. Please."

I thought back to that horrible day two years ago when Saarien had me tied to a chair, ready to dump a can of cane diesel on me and light me up. He had shot Wash in the gut. He had worn this look of triumph, like he'd won every World Cup in history. I looked at this ruined creature begging and snorted. "You're going to have to work a whole lot harder than that to earn my trust, Saarien. Anyone from your group so much as looks at me funny, and I'm going straight to Soni, and you're going back to Maersk." I looked up at the goons. "Could I please get by? Gwendolyn? Kazys?"

Gwendolyn stared down at me, her mouth a hard, thin line. She rolled one of her shoulders, and I heard bones grinding together.

"I'm sorry for everything I said about people in your profession," I said. "That was wrong. I think you're absolutely right to go on strike. The Union has been terrible to former security services personnel."

Gwendolyn and Kazys exchanged glances. "Talk is cheap," said Gwendolyn.

"But I'm sure your rates aren't," I said. "Class Two Mechanist, right?"

She snorted. "You're really going to try and buy us off?"

"No, but I will help hook you up with that better gig if you want." I nodded to Kazys. "You, too."

"It's all right," said Saarien. "Friends, let's let Padma go on her way. Please."

The two former goons took a few steps back. The air felt cooler and freer and *man* were those two big. I nodded my thanks and walked out of the alley, doing my best to keep my steps straight. My head spun as all the blood rushed to the rest of my body.

Onanefe stood by the Temple door, fiddling with the ruins of his mustache. His eyes didn't leave Gwendolyn and Kazys, even when I staggered by and grabbed his elbow. He didn't turn his head until we got to the mouth of the alley. "You okay?" he asked.

"Yeah, just feels like I've done a three-g drop down the cable."

"I have no idea what that means."

"Just imagine all the blood in your body getting squished in place so your brain doesn't get any. Also, where the hell were you? What about sticking by me?"

"I don't get involved with goons," he said. "I've had

clients who employ them, and they're nasty business. Like having sentient bulldozers."

"They're not that bad, once you get to know 'em."

"I'm perfectly happy not doing that, thanks."

I grinned. "Do you mean to tell me that the big bad cane cutter is afraid of a little goon?"

"No, just the big ones, which is all of them." He took one more glance back down the alley at Gwendolyn and Kazys and shuddered. "You learn anything?"

I told him about Saarien's guilty looks and his babbling. "He seemed more worried about how the whole thing looked than how it was going."

"That doesn't sound like an evil mastermind," said Onanefe.

"No," I said. "I have the feeling Saarien's gotten in way over his head."

"Then what's your plan?"

My stomach grumbled, and I blinked up the time: one in the afternoon. Lunch wasn't a bad idea; getting to the nearest of my backup Six O'Clock rooms was better.

"We need to go to Bakaara Market," I said.

Onanefe blanched. "That's five klicks away!"

"Six. We'll probably have to take side alleys."

Onanefe pointed at the vendors winding their way through the crowd. "Whatever you need, I'm sure we can find it here."

I doubt it, I wanted to say. I kept a crate of Old Windswept and candles in the back of a stall in the northeast corner of Bakaara Market. The woman who owned the stall, Hawa Said, was a sweet grandmother who led a knitting circle of little old ladies called the Needle Nanas that made baby clothes. Hawa had once been a Ward Chair and had never lost her taste for the action, so she also led the Nanas to every Union committee meeting to raise hell. Rumors floated around the neighborhood that the Nanas also ran a protection racket in Bakaara, which wouldn't surprise me considering how much Hawa charged me every month.

I just shook my head and walked up Lutyen. "Bakaara. And I should remind you that *you* insisted on sticking with me. You can't hack a little walk?"

He snorted. "Six klicks is nothing. When I was starting out, it was a ten-K walk to our work sites, and that was with my tools."

"Was it uphill both ways? With a headwind?"

"Yes, in fact it was." He gave me a sideways smirk. "Well, not uphill. But I got onshore winds going to work sites, and offshore on the way home. It made riding my bike that much harder."

"Looks like you did well enough to jump up to a truck."

He shook his head. "That damn thing. It eats as much as my teenage nephews. Every time it breaks down, I wonder if it was worth the expense. And it's getting harder to find parts or a mechanic I can afford. You know, the guy I used to go to, he was Freeborn, moved to the city and picked up the trade. He had a great business going, and then the Materiél Committee decided there weren't enough serviceable Hanumans on the planet to push for better prices for parts."

Onanefe ran his lower lip under his teeth. His mustache's tips twitched. "So, my guy figures, okay, he can start making the parts himself, right? He rustles up a metallurgist who knows a gal with a forge, talks a couple of design guys into making templates. He's going to become his own supplier, right? And it works out for a while, enough to recoup some of his costs and keep my truck running. Until the lady who runs the forge gets sick and can't work anymore. The whole supply chain collapses almost overnight. Who does my guy have to turn to? Who do *I* have to turn to?"

"The Union?" I offered.

His face darkened. "Why would we do that?"

"Because if enough owners of MacDonald Heavy Hanumans screamed bloody murder at the people who live off dues, then maybe you'd still be getting parts. Or they'd have found someone else willing to run the forge. Or found some other way to get you what you need." I rubbed my fingers together. "If you want to play, you got to pay."

"Pay. Pfft."

"Says the man who wants his fifty K."

"I had a contract for goods rendered, not that piracy you call 'dues'."

"You make it sound so *dirty*," I said, giving him a wiggle of my eyebrows.

"And you don't think it is?" He pointed at the globe on my cheek. "You once signed your life away, *literally* signed it away. You come here, and what do you do? Sign up with another outfit that takes a chunk of your pay."

"That's how society works," I said.

"That's not how it *has* to work."

"Oh, Christ," I said. "Are you going to start talking about anarcho-syndicalism or some other crap like that?"

"You think tramping on human liberty is crap?"

I stopped and held up a finger. "I think *talking* instead of *working* is crap. I think trying to organize people without listening to them is crap. And I think hearing the same recycled labor theory glurge over and over again is complete and utter crap."

Onanefe's mustache twitched. "You don't have to be so harsh about it."

I let out a breath as a group of ugly-looking people wearing glass Temple pins filtered past us. They all had the posture of someone ready to fight. I scooted to the other side of the street. "Every six months, some kid gets to the

Marxism section on the Public Library, and then there's a lot of speeches and noise without anyone doing the work." I held out my hands at the milling, listless crowd. "This is what speeches get you. Everyone is pissed off, but no one is *asking* for anything, let alone *demanding*. All the talk about 'history's select' smacks of people who want to vent and be famous for a couple of days without doing the goddamn work. I've stuck with the Union because there are people in it who do the work, every day."

Onanefe *hmph*ed. "Looks like they've been slacking on the job."

"No arguments there."

Onanefe smirked. "So, is that what you're going to do at Bakaara? *The work*?" The jerk actually made air quotes with those last words.

"What, you don't think I can?"

He smiled and shook his head. "The time for any of you Union people to quit gabbling and do *the work*" – he wiggled his fingers again, his smirk growing more punchable by the moment – "was about twenty years ago when y'all were prepping the Contract. *That* was when you could have built a true coalition between Freeborn and Union, back when the traffic was high, the prices were strong, and we *all* had a real dose of power. But no, you had to piss it away."

"First of all, twenty years ago, I was still living the Life Corporate," I said, dodging a woman selling pre-soaked rags (*Keep the riot gas away, only five yuan a pop!*). "So you can stow that 'you Union people' crap right the hell now. And second, I have no idea what you're talking about."

Onanefe narrowed his eyes. "I thought you were supposed to be a big wheel in the Union."

"I was just a Ward Chair. Where did you get that idea?"

"Your theme song." He cleared his throat and belted out, in a booming basso:

*"When she sits at the table
Negotiations stop
When she lists her demands
The Sky Queen comes on top!"*

I groaned. "That bloody song."

He put his hand to his chest and opened his eyes wide. "Do you mean to tell me that the oral traditions of Santee Anchorage aren't *accurate*?" He held that look of feigned outrage for a moment before bursting out laughing. "No, seriously, I just heard through the grapevine that you had the Executive Council's ear."

"The grapevine is wrong," I said. "After my little trip up the cable, none of them would touch me if I were covered in money."

"Which brings me back to what I was talking about," said Onanefe. "All the cash that was left on the table. Well, it was hypothetical cash, but still…"

"What money?"

Now he looked surprised for real. "You really don't know? Two Contracts ago, the Union and all the Freeborn were on the verge of uniting forces. Instead of the Union doing all the negotiations with the Big Three, we'd enter into a compact and do it together. Everything would be distributed fairly: profits, benefits, education, health care, tech. There would be no more trickling down of money from the city to the kampong."

This was all news to me. "Go on."

He shrugged. "Not much else to tell. Depending on who you talk to, one side said the other overreached, and the whole thing collapsed."

"What did the Freeborn want?"

"The usual: a bigger cut of cane profits, better infrastructure, more clinics in the kampong. Plus an acknowledgement of the Freeborn contribution to the thriving mess that is Santee Anchorage."

I kept the guffaw in check. "Since when is that *not* acknowledged?"

He stopped and shook a finger at me. "See? That's just what I'm talking about. You want to dismiss me."

"I do not!"

"Are you saying I don't know what my own life has been like?" said Onanefe, his eyebrows beetling. "I was *born* on Santee. My parents, and their parents' parents? Born here. I grew up in the shadow of the Union pushing us around, calling us peasants because we didn't want to join up."

"And where did your great-grandparents come from?" I said, crossing my arms. "Did they spontaneously generate out of the ground?"

His mouth quirked. "No, they were Breaches."

"Uh-huh. That 'We Were Here First' argument doesn't wash, and you know it. Trace any Freeborn family back, and they came from Breaches or Shareholders or *someone* connected to the Union. And the Union keeps money and gear flowing until we get enough homegrown science and industry to cut ourselves loose from the Big Three. You want to tell me of a single Freeborn scientist or engineer whose work has been turned away? Can you name one?"

"That's beside the point," said Onanefe. "We have to rely on the Union, and you – I mean, the Union leadership knows it. Just like they know the Union depends on the Big Three. We're all dependents. The people who walked away from the table twenty years ago knew that, and the people on the street today know that."

"And you think this strike is going to stop that?"

His face softened. "I know there are just as many Union people marching as there are Freeborn. Is that such a bad thing?"

"It is when no one knows what they're marching *for*."

"You think that?"

"I know it."

Onanefe crossed his arms over his chest. "And what do you base that assertion upon?"

I gave him a tiny smile. "You know, for a guy who spends his days cutting cane, you sound a lot more like one of us gabbling Union people."

He shrugged. "You gotta learn how to play the game if you want to win. I study, you know?"

"And so do I, which is why this is nothing like the last two strikes I've seen. You make your demands before you hit the streets, not the other way around. This is theater."

"You wanna bet?"

I held out a hand. "I'll bet you a case of Old Windswept."

Onanefe considered this. "Which kind?"

I made a face. "Standard, of course."

"Not a bottle of Ten-Year?"

I blew him a raspberry. "Don't you start on me, too. There's no such thing as Ten-Year. That was Estella Tonggow's magical marketing bullshit. But the *two* cases of Standard I'm betting are real."

"Okay, then." He reached for my hand, then stopped. "And what if you win? 'Cause I'm not giving up the fifty K."

"Then you give up your cut," I said. "And, before you protest about me ripping you off, I'll make sure it's rum made before I took over. *That* I still have."

He took my hand. "You are on."

We shook on it. I let go and asked the first passer-by, a man with a young girl perched on his shoulders, "Excuse me, could you tell me why you're marching today?"

For the rest of the way to Bakaara Market, we talked to everyone going our way who would talk back. I heard complaints about preschool cutbacks, about broken sidewalks, about how the latest pai firmware update made this one guy's implant play *The Lincolnshire Poacher* in the middle of the night, every night, for a month. The only people who wouldn't talk to me were the ones wearing Temple pins. They scooted away as soon as I approached them.

I recorded all of it, making as much space as I could on my buffer. And, with every interview, I got confirmation: everyone was angry, everyone wanted something done about what was making them angry, but no one had any plans on how to accomplish that.

"I just heard people were marching," said a man handing out shelled coconuts. He had parked a loaded bakfiets on the corner of Jodpur and Fleetwood. "And I figured, hey, it's about time I did, too."

"But you're standing here," I said.

He shrugged. "All my stock's going to rot. Might as well write it off and keep people from dehydrating."

"So what do you hope to get from being out here?"

He whacked at a coconut with a machete, then handed me the cleaned-up fruit and a straw. "I want the Executive Committee to do their goddamn jobs."

I thanked him for his time and walked up Jodpur, sipping my coconut water. Onanefe called to me from across the street, and I wove my way through the crowd. He had a wood cup full of lychees in his hand, and he offered me one. "Well?"

"I know what I saw and heard."

"Which is?"

"Six kilometers of angry people with no focus."

He made a face, then spat out a lychee. "We're still not at Bakaara. I'm not giving up."

"You might want to," I said, offering him the coconut. "Not even the Freeborn I talked with had any idea of why they were marching. Everyone's out in the streets because everyone's out in the streets."

"I just don't get this," said Onanefe. "Last time, we all had our act together. We had solidarity."

"There's that Union talk again."

He gave me a sideways glare. "I'm not so high-and-mighty that I can't rip off a perfectly good idea to suit my own needs, okay? Besides, if there's any one thing we Freeborn need, it's sticking together."

"Well, you're all certainly following each other out of the kampong and into the streets." I tried not to smirk as we rounded the corner to the edge of Bakaara Market.

Onanefe stepped in front of me and turned around. "I didn't get a good enough representative sample."

I laughed. "No one likes a sore loser."

"It wasn't enough! This is a heavy Union route you took us on, and there will be a lot more Freeborn in the market."

I bowed. "Of course, Your Quantitativeness."

He *hmph*ed. "You don't have to get sarcastic about it."

Any other day, Bakaara Market would have been a great place to visit. It was one of the first structures the first Breaches had built, a beautiful open-air lattice of coral steel, caneplas roof tiles, and PV cells. It kept cool in the day and warm at night, thanks to the system of louvered shades that ringed the lattice. It stayed open twenty-six hours a day, sold just about everything there was to sell, and was now a complete and utter mess.

People jammed the aisles, grabbing and pushing for anything left in the stalls. Two men held a tug-of-war over a packet of biryani spice mix next to a table stained with turmeric and paprika. Old ladies wrestled for the remaining packages of lug nuts at Bernice's Pick-A-Peck-Of-Parts. Kids wailed, Union and Freeborn people yelled at each other, and–

Something in the back of my head snapped. I had no idea if it was The Fear trying to get loose, or if it was the stress of the previous day, or what. I just knew I had had my fill of this bullshit and that it was time for it to end. I grabbed the wrench from my trouser loop, climbed atop a table, and started whacking the wrench on a coral steel strut. After a minute, the crowd at my feet stilled and looked up.

"WHAT ARE YOU DOING?" I bellowed. People winced and clutched their heads. I forgot that my pai was still pinging everyone nearby, so my words blasted right into their eyeballs. A few people gave me smiles; the rest glared.

I pointed my wrench at the mob. "This is not how it's supposed to go. Whatever's gotten you angry, is it bad enough to get you to turn on strangers? On your neighbors?"

"There's no food!" yelled someone.

"That's because the Freeborn are blocking the farms!" yelled someone else.

"That's a lie!"

"You're a liar!"

The squabbling started up. I banged the wrench on the strut so hard that sparks flew. "ENOUGH!" I yelled. I could feel the feedback from the nearby pais. The crowd stilled again.

"Everyone here has gotten screwed at some point in their lives," I said. "I used to be a Ward Chair, and now I muck out the holding tanks at the bottom of the Brushhead water works. I spend every day covered in filth. I'm sure a lot of you do, too.

"And you know what keeps me going? It's the knowledge that, as bad as things may get for me, I'm not owned by WalWa anymore. I know that there are people here on Santee really looking out for me, even though I have to kick them in the ass to remind them of that."

A mild titter traveled through the crowd. A few of them whispered to each other, and I caught them saying my name or *Sky Queen*. That damn song...

I cleared my throat. "I know a lot of you are angry because you haven't gotten what you think you've earned. A lot of you think you've been ripped off by your bosses, or by the Union, or by the person who sells you vegetables. The more I've talked with people, the more I'm convinced that you're right. Things have gone bad with the Union. It's not living up to its end of the bargain.

"But is this the way to hold them to it? Fighting each other over tea and bolts? This is the kind of crap that the Big Three *loves*. When we fight each other, we forget to fight *them*. And do you want to let the Big Three win?"

The people looked at me, then at each other.

I sagged, then leaned toward the crowd. "Really? Contract Time is less than a year away. The Big Three are betting that we won't have our act together so they can slip some new evil under our noses. You want that? You want to make even *less* than you do now?"

People shook their heads. I heard a few *No*s here and there.

"Then you have to *want* a better life. You have to *want* to work together, 'cause that's the only thing we've got. When we're united, Union and Freeborn, we are unstoppable. We have to work together. We have to *fight* together. And you look like people who want to fight. Am I right?"

That got a few cheers.

"I said, do you want to *fight*?"

That got even more.

"Then start talking it out *here*, then you take it to your Ward Chairs. Take it to the Union Hall. Even if you're Freeborn, 'cause whatever the Big Three are planning to do will screw *you* even harder."

I jumped off the table and pointed at the first person I saw, a Union woman clutching a stack of motherboards. "You," I said, "what are you pissed off about?"

She held out the circuitry. "I can't operate my CNC mill with this crap."

And so on for another two hours. I ran out of buffer space on my pai recording one story after another about pay cuts, evaporating benefits, or promised equipment never arriving. I got the names of everyone involved: the Ward Chairs who were supposed to make things happen, the Committees that were accountable, the endless list of promises broken to everyone, Union and Freeborn alike. I cadged a notebook from a bookbinder's stall and a bunch of colored pencils from an art supplier, and even then I ran out of room. I had a whole volume of *How I Got Screwed By The Union*, written by the people of Bakaara Market.

I blinked up the time: five o'clock. My hand hurt from writing. My eye twitched from all the blinking. I thanked my last interviewee and found Onanefe talking to a Freeborn woman. He scribbled in a notebook, nodding as the woman talked about water cutbacks. When he saw me, he thanked her and stuffed the notebook in his satchel. "You finally ready to go shopping?" he asked.

"Food first." I nodded to his satchel. "You been busy?"

He shrugged. "A lotta people want to talk. I like to listen."

"And record."

"That a crime?"

I shook my head. "Looks like someone doing the work."

He made a face. "I think I'd rather do the eating."

"Then follow me," I said. "I know a place with great tacos."

"I suppose I'm buying?"

"No, because I get tacos on credit."

He opened his eyes wide. "I think I have much to learn from you."

I threw him a very sloppy wink. "Stick with me, mister. I'll take you places."

We wove our way through the stalls. The mood had calmed, though I could see tension on everyone's faces, as if they were still waiting for *something* to happen. The vendors kept their patter to a minimum. Everyone kept blinking madly, the sign of pais on the fritz. The sharp wave of panic had died down, but I could feel the anger running through the people, like a low-level electric current just waiting for a gap to jump.

"What's got you angry?" asked Onanefe.

I shrugged. "The usual. The unfairness of entropy. Man's inhumanity to man. The fact that my favorite konbini upcharges for kimchi."

He shook his head. "You want to keep it to yourself, fine."

"I don't *know* you," I said, giving him a broad *fuck-you* smile. "We're not friends. We're not colleagues. *You* claim I owe you money, so that means we have a transactional relationship. Feelings aren't part of that transaction."

"Even though we have the same goal?"

"We do? That's news to me."

He smiled as he wagged his finger. "I watched you today. Every time you talked with someone, you lit up. You *like* this."

"Because I know I'm going to use it to get Leticia Smythe off her ass. Never underestimate the motivational power of spite."

"So you've been done wrong, too?"

I gave him a little shrug. "I guess. Spend enough time wading in muck, you'll think *everyone's* done you wrong."

Next to us was a table covered in coiled multi-colored

network cables. Two men were arguing about the esoterica of network protocol and blaming each other for their lack of pai access. A pair of cops stood by, not looking at the ever-heating argument. Soni would have had their heads if she'd seen her people not breaking up arguments before they turned into brawls.

Both of the arguers, I couldn't help but notice, wore a Temple pin. Even Saarien's people were losing their cool. "But you know what? Right now, I just want to get dinner. We can worry about Letty later."

"What, you think she's gonna pay attention to you?"

"I'll make sure she does."

And that's when the network cables exploded.

TWELVE

My brain wasn't sure how to process that. One moment, I was looking at a table full of cables; the next, the cables flew at me like a forest of striking cane vipers. There was no flash, no bang, no puff of smoke. Just a thousand noodles of wire and caneplas shooting toward our heads. They lashed around my shoulders and neck, and I fell to the ground under their weight.

I took a moment to catch my breath and tamp down my rising panic. I wasn't on fire. I looked over at Onanefe. He wasn't on fire either. That was good. I could work with that.

"Here." I reached for him, and another wave of cables flew over us, followed by a table, two chairs, and a few hundred people.

Three of them stepped on us before I could grab Onanefe and pull him toward me. I wrapped my arms over his head and held on tight. Boots came down on my legs, my hips. Someone tripped and landed on my side, squeezing all the air out of my lungs. I let fly with an elbow while I gasped in a breath. Onanefe's eyes were wide with panic. I couldn't hear his muffled words over the roar of the mob. I held him closer, wrapping a leg over his hip. "It's going to be okay!"

I yelled, my own voice fighting to get through the cables covering my face.

The Fear hissed: *You're going to miss Six O'Clock, and all because you saved this guy who says you owe him money. What is he to you? A creditor. Who saves someone you owe money? You're an idiot.*

"Shut it," I hissed under my breath. A foot came down on my back. Three people stepped on Onanefe, and he howled. I held him closer. To hell with The Fear. I wasn't going to let anyone get trampled. I wormed both of us against the overturned table until we both huddled against the ragged tabletop. People jostled the table as they bumped the ends. The world was a white noise haze of rushing bodies, screams, and the table banging on the pourform ground.

I didn't know how long it took for the noise to die down. I waited until the table stopped moving for a whole minute before I threw off the cables and gave Onanefe a nudge. "You still alive?"

He groaned. "I think I broke a rib." He tried to get up, then went right back down. "Or three."

I took my multi-tool from my trousers, thankful it hadn't tumbled out in the chaos. I snapped open the shears and cut away the cables around his body. "Just stay still. I'll find help."

Onanefe gave a weak chuckle. "I think the help went with the mob. What was that?"

"No idea." I pulled cables off his neck, trying not to touch the fresh lashes the cables had made on his skin. "Can you breathe?"

He inhaled and winced.

"Good enough." I got under his arm and helped him up. "Please don't faint on me."

We stood all the way up. It looked like a hurricane had swept through the Market. Everything that wasn't made of coral steel had been smashed to pieces. Awnings were torn apart, tables snapped in half, and fruit, clothes, and electronic components lay scattered on the ground. There were a few other wounded people with bloodied faces and limbs hanging at weird angles.

But as I looked toward the west edge where Hawa kept her stall, I saw no damage. The line of wreckage moved in a thin, straight line from Parkhurst to Djimon, two hundred meters long. It was like a stampede of very narrow bison had plowed its way through the Market.

The small amount of damage wasn't enough to keep the other vendors open, however. As I helped Onanefe toward Hawa's stall, I saw everyone had closed up shop. What couldn't be rolled up, stowed, or boxed was simply dumped into wheelbarrows and bakfietsen and taken away. It looked like someone had hit the hurricane warning alarm, the one that meant get the hell out now.

Hawa's stall was one of the few permanent ones, more of an open-air office than a tent. The front was all display boards, but the back was a pourform shed with enough room for four people. By the time we got there, the coral steel door to the shed was closed, and chicken wire wrapped around the now-emptied front. An embroidered sign (*All done for the day, thank you!*) hung from the wire. Above the sign was the crocheted figure of a woman holding a spiked cricket bat. Tiny crocheted heads hung from the woman's belt, their eyes now adorable stitched X's.

"Hawa!" I yelled, banging on the chicken wire with my free hand. "I need you!"

"We're closed!" came Hawa's voice from behind the door.

"I can see that, but I still need you! It's Padma!"

There was a horrible pause, and then the door's multiple locks clacked. Hawa opened the door enough to see me and cursed. She was an elegant woman who decorated her hand-knitted hijab with strings of glass beads. They rattled as she shook her head. "This isn't a good time."

"I pay you five hundred yuan a month for times just like this."

She *tch*ed, wrinkling the starfield and sextant tattooed on her cheek. "I've got all my stock in here, plus my granddaughter."

"Then we'll be very careful and polite as we take shelter. You gonna let us in, or do I have to start telling everyone that you farm out your needlework?"

"Shh!" She strode to the chicken wire and unwrapped it. "You want to ruin me?"

I helped Onanefe through the gap. "Of course not. I love the scarves you make."

Hawa gave Onanefe the hairy eyeball. "Who's this?"

He straightened up enough to give Hawa a bow. "Asalam malakum, sister."

"Wa alaikum salaam." She nodded. "At least he's got manners. More than I can say for you, Padma, showing up in the middle of a riot. Get your asses inside."

Hawa slammed the door behind us and threw four bolts into place. The pourform walls kept the inside of the shed cool, though I felt little balls of heat from the two lamps overhead. Stacks of knitwear went from floor to ceiling. A teenage girl sat at a tiny table, knitting needles in hand. I eased Onanefe into the chair opposite her. The girl looked at him, then gripped her needles together, points facing him. He gave her a polite nod before going back to sweating and wincing.

"How long you been holed up in here?" I asked.

"Long enough." Hawa's copper bracelets rattled as she fussed over a tiny teapot with equally tiny copper cups. They looked like giant thimbles. She made a tall, precise pour into each one. The smell of heavy mint filled the office.

"I opened up this morning and could tell it was going to be a weird day. Everybody was snapping up staples or meds or anything that could make for a good weapon. And no one knew why! No one talked about what they were worried about, just that they were worried." She handed each of us a cup and toasted us. "One gulp. You lose flavor if you sip."

We downed our tea, and I felt something like relief rush from the back of my head down to my toes. Except for the bus ride and hiding from the human tsunami, I had been on my feet all day. I also hadn't eaten since that guy gave me a coconut hours ago. I nodded to Onanefe. "You got any pain meds? He got stepped on."

Hawa shook her head. "My first aid kit got boosted yesterday. Why don't you give him a slug of that rum?"

I felt the blood rush out of my face. "I don't know what you're talking about."

She clucked her tongue. "Oh, please. You think I don't know what's in your stash?"

"I paid you to keep it, no questions asked!"

She shrugged. "I didn't ask. I just looked. A case of Old Windswept and some candles? Is that really worth five Cs a month?"

Onanefe turned to me. "Seriously? What is it, some kinda special blend?"

Hawa laughed. "No, it's just the plain stuff. From what I understand, you make a good rum, but it can't be *that* good."

"I want a refund," I said. "Right now. All of it."

Hawa pointed at the door. "Then you're welcome to step outside and talk to my banker. She's probably ransacking the neighboring stalls."

I stood up. I clenched my hands so tightly that the tea cup bent. "Where is it?"

Hawa made a big show of sifting through the piles of

knitwear. In the middle of a stack of onesies was a canvas
sack. She smiled as she reached in, her bracelets rattling.
"Seriously?" I said. "Five hundred for a *bag*?"

She waved me off. "You know what the secret is to
maintaining a good holding company? Misdirection." She
pulled a battered pad from the bag and tapped its screen.
The lamps winked out, then blacklight LEDs embedded
in the ceiling winked on. The pourform walls came alive
with star charts and circuitry diagrams. Hawa hummed as
she ran her fingers over the constellations and tapped at a
scrawled keypad on the wall. She nodded to Onanefe. "Can
you scoot ten centimeters to your left, dear? I don't want
you to get a concussion."

Onanefe slid to the side. Hawa put her palm flat against
an outline of a hand (decorated, I noticed, with feathers,
eyes, and a beak), and the portion of the wall where
Onanefe's head had been *chunk*ed open. Hawa tugged at the
panel of pourform, and two wire racks on rails slid up from
the ground. In the racks were bundles of blue boys, three
foil bags covered in biohazard stamps, a khanjar in a silver
sheath, what looked like the components of an automatic
pistol, boxes of ammunition, and, tucked behind a skein of
purple yarn, a crate holding my candles and my bottles of
Old Windswept.

Hawa pulled a candle and a bottle out of the rack. "Is this
worth your five hundred?"

I plucked the bottle out of her hands and grabbed a
candle out of the crate. "Thank you. Now, if you'll excuse
me." I walked to the door and started throwing bolts.

"What do you think you're doing?" said Hawa.

"Going out. I need some privacy."

Hawa gawped. "To drink? Are you nuts?"

"I'll be right back."

"I think not," said Hawa. "You step out of here, Padma,

I'm locking the door behind you. It's insane outside, and I'm not going to let it get in here."

"But you let us in!"

"That was before I knew you were going to go right back out," she said. "As of a few minutes ago, you've reclaimed your stuff. That means our deal is done. You want to have a nightcap in the middle of all that madness, you go on ahead. But you can't come back in."

"You got any matches?"

Hawa crossed her arms over her chest. "What, it's not enough to wade into a riot? You want to start a fire, too?"

"No questions asked," I said. "You got a light, or what?"

Hawa's beads clacked as she tilted her head to the side. "Maybe. You can't tell me why you're going to commit suicide first?"

"Good Lord, Hawa, could you knock off the theatrics? There is no angry mob. There is no riot."

Onanefe groaned.

"Okay, not anymore," I said.

"You got some kind of problem? Let me help you." Hawa put her hands on my arms and tugged. "Whatever it is–"

"Christ Almighty, I am not an alcoholic, okay? I'm not some rummy who needs to get liquored up to deal with stress! I just have to step out for all of sixty seconds, and then I'm done." I clicked the bolts.

Hawa moved to block the door. "Padma, please. Don't do this. Whatever you need to do out there can wait until it's safe."

The Fear hissed. I blinked up the time. Five forty-seven. "No, it can't," I said. I gave her a kiss on the cheek, kicked open the bolt in the floor, and went outside.

I shivered even though it wasn't cold. The sun had started its dip toward the horizon, and everything looked angry and red: the sky, the Market, the people. I clutched the crate as a pack of women holding cricket bats sifted through the wreckage next to Hawa's stall. They all wore gray t-shirts with SECURITY printed on the front and back. They couldn't have been younger than thirty, but they all looked old and hard as they squinted into the failing light.

"Oy!"

I turned. Onanefe held onto a strut, gasping as he took an unsure step toward me. "We had a deal!"

"No, we had a bet. Which you lost."

"Semantics." He screwed his face and winced as he walked toward us. "Ladies, good evening. You mind if I talk with my colleague?"

The women looked at each other, their wariness transferring from me to Onanefe. I held up a hand. "It's okay. He's okay." They shrugged, then moved on to another pile of wreckage.

I shook my head. "I'm not going to run off and leave you stranded, okay? I just have something to do."

"That you can't do inside? Where it's safe? And there's tea?"

"I need privacy."

Onanefe narrowed his eyes, then shook his head. "Look, I understand about habits, okay? I've had plenty of friends who get hooked, and–"

"Oh, fuck you," I said. "You can take your concern and sanctimony and shove 'em up your ass, okay? I am not an addict off to get a fix. I have something I need to do at six o'clock, and if I don't, things will get unpleasant for both of us."

He cocked his head. "What, are you some kind of werewolf?"

"None of your business."

"You don't trust me?"

"I don't *know* you!" I turned and got in his face. "You

miraculously showed up at my flat when it was on fire, then you miraculously said I owe you a boatload of money. You know what that sounds like to me? A setup. A great big setup to relieve me of something, and I don't have the time, the energy, or the network connection to figure it out. What I *do* have" – I jabbed a finger in his shoulder; his cheek twitched at my touch – "is a pain in my ass and an appointment at six. Guess which one is more important to me now?"

I took a step back. "Besides, if there's anyone who shouldn't have to prove trust, it's me. I saved your ass from getting crushed. *You* don't get to lecture *me* about trust."

He gritted his teeth, and his eyes unfocused for a moment. When he looked back at me, he nodded. "You're right. You're absolutely right. You got something to take care of, okay. I just –" He bit his lip and looked away. "I know your reputation, that you're this badass, that you don't take any crap. But I saw something else in you today. You worry. You care. You give a shit. And right now? Santee needs more people like that. And it fucking kills me to think that you're going to take that bottle and wander out here and–"

"And all that can wait for five minutes. I promise." I patted him on the arm and walked away as quickly as I could without making it look like I was running.

I passed an abandoned food stall, the coals under the grill smoldering. A corner of the stall's dark blue awning flapped loose. I set the bottle and candle down next to the grill and set myself up. The awning came down with a few sharp tugs. The stall's owner had left all her tools out, including a bundle of rags for cleaning the grill. I wrapped a rag around a spatula, dipped it in a bowl of cooking oil, then set it on the grill. It *whoosh*ed into flame, and I lit the candle. I plopped on the ground in front of the candle and threw the awning over me.

I blinked up the time: five fifty-nine.

There I sat, underneath a canvass tent in the ruins of one of the biggest markets in Santee City. There I was, me and my candle and my bottle and my wrecked brain as my city and probably my whole planet spun out of control. I saw my place in the middle of all that mess, one lone woman who had people hounding her for money or favors or blood. This was not where I wanted to be. I wanted to be in my flat, listening to the Six O'Clock sounds of Brushhead, the beeping of the tuk-tuk horns, the ringing of the bells at Our Lady of the Big Shoulders, and the glorious sounds of the muezzin at the Emerald Masjid. I wanted to hear people working and living and loving, not the hostile silence that surrounded me.

I took a breath and cracked the seal on the bottle. The smell of Old Windswept, that smell of pear and cinnamon wafted upward, overpowering the must and smoke. For a moment, I knew right where I was: in a makeshift tent in Bakaara Market in Howlwadaag, on the northeast edge of Santee City. I let my mind's eye fly upwards, above the haze and the crowded streets, above the network-dark buildings and cafés, up and up past the orbital anchor and out into Occupied Space, higher and farther than the ripples of today's madness could travel. I was a speck, an invisible dot on an invisible dot in an ocean of stars I could never comprehend, but I knew where I was. I drank, took a breath, then took a second drink. Why not?

I threw aside the tent. Where I wanted to be was a long way from where I was. I would get there. I would get Onanefe and his crew squared, I would get Letty squared, I would get this entire goddamn planet squared... it would just have to wait until I was done here.

Onanefe was right where I'd left him. I handed him the bottle. "Done."

He held the bottle up to the failing light and sloshed the

rum. "Looks like you barely started." He unscrewed the cap and sniffed. His face mellowed. "You mind?"

I shrugged. "Help yourself."

He took a long pull, then coughed. "Ho," he breathed. "Strong, but smooth."

"That was from the first batch I made after I took over. I was terrified I'd get it wrong, send the whole place under."

He took a sniff, then capped the bottle. "You got it right. Madame Tonggow would always send us off with a bottle after we delivered. Everyone else on the crew cracked theirs right away, but I never opened mine. Figured I'd save them for special occasions."

I laughed. "You know there's a market for the stuff she made? You could probably sell those bottles and get a better chunk than what you think I owe you."

He raised an eyebrow. "Fifty thousand yuan worth of rum?"

"Try a hundred K." I shook my head. "Collectors are weird. They came sniffing around after I took over, offering me cash for used barrels. They all wanted a piece of her."

He nodded. "Madame Tonggow would talk about stuff like that. People always coming from the Co-Op, pestering her about selling bits of equipment or buying into weird schemes. She'd give 'em that smile, the one that says, 'Yes, dear, that's nice. Now shove off.'"

"I wish I'd spent more time with her. I was so focused on buying the distillery that we didn't do much more than talk business." I looked at the bottle and contemplated another pull. I contemplated a lot of pulls. Bad things were happening out there in the growing dark, not just in the Market, but in the rest of the city. I really had to keep myself sharp.

I took another pull and handed him the bottle. "She probably could have helped me deal with those assholes from the Co-Op. Did you know they wanted my cane?"

Onanefe coughed as he finished his swig. "Maybe I should send *them* the bill."

I snorted. "You'd have even less chance of getting it, then. The Co-Op Board got caught up in some stupid speculation scheme, and with the labor stoppage…"

Somewhere in the back of my brain, a thought came loose and bumped into a whole lot of other thoughts, like a pachinko ball plinking its way down the pegs. "The Co-Op doesn't have cane. The cane isn't coming because you guys have stopped working. You've stopped working because you haven't gotten paid."

"What's that?"

I focused on Onanefe, fighting through the buzz. "Who else hasn't been getting paid?"

He opened his mouth, then clamped it shut as he sat back. "Well, *everyone*. All the crews."

"Heirloom and industrial?"

He laughed. "We don't discriminate. We get a call to cut, we go."

"But it wasn't like you were getting paid for one and not the other, right?"

"Right. Why?"

"Because…" I put my head in my hands and squeezed. This was too much to think about with those three shots of rum and a long day in the sun. I was so tired. My skull hurt. I didn't want to piece this all together. I wanted someone else to do the work and let me go back to my distillery and my horrible job in the bowels of the water works.

The horrible job that paid off my crushing debt. The debt that would go away if I did what Letty asked, but I couldn't do that anymore because the strike had taken on a life of its own. I couldn't stop it, Saarien couldn't stop it, Letty sure couldn't stop it. The only way to stop a strike was to give the people what they wanted or wait until they broke. And since there had been no list of demands…

"She wants this to happen," I breathed. The high from the rum evaporated, leaving me sick to my stomach. "She wants the strike to happen, and to burn itself out. Why?"

"Who is 'she'?"

"The Prez."

"Letty?"

I nodded. "She burnt my building down on purpose."

"She was *there*?"

I narrowed my eyes. "Do you know her? And I mean know her as a person, not as the Prez?"

Onanefe fiddled with his mustache. "It's complicated."

"Don't you dare tell me you were an item, 'cause that's the last bit of weirdness I need right now."

"Worse. We were political partners. Back in the day."

I cocked my head and smiled. "Holy crap. You're with the FOC, aren't you?"

He straightened up. "And proud of it. Hell, I helped found our local chapter with Letty." He shook his head. "Then she took off for the city and joined the Union."

"How long ago was that?"

"Two Contracts. Ah." He sighed and looked out into the distance. "We'd spent two years going from one farm to the next, talking with every Freeborn about working together. The old-timers wanted to defer to the Union, but Letty and me, we wanted Freeborn seats at the table. We'd seen our parents and *their* parents work their tails off, taking *pride* in how they'd remained free and independent when they were working for jiao on the yuan."

He sucked his teeth. "My folks were good people, but they were scared. They didn't want to risk the little they had asking for what they were worth. Letty and I weren't scared. We were going to make things better."

I looked at the ruins of the Market. "I don't suppose this is the 'better' you had in mind?"

He uncapped the bottle and took a long, long drink.

Another thought plinked into my brain. "Were you in Brushhead to meet with Letty?"

He coughed, and a little of the rum splashed onto his lips. "I really can't talk about that."

That was enough for me. I stood up, wobbly as I was. "You and I are going to end this shit. Right now."

"We are?"

"Yep." I grabbed his arm and yanked him to his feet. "Whatever secret business you and Letty were going to hammer out, we're going to make it happen."

He winced. "I really don't know what you're talking about."

"Come off it, Onanefe. You and Letty were going to meet, but Letty set fire to my place. She got to whisk herself away from whatever it was you were going to discuss, and now the strike has turned to chaos. There's no organization. There's no discipline. There's just a whole lot of angry people breaking stuff, and once that blows over, we'll go right back to status quo. Whatever it was you wanted to change won't happen unless *we* make it happen. So come on."

"Where?"

I sniffed the air and caught a whiff of shawarma. "Over there. It's never a good idea to talk treason on an empty stomach. And you're buying."

THIRTEEN

Onanefe protested for a few meters, but the sudden smell of roasting eggplant and baking bread perked him right up. One of the food stalls had reopened, and a few dozen people huddled over their plates of kumara cakes and pita. Even the tough-looking security women ate there, their bats tucked under their arms. The man running the stand wouldn't take our money. "No point in letting this spoil, and the banks are closed, and what the hell," he said, handing over two plates. "Solidarity, wha'?" I handed him the bottle of Old Windswept. He winked, and the smiley-face tattoo on his cheek crinkled as he took a drink.

We shoveled food into our mouths. I didn't bother to slow myself down. This wasn't a time to savor. It was a time to plan and get angry. "We won't be able to find her, so we'll have to draw her out," I said, wiping the last of the thoom off the plate with my thumb. Oh, a thousand blessings on thoom, that most delicious and anti-social of condiments.

He munched on his shawarma. "How should we start?"

"The old-fashioned way would be to just complain to a few people and wait for word to get out on the Public. You get enough complaining and some minion would scurry over to take reports and assure everyone that things would get done."

Onanefe rubbed his mustache. "Except the whole city is complaining right now. And the Public's down."

"Right. Which means we have to boost our signal above the noise." I gave him a nod. "What would you do?"

Now he gave his mustache such a twirling that the ends began to stay in tight curls. "It's not enough to complain. We have to get her angry. We have to call her integrity into question."

I nodded. "We need focus." I looked at people around us until I saw what I needed. "And there it is."

I grabbed one of the security guards and said, "Hey, you know who I am?"

She stopped chewing long enough to size me up. She finished and swallowed. "Should I?"

I pointed at the ink on her cheek, a megaphone. "You used to do Big Three PR."

She bristled. "I'm a security consultant now."

"And what I have to tell you concerns not only the security of this market, but of the entire Union. The entire planet, even. What's your name?"

"Who wants to know?"

I moved my plate to my left hand and held out my right. "Padma Mehta. I'm with the Stipend and Benefits Reinstatment Committee."

She took a moment before shaking my hand. "Thoj KajSiab. What committee is that?"

"The one I'm starting right now, and I'd like you to join me. What are you getting paid to work here?"

"Fifteen yuan an hour."

"And no hazard pay?"

KajSiab made a face. "For what?"

"Are you kidding? For the riot!"

The women looked at each other, their faces bunched up in worry. KajSiab cleared her throat and leaned in. "We're, uh, not supposed to call it that."

I looked at the smashed produce on the ground and the tattered tents flipping in the evening breeze. "What was it then?"

KajSiab swallowed. "A spontaneous human outburst incident."

I laughed. "Where did *that* come from?"

KajSiab swallowed. "Look, this is a really weird time, okay? We get discounts on food for our families by working here. If we upset our boss, we're out of a gig. And this is the best gig I can get right now."

I nodded. "I've been hearing that a lot. Which is all the more reason for you all to be pissed off. This isn't how things are supposed to work here. It's bad enough when the Big Three are messing with us. This is a Union job, isn't it?"

KajSiab and her co-workers gave me small nods. "The manager didn't want to pay police rates."

"Doesn't matter. You're getting hosed." I felt that warm glow of righteous indignation I used to get from my old organizing days. Some WalWa middle manager would try to cut back on hours or say they had to freeze wages, and I would get to march into Thronehill and whale on the Corporate drones until money fell out of their ears. It was a glorious feeling to have that rage back, all made just a little nauseating by the fact that I was defending Union people from a Union screwing.

KajSiab's face got a little harder. "Then what do we do?"

I smiled. "The first thing you do is talk with everyone who works with you and get names and times of meetings. We can't pull up anything from the Public to back up your testimony, but we can sure as hell start preparing things."

She snorted. "More talking?"

"No, *focused* talking. Because after we're done here, we're going to find out who else is in the same boat as you. Who else isn't getting their fair wages? Who else is having their livelihoods stolen through paperwork? I've seen a lot of angry people all day, and, believe you me, we got allies out there. But if we want the Prez's ear, we need to be prepared. Are you in? Or do you want to go back to scrounging for leftover tabbouli?"

The security women made faces as they weighed their options. "The tabblouli's not *that* bad," said one.

"The quality of the food isn't the point," said KajSiab, flexing her arms. "This woman's right. What happened today was a full-on riot, and we got sent out here with no armor, no instructions, no police backup." She nodded and put a meaty hand on my shoulder. "I'm with you, Padma."

The other women all piped in with a chorus of, "Me, too"s. I sighed and flushed away a little more of my buffer to make room for whatever they were about to tell me. I made sure to keep everything Vikram had said. One of these days, I'd have to get a memory upgrade, even if it meant letting some tech jab needles in my eye. I hadn't needed to remember much before, but now? Now meant having to remember everything.

By the time the shawarma stand was out of food, the security women had brought over other merchants, and they told us about how they'd had to pay extra rent for security measures that never arrived. "We're ruined!" said one, a middle-aged guy with welding spot scars up and down his arms. "I put everything into my business, and it all got washed away by those looters! And now I can't find the Market manager or my Union rep or anyone!"

I nodded and blinked in his testimony. "I'm going to make sure you get restitution. Can you find anyone else who's gotten nailed by this... what did you call it?"

He snorted, and his tattoo – an old clipper ship – moved like it was rolling over a massive wave. "It was an 'enhanced logistical fee.' Never heard such garbage before, but Luc, y'know, the Market manager, he said I couldn't keep my stall if I didn't kick in."

"You know anyone in your Ward who had to pay it?"

"Only everyone," he said. "Didn't matter what their trade was. Hell, even my wife, she runs a kindergarten, *she* had to pay. What, the kids are gonna riot? Please."

I nodded. "That is indeed some serious bullshit. And we're going to take this right to your manager, and then to whoever told *him* to put the squeeze on you, all the way up to Letty Arbusto Smythe. 'Cause you *know* this is because she's falling down on the job."

He shrugged. "Yeah, but you think it'll really change anything?"

"We won't know unless we do it." I patted him on the shoulder.

Onanefe was talking with a few Freeborn men who also had market stalls. Their conversation slowed as I approached, but Onanefe prodded one of them on the arm. "What's your problem?"

The man rubbed his arm, then fiddled with his rolled-up shirtsleeve. "I don't know her."

"You don't know me, either," said Onanefe.

"But I know *about* you." The man nodded at me. "Her? She's just another Ink."

"Not just any Ink," I said, giving him my winningest smile. "I'm the one who's going to help you get back what you lost."

"And what's that?"

I let the smile fade. "Nothing less than your pride."

The men exploded into laughter. "Wow, she's *good*," said one of them, clapping Onanefe on the back. "I might actually buy her bullshit."

"It's not," said Onanefe. "We're going straight to the Prez's office, and Padma here is going to kick in the door."

The men stopped laughing. "You serious?"

"As a heart attack," I said. "Whatever you've told Onanefe, we need it to build our case. We're going to take her down. Tell everyone you know."

After a few more mutterings and handshakes, the Freeborn left the Market. So had everyone else. By now, night had fallen, and none of the streetlamps had come on. The purple moon was a quarter full, strong enough to help me see faces but too weak to see in the shadows. "You think your friend will let us back in?" asked Onanefe. "It feels a little bleak out here."

"We need to find more people," I said, walking toward Shahjahan Road. "I figure we'll spend another couple of hours talking with marchers, and that should boost the signal enough to get Letty's attention."

He shivered and rubbed his arms. "It's just that, you know, it's dark."

I stopped at the edge of the Market. "You're from the kampong!"

"Where we use *lights*." He shook his head and looked up at the darkened buildings that surrounded the Market. "You ever march through a cane field in the middle of the night? It's not fun. You got cane vipers, cane toads, cane *rats*... You ever seen a cane rat?"

A bottle smashed on the ground nearby, followed by a high-pitched howl. Onanefe tensed, his fists up. I pulled him with me into the shadows of a shuttered konbini. "What was that?" he whispered, his voice hoarse.

"Probably nothing," I lied. Down the street, there was another tinkling of shattered glass and another howl, like a drunken wolf declaring it was on the hunt. Other howls joined in, a chorus of anger. It gave way to a harsh clanging, a thousand kids bashing rebar on molasses barrels, all out of rhythm. Down Shahjahan, an orange light appeared. It grew brighter as the noise got louder, and I pulled Onanefe past the konbini until we got to an alley. I took a quick glance: it wasn't a dead end, so we still had an escape route. We hid behind a rubbish bin as the sound bounced off the buildings and echoed through the empty Market.

The marchers that we saw today were calm and buoyant. The mass of people that worked its way down Shahjahan was anything but. They carried crowbars and hammers and whatever implements of destruction they could find. Torches made of rags dipped in cane diesel lit their way, the greasy flames casting harsh faces into relief. There were no signs, no chants, just a susurrus filled with frustration and barely contained rage.

Onanefe breathed out. "There's an angry mob if ever I've seen one."

"Yeah, but whose?"

"What do you mean? It's a mob. It's angry. They have *torches*, for God's sake."

"Yeah, but are they Union? Freeborn? Are they with Letty? Rank-and-file? I can't make out any faces."

"You'll pardon me if I don't walk out and ask. Hey!"

I left Onanefe behind the bin and tip-toed to the edge of the alley's darkness. It was a mixed bag: Union and Freeborn, men and women, old and young. They all had the glass fist pin of the Temple of the New Holy Light on their shirts.

Then one of them looked at me.

I was hidden in the shadows. One of them turned for a brief moment, and the torch light reflected in her cold, hardened face.

It was Saraphina Moss, the woman with the shark eyes.

I made myself as small as I could. I recognized a few more faces in the crowd, people I'd seen milling around the Temples I'd visited. I crept back to Onanefe. "They're with Saarien. Maybe all of them."

His eyes grew wide. "What the hell is he *doing*?"

"Immanitizing the Labor Eschaton. Let's get out of here." I pulled him away from the mob to the other end of the alley. Onanefe winced as I grabbed his arm, and he doubled over, knocking aside a crate full of empty bottles. They crashed to the ground, loud enough for anyone to hear over the steady drumbeat of feet on Shahjahan.

The feet came to a quick stop. Flashlights blinded us, and a dozen people yelled "Stop!"

We didn't.

We also didn't get very far, what with Onanefe's busted ribs. I managed to swing him out of the alley onto Proctor Avenue. Everyone on Proctor painted their houses bright colors and let their kids play in the streets. Now, as the torches flickered and the flashlights danced, the street turned into scenes out of a nightmare: slashes of orange wall, doorways glowing red, and the purple moon turning the darkened streetlights into looming sentries.

Onanefe groaned as his legs gave out. I lowered him in a doorway as the mob crowded around us. I didn't flinch from the lights. "Good. You're here. This man needs help."

The few angry faces I could see looked at each other. "Why did you run from us?" asked a woman.

"That's entirely beside the point," I said, stepping up to the woman. She stood in front of a few hundred people. Her hair was tied into a precise bun on the top of her head. A Temple pin glinted on her coveralls, and a pair of welding goggles hung from her neck. Her tattoo, a flame, made this woman a rare sight: someone who'd kept the same job even after Breaching. "My friend got crushed during the riot in the Market. He needs to see a doctor."

The woman blinked, and I could see her eyes focus in the torchlight. I hadn't realized that I'd taken that look for granted. All day long, I'd talked with people who hadn't used their pais because the Public was down. She looked like it was still running. "Excuse me," I said, "but do you actually have access? Is the Public back up?"

That broke her concentration. She pointed her flashlight at my face, and I threw up my hands to block the glare. "You need to keep quiet."

I snorted. "Man, if I had a blue boy for every time someone said that to me."

"Could you please not antagonize these nice people until we've gotten some help?" said Onanefe. "My side's killing me."

"Sorry," I mumbled. "Force of habit."

He sighed. "Your habits are going to kill *you*."

The welder shone her light on Onanefe. "You, too. Quiet."

He nodded and shielded his eyes.

The welder blinked again. I looked around the crowd to see if anyone else had that faraway stare, but I couldn't tell from the torchlight. Eyes were hollowed out by shadow, and exhaustion turned faces into death masks. I knew that one day of action couldn't have done this. People had been tired and angry for a long, long time, and all that simmering resentment had been given voice. It didn't have to be Saarien leading the charge. It could have been anyone who was willing to get them to focus their anger enough to pop.

The welder's face softened a bit. "We can help." She nudged the people next to her, and the crowd parted. I helped Onanefe to his feet and led him into the ocean of angry, tired faces. The welder walked behind us, and the crowd came back together in her wake.

"I'm afraid I can't blink up your name like you can with mine," I said, glancing over my shoulder. She answered by pursing her lips in a thin smile. "What may I call you?" She just put a finger to her lips, and I sighed. To hell with it.

We got to the edge of the crowd, and the welder got in front. As we walked up Proctor, the crowd shuffled back toward the alley, off to join with the rest of the masses stomping up Shahjahan. Within minutes, the street was empty but for the three of us.

She led us to one of the row houses and beckoned us up the stairs to the stoop. She knocked three times, then once. The same pattern came back from the inside, and six locks clicked loose. The door opened a crack, and she motioned for us to go inside. I peeked in and saw nothing but darkness.

This was a bad idea. My gut knew it was a bad idea. Even The Fear hissed this was a bad idea. Then Onanefe shuddered and yelped. "Can't breathe," he gasped.

I turned to the welder to ask if someone could come out here, but she was gone, faded into the shadows. Onanefe groaned and sagged from my grip. "No, no, come on, get up," I said, fighting his bulk as we slipped to the ground. "Help! HELP!"

The door flew open, and metal glinted in the moonlight. My brain screamed *MACHETE* just in time for my leg to lash out. I connected with something solid, and there was a muffled scream from above me. Then my attacker fell on top of me, his chest hitting my shoulder. The machete *clang*ed off the stoop's pourform bannister. I let go of Onanefe and reached behind me until I felt hair. I grabbed as much of it as I could and brought my attacker's head down on the bannister. I felt the crunch of cartilage on pourform, heard a wet scream fill my ears. I shoved the wailing weight off me, back toward the door. There was a stumble of bodies, a mass of shoving and *Get 'em*!s. I scooped up Onanefe and dragged him down the steps. "HELP! SOMEONE HELP!" I yelled. "THEY'RE KILLING US!"

We got to the street, Onanefe now dead weight as I pulled him away. The people in the murder house had gotten their feet and clattered after us. I set Onanefe down and turned, my feet planted, my fists up. "Come on, you fuckers! Come on and try to take me!"

They stopped a few meters away. I could make out three shapes in the moonlight, all of them hunched forward and hungry. They held up their machetes, the purple moon dancing on the blades. One giggled, then let loose with that howl I'd heard on Shahjahan. I pointed at the one in the middle. "You! You're going to lose an eye. You're gonna kill me, but everyone will know I took your eye."

He laughed, that cocky sound of someone who knew he was hearing bullshit. It probably was. But I'd sure give it a go. "You talk way too much," he said, then lifted his machete.

A lifetime ago, back in the WalWa Business Academy, I learned the delicate art of street fighting. Baily Barnes, our instructor, first taught us ballroom dancing so we could get used to being close to other people, feeling how they moved, feeling their weight close in. We learned the importance of protecting our partners as we spun each other around the squeaky floorboards. After six months and two regional competitions (I came in fourth place in the rhumba), he changed up the curriculum. "Fighting," said Baily, "is just dancing. Except your job is to fuck up your partner before *she* fucks you up."

When my new dance partner brought the blade down, I stepped toward him. He was a bit taller, which made it that much easier for me to spin into his body. I grabbed his wrist and tugged, adding my momentum to his as I drove the back of my head into his nose. I felt the wet pop and dug my thumbnails into the meaty base of his thumb. The machete clattered to the ground. I kicked it aside and spun away, leaving my partner staggering.

His friends weren't sure what to do, so I charged them. They outweighed me by twenty kilos, but I outmatched them in anger. I actually heard myself scream as I brought a knee into one of their crotches. Screaming, Baily had said, was bad for the ballroom judges, but it was a great thing to do in a fight. My voice bounced off the silent buildings, echoed off the pavement. The man yelped as I grabbed his hair and pushed his head to the ground. I screamed again as I smacked his forehead on the street, forcing myself to stop as The Fear egged me on: *More! More!*

This dance partner, he swung at my ankle. It hurt enough to let go. That gave him enough opening to launch himself at my shins. I tried to hop back, but he connected. My ass hit the pavement, and sharp pain shot up my spine. I couldn't stop the yelp, but I could still kick. One boot sole to the crown of his head. One boot heel to the back of his head. He stopped moving. That left the third.

He was the biggest of all of them, but I could see his shoulders quivering in the moonlight. Either he was high or he was freaked out. I got to my feet and snarled, the way a cornered dog does before it goes for the throat. I took a false stompy step toward him and howled, louder and crazier than I knew he could ever go. He dropped his machete and ran.

"Hey."

I glanced to Onanefe. He was on his feet, but only because my first dance partner had a machete to the cane cutter's throat. His eyes were calm, though his forehead shone from the sweat. The man smiled, his face painted black from the blood running down his nose.

"Put it down and walk away," I said. "I don't care why you want to hurt us. Just go right now and this can all end."

He shook his head and pointed the machete at me. "You're going to be my bonus."

A light flickered on in a front porch.

We froze at the soft *click* of the LED bulb. It was a gentle bluish light, the kind that meant it was time to go home, have dinner, read a book. The kind of the light that said *safe*.

Another porch light switched on. Then another, and another, until the entire block was lit up like any other day. Front doors opened, spilling warm orange light into the narrow street. People walked out on their stoops and aimed flashlights at us. They came out into the streets: families, retirees, singles in various states of undress. Within minutes, we were surrounded.

"Back off!" yelled the bloodied man. "I'll cut them both! You can't stop me!"

The crowd was silent. People in their bathrobes and shirtsleeves stared at him.

"None of you can get in my way!" yelled the man.

A rock sailed out of the crowd and beaned him on the forehead. His eyes rolled up in the back of his skull, and he fell over like a dropped plank. Onanefe looked down, then took a wobbly step toward me. I closed the distance and helped him stay upright. "Does this all count as doing the work?" he asked, giving me a weak smile.

"With overtime," I said.

A blue light bounced off the buildings, and the crowd parted. There, for the first time in two days, was a yellow-and-black police bumblecar, its bubble lights clicking and rotating. Behind it was a beat-up ambulance. The caravan pulled up in front of us, and the bumblecar's driver side door swung open. The driver herself took her sweet damn time climbing down and walking over. "Well," said Soni Baghram. "This looks like quite the scene."

Two paramedics ran from the ambulance; they looked at the men on the ground. "Forget those assholes," I said. "Help *here*." They eased Onanefe onto a stretcher.

Soni was wearing her street uniform, but the other cops that got out were in black-and-yellow riot gear. The plates on their legs and chests clattered as they hunkered over the unconscious thugs. Soni took off her cloth patrol cap and whapped it in the palm of her hand. The stubble on her shaved head stood up in the night chill. She looked at the bloodied men on the ground, then gave her head a single shake. "Quite a scene, indeed."

"Where in the holy hell have you people *been*?" I yelled. "This city's a mess, and the police have been nowhere!"

The crowd tittered. I heard mumbles of *She's right* and *Where* were *they?*

Soni pointed at me. "You and I have a lot to talk about."

"I'm sure we do," I said, crossing my arms.

Soni looked around. "I'd prefer we talk inside. And far away from here."

"Do you?"

Soni leaned in close. "Padma, I've got riot squads standing by all over the city. I've got precinct houses on lockdown. I'm trying to keep the mob from dropping the torches and getting the pitchforks. Help me out."

I didn't move.

She sighed and rolled her eyes. "Jesus. *Please.*"

I nodded and pointed at the ambulance. "Wherever he goes, I go."

Soni worked her jaw. "This one's one of us, right? Not another Ghost?"

I gave Soni the finger. She threw her hands in the air. "Fine! Jesus, I just want to talk, not hold a crisis negotiation.

We'll all go in the ambo."

One of the cops nodded to the men in black. "What about them?"

"They get the premium seats with you, officer." Soni walked to the ambo. "You coming?"

I climbed in after her. Onanefe lay on the stretcher, an oxygen mask on his face. "This feels nice," he said.

"I gave him a little painkiller," said the EMT, putting away a syringe. "Nothing too strong. We're saving it for later."

"What's later?" I said.

"Oh, just the end of the world," said Soni. The driver slammed the doors shut, and off we rolled into the night.

FOURTEEN

Soni sagged against the ambulance's bulkhead. In the soft LED light, I could see bags the size of cricket balls under her eyes. Even her head stubble looked tired. "This is just about the perfect way to cap off today," she said. "Every precinct has been on tactical alert since the strike started, and that means making all my people wear armor while carrying half their bodyweight in water bottles and riot foam. You know how unbreathable our armor is?"

"Is that why you're not in it?"

She gave me a weak smile. "The advantages of command. My armor is back at the Fourteenth Street Precinct, air drying in my office. I've been on my feet since four this morning." She closed her eyes. "Believe it or not, I am happy to see you. I heard about you walking around today, talking with people. But you vanished for a bit after the fire at your building."

"I went back to Tanque."

She made a face. "How? The outbound buses had stopped."

I opened my mouth to say, *Letty gave me a ride*, and realized I had no idea whose side Soni was on. That made my stomach roil. We had pissed each other off as much as we'd made each other laugh. Maybe more. I could count the people I trusted on one hand, and she was right there. That was before all of this chaos, and I now had no clue where she stood. Was she loyal to Letty? Saarien? The general good? How the hell do you ask your friend if she's really on your side?

"I got a lift," I said.

"And you didn't think to call?"

"Well, Soni, considering how the fire brigade didn't bother to show up, I wasn't sure what would happen with the police."

She didn't protest. "Yeah. I'm sorry I couldn't spare the hands. I had to deal with looting on Kuttner."

Now it was my turn to make a face. "There's nothing but clinics there."

Soni sighed and nodded. "A bunch of footie thugs raided the dispensaries. Made off with a whole lot of painkillers. Everyone's convinced the city's going to burn and we won't be able to buy meds for a year. Half my people are just standing guard at every chemist in town."

I rubbed my temples. "Soni, what the hell is going on? This apocalyptic crap pops up every now and then, but it's never more than a dozen people. The whole city's losing it."

She quirked her mouth. "I'm sure you've heard about our friend, the Good Reverend Saarien?"

I nodded. "I even went to see him."

Her eyes went wide. "What the hell for?"

"Because I was helping Keiko Nakamura. Remember her? Runs that omusubi-ya?"

Soni's face darkened, and she looked at the EMT. "Would you mind leaving us for a moment?"

"I have to monitor this guy," said the EMT.

"I can handle that." She jerked her head toward the front

of the ambulance. The EMT shook her head, the beads in her cornrows clattering. She threw her hands in the air and climbed into the front, sliding a panel behind her. Soni looked out the back of the ambulance. "This isn't how it was supposed to go."

I cocked my head. "What horrible thing are you not telling me?"

Soni clacked her teeth. "Did I ever tell you about the night I came to Santee?"

I wracked my brain for the memory. "No," I said. "I don't think you ever have."

Soni cleared her throat and settled into her seat. "The last time I was in transit was en route to some job… you know, some shitty colony where I'd do accounting for the next decade before moving on to another assignment. A week out from the Red Line, the ship's cryo malfunctioned. I woke up, thinking I'd arrived, and then I saw all these bald, angry people standing around in their underpants."

"Bald?"

Soni rolled her eyes. "LiaoCon policy for transit was to shave everyone's heads. Helped with the hibernant or something. Anyway, the crew tried to keep us in check, but then word got around that the nearest repair ship was eight months out. There wasn't enough food and water for everyone who was awake. The crew just didn't care enough to stop their cargo from taking over; they locked themselves in the hold. Everyone started panicking, so, as Senior Managing Accountant, I sat down, did the math and figured the only way out was through. We could stretch the food and water, spend the whole time doing as little as possible to conserve air. Santee was the closest destination, so I sent out a punch probe to let 'em know we were coming, and we jumped.

"I spent all my time breaking up fights and stopping a

couple of suicidal people from venting all of us into space –
you know, that old *if I go I'm taking everyone with me* attitude.
The relief ship – a Union one – made it just in time. All of
us were glued to the monitors, watching it get closer and
closer, just counting the minutes of air and the calories left.
Another two hours and we would have been dead."

She picked at a fingernail. "Anyway, two years later,
we arrive at Santee. I'm still babysitting everyone, playing
the go-between, keeping everyone calm. All I could think
about was getting off the ship and doing *anything* that didn't
involve people. I actually got offered a job in Thronehill, but
the relief crew had convinced me that the best thing to do
was Breach. I went down the cable, slept for a week, then
wandered into the Union Hall to declare myself in Breach
of my Indenture."

She laughed at the memory, a warm smile spreading
across her face. "And there's this cop at the Hall, the precinct
lieutenant, a woman named Danai Skalter."

"I don't think I know her."

Soni waved a hand. "She had a heart attack the week
before you showed up in Brushhead. She was a hard, hard
woman. Had the department records for chin-ups *and* the
number of ribs eaten at one sitting. She was standing by
the terminal where I got my pai reburned and said, 'I hear
you're good with people. Thought about becoming a cop?'
And I just laughed. That was the last thing I wanted.

"But she needled me for weeks until I finally gave in. She
swore up and down that I'd never have to sit behind a desk,
never lack for action, never have to run spreadsheets again."

Soni looked at me. "Do you know what happens
when you get promoted to chief of police? It's nothing
but spreadsheets. Payroll. Overtime. Reimbursements.
Equipment. I'm an accountant again, and it sucks."

"I'm really sorry to hear that," I said, "but I have no idea what it has to do with you not being around when the city needed you *now*."

"Department budgets are disappearing. Not the money, but the actual spreadsheets. Before the Public went out, I lost access to deployment schedules. I couldn't tell how many officers were on sick leave or vacation or just plain didn't show up to work. It all sounds like another Ghost Squad action, but..." She gritted her teeth so hard they squeaked. "I think someone in the Union is egging people to strike. I think it's to cover something up. I don't know what. I don't think it's something like starting a fire on one side of town to distract people from a robbery on the other. It's bigger and weirder."

"Letty Smythe set fire to her building."

Soni and I looked down at Onanefe. A great, stoned grin broke across his face. "Padma told me about it."

Soni glared at me. "You didn't think this was pertinent?"

"I didn't know whose side you were on until now."

Her face fell. "You know, you've said a lot of hurtful things to me over the years. I think this tops it."

"Well, I'm *sorry*, but I've never had the President of our Union try to kill me before. It's not like there's a manual that tells me who I can and can't trust."

She jerked a thumb at her chest. "You can trust *me*."

I pointed at the badge on her blouse. "You? Or that?"

Soni's face froze in a mask of rage. Her nostrils flared as she breathed in and out. "You have any idea how many people are in this city? And all of us police with nothing but orders to maintain the peace." She slapped at her badge. "I've been keeping my oath. I have to, seeing how no one above me is."

We stared at each other. "You guys *are* friends, right?" said Onanefe.

I nodded. "We are. I'm sorry." I held out a hand.

Soni flicked her eyes toward it and sighed. "You know how many times we've done this?"

"Only every crisis," I said. "The rest of the time we're downright pleasant."

She took my hand and squeezed. "You're an asshole, you know that?"

I smiled. "Yeah, but at least you'll always know where I stand."

Onanefe grinned. "You *are* friends."

I patted his shoulder. "You're going to be hating life once those meds wear off."

He made a face. "I still hurt like hell. The drugs just keep me from caring about it."

"What happened to you?" said Soni. "And why has Padma latched on to you?"

Onanefe propped himself up. "My name is Onanefe, and I am the best damn cane cutter on this planet." He winced, then sank back in the gurney.

"He's also involved with the FOC," I said. "He and Letty were in the same chapter."

"And what a chapter it was!" Onanefe waved his arms and began to sing: *I had a job once cutting cane, worked all day through blood and pain...*

That sparked a memory: the Temple on Lutyen, that service before the strike began. "What song is that?"

"Old Freeborn work song," said Onanefe. "It's got a good rhythm for cutting and packing. Plus, if you get the whole crew singing, it'll scare away the rats and vipers. Also…"

He grinned and beckoned me to come closer. I leaned towards his mouth. "It was our secret signal to other FOC members: time to kick ass." He clamped his hands over his mouth, his eyes big and his pupils pinpricks. Then he laughed, big and hoarse. "Oh, shit, I've given away our secret signal!" He grabbed Soni's arm. "Officer, please show some mercy! Don't throw me in solitary! I'm too pretty for prison!"

Soni smiled and patted Onanefe's hand. "We don't do that anymore, dear."

"Thank Christ! Praise the Di-Lặc Buddha! 'Cause I really like people, and being alone sucks." He closed his eyes and passed out.

We both froze. I reached for his neck and felt a strong pulse. Then I felt a strong snore. I shook my head. "Lightweight."

"Too right," said Soni. "You think you can tell me about the alleged arson at your building?"

As we edged through the streets, I told Soni everything. Almost everything. Six O'Clock was off limits, even for her. Fortunately, she was more concerned with the threats from the Co-Op, Letty, the guy with the knife, the guys with the machetes, and the human tsunami at Bakaara Market.

She had her chin cupped in her hand. "That doesn't fit."

"What?"

Her eyebrows furrowed. "Bakaara. I had people stationed at every public market. Hell, I had *twice* the usual number."

"I know. I saw them."

She rubbed her temples. "I had comms running through old radio rigs."

"Yeah?"

She nodded, her eyes not focusing on me. "And I didn't hear anything about a riot there." She knocked on the partition to the front seat. One of the EMTs slid it open. "Change of plans," said Soni. "Go to the Twenty-Eighth."

The EMT balked. "But the crowds–"

"Turn on the sirens, step on the gas, and get us there."

The EMT gave a quick nod and slid the partition shut. A moment later, the sirens blared overhead and we picked up speed. "Why aren't we going to a hospital?"

"Because I can't keep you safe there."

"What, *now* you're interested in my health and well-being?"

"I never stopped. But I can't take you with me, and I'm not going to leave you at the hospital. You've had three attempts on your life today."

"I only recall two."

"Bakaara." Soni's face darkened. "What happened there was a hit."

"No, it was a panic. People were worried about food, and there were all these rumors flying around–"

"And none of my people at the Market calmed things down," said Soni, rising from her seat. She hovered above Onanefe for a moment, her eyes burning, before she eased herself back down. "They had standing orders to keep the crowd calm, even if it meant shutting the place down. What you saw? When you got there? That shouldn't have happened." She shook her head. "This all sounds like the provocateur games I heard all over the city in precincts that I lost contact with. If it happened here, it's because someone above me *ordered it*. Someone wants you dead. I don't. End of discussion."

I felt a cold knot in my gut, the kind that came in between the last hurricane siren and the storm making landfall. Something bad was coming, and the lizard part of my brain screamed, *Run! Run far and fast!* The monkey parts all said, *No, forget that, we're staying* here. Stupid monkey brains. "You really think so?"

Soni nodded. "What happened at Bakaara was a classic, sloppy cover-up. Set off a panic, take out the target in the crush. The guys with the machetes cinches it for me. They were trying to finish off what the knife attack and the riot couldn't. What do all these incidents have in common?"

I sighed. "The Temple pins. But why me?"

She shook her head. "Finding that out is not really my job now. Keeping you from getting killed is. I'm going to put you in protective custody in a precinct house in Rongotai. I handpicked everyone there."

I nodded. "Not to sound snotty, but did you do the same with the people at Bakaara?"

Soni shook her head and shrugged. "Maybe? I've sent out a lot of deployment orders on paper. Now I'm starting to wonder if any of them got through."

"All the same, I really don't want to be locked up right now."

Soni grunted. "You'd rather be out there, waiting for someone to chop you to pieces?"

"I don't like being caged."

"Christ, Padma, I'm not going to lock you in a cell!"

"No, but you're going to keep me from figuring this out."

"I'm sorry, I had no idea you'd become a deputized detective."

"I haven't."

"Exactly. That's why your ass is going to sit tight while the professionals figure it out."

"Oh, like *you* did, right? I forgot: 'professional' means 'I'm going to look out for the other people in my profession first.'"

Soni made a fist, then relaxed it. She looked at me and said, in a low, missile silo hiss, "You want me to arrest you? 'Cause I can do that, too. I know how much you like to make a production out of everything."

"I'm on your side, remember? Solidarity and friendship and all that?"

She nodded. "Which is why I want you safe at the Twenty-Eighth Precinct, surrounded by people who are pointing their weapons *away* from you."

I looked at Soni's grim face for a moment, then slid the

partition. The EMTs jumped as I stuck my head through. "Hi, there! Stop the bus, please."

"What?" said the driver.

Soni muscled next to me. "Ignore her. Keep going."

I wracked my brains. What would get their attention? Money? Rum? Yes, rum! "If you stop the ambulance and let me out," I said, "I'll give you both a bottle of Old Windswept Ten-Year."

The EMTs looked at each other. I sighed. "Okay. Two bottles."

The driver put on the brakes. "What the hell are you doing?" yelled Soni.

The wave tattooed on the driver's cheek curled as he gave her a pained look. "Chief, I could get half a year's salary for that!"

"Who's going to buy it?" said Soni. "Are you going to convince a bunch of Shareholders to invest in your bottle? Are you going to dole it out, one shot at a time?"

"But…" The driver's head wobbled, like a kid who was trying to convince his mom that an extra slice of pie was, in fact, a great idea. "It's from Tonggow's stash."

Soni ground her jaw and stared at me. "You are an idiot."

I smiled as I eased toward the back door. "I'm just using what little leverage I've got left."

She shook her head. "Then I'm sorry I have to use mine." She lunged across Onanefe, grabbed my right wrist, and cranked it so hard I felt the pain at the bottom of my spine. I couldn't yell as she slapped a handcuff on me. She clipped the other end to the handrail of Onanefe's gurney.

"You cuffed me!" I yelled.

"Wasn't the first time, probably won't be the last." She touched the driver on the shoulder. "I don't want to do the same to you and your partner. Drive."

The driver hesitated. "Four bottles each!" I called out.

"Two to sell now, two to hide for the future."

"That's enough!" yelled Soni. She turned to the driver. "Get us to the Twenty-Eighth right the hell now, or I will subdue and detain both of you."

I could see the EMTs looking at each other. "Five bottles!" I yelled.

The driver put the ambulance into park. Soni swore under her breath and pulled a taser from her belt. "Soni!" I yelled.

She glared at me. "I have had enough of your bullshit, Padma. I am trying to *help* you, and you want to throw money around, buy your way out of trouble? It doesn't work like that. You can't just–"

She froze, then flopped forward across Onanefe's face. Behind her, the EMT with the cornrows held a drained syringe. "Five bottles each, right?"

I nodded. "I hope you're okay with me not having them *now*, right?"

"You keep 'em at the distillery?"

I nodded. "Think you can help me out?" I rattled the cuffs.

She gave me the once-over, then turned back into her seat. "After we get to Tanque."

The driver shifted into the gear, and the ambulance lurched forward. My guts shifted. Of course I didn't have any Ten-Year at the distillery. I didn't have any, period, but now was not the time to reveal that bit of poor business planning. I had to get out of here.

I reached for Soni, but the handcuff chain was too short. The vertical bars on the gurney's handrail kept me from sliding closer to her. I reached across with my left hand, but I still couldn't reach her. Then I realized I was, indeed, a dumbass. I was still dancing, and dancers moved in all directions.

I put my back to the gurney and reached out my left

hand. I got a firm grip on Soni's collar and pulled. She flopped to the ground in front of me. I pulled on her collar again, only to have her blouse come untucked. I gave it another yank; her blouse tore at the seams in her armpits, revealing a simple body armor vest. She didn't move.

"What's going on?" yelled the driver.

"Nothing. Make sure to avoid the Brapati Causeway. It'll be jammed."

I reached for Soni's belt, but it was too far. I tugged on her wrist. She slid toward me until her boot caught in the gurney's wheels. I pulled harder, but that only made the gurney rattle. Above me, Onanefe groaned, "Oy, my *head*." The ambulance bumped over something, and he tumbled on top of Soni.

The EMT with cornrows stepped through the partition and stopped. It must have been a hell of a scene: me tugging on an unconscious and shirtless Soni as Onanefe made apologies and tried to get to his feet in the cramped space. The EMT held up the syringe. "I really wanted to save this for people who need it."

"You can just let us go," I said.

She shook her head. "I got mouths to feed. Those bottles will go a long way."

Onanefe looked up. "Bottles?"

The EMT loomed over Onanefe. I couldn't reach Soni's belt, but I could reach her hand, the other that held the taser. I grabbed it, flicked off the safety, and fired. The EMT shuddered as fifty thousand volts locked her muscles. She collapsed on top of Onanefe, who yelped.

The driver screeched to a halt and killed the bubble lights. He couldn't get in through the partition, so he ran to the back and threw open the doors. For a moment, all I saw was his darkened outline against the starry night sky. The syringe in his hand flashed in the light, and I lashed out with a boot to his nose. He flew backwards, his head smacking on the pavement.

Onanefe shoved the EMT off him and surveyed the scene. "We're in trouble, aren't we?"

"Such trouble. Help me get her on the gurney."

Onanefe looked at the two unconscious women. "Which one?"

"Soni, the cop."

"Why her?"

I rattled the handcuff. "Oh," he said. We got her on the gurney, and I searched her belt. No key. "Look on the floor, maybe the key fell."

Sirens floated over the night air. "We don't have time," said Onanefe. "Come on!"

"I'm a little stuck!"

"Then we bring her with us."

It was awkward as hell, but we got the gurney out of the ambulance. We had stopped in a darkened residential block, not unlike the one we'd left. In fact, the more I looked around, the more I realized we'd only gone around in circles. "We're still in Howlwadaag," I said.

"You sure?"

I pointed at the rowhouses. "Those EMTs, they were in on it."

"On what?"

"It, the… you know what? Let's get inside before someone tries to kill us again, okay? And then we can talk."

A high-pitched howl, that hunting sound, bounced off the houses. "Yeah, that works for me," said Onanefe. He grabbed two bags of medical supplies and tossed them onto the gurney between Soni's legs. We rolled away from the ambulance as quickly as we could, the gurney's wheels rattling and bouncing over the damp, cracked pavement.

FIFTEEN

Fifteen nerve-shattering minutes later, we found an abandoned konbini. The door hung from its hinges, and the shelves that remained standing had been picked clean. The smell from smashed jars hung in the air: chutney and pickles and yogurt going bad. A wet spot on the floor slipped me up, and I went down, my cuffed wrist catching on the handrail. I bit my lower lip to keep from yelling.

The back office was open and emptied. The gurney's wheels bumped against the legs of a small, overturned desk. With some choice shoving and cussing, we got Soni inside. I dug a chemical light out of the medical bag and cracked it. The room took on a sickly green glow, made even worse when Onanefe closed the office door behind us. Soni's gentle snoring filled the room.

I sat on the gurney. "Well, I'd say I've been in worse situations, but I'd be lying. This is bad."

Onanefe nodded. "How long do you think your friend will be out?"

"No idea. You only got a couple of CCs. Looks like she took the full load."

"Is there anything that could wake her up?"

I looked in the medical bag. "Probably."

"Do you know anything about medicine?"

"Nope. You?"

"Nope."

"Terrific."

Soni snorted, then resumed her slow, steady breathing.

"She's going to be *pissed* when she wakes up," I said. "Too bad I can't restrain *her*."

We checked her again for handcuff keys, but found nothing. At least I had time to look over the gurney's handrail construction. It was made of three horizontal aluminum pipes fastened to two verticals. The whole thing could collapse, thanks to the rivets punched through the horizontals. The rivets wouldn't budge, but the verts were bolted to the frame of the gurney. Four hex-head bolts held it in place; I could unscrew the nuts and only remain attached to a bunch of pipework. At least it would be portable. I took out my trusty multi-tool, snapped the pliers into place, and got to work.

"I imagine someone will come looking for her," said Onanefe. "It's not like police chiefs are allowed to vanish in the middle of a crisis."

"Unless someone wants her to." I told Onanefe about Soni's getting locked out of police decisions and her suspicions about Bakaara.

Onanefe brushed his mustache. "You don't think those EMTs are part of this, do you? I mean, attacking your friend and all."

"Ah," I said, catching the first nut as it fell free into my palm. "No, that was probably me." I told him about the bribe. By the time I was done, Onanefe's mouth hung open.

"*Ten-Year*? You're sitting on a cache of *Ten-Year*?"

"Of course I'm not! There is no such thing as Ten-Year!" I got to work on the second nut. "Tonggow sold the last batch before I took over."

"But everyone says–"

"Everyone says exactly what Tonggow had fed them and what *I* have fed them," I said. "It's not anything special. I mean," and I started laughing here, "if I had rum that expensive, don't you think I'd have sold it? Don't you think I would have bought a ship and crewed it and sailed from one end of Occupied Space to the other instead of staying here?"

Onanefe cocked his head, and he smiled. "No. I think you'd have stayed here regardless. I think you like this place."

The second nut came loose, then slipped out of my grip. I let it go. It's not like I needed to put the handrail back together. "Really? What gives you that impression?"

"You're working way too hard to hang on to what you've got. You're tied into Santee like the most radical member of the FOC. This place is in your blood."

"That's a really nice load of crap you're selling," I said, struggling with the third nut. It had gone on cock-eyed, and the bolt had been partially stripped. "No wonder you guys don't have a seat at the table."

"Why do so many people come here? Why not any other Union-run world?"

"Because it's the last resort before jumping Beyond."

"But it hasn't always been. Santee is *special*." He closed his eyes as he took a breath. "It's that feeling when the wind comes in off the ocean at dusk. All those smells, all these people, all this *life*. People hear about Santee, about how good we got it, even when we're working our asses off or we're at each other's throats. This is a good place that we've made. Don't you think?"

The third nut refused to budge. I rattled the bolt, pounded it with the butt of the multi-tool, but it remained stuck. I looked at the remaining nut and hoped removing it would be enough. Maybe I could just pry the thing loose. I got to work on the fourth nut, hoping it wouldn't surprise me. "You know I used to be a Union recruiter, right? You don't have to sell me on this place."

He chuckled. "Sorry. Force of habit." He watched me unscrew the nut. "You miss it? Recruiting?"

The nut spun away. "Not anymore. It was really fun when I started out. Traffic was great, so it was easy to convince people to jump ship. I could just borrow a rooftop transmitter and blast the Public's live feed into space. People would slide down the cable just to see what was going on down here. They'd had it with being Indentures. Most of them fit in nicely. A few didn't. But none of them ever went to Thronehill to turn themselves in. They were done with being property." I tapped the tattoo on my cheek. "I hope you never go through that. No matter how much I got paid or how good the bennies were, I always knew I belonged to Walton Warumbo Universal Unlimited. I could be replaced, just like any old part."

The fourth nut fell free and danced on the pourform floor for a moment. I scooped it up and showed it to Onanefe. "All the training, all the schooling, all the pats on the back, I might as well have been this. Once I was no longer useful, I would be removed and tossed aside, stuck into some other slot that WalWa thought needed filling." I tossed the nut into a corner of the office. "Give me a hand, would you, please?"

We rolled the gurney against the wall and collapsed the sides so the bed was only a few centimeters above the floor. We put our backs to the opposite wall and grabbed the handrail. I planted my feet on the gurney's frame and nodded at him to follow suit.

"I don't know how much help I'll be with this busted

rib," said Onanefe, grunting as he put his boots on the rails.

"Just do what you can. Ready?"

He nodded.

We pulled on the handrail. The bar strained against the stripped nut, and I could swear the thing moved a few millimeters closer to us. Onanefe huffed and puffed. "A break, please."

We relaxed. I kept my grip on the handrail, willing the nut to turn into gelatin. It didn't comply. "Did you have anything to do with the strike?" I asked.

Onanefe took a moment before shaking his head. "Don't get me wrong, I would have loved for us to strike. I have a list of demands as long as my arm, but what I didn't have was a disciplined movement. It's easy to get angry people to march, but a strike? That's a different beast." He nodded at me. "You know what it's like, right? Making sure the demands are clear, keeping people on the picket lines, making sure no one folds and goes home when they're tired of occupying the manager's office."

I nodded. "It sucks."

"It does indeed." He gripped the handrail again. "Which is why this has been such a disaster. It's going to set us back until after *this* Contract. All of us."

"If we aren't killed first."

We pulled again. This time, I heard the distinct whine of metal on metal; the nut was giving way. I hoped it was weaker than the handrail, or this would be for naught.

Onanefe begged off, and we relaxed. "So, the FOC isn't getting people to leave the kampong?"

"I didn't say that. I've no doubt they're stirring the pot. The problem is that they're not working with a recipe. There are a couple of hotheads who've been screaming for us to *do something*, but none of those somethings have been enough. No one wants to negotiate. No one wants to talk.

And I'm talking about doing that with the other Freeborn. We're not this monolith, you know."

"Neither is the Union," I said. "That was always the part I hated the most: convincing people to quit being stupid and just listen to me."

He snorted. "Well, with a pitch like that, how could they refuse?"

I waved him off. "I'm bright enough not to say it like that to their faces, even though that's the job. My first organizing gig was when WalWa wanted to shut down the micro-cleaner plant at Brushhead."

He nodded. "I remember that. Didn't you guys strip the place clean?"

I grinned. "That part everyone knows about, because I made sure to tell as many people as possible. What I didn't talk about was the incredible hassle of getting all those people to go into the plant in the first place."

He made a face. "You kidding? I thought anyone with ink would be happy to smash a Big Three facility into tiny pieces."

"And you'd be right. But that would have solved nothing. Everyone would have been out of work, which meant they wouldn't have gotten paid, which meant they couldn't make rent, and on and on until your jobless angry mob is a jobless, homeless, *hungry*, angry mob. We had to make a point to WalWa, and we had to get something for ourselves in the process. No one wanted to listen. They just wanted to break things."

"What did you do?"

I smiled. "I did the work. I talked with every floor manager, every worker, every spouse. I found out they were fine with losing their jobs – 'cause the jobs sucked – but they were worried about where they'd live. One of them, this extruder tech named Mesh Lollabrigida, she had the bright idea to turn the plant into housing. And that meant bringing in architects, builders, all the people who could make that happen. And no one wanted to do it, not for free, anyway. The Union didn't want to pay for it, the employees didn't have the cash to pool together, and the whole thing would have fallen apart except for me bullshitting everyone into it."

I laughed at the memory. "I had this one machinist, a guy named Giacomo Teff, who was great at taking lathes apart. There were six in there, big industrial pieces, and they were obsolete and dangerous. Every couple of months, they'd slip a gear and change speed, and some poor operator would lose control of whatever they were working on and get sent to the hospital. He was the only one who could keep them working.

"One of the architects, Smitty Pryde, said the lathes could be repurposed into rooftop windmills. The place needed power, everyone hated the lathes, so I asked Giacomo to do his thing. He refused. Said it would be sacrilege to dismantle the lathes, even though we both knew they would never be turned on again. He was so attached to them, even though they'd cost him a finger." I waved my pinkie in the air, then popped it down.

Onanefe grimaced. "What did you do?"

"I kept on at him, kept pointing out that the lathes did more good apart than whole. He kept saying if the plant was closing, he wasn't going to take orders from anyone ever again. I thought he was just being a stubborn ass until I asked the other machinists, and they told me that Giacomo and Smitty were neighbors who shared a common wall. When Giacomo got home from the night shift, Smitty was awake, messing around with his windmills. Giacomo couldn't stand the noise, and he couldn't stand Smitty. Giacomo didn't want to give Smitty the satisfaction."

"And?"

I shrugged. "And I had a brilliant insight: Giacomo was in charge of the construction and maintenance of the windmills. He got to boss Smitty around. Smitty didn't like it, but he wanted to see his designs happen in real life. Took me six hours to deal with that, but it worked."

Onanefe sighed as he fiddled with his mustache. "People, right? That's the problem with the FOC: no one wants to talk about what they want 'cause they're afraid they won't get it. Or that they'll get it and be disappointed they didn't ask for more. I keep telling everyone we need small, discrete goals that add up to a big payoff, but everyone wants the big sweeping changes now. Big changes have a tendency to knock innocent bystanders aside. I'd rather minimize that."

I nodded. "When all this settles, and if I'm still alive, I'm going to make sure you talk with the right people."

"You think someone's going to get you?"

I shrugged. "First time's an accident, second time's a coincidence, third time's a trap filled with machete-swinging nutbars."

"You think it's Letty? She did set fire to your building."

"True, but I think that was more of a ploy to freak me out. If she wanted me dead, wouldn't she have done it then and there? Knocked me out, left me to burn?"

"Then who?"

I had no problem remembering the Temple pins on the mob on Shahjahan. I rewound my buffer to the kid who'd stabbed me. He did indeed have a Temple pin attached to the collar of his jumpsuit. I zipped ahead to the riot at Bakaara, and crawled through the footage. There were those guys arguing, there were the cops, there were–

Wait. The men getting worked up at the cable stall. They had a pin.

So did the cops.

They were all made of glass.

"Hey," said Onanefe. "You okay?"

I let out a breath as the whole thing formed like a fresh soap bubble. "Evanrute Saarien once had a glass-blowing operation. He also had people who built a covert refinery underground where there was no pai reception. Son of a bitch."

"What?"

"It *is* Saarien. All of the people who attacked us, they wore glass Temple pins. Even at Bakaara. *That's* how they're communicating, even with the Public down. Saarien's running this whole deal."

He furrowed his eyebrows. "But I thought he was this meek little lamb now."

I shook my head. "No, that was just another act. I should have seen through it. Every time Saarien talked to me, there was someone else around. He always had *witnesses*. He didn't want anything to mess with his image as a non-violent man of the cloth." I gave Soni a prod. "Now I really want her to wake up so she can go arrest that asshole."

"But why?" said Onanefe. "I don't see that. The man's built himself this movement. He can get the entire planet to come here and flood the streets. Why try and off you?"

I sat back, the handrail dangling from my fingertips. "He talked about wanting to keep the first attack quiet because he didn't want people to get worked up over my death."

"That was nice of him."

"Wasn't it? Except now I think he would have been perfectly happy to see me killed. If there were any kind of unrest, he'd be able to step in and play the great peacemaker. 'Let's rally around the death of dear Sister Padma' and all that." I rested my chin in my hands. "Plus, there's always good old revenge."

"For putting him in jail?"

I shrugged. "Why not? He lost everything. And what he's got now may be big, but it's not *as* big."

"You don't think commanding a planet-wide strike is big?"

"You and I would, because we are not insane. Saarien wanted to upend the entire economy. Not just Santee. All of Occupied Space. He wanted the biggest platform possible to stage his great victory in The Struggle."

"Hm." Onanefe pulled his knees in to his chest and wrapped his arms around his shins. The big cane cutter suddenly looked small. "Then why not another knife attack? Why something like the market or the machetes?"

I wound up to the footage of the machete men. They all had handsome faces, but there was a darkness in their smiles that said: *we* like *hurting people*. Saarien had that look when he tried to immolate me. I couldn't see any Temple pins on them, but I didn't need to. People who cultivated that look didn't need any outside markers. They wore it in their eyes.

"Maybe when the first attack didn't work, Saarien figured I'd outlived my usefulness," I said. "He used Bakaara as cover to get me crushed to death. And when *that* didn't work, he set up that ambush. He doesn't just want to win. He wants to dominate. And he'll do it by scaring the living crap out of anyone in the Union or the FOC by having hit squads. It would have been a very messy, very public way to die."

Onanefe *hmm*ed. "Then how does he wind it down?"

I clanged the handrail with my foot. "I don't think he does. It would take a lot of work and a lot of talking, and I haven't seen any signs of that. People are scared, they're passing around rumors, they don't know what's up. He'll let the rioting burn itself out, then step up as hero and savior."

"How?"

"We know he's got his own communications lines. We know he's got stockpiles of food and meds at his Temples. I bet he's got bigger caches all over the city. Hell, he built a state-of-the-art refinery underground. He can send out gangs like the one we saw at Shahjahan, subdue any opposition, buy everyone else off with food. The Union leadership will collapse, and then he's in charge." I gripped the handrail and replanted my feet on the gurney's frame. "I have no idea what happens next. Maybe he'll just fiddle while Santee burns. Maybe he'll be the great leader we need. Either way, I'm not going to sit here and wait it out. I'm going to go out and do *something*."

Onanefe took hold of the handrail. "That sounds like an epitaph."

"I didn't say it would be something *smart*."

"*Definitely* an epitaph."

"I've written better. Come on. Let's get me loose."

We squared our shoulders to the handrail, gave each other a nod, and *pulled*. There was a screech, and the nut popped off the bolt, straight into my right eye.

I didn't even have time to cuss. I just let go of the handrail and put both hands over my eye. I was vaguely aware of the thing still cuffed to my wrist, but the mild pain of the handrail bumping into my torso was nothing compared to the burning in my face. I could see nothing but dull orange.

Eventually, I opened my unjabbed eye. Onanefe crouched in front of me, worry lining his face. "There's no blood, but that looked bad."

"Another epitaph," I said. My right eye throbbed. "I really don't want to move my hands."

Five dull *boom*s sounded in the distance, like all the bass drummers in the Brushhead Memorial Band warming up. A moment later, the building shook.

"Does that happen a lot in the city?" asked Onanefe.

I shrugged. "Could be heavy equipment. Maybe someone's building barricades."

"For what?"

"For whatever's coming next."

Three *boom*s, a little louder. I felt them in the pit of my stomach.

"I don't think I like what's coming next. You think we should go?"

I looked at Soni with my good eye. "All three of us are in no condition to run."

Onanefe dug through the medical bags until he held up a spray stick. "This says it's a topical painkiller."

"Does it say to keep away from eyes?"

He looked at the label. "I don't think so."

"Maybe we should wait to find a pro."

Another four *boom*s came from down the street. This time, the air filled with the smashing crunch of houses collapsing. One of the konbini's walls buckled, and I jumped up to cover Soni as ceiling tiles rained down. The panels tumbling on my back helped me forget the pain in my eye for a while.

When the shaking stopped, I opened my good eye, only to jam it shut again quickly. What felt like sandpaper rubbed the inside of my eye, probably grit from the plastered ceiling and the busted tiles. I coughed and put an arm over my mouth; I got a lungful of dust in return. "We need to go!" I managed to say. I felt something move to my right, and Onanefe croaked, "Can't." He coughed, and the gurney shook.

Everything from my nose down to my lungs burned. I could smell nothing but the must of plaster powder. The air in the office was getting impossible to breathe. We had to get out.

I nudged the gurney toward where I remembered the

door was. The wheels jammed on the debris that crunched under my boots, and the frame bumped into the doorframe. Onanefe held on for dear life as I shoved and shook the gurney through the dust. It battered my face as I fought towards what I hoped was the door.

Screams filled the night air. Screams from sirens, screams from shattered pipes, screams from wounded men. I didn't want to open my eyes, but I also didn't want to be killed by something I couldn't see. I scrabbled around until I got a grip on the medical bags. I dug inside them until I felt a squishy caneplas bag that I hoped was full of saline. I forced my left eye open enough to make sure; in the dim light, I saw "NaCl" on the label. I tore it open and splashed the solution into my face. It stung like ocean water, but it was enough to wash away the dust. My right eye stayed swollen shut.

Onanefe had shielded Soni's lower torso. Dust made a trail from the crown of his head down to his tailbone. I helped him stand up and cleaned his face. Gray slurry ran down his cheeks, dripping off his chin. He sputtered as he wiped it away with his sleeve. "Is she okay?" he said, nodding at Soni.

The top of her body, where we had shielded her, was dusted with a few particles of plaster. Everything from her waist down was now a dingy gray. I gave her a prod, and she snorted.

"Okay enough." I coughed more dust out of my lungs, then made the mistake of looking up.

Of the twenty shophouses on the street, five of them had been stomped flat. Gouts of flame rolled up from the wreckage, lighting the clouds of greasy smoke that loomed overhead. Frantic rescuers dug at the rubble and shoved aside the wreckage of a tuk-tuk. People wandered the shattered sidewalk, arms hanging loose at the wrong angles. In the flicker, I could see bodies and pieces of bodies hanging off crooked streetlamps. I grabbed the medical bags. "Stay with Soni," I said, walking toward the closest fire. If Onanefe protested, I couldn't hear it over the wailing.

A man not much older than me stood on the sidewalk, holding another man in his arms. Both of them were covered in soot and blood; their skin shone in the firelight. As I got closer I saw the unconscious man had a face full of glass shards and burns across the side of his head. "What happened?" I said as I eased them to the ground.

The crying man just sniffed and looked down at his partner. I dug into the bags and realized I had no idea what to do with their contents. There were packs of loaded syringes, rolls of gauze, bottles of pills. I'd been through disasters before, but I didn't know much more past basic first aid.

The crying man let out another sob. I pulled out an antibiotic spray and squirted wherever I saw blood. There was a pair of caneplas exam gloves, but they were too small. I put them on anyway and started wrapping both of their wounds with gauze. That got the crying man calm, though he never took his eyes off his partner. "What happened?" I asked again.

He wiped blood off his cheek; there was ink there, but I couldn't make it out. "We were having a block meeting at the Pulaski's, and then–"

Another *boom* shook the air. Three blocks east, a lick of flame curled toward the sky. I shivered as three more explosions sent fire and debris upward. The night sky glowed red and orange under a cloud cover of smoke. The city wasn't just on fire. It was exploding.

A hand clamped on my shoulder, and I yelped. I turned and saw Soni, her eyes fixed on the distance. Onanefe stood with her. She looked down at me and said, "What do you want to do?"

I swallowed a lump out of my throat. "Whatever we can."

She nodded and clicked on the radio on her belt. "I've heard worse plans."

SIXTEEN

We turned the ruined konbini into our triage hospital. Onanefe and I walked up and down the street, helping people to the space we cleared inside. The konbini's roof had stayed intact, so we shoved the shelves to the sides to make room. In less than fifteen minutes, we had thirty people with burns, cuts, broken legs, and concussions all laid out on the floor.

We worked until our legs and the bags of meds were out. The three of us huddled together in a corner of the konbini. When I woke up, weak dawn light was trying to break in through the shattered storefront. I wormed my way out from between Soni and Onanefe and walked outside.

The damage looked even worse now that I could see it. The fires had died down thanks to the survivors' efforts, but not before half the buildings had been burned to the ground. The stench of ash and charred meat hung in the air, like a barbeque gone horribly wrong. I didn't want to think about what caused the smell. Overhead, crows made lazy circles, their *caws* soft and distant.

Soni called out to me. She stood in the ruined doorway, holding up a spray bottle. "I think this is a painkiller. Forgot

I had it in my utility belt."

"Give it to that lady with the broken hip," I said. "We need to keep her calm."

"I'd like to put a bit in your eye."

I waved her off. "It's not like I can use my pai right now," I said.

"It's not your pai I'm worried about," she said.

"I don't want it," I said.

Soni grumbled. "Can I put a bandage on your eye, then? Or do you want to save those, too?"

I sighed. "Fine. If it'll get you off my back."

Soni popped a fist-sized gauze pad out of a pouch on her belt. I held still long enough for her to tape it over my right eye. "We'll have to get you to a doctor."

"Them first," I said, pointing at our patients. "Can't you raise anyone?"

Soni held up her radio, a tiny handheld unit. Someone had taken a pen to its backing and drawn an angry cat. It stretched a paw and showed a mouth full of teeth. "Total silence. Our relays got knocked out."

"You sure?"

She nodded. "We had one on top of the house that got blown up."

"You think that was on purpose?"

"I don't know." She shrugged. "I don't have a clue what's going on now, Padma. I keep hearing sirens, but I've yet to see an ambo or a patrol wagon. We have to get out of this neighborhood and start talking to other people, find EMTs, other police, doctors, whatever."

Onanefe joined us. "Is that the plan? Leaving?"

"It's *a* plan," said Soni, "and it involves me. I'm the least injured, and the only one with a badge."

"You think that matters right now?" I said. "Christ, someone's setting off *bombs*."

"We don't know that," said Soni. "It could be crap piping, makeshift heaters, or just plain bad luck."

I swept my hand over the ruined street. "You can't possibly believe that."

She gave me a hard look. "I *have* to," she said. "Otherwise, it means our city's coming apart at the seams, and I'm not ready to believe *that*. Not yet. Not until I know that all the people under my command have given up or gotten themselves killed."

I sighed. Of course. Someone at Soni's level had to have hundreds of people working under her. She wasn't the type *not* to worry about them during a crisis. "You're right. But I still want to go with you."

She shook her head. "You're hurt. It's going to be hard enough to get around."

"I got a bolt to the face, not a concussion."

"Did you just get magical diagnostic power?" said Soni. "You might have a blood clot working its way to your brain. What happens if we're walking and you stroke out?"

"Probably the same thing that would happen if I stayed *here*. I'm going."

"No, you're not. That's an order."

I laughed. "Are you fucking kidding me? You can't order me."

"The hell I can't. This is a civil disturbance, and as the chief of police I have the power to–"

I blew a raspberry. "You don't have the power to do squat unless the Prez says so, and you know it."

She narrowed her eyes. "The same Prez who set fire to your house? That's who you're going to defer to?"

"Hell, no," I said. "But I'm also not deferring to someone wearing a badge, because many other people with badges have completely failed to do their jobs. *You* haven't, Soni. You take that badge seriously. But what about the people you'd sent to Bakaara? They can't be the only police like that in the city."

Soni clenched her jaw for a moment, then sighed. "I hate it when you're right about stuff like this."

"Me, too. Can we go now?"

"I can. You can't."

"Why not?"

"You've only got one eye."

"Oh, like that's gonna stop me."

"Yeah?" Soni walked to my right side and said, "How many fingers am I holding up?"

I gave her the bird.

"Wrong!" She put her hand in front of my left eye; she had shaped it into a gun, her thumb cocked back. "We're walking along, someone sneaks up on your right side, you can't see anything until it's too late."

"Then I'll walk on your left."

"Dammit, Padma! I'm trying to keep you from getting hurt!"

I tapped the bandage. "Too late."

Soni swore. "You're impossible, you know that?"

"That's why you trust me."

Behind us, Onanefe cleared his throat. I rolled my eye as I turned. "You have something to add?"

"I do," he said. "Me."

"Oh, *hell*, no," said Soni. "I will have enough to worry about without both of you invalids coming along."

Onanefe smiled, the first time he had without wincing in pain. "While you two were arguing, I helped myself to Chief Baghram's painkillers. Not all of them, mind you, but enough so I don't have to think about my chest exploding. Now that I have a clear head, I have something to point out."

I put my hands on my hips. "Yes?"

His mustache widened with his grin. "What we are

seeing is a breakdown of trust. There's no trust between you two, or between the citizenry and the police, or between the Freeborn and the Union. That's the thread that's run through every discussion we've had, Padma: people don't trust anything right now. People didn't trust they'd get paid or get to keep their jobs or their homes, and they got *angry*."

"Angry enough to start blowing up their own neighborhoods?" I said.

Onanefe shook his head. "These bombings are meant to reinforce that mistrust. I would argue that this is all deliberate. We're seeing an orchestrated campaign."

Soni's eyes narrowed, and her mouth became a line so hard it could have shattered diamond. "And how do you know this?"

Onanefe's smile never flagged. "Because it's what we talked about doing two Contracts ago."

Soni now gave Onanefe her full Cop Face. He flinched the tiniest bit. "Who, exactly, is *we*?"

Onanefe's eyes flicked to me. I nodded: *tell her the fucking truth*. He cleared his throat and said, "I'm on the Executive Committee of the FOC."

Soni stiffened for the briefest of moments. Her arm was a blue blur as she grabbed Onanefe's wrist and spun him around. He didn't say anything when she jammed him against the front of the konbini, but that was probably because his face was squished.

"Do you have any idea what you assholes did two Contracts ago?" she hissed. "I was a rookie, and I had to do clean-up duty after every one of your bombings." She looked at me. "You really know how to pick your company, Padma. First that Ghost, now this terrorist."

I held my hands out. "I think you might be overreacting a bit, Soni."

"This?" She laughed. "No, this is a calm, measured

response. If I were overreacting, your friend here would be weeping."

"All the same, I don't think he or his group is responsible for all of this."

"Then that can come out in court," said Soni.

"For what?" I said.

"Consorting with terrorists."

"So, what, you're going to drag him to the nearest cell? Lock him away? He helped me keep you safe while you were unconscious."

Soni turned and looked at me, her face screwed up in hatred. "The FOC killed police. They bombed precinct houses."

"That wasn't us!" yelled Onanefe.

"Then who was it?"

"I don't know!"

"This is a waste of time." Soni pulled a zip-tie off her belt and looped it around his wrists. She cranked them extra tight. "You want to talk about trust now? I'd *love* to hear you talk about trust." She let him go and stepped back.

Onanefe turned with care. He looked me in the eye as he took a breath. "Twenty-two years ago, the FOC's Executive Committee met to determine what we would do during the upcoming Contract. A small faction wanted to engage in a bombing campaign. They thought the only way to get the Union to pay attention to us was to show strength. I argued against it because, surprise, no one would trust us if we started blowing people up. Leticia Arbusto Smythe was on the committee with me. We were on the same side. It took a week of debate, but we finally prevailed. There would be no bombings."

He cleared his throat. "And they happened anyway. None of the people in the faction claimed responsibility. In fact" – he looked Soni in the eye – "they all turned themselves in to the police as a show of good faith. It never went to trial, because there were never any charges. We didn't do it, and if we knew who did we'd have turned their asses in."

Soni shook her head. "Not good enough."

Onanefe sagged. "What more do you want? It was good enough for the police back then."

"That was then. I was only a rookie. Now I'm the chief of police. I've had my comms cut, my people moved, and my city on fire. I need to know who was in that faction, because it's a pretty good bet they're behind this now."

"Then you can go to Lonxia Cemetery, 'cause that's where they are now."

Soni nodded. "So, they're meeting there?"

And then she saw Onanefe's eyes, the way he tried to keep them open despite the tears welling up. She cleared her throat. "Ah."

And then I remembered: the Hanuman, sparkling clean with the cane wreaths on the front grill. Onanefe and his crew, all in white as they rushed into my burning building. "Whose funeral was it?"

"Does it matter?" he said, his voice breaking.

"If he was buried at Lonxia, he lived in my neighborhood. I'd like to know the name. Yes."

He coughed. "Milt Gorsky was a cutter and a Zen priest. He spent all his down time teaching kids to read. He used to cry whenever he found dead animals after a cane burn. He was the friendliest man you ever met, which is why it shocked me when he proposed the bombing campaign. Even though he planned it to make sure no one would get injured – giving everyone plenty of warning, making sure only to take out the target building – it hurt me to think he'd do that. We were such good friends until he made that proposal. I hadn't spoken to him since the vote."

He snuffled and didn't look away. "He died last week,

alone, in some grubby bedsit in Faoshue. He left a handwritten will that just said he wanted to be at Lonxia because he liked the shade there. He'd spent enough of his time in the sun."

I flashed back to Meiumi Greene-with-an-e. She wanted to come into town for *Uncle Gorsky*'s funeral. "Are they all there? The ones who wanted the bombings?"

Onanefe nodded. "Milt was the last one of them left."

I looked at Soni. "You know about this?"

She shook her head. "It must not have looked like a suspicious death, or I would've gotten a call."

"Milt was always in poor health," said Onanefe. "And considering how nasty his place was, it looked like he hadn't gotten better. Dirty dishes in the sink, spoiled food in the fridge. That kind of thing."

"You were there?" said Soni. "After he died?"

Onanefe nodded. "I knew his landlady. She called me after the police went in to investigate the smell." He coughed again and shuddered. "He'd been in there a while. A couple of months, the coroner said."

Soni rubbed the top of her head. Her eyes were still hard, but the thin line of her mouth had shifted like a fault line. "Did all of them die like that? Natural causes?"

Onanefe bit his lip as his head bobbed from side to side. "Susan Broyles had a heart attack. Thanchanok Morrison drowned. Jimmy Nguyen got hit by a tuk-tuk. But he was also really drunk, and considering how much he liked his rum, that's practically natural causes."

"When did this all happen?"

He shrugged. "I dunno. In the past few years. They were in their fifties when we met. Letty and I were the youngest ones on the committee."

Soni's line of questioning clicked in my head. "You said everyone who voted for the bombings died," I said. "What about the people who voted against them? Are they all still alive?"

"Hm." Onanefe rubbed his mustache. "There were seven of us on the Executive Committee. Of the four who voted against, there's just me, Letty, and Marquise Spadinet. Louellen Prima, she was the chair, and the whole thing broke her heart. She died a few weeks after the vote. Marquise moved to the other side of Santee after the bombings. She didn't want anything to do with us anymore. Haven't heard from her in years."

"What are you thinking?" said Soni.

"I'm thinking it would be nice to find a working phone and see if Marquise is still alive."

Soni narrowed her eyes. "Why wouldn't she be?"

"Because she's the last FOC member at that vote, excepting Onanefe and Letty."

"What, you think *she's* behind this?" said Soni.

"Maybe. I don't know," I said, looking at Onanefe. "What was Milt's proposal? What was his plan?"

Onanefe took a deep breath. "He was going to pack tuk-tuks with fertilizer bombs. Small enough to take out a storefront, knock a Union office out of commission, that kind of thing."

I nodded. "The other day, one of Jilly's drivers told me that a lot of tuk-tuks have been boosted. And I've heard complaints of how hard it's been to hail a ride over the past month."

Soni cocked her head. "You don't think...?"

I nodded. "When we got outside this morning, I saw a shophouse blow up. A tuk-tuk was parked in front of it."

"You sure?"

"I realize my memory isn't as accurate as my pai's feed, but, yeah. I thought the house had exploded, but maybe it was the tuk-tuk. Maybe someone's carrying out Milt's plan."

"Who else knew the details?" said Soni.

Onanefe put his head in his hands. "Just us. And whatever police were in on the interrogations."

I looked at Soni. "You think you can find out who they were?"

Soni shook her head. "Not with the Public down. But I can't believe any police are doing this."

"Yeah? Like you can't believe your people just stood by at Bakaara?" I hunkered down in front of her. "Two days ago, I would have laughed in your face if you told me that. I would have laughed if you'd told me the President of the Union would have set my building on fire. But now?" I took her hands. "We're all getting played, Soni. And I don't know about you, but it really pisses me off."

She smiled. "I do like it when you get pissed off. Things happen."

"Damn straight. You want to make them happen with me?"

"What do you have in mind?"

I nodded to Onanefe. "Cut him loose, first. We need him."

Soni's smile faded. "You're going to have to explain a little bit before I do that."

I grinned. "Like the man said, it's all about trust. We need to build a case."

"That's what I wanted to do before you started insisting on coming along."

"And if you don't, you're not going to get much done. What have we not seen this morning? What would be here on any other day, during any other crisis?"

Soni grunted as she surveyed the street. "I agree that the emergency response has... sucked."

"It's been non-existent," I said. "Whether that's because

someone on high is pulling strings or police are freaked out, I don't know. What I do know is that having them hide is only going to encourage more chaos. There has to be a presence out here that says, *We see there's a problem, and we are working on it.*"

"And you think that presence should be the three of us?"

I nodded.

"Mm-hm." Soni leaned on her thighs, tenting her fingers together. "I cannot wait to hear how you're going to make that happen."

"We're going to talk to people."

Soni looked at Onanefe. "Are you buying this?"

He shrugged. "I'm willing to hear some details."

"Good, because I think you're going to love this," I said, bouncing on the balls of my feet.

"I'm worried about how excited you are," said Soni.

"That means I'm on to something. We are going to talk to people, and we are going to say one simple thing: we hear you."

Onanefe and Soni stared at me for a moment. "Did you hit your head?" said Soni.

"Possibly, but it has nothing to do with this. We need to reassure the citizenry that this crisis is going to pass, and that we're all going to get through it by working together."

Onanefe shook his head. "I think your friend's right. That's delusional."

"It's what's going to work, because it's what *always* works."

"Talking?" said Soni.

"And listening. The listening is more important than the talking."

Soni sat back. "Jesus, Padma, this is not the time to sing songs and have everyone hold hands."

"Why not?"

"Because someone is setting off *bombs*?"

"And that's why people will be reassured that Chief Soni Baghram of the Santee City Police Department is walking the streets instead of hiding inside an emergency bunker."

"And what can Chief Baghram do on her own?" said Soni. "Especially now that she's out of medical supplies?"

"She's going to become the rallying point for all emergency personnel who still believe in what their badges represent," I said, tapping the metal star on her chest. "Serve and protect, right?"

She mulled this over, her eyes focused on the smoldering shophouses. "Suppose I go out there. Why does he come along?"

"Ah." I strode to Onanefe and put an arm around his shoulder. "Our friend from the FOC is going with us to show that the Freeborn are valued members of society, and that their fears will be allayed and their demands will be met."

"Really?" said Soni. "Just from having him along?"

"Absolutely," I said. "This man, like you, stands for something important: not taking any more bullshit."

"This is true," he said.

"There will be Freeborn who know him by reputation," I said. "And there will be sympathetic Union people who know what Onanefe stands for. Everyone will see him walking with the chief of police and a beloved hero of the Union."

"Beloved?" said Soni.

"You bet your ass I'm beloved. That's why you're going to come with me. We're going to show everyone how trust is supposed to work." I patted Onanefe's shoulder. "That's what you had in mind, right? We all need each other. No one side is strong enough to prevail. If the police are considered untrustworthy, Soni's useless. If the Freeborn are untrustworthy, you're useless. If the Union is untrustworthy, I'm useless. So, let's all be useless *together*."

Soni and Onanefe stared at me. "That is the worst speech I have ever heard," said Soni.

"It's a rough draft. I can always edit later," I said. "But you get what I'm saying, right?"

"The Kum Ba Ya solution *never* works," said Soni.

"That's because it's bullshit," I said. "Holding hands and singing songs around a campfire means no one listens. No one learns why the others are pissed off. There's no reconciliation. *That's* what we need, and we're not going to get it from Letty, because she's the one pulling all the strings."

"She is?" said Onanefe.

I nodded. "That's the case we're going to build. I thought this was all Saarien and his whackjobs running around, but now I think *he's* getting played, too."

"What makes you think Letty's behind this?" said Soni.

"Him," I said, tapping Onanefe on the shoulder. "The loose end."

"The what?" he said.

"You were at the vote. You knew what the bombing plan was. And you were at Milt's funeral."

"So?"

"Was Letty there?"

"Yeah."

I looked at Soni. "Milt's funeral was the morning Letty visited me. She came to my place and started that fire, knowing it would draw Onanefe and his crew. And she ensured their arrival by getting the police and fire chiefs to shift their officers around so there was no timely response."

Soni made a face. "That's pretty thin."

"Not when you take into account everything that's happened since. When Onanefe didn't snuff it at the fire, someone tried to stab me. Except he was going for Onanefe."

Onanefe shook his head. "He was pretty fixed on you, Padma."

"Then why was he yelling, 'You're in my way'? I thought he meant that figuratively, but he didn't. I got in between you and the knife. After he stabbed me, he wasn't angry; he was *mortified*." I looked at Soni. "As soon as I get my pai working, I'll show you the footage."

"What about Bakaara?" said Onanefe.

"That was cover," I said. "Soni said all her officers had been pulled back. We saw people shaking their heads and arguing about the Public being wonky *right before* the riot. That means someone monkeyed with their pais. The only ones who can order that are the Executive Committee."

"But the people who run the Public are on strike," said Soni.

"Are they?" I said. "Are any of the people who actually run the city marching? Have you heard from any of them? Have you seen any demands, any speeches, any signs indicating that the people who do the work don't want to? No. The only person who's been broadcasting is Saarien, because he's just cover for what Letty's doing."

"Which is?"

"That part, I have no idea." I shrugged. "I don't know what her game is, but I know she's the one running it. I just *know* it."

"Your gut instincts won't be any good in court," said Soni.

"It will in the court of public opinion," I said. "And that's where we have to try this. That's why we have to get into the streets. No one has challenged Letty's narrative. No one's countered her story that everything is hopeless, that we're all doomed. We have to do that. We have to give people some *hope*."

Soni tucked her chin in her hand. "This still sounds Kum Ba Ya."

"Talk without works is dead," I said. "And we are going to do the work."

Onanefe grinned. "I'm ready to do the work." He turned his back to Soni and raised his cuffed hands. "If you please?"

Soni rubbed her head, her hand sliding back and forth over her scalp stubble. "Where do we go first?"

I looked at the street signs and finally got my bearings. "Back to Bakaara Market."

"Why?"

I smiled. "Because I've got a case of rum stored there."

SEVENTEEN

Soni was pissed, and she spent the next ten blocks making sure I knew it. "When I joined the police, you know what they taught us first?"

"Hairstyling?"

Soni glared. "That the very worst thing to do in this job was to offer someone a drink."

"Your instructors must have been a ton of fun."

She stepped in front of me and held up her hand. "I'm serious, Padma. I know rum makes this world go 'round, but right now the city is full of angry, terrified people. Throwing booze into the mix is going to make things worse."

"It's going to get them to come out of their houses and relax."

"Not today it won't," said Soni. "We've both been at Big Lily's at last call. People who've been nursing grudges for months will find that excuse to throw a punch, and then no amount of talking can calm them down."

"Then what do you suggest?" I couldn't help but laugh, I felt so light. "Do we wait until another bomb goes off? Do we wait until people break out the power tools and start slashing each other to pieces? 'Cause that's what's next,

Soni. We have to do something. We have to make a choice."

"Throwing a party is not the best choice to make."

"Really? I think everyone would much rather have a party than a bloodbath. Besides, it's Saturday."

"Is it?" said Onanefe. "I've lost all track of time."

"It is *not* Saturday," said Soni, blinking furiously. "It's only Thursday."

"I think people would rather have my Saturday than your Thursday."

"Can we split the difference and call it Friday?" said Onanefe.

I clapped my hands and laughed. "Yes! Here's a man who gets it." I looped my arm through his and looked at Soni. "You coming, or what?"

She shook her head. "I know the Public isn't up, but I'm going on record right now by saying that whatever happens next will be all *your* fault."

"Wouldn't be the first time someone said that." I offered my other arm to her. She took it, but gripped hard enough for me to know she wasn't in the mood for bullshit.

As we approached Bakaara, I saw that KajSiab and her security people had been busy during the night. Anything that hadn't been bolted down had been turned into a barricade that ran around the perimeter of the Market. Empty kegs and molasses drums propped up head-high walls made of smashed tables and stall counters. As we got closer, I saw sparkles along the top of the barricade: smashed glass held in place with molasses paste.

In front of us, there was a break in the barricade. Three security women stood there, eyeballing us as they showed us their cricket bats. One of them told us to hold up our hands, and we complied. As the guards frisked us, I recognized KajSiab among them. "What gives, KajSiab?"

She gave me a wary look, then nodded, as if to say it

was okay I addressed her by name. "We've got all kinds of people here seeking refuge, and we have to make sure no one brings anything dangerous inside." She allowed me a small smile. "I'm glad you're alive."

"Was I not supposed to be?"

KajSiab shrugged. "We'd heard you got chopped to pieces by a bunch of Freeborn."

Onanefe curled his lip. "Says who?"

KajSiab gave him the onceover, spending a long time looking at the lack of ink on his face. "I dunno. There's all kinds of rumors floating around: the Prez is dead, WalWa is reclaiming the planet."

"I heard the Prez ran up the cable last night, and she's hiding out on the anchor," said the woman who'd frisked me.

"Where'd you hear *that*?" I said.

She shrugged. "Like KajSiab said. All kinds of rumors. Some guy fixing the water filter was talking about it." She laughed. "Of course, he also said the Co-Op was giving away free rum, so he was probably full of it."

I looked at Soni, who shook her head so hard I thought it would fall off. "Funny you should mention rum," I said. "Does anyone feel like a drink?"

KajSiab snorted. "Are you serious?"

"I'm a member of the Co-Op," I said. "I never joke about rum."

She giggled, and I tried to put on my best I Am Completely Serious face. It must have worked, because KajSiab lowered her cricket bat. "I'm listening."

I threw Soni an eyebrow wiggle before turning to KajSiab. "Throughout this city, I have many cases of Old Windswept rum. Some of it is the standard production batch, but there are a few bottles of the really good stuff here and there. I want people to come out of their hiding places, bring their grills and their food and whatever they've got, and I want us all to sit down and eat and talk. After all" – I spread my arms out like I wanted to give the entire Market a hug – "it's Friday."

KajSiab furrowed her brows. "No it isn't. It's Thursday."

"It's Friday now," I said. "Are you going to let me in to get my rum?"

KajSiab fiddled with the bat. "Where is it, exactly?"

I dialed up the smile another notch as I shook my head. "My rum is not for people to horde, KajSiab. It's for sharing, and I'm the one who's going to pass around the goods. There's a case in here, certainly, but you won't be able to get it."

She hefted the bat, slapping it in the flat of her hand. "Is that a challenge? I'm pretty good at challenges."

"I'm sure you are," I said, taking a small step toward her. "How much liquor can you hold?"

Her eyebrows drifted up like freshly released balloons. "*That* is definitely a challenge." She stepped aside, and I beckoned Onanefe and Soni to follow me into the ruins of Bakaara Market.

"This is not going to work," Soni whispered as we walked through the Market.

Looking around, I wanted to agree. Whatever goods had been out in the open yesterday were gone. Bakaara had been stripped bare of anything edible or valuable. People huddled around the last embers on the grills, and kids picked through the compost bins. A little girl popped out of one bin and held a pineapple core aloft. The kids all skittered away as we approached. "Holy shit," I muttered. "It's only been a *day*."

"Everyone's hoarding the last of the food," said KajSiab. "We probably spent more time keeping people from raiding the stalls than we did building the barricades. The worst rumor that came tearing through is that every grocery warehouse and farm is on fire. With the Public down, there's no way to verify, so..." She rubbed her eyes and sighed. "I've been up all night, and I'm really goddamn hungry, and I can't even find so much as an almond. I know I'm gonna be a bear by dinner time. What's gonna happen everywhere else? Where's the goddamn Union?"

"It's right here," I said, tapping my cheek. I pointed at KajSiab's tattoo. "And here." I nodded at Soni. "There, too."

KajSiab glanced at Onanefe. "What about him?"

"He's still thinking about it," said Onanefe, "though he agrees with the sentiment."

KajSiab tapped her ever-present cricket bat against the sole of her boot. "Which is?"

He gave her the most sincere smile I'd seen him wear. "That we're all in this together. Right?"

KajSiab mulled this over for a moment before giving him a curt nod. "Fair enough. But why hasn't the Prez said anything? Shit, she could have printed up *flyers* or something by now."

I looked at Soni, who shrugged: *You want to make the case, do it.* I felt like I was about to jump off a cliff into an ocean full of sharks. Hungry sharks. With machine guns. And herpes.

I cleared my throat and said, "Letty Arbusto Smythe is making this all happen. She's shut down the Public, made the cops withdraw, and let our city fall apart." I pointed at Onanefe. "She put out a hit on Onanefe, 'cause he's part of the FOC. She wants this chaos."

KajSiab's face soured. "That's insane. Why?"

"I don't know yet," I said. "But I know if she wanted it to stop, she would have done it by now. *I* want it to stop, and that's what we're gonna do. And we start by getting everyone out of their hidey-holes and acting like people."

We rounded a corner, and the sweet smell of crushed cane washed over me. I wanted to turn right around and head back to the distillery. Soni was right: no one was going to talk, not even if I served all the rum in the world. I could leave right now and hole up until Letty finished doing whatever it was she planned.

We stopped in front of a ruined stall, a sign proclaiming *BEST CANE JUICE IN TOWN* flapping in the breeze. Two little boys, probably eight years old, crouched next to a smashed cane press. They started when I cleared my throat and brandished splintered cane stalks like swords. Both wore forest green Nortec United football jerseys. Their faces were smears of dirt and dust, and the ants that crawled over the press's rollers ran over the boys' sandaled feet.

I held out my hands and waited. The boys' eyes were big, and they looked *through* me. I had no idea what these kids had seen in the past twenty-four hours, but the blank looks on their faces told me it had been horrible. I tried to make my face as calm and friendly as possible, which was a neat trick because the possibility of a face-full of splintered cane was terrifying.

After a minute, they lowered the stalks. I hunkered down in front of them. "My name's Padma. You two okay?" They kept staring.

I got the emergency date bars out of my trouser pocket, and the boys focused on the soft, brown rectangles in my hands. "Do you have families?"

The boys didn't take their eyes off the bars as they nodded.

"These are yours," I said, "but only if you run and tell everyone to bring whatever food and cooking fuel they have to Hawa Said's stall, okay? Tell them Padma Mehta's throwing a party, and that it's not a joke."

I handed them the bars, and they snatched them so fast

their fingernails scratched my palms. They stuffed the bars in their mouths and ran away, full tilt boogie.

"We're calling it a party now?" said Soni, her arms crossed.

"Anything to get people to remember that we're not supposed to live like this." I stood up and showed Soni the red marks on my palms. "One week, and we've got kids digging in the compost bins for food. Sweet Working Christ."

"It's only going to get worse," said KajSiab. "All those stories we got about the Tsokusa Blight, about how the food just turned to dust." She shuddered.

"We don't have to worry about *that*," I said. "We're dealing with a distribution problem, not supply."

"Not yet," said Soni.

"You know, you are just a radiant ball of sunshine right now," I said. "I look forward to your positive attitude helping with the proceedings."

She quirked her mouth. "I'm sorry. I'm just worried about Millie."

Oh, shit. Sixteen hours, and I hadn't thought to ask about her wife. "You want to check on her?"

"Of course I do. But I can't. Because my comms don't work." She plucked her radio off her belt and waved it around before tossing it on the ground. "Plus the battery is now dead."

"We'll get you a battery."

She laughed, a sound like sandpaper on glass. "Terrific. I'll be able to keep hearing nothing but static."

"I can send a runner," said KajSiab.

"No, thank you," said Soni. "For now, I'm going to stick with Padma's plan. Assuming there *is* a plan?"

"Of course," I said, making a mental note to ignore Soni and have KajSiab check on Millie anyway. We rounded the corner to Hawa's stall. "And it starts with a proper breakfast."

Black scorch marks streaked up the pourform sides of Hawa's stall. The chicken wire that had covered the front lay in the market aisle. A nightmare of nicks and scratches decorated the door. The embroidered sign and the crocheted doll were on the ground, stomped flat and darkened by boot treads. I banged on the door and put my head close. "Hawa! It's Padma Mehta!"

"I don't care!" came a muffled reply from behind the door.

"Hawa, I need to get my rum!"

"Now I don't care even more! Go away!"

"What, are you reneging on our deal?"

"Our deal didn't cover riots! And, yes, this time, there *was* a riot! Those animals tried to burn down my stall!"

"Your stall is made of unburnable pourform. Plus you've got fans and secret lights and all kinds of stuff in there."

"And they're only good protection as long as my door is closed and locked! Take your angry mob and piss off!"

"There is no mob! It's me and Onanefe and KajSiab and Soni Baghram."

There was a rustle behind us. I spun around, ready to fight, only to see the two boys who had been scavenging cane. They had brought along two other boys. One of them held half a baguette. The other held a mesh bag with two oranges. I crouched where I stood so I could get at eye level with the youngest. His football jersey was three sizes too big and came down to his knees. I smiled. "Are these your brothers?"

He shook his head. "Friends."

I nodded to the older boys. "I'm glad you brought something. Are your parents coming?"

"My dad says you're full of crap," said the tallest boy. "Says this is all some plot to get people to come out and get killed."

"But you're here."

He shrugged. "I'm tired of hiding. We're in this basement, and it smells like farts."

"Good reason to come out. We'll get things started in a moment." I banged on the door again. "Come on, Hawa. Everyone needs a little normality. Can we get some of that? Please? Or do you want me to send these kids back to the fart chamber?"

"I have no way of knowing if you're telling the truth."

"Are you kidding? Just turn on the cameras!"

"All my external cameras got smashed during the night. They got the backups, too. Nothing on the radio, the Public's still out."

"You still got food and light?"

"Why?" Her voice grew hard. "You want to try and take it?"

"No, but I had hoped you'd bring it out to the party."

There was a pause. "I'm sorry, I must have misheard. The Padma Mehta I know wouldn't be so stupid as to throw a party in the middle of turmoil."

"I'm trying to calm things down because no one else will."

"That's the police's job. Since when are you the police?"

"Since they were told to stand down."

"Who would do that?"

"The Prez."

Hawa laughed. "You know, of all the ploys to get me to open my door, this is a good one."

"I'm not joking, Hawa. The higher-ups aren't doing their job, so it's up to the rest of us to calm things down."

"By throwing a party?"

"You don't think that's the best time to fire up the grill and start passing the punch?"

"I hate punch."

"Then I'll get you some pineapple juice. Come on, Hawa! Would you turn away a neighbor?"

"We're not neighbors!" she laughed. "You live in Brushhead! That's way the hell over on the other side of town!"

"Yet I shop in Bakaara every week. I buy embroidery from you. I *talk* with you, and that makes us neighbors. All of us. And I'm asking you, as a neighbor, to come outside and break some bread with us."

"I have plenty of bread in here, thanks."

"But you don't have *us*, and *we* are *inviting* you to join us. Would you turn aside my hospitality?"

This time, the silence dragged on for a good minute. There was nothing but silence from the inside of Hawa's stall. I held my breath so I could hear anything: a murmured argument, a machete sliding out of a sheath. Nothing.

The door rattled, like someone was pressing on it from the other side. I put my ear close. "How can I trust you?" said Hawa.

"The same way we've always trusted each other," I said. "You open up and take a risk."

She laughed. "Good God, is that the best you've got? You really think that's going to convince me?"

"Yes," I said, "because you still have that fist tattooed on your face. You might not be a Ward Chair anymore, Hawa, but I know you still believe in what the Union stands for. An injury to one is an injury to all, and we need to work together to get justice for those injuries. It's easy to stand together when it's us versus the Big Three, but now we've got our own people screwing each other over. You wouldn't have stood for that when you were organizing, and I don't think you'll stand for it now."

I held my breath so I could hear whatever noises came from inside the stall. For a moment, there was nothing, then a gentle drumming against the door. "And you really think that asking everyone to put aside their grudges and have a barbeque is going to solve all this?"

"It'll get us talking with each other instead of killing each other. I think it's the start we need. And I don't see anyone else trying it."

"That's terrible logic."

I laughed. "It's all I got left, Hawa. That, and all the rum I've got scattered around the city. Won't you come out and join us?"

There was a *clack* like a rifle bolt, and I leaped back. A narrow panel in the door opened just enough for one of Hawa's bloodshot and drooping eyes to peer out. I heard a faint tap and glanced down; the business end of a knitting needle pointed right at my chest from a second panel. "Anything happens to my granddaughter," came Hawa's voice from behind the door, "and I swear to God Almighty, Padma, you'll be the first person I stick. This one's extra sharp."

"If anything happens, I'll stick myself," I said, holding my hands up.

Hawa's eye flicked around at the people standing behind me before withdrawing into the shadows. The door slammed shut. Six *clacks* came from behind the door, and it flew open. Hawa took a cautious step out of the stall. She held her head high as she looked at us, daring anyone to make a move. She still had the needle, but she pointed it at the ground. "You know I take offers of hospitality seriously, right?"

"I wouldn't have done it otherwise."

She nodded. I held out my hands. "Are you going to join us?"

Hawa grunted and took my hands. She squeezed tight, then pulled me in for a hug that hurt. After thumping me on the back, she let go and said, "You know, kid, if you're going to pull this in front of the mob, you're going to get your head handed to you."

"I hope the mob will smell what we're cooking and join us."

The boy with the oranges held up the bag. Hawa raised an eyebrow. "I suppose you'll want me to bring something to this little shindig?"

"If you like," I said. "I just need my rum."

She nodded back into the stall. "Go in and get it. I didn't bother to put it away. If another riot swept through, I was going to turn them into Molotovs."

I froze. "You were going to mess with my rum?"

She shrugged. "I would have paid you back."

"My rum is priceless."

"It goes for thirty yuan a bottle at the konbini." She took an orange from the kid, then motioned everyone to follow her inside. "It's a good thing for you the Prophet – peace unto him – forbids me to profit from selling alcohol."

"But you can hang on to it?"

She stopped in the doorway, the beads on her scarf clicking as she whipped her head back to me. "Holding isn't the same as selling. It isn't the same as using, either." She patted the boy with the oranges on the cheek and entered the stall.

I followed her into the stuffy dark. Hawa's granddaughter hadn't moved from her spot, but the blanket she'd been working on had grown half a meter. A pair of sharpened knitting needles sat on the table within her reach. She only looked up as the four boys entered. Her nose wrinkled, and she went back to her purling.

Hawa ran her hands over the stars on the walls. Shelves and cabinets popped open, and she handed out jars of pickled turnips, loaves of vacuum-packed bread, and can after can of chickpeas. "How do you fit all this in here?" said Onanefe as he struggled with his stack of food.

"Excellent engineering," said Hawa, kicking open the panel that had held my rum. "Plus twenty years of hiding stuff from the police."

"Ahem," said Soni, her arms full of water filtration packets.

"Oh, like you didn't know what I was doing," said Hawa.

"I knew you were never doing anything *dangerous*," said Soni.

"I could have been."

"Ladies, please," I said. "You're both badass. Can we get on with it?"

Soni grumbled and headed outside. I picked up the case of Old Windswept and gave it a gentle shake. The triangular bottles rattled against the sides of the crate, their bumpy sides clinking. A thin layer of dust coated the green glass, turning the rum inside the color of industrial pollution. I didn't like to think of my rum like that, so I set the case down and gave each bottle top a wipe with the inside of my shirt. The bottles, and the rum, now looked more appealing.

Outside the stall, everyone had piled the food on the now-upright table. The kids had multiplied, probably summoned by the smell of the hibachi that Onanefe was fanning. A few other adults had arrived, and some of them had brought food: packages of fish jerky, wreaths of noodles, and a bunch of plantains. No one looked happy, and one Freeborn woman shot me dirty looks, but they milled about the table, waiting for an excuse to tuck in.

I put a bottle of Old Windswept on the table and cracked the top. "I know it's early, but would anyone care for a taste? I'm afraid we don't have cups."

"We do now," said KajSiab, setting bamboo plates and mugs on the table. She shrugged. "Murray Henson wasn't at his homewares stall, so I left a note."

I poured a tiny sip into a teacup and handed it to her. "Cheers."

She downed the rum in one gulp, then sucked in a breath. "Oh, my. That is nice. You going to have some?"

"Maybe later," I said, looking to Hawa. "Were you really going to sell my stash?"

She shook her head, the beads clicking. "It would have been haram. Besides, there wouldn't have been any profit in it."

"You could have gotten more than thirty yuan a bottle," I said, shooing the boys away from the rum.

Hawa chuckled. "Whatever the margin, it's haram. You should make sure those sales people from your Co-Op know that."

"What sales people?"

She waved her hand in the air, like she was chasing away a trifling thought. "It was weeks ago. Some nice young lady showed up at closing time, going from stall to stall. Talking about buying shares of some Co-Op fund. I told her not to waste her time with the faithful, just to keep on walking–"

I put a hand on her wrist. "Shares in *what*?"

She shrugged. "A mutual fund, something like that. Said it was going to let us all become investors in the Co-Op. She was very kind, with really incredible skin. I'll give you that, Padma. You put your best-looking salespeople out there..."

But I didn't hear the rest of Hawa's complaint. I couldn't for the sound of all the gears clicking in my head. Vikram's fears about the harvest, Letty's fears about not meeting the budget, everyone's fears of not having enough money for food and meds: my brain rolled them around and around until the pieces fit. "Holy fucking shit. That's what she's doing."

Hawa eased her hand out of my grip. "You all right?"

"No," I said. "None of us are."

"We're not?" said Soni.

"I know what Letty's game is. I know why she's letting this strike drag on. I know why she's letting everyone get pissed off. Oh, my God, I can't believe I voted for her."

"What are you going on about?" said Onanefe.

I pointed at him. "Don't you get it? She's changing her vote. She wants to blow everything up."

EIGHTEEN

"Okay," said the man with the missing ear and the abacus tattooed on his cheek. Once again, I wished the goddamn Public was fixed so I could ping this guy and find out his name. "Explain this to us like we're stupid."

"What, were you in WalWa middle management?"

That got a laugh from the crowd. There were now a few hundred people gathered around Hawa's stall, all of them munching on tacos or sipping bowls of the stew we'd knocked together from second-hand vegetables and questionable cuts of meat. I recognized a few faces, merchants and rabble-rousers and attractive street poets who'd drifted in and out of my orbit every time I came to Bakaara. They were fed, and calm, and attentive. They were also angry, and I was making sure their anger had focus.

I tapped the marker on the side of Hawa's stall. She had protested when I started scribbling on her table, so I started writing on the pourform walls with a packet of marker pens the kids had found. Longshore crews used pens like this to scribble on the sides of cargo cans before they went up the cable. The ink was durable enough to deal with the hazards of deep space, and the colors were electric and vibrant.

Hawa's gray stall now looked like the aftermath of a fight between a bunch of MBAs and abstract expressionists.

"Where does money come from?" I held the marker to a box at the very top of my chart. It had a single yuan symbol.

Abacus Cheek said, "Well, when an economist and a central planner love each other very much..." A titter ran through the crowd.

I pointed the marker at the man. "Mister, maybe *you* ought to be talking instead of me."

He waved me off. "Sorry about the heckling. I just been hiding under my couch for the past few days, and... you know. Letting off steam."

"No, please, keep it up," I said. "I'm terrible at being funny."

"That's not what I've seen," said Soni, leaning against a coral steel beam. Another laugh. It was good to hear that instead of shouting. "But if you're talking about *value*, it comes from us. Our work."

"Right you are, Chief Accountant." I touched the capped marker to the yuan symbol. "We all know what our work is worth, because the Union and the Big Three have sat down and hammered it all out. We know what the price of cane is, we know what the price of meds are, we know how to trade one for the other. And it's worked pretty well until it hasn't."

Below the yuan box was a green box with the word CANE. One of the kids, Jianji, stood on a bench, filling that box with black dots. He gave me a look to see if he should stop; I shrugged, so he kept on dotting. "When the black stripe hit the fields, it meant that we couldn't sell cane until Thronehill certified our crops were clean. Since they're a bunch of dicks, they still haven't done that, even though everybody who knows anything about cane can tell you we're good to go. The Union, of course, had prepared for this, in the form of something new and exciting from my friends at the Co-Op."

The kids had drawn arrows between the CANE box and the silver CO-OP box. Below the CO-OP was the word MUTUAL FUND in blue. "For the price of a single blue boy, you can buy twenty shares of the Santee Anchorage Rum Co-Operative Mutual Fund. Eventually, you sell those shares, and you hope that the price has gone up enough so you get back more than you put in. But the big question is: what are they shares *of*?"

Everyone looked at each other. Even Abacus Cheek was quiet. "The Co-Op, right?" said Onanefe.

"And what does the Co-Op produce?"

"RUM!" everyone answered, holding their cups aloft. Against Soni's protests, we had made a simple bumboo by grabbing an empty molasses barrel and filling it with water, lime juice, honey, whatever spices we could cadge from Little Jan Sørensen, and Old Windswept. It was a pretty weak punch, but it meant my case would go a lot farther.

"Correct!" I called out. "The Co-Op ensures that we'll make rum to a certain quality, sell it at a certain price, and that everyone will back up everyone else if need be. A union for boozers."

"Best kind," said Abacus Cheek.

"You'd think so," I said. "Because whenever there's a serious crisis, the Co-Op falls apart like wet ricewheat paper. For example." I tapped the CANE box and smeared one of Jianji's fresh dots. He gave me a glare, and I glared right back until he backed off. Now was not the time to let an eight-year-old interrupt me over a tiff on artistic integrity. "Vytai Bloombeck's gengineered black stripe was a wild card that none of us had prepared for. We could handle small outbreaks, because that would mean losing only a few thousand hectares at most. Bloombeck's black stripe cost us fifty million hectares, then put the other five billion out of commission. Neither the Union nor the Co-Op had plans for that because, as far as I can tell, it was too terrifying an idea. Too big a failure to contemplate."

I spread my hands to the crowd. "Except it's happened, and now we're here on day seven of a planet-wide strike that no one seems to have expected, with the exception of the congregants at the Temple of the New Holy Light. And they were prepared because Leticia Arbusto Smythe" – I tapped a box with LETTY in red letters – "is the one really in charge. Not just of the Union. But of the Temple, of the FOC, of this entire strike. She's behind the Mutual Fund, too, in clear violation of the Union's Second Clause, which states that the Union shall not do anything it's not contracted to do, including selling shares in rum-backed securities. She's calling the shots, and she's not going to stop until everyone's burned themselves out."

That got me stony silence from everyone with ink on their faces. Even the Freeborn looked uncomfortable. "That's a hell of a thing to say," said Abacus Cheek. "That's some Ghost Squad shit there."

"I wish it were Ghosts," I said. "I wish I could point at Thronehill and say that it's all the Big Three's fault. It would be a hell of a lot easier to get everyone on the same page and march on the Colonial Directorate and remind those fuckers that they don't manage *us*, no matter what the Contract says. *We* manage ourselves. *We* make this planet run. People like us on every world in Occupied Space, *we* make sure there *is* an Occupied Space."

I cleared my throat. This next part made my guts shrivel and my stomach flip. If I couldn't sell it here, then I couldn't sell it anywhere. This crowd, these people, Union and Freeborn, cops and marchers, the scared and hungry, they were everywhere in Santee City. I took a breath and plunged in.

"And that's why it kills me to accuse Letty of not only letting this chaos happen, but of orchestrating it. She told the Chief of Police to stand down, she let gangs of criminals come back from Maersk, and she goaded Evanrute Saarien into pushing for a planet-wide strike when she *knew* our food and medical stores were at their lowest. She strong-armed the Co-Op into forming the Mutual Fund as a backup plan, then used her assistants to push shares on everyone with spare cash. But she didn't make any contingencies for the lifter getting cut."

"By you," said Abacus Cheek.

I nodded. "By me. And I will spend the rest of my life living with the consequences of my choice, but I won't apologize for it. If Bloombeck's black stripe had gotten to the anchor, if it had spread to just one ship–"

"If," said a woman holding a burrito. She had stars inked on her face and forearms that looked like they were made of coral steel. "That was all just a possibility, but you went ahead and did it. You cost me work."

"I know," I said, looking at her right in the eyes. "And I'm sorry that happened. But if I hadn't–"

"If you hadn't, some other world *might* have gotten in trouble," she said. "*Might*. You have no idea what would have happened. But that didn't stop you, O Great Sky Queen Of Justice. You were up there, and you made a choice on your own, just like some Big Three executive. You didn't consult your fellow members. You didn't ask for a vote."

"If I could have, I would have. The Ghosts had smashed all the comms on the platform, they'd scrambled the Public lines... oh, and they also had control over our pais. I was sitting on a pile of contaminated molasses. Would you rather I had let it go? I could have done that, and then the Ghost who had hijacked the lifter would have hijacked a ship and *jumped from orbit*. It would be tough to have a vote as you're being vaporized."

She snorted. "Rah, rah. You save us, and you still screw us. All for what?"

"To save everyone else." I pointed at the fist on my face. "Remember this? We all fight together, or we die alone. That means fighting for everyone else who's Union, even if they'll never know you're helping them. It wasn't an abstract decision. I was doing what I was supposed to do."

"Deciding everyone's fates on your own?"

I shook my head. "Going up the cable meant helping everyone else in the Union. If I had stayed on the ground when that bad molasses hit orbit, then what good would I have been? If Bloombeck's black stripe had spread, it would have wiped out cane, and that would have wiped out everyone else's livelihoods. If I let that happen, then what good am I? If we're not going to stand up for each other, if we're not going to take care of each other, then why be a Union? I hated making that choice, but I would do it again. Some Big Three assholes came here and wanted to burn us to ash. You're goddamn right I blew up the lifter, because I know that any of you would have done the same.

"And now someone's screwing with us, and it's not just one of our own, it's our President. We *chose* her to make the hard choices that are supposed to benefit us all, and it turns out she's not making them. She's not doing anything to ensure the Union can pay out benefits or disburse cash to all the subcommittees that run our city. And there *are* choices she could make. She could ask all of us to cut back, or to share what we've got, or to work together to get the cane recertified so we can get some cash rolling in. She could work with the Co-Op to put the freeze on all those Mutual Fund shares. She could, God forbid, work with all the Freeborn who have been demanding seats at the table.

We could come up with solutions together.

"But she's not doing any of that. She's winding us all up, letting criminals loose from Maersk, and giving them machetes or churches. She's made us afraid of each other, all in the hope that we'll be so busy hoarding cans of pickles or fighting each other that we won't turn on *her*."

That silenced the crowd. I had to get them buzzing again. "I don't like pointing fingers at Letty. I don't make these accusations lightly. I'm not the police, I'm not the courts. I'm just a rank-and-file member who thinks the Executive Council has lost sight of what it's supposed to do. Letty and the rest have forgotten the First Clause: the Union exists to protect its members from the Big Three. How can she do that when she can't protect the members from *her*?"

Abacus Cheek rubbed his face as he rocked back and forth. It was so quiet I could hear his boots squeak on the pavement. "Then what do you propose we do?"

"We start with what we're doing now," I said. "We remember why we Breached our Indentures with the Big Three." I nodded to Onanefe. "Or we remember why we didn't join the Union. We break out the bottles and the grills and the tortilla presses, and we sit down and eat and talk. We remember that *this* is the life we chose, everything that goes with it, even the crap work and the miserable hours and how nasty the air smells when the palm crabs are mating."

Jianji gagged. "That's the worst."

"Indeed," I said, giving him my marker. He got to work drawing stars around all the boxes. "This is how the Union started in the first place. Somewhere, back in the mists of time, a bunch of people got pissed off with the Big Three and Breached. They worked together to find gigs on their own terms, they looked out for each other, and they did their best not to climb over each other. We've all had lean times, and we've all dealt with disasters and crap Contracts and getting stuck in horrible Slots. Hell, I used to be a Ward Chair, and now I muck out the mains in the Brushhead Water Works."

"But you own a distillery," said Star Woman.

"No amount of rum will ever make up what I owe for blowing up the lifter," I said. "And I know my wages won't, either. But it's part of taking responsibility for my choice, and I'll keep doing it until the day I'm ready to become compost. I stand by what I did, and it's time for Letty to do the same."

I waved my hand at the lower part of my presentation. "Every movement needs goals. This chaos sweeping over our city has none. So we're going to whip some demands on the mob. Number One: turn on the damn Public."

"I'm missing my stories!" called Big Jan from the grill. Finally, another laugh from the crowd.

"Number Two: we do what we're doing here, but for the entire city. Everyone empties their larders to make sure everyone gets fed. No more hoarding, no more price gouging. If it took a week for our city to fall apart, then it'll take a month to get us back on our feet.

"Number Three: full accounting of the Union's finances, including any connections between the Union and the Co-Op's Mutual Fund." I touched the words on the wall. "This is a big one, because it's going to show what's been happening with the money. We all need to know what's happened with our dues, with the money earned through the Contract, and just what the hell happened with all those Mutual shares. This is the kind of thing that will get people tossed into prison.

"Number Four: Letty and the entire Executive Committee are out, and they're banned from any committee work for ten years. Same goes for anyone else responsible for the riots."

"Why not ban them for life?" said one of the crowd.

"Because we still need the people we've got if we're going to keep Santee from sliding back to the Industrial Age. We're not the Big Three. We don't have an endless supply of skilled workers. Plus we still have to live with each other, and that means reconciling with the people who've wronged us. If someone committed crimes, they need to be charged and tried. But if they just got caught up in the madness, then we need to work together and move forward. No grudges. That's poison."

"So, cookouts and presentations are what's going to stop this mess?"

"If everyone's busy eating and talking, they're not hiding and hoarding," I said. "Twenty-four hours ago, this place was in riot. Now you're all here eating tacos and drinking bumboo. I think there are more people like us all throughout Santee. I would even say that the vast majority of people would rather talk and eat and drink instead of fight each other for a pack of dried beans. Don't you think so?"

Nods. A lot of unsure faces.

"Seriously? Are the tacos that bad? If they suck, then we need to get something better. Come on!"

I pushed through the crowd, stepping over people as they munched away. I got two stalls away when I realized no one was following me. "I'm completely serious," I said. "It's not enough for us to get you here. We need to take this to another neighborhood. Soni! You know this city better than I do. Where should we go next to get something to eat?"

Soni coughed. "I could really go for doubles over in Bluffton."

I snapped my fingers and grinned. "Perfect! You talking about Jaffa's? Let's go!" I grabbed the closest able-bodied people and hauled them to their feet. "We are going to

Jaffa's, and we're going to ask Min-Na James to fire up the cooker and make us some by-God doubles."

"What are doubles?" asked the woman I had pulled up. She had a crane tattooed on her cheek.

"Well, you're not going to find out by sitting here." We passed the remains of a dry goods stand, and the glint of glass caught my eye. I scooped up two liter jars full of chickpeas. Serendipity. "By the way, what's your name? 'Cause I'd rather not call you Crane Face while we walk and talk."

Half the crowd followed me, all of them buzzed on excitement and bumboo. I told Sharon, my new friend, all about the curried channa and the chutneys and the crunchy bara that make up perfect doubles. She told me about how she worked a Contract Slot on the Sou's Reach reconstruction project because no one else could do her job. Also because no one wanted to be near the rotting molasses mess that Saarien had presided over during his tenure as Ward Chair. She wasn't that keen on reconciling with him. I wasn't either and said as much, but I pointed out that we would have to work with the fucker if we were going to get through this mess together.

Jaffa's was two kilometers away, and I led the hundred or so that followed me through the streets. I made a point of talking as loud as I could, and my voice bounced off the shuttered rowhouses. People had broken out the hurricane shutters, and the coral steel slats not scored with soot glinted in the late morning light. Piles of burned garbage smoldered in the gutters, and someone had painted a giant red Union fist in the middle of the street. Someone else had added a raised middle finger in white.

A few doors opened as we passed, and the wary faces of men, women, and children peeked out. I made a point of waving at everyone who made eye contact with me. "We're going to Jaffa's!" I yelled. Most of them slipped back into their houses, the doors banging shut. A few joined our little parade, though, and I made sure that anyone who was hungry got something to munch on.

Jaffa's sat on the corner of Vicarage Street and Ham Park Road. A cloud of frying oil and curried chickpeas should have hovered over the intersection. Now there was just the stench of ash and rotting trash. The shop wasn't just closed. Min-Na had put up the hurricane shields, then hammered boards across the door and the windows. For a finishing touch, he'd splashed paint across the front: CLOSED UNTIL YOU SORT OUT THIS BULLSHIT. I knocked on the door, the hurricane shield rattling under my knuckles. "Min-Na! How much for doubles?"

A rock crashed next to my feet. I yelped and hopped back. Min-Na James and his son stood atop the flat roof. Both of them had fist-sized rocks in their hands, and their arms were cocked back. They had tied their dreadlocks back into tight braids, and their faces were hard and exhausted.

"Can't you read?" yelled Min-Na.

"Well, I'm trying to sort out the bullshit. Does that warrant some lunch?"

Min-Na narrowed his eyes as he looked at the lot of us; one of his dreadlocks drifted out of his hair clip and flopped across his temple. "What are you talking about?"

"I said, we're working things out. I'm really hungry and would really like doubles. You open or what?"

He lowered his arm, then leaned over the edge of the roof. "Are you serious?"

I held up the jars of chickpeas. "Even brought something in case your stocks were running low."

Min-Na looked at the jars. "I hope you don't expect me to feed everyone with *that*."

I looked back at the people behind me. There were a

lot of new faces, and some of the buttoned-up houses had opened. I turned back to Min-Na. "How much would you need?"

Within the hour, the shutters at Jaffa's were off. The three cafés and the ramen-ya farther up Vicarage had also opened up, but the smell of curry and frying bara overpowered everything else. Min-Na had turned his nose up at my offerings. ("They're dried, and that'll take a day to soak into usefulness," he'd said, handing the jars to his son before opening up his walk-in fridge.) His eyes were dead tired, but he smiled as he stirred giant pots of simmering chickpeas in the kitchen. His son poured curry on the baras and handed the doubles out. People crunched their food, leaning forward to keep the sauce from dribbling down their clothes.

I found a closed-up flower shop whose owners didn't respond to my rapping on the hurricane shields. After getting the pens back from Jianji and his friends, I redrew my diagram from Bakaara, linking all the different groups that had failed us. If my professors from B-School hadn't had heart attacks when they'd heard I'd Breached, this cobbled-together chart would have done the job. Precision counted, not just in data but in presentation. I'd done so well in my classes, and, now, sixteen years later, I was writing on walls in an attempt to convince people to stop fighting and work together.

This time, I didn't try to get everyone's attention. I just talked with the people who drifted over, food in hand, to find out what I was doing. A few turned away as soon as I told them, but most stayed and listened. A lot of them argued, saying that this was all the fault of the Freeborn or the Union (and a lot of that depended on whether the speaker had a tattoo on their cheek or not). Everyone took pictures with their pais, saying they'd pass around what they saw through peer-to-peer. I reminded them to pass around food through the same method.

One woman with a metal Temple pin on her shirt gave me an angry stare as she wiped at the boxes. The ink didn't smear, so she just rubbed harder. Finally, she banged on the shutter and got in my face. "We are *not* dupes!" she yelled, a finger held up to my nose.

I smiled. She huffed and walked away.

"That wasn't pleasant," said Onanefe. He had stood a few meters away and let me do the talking.

"No, but it's to be expected," I said. "No one likes finding out that the thing they believe in is hurting people. I'm sure I'll get plenty of Union people screaming at me soon enough, calling me a traitor and a parasite and all that." I shrugged. "As long as no one's swinging machetes, they can yell all they want."

"You think this is going to be enough?" He took a bite of his doubles, cradling the bara and leaning forward like a pro. "These little block parties?"

"They'll have to be," I said. "If we can get more people out into the streets to eat and talk, I think we'll have a breakthrough by dinner."

"You've got a lot faith in the people."

"I have faith in their stomachs and their need for someone to do something."

"But not themselves?"

"I am always willing to step aside if someone who isn't insane wants to take the lead," I said, wishing I'd gotten a second doubles for myself. "That person has yet to show up."

"Give it time," said Onanefe. "Once word gets around about the free grub, you're going to have everyone showing up, including the nutbars."

"Maybe," I said, my stomach growling. "But first, I'm

getting seconds."

Min-Na stood at the door as I entered his place. "Hope you've got a line on some more food," he said. "At this rate, I'll be out in a day."

"In a day, I hope everyone will be spending money again," I said. "In the meantime, could you make me one more with extra pommecythere chow?"

"We're all out," he said. "Unless you want to go in the back and make more."

I nodded. "Tell me what to do, and I'm on it."

He grunted and handed me a key. "The pantry's behind, in the alley. Get everything you can carry. They're about to go bad. And don't lose my key!"

I walked through the kitchen to the alley. A pantry shed as big me stood against the café's back wall. Inside were sacks of pommecythere, all orange and spikey and fuzzy. I scratched the skin off one and took a whiff, and the smell like sweet mango and sharp orange floated into my nose. I chuckled as I scooped up the bag. Twenty-four hours ago, I was hiding in a burnt-out konbini. Now everything almost felt like normal. I'd make the chow for Min-Na, hit a few more neighborhoods, then get home to Brushhead to rally Big Lily and everyone else. Tomorrow, we'd press our case against Letty and end all this bullshit.

Someone bumped my shoulder. "Jesus, Min-Na, I haven't lost your key–"

I had just enough time to register Jennifer's smooth face and dead eyes before she put a black bag over my head. I smelled the harsh tang of chloroform, and I was out.

NINETEEN

I woke with a start, the bag still over my head. I was on my side, my hands bound behind my back. I strained; the caneplas zip tie cut into my wrists. The floor jumped, and I bashed my shoulder (the one that I'd forgotten had been stabbed until *now*) into something heavy and metal. I fought to get up, but I just knocked my head against whatever had hurt my shoulder. I rolled on the floor for a bit until my head cleared.

"Don't thrash," said Jennifer from my left. It was the older one. "The Prez wants you unbruised."

I tensed, then let out a breath as I got to my knees. "Should I be happy that she hasn't killed me, yet?"

Jennifer snorted. "You think this is all about you. No wonder you were so bad at being a Ward Chair."

"I was a *great* Ward Chair, because I made a point of not trying to murder anyone else."

"If the Prez wanted you dead, you'd be dead."

"What about you? You want me dead?"

The floor bumped, and I realized we were in the back of a lorry. "Well?"

Jennifer cleared her throat. "Just don't talk. It's easier if you don't talk."

I felt a hand on my neck, and that was answer enough. I took a guess where the hand's owner's nose was and drove my head up as hard as I could. I made contact but didn't hear that satisfying *crunch*. Instead, I got a harsh laugh. "You can't hurt me, remember?" she said. "That whole reinforced skeleton. Just stay down. She wants you unbruised, but she didn't say anything about unhurt."

"What's in it for you? Or do you just like cracking skulls while your sister sells Mutual shares?"

"I told you to stop talking."

"Why? Letty's going to kill me when she's done with me. Whatever her scheme is, it's going to end up with a lot more people hurt or dead. She'll probably do the same to you and your sister. She doesn't care about you or me or anything but hanging on to power, Jennifer. She's letting our city burn. She's setting off car bombs. She's–"

That got me a zap from a taser. My body stiffened, and the scream froze in my throat. *Fuck*, I hated tasers.

I fought for breath. "Jennifer, people will *die*." I ran through my brief interactions with her and tried to think of a single time she'd shown weakness. Everyone had one. What was hers?

Agamjot Patil. Jennifer froze when she saw Agamjot unconscious on the floor. "Did you really Breach so you could see kids die?"

Jennifer whipped the bag off my face and held the taser up to my nose. "I swear to fucking God I will put this into your eyeballs and pull the trigger."

Bingo. "You went through all the trouble to Breach. You pulled your little sister with you before she signed an Indenture Contract. You didn't want her to do the same shit you did in Security Services. You wanted to get her away from all that."

The taser shook, the leads bobbling at the edges of my

vision. I kept my eyes open as The Fear snickered, *This is either the biggest gamble or the stupidest thing you've ever done.*

"What's in it for you?"

Jennifer backed away and put the taser in her belt. "She knows where our littlest sister is." Her voice was flat, and she stared off into a corner of the lorry. "I was the first, something that came out of LiaoCon's Advanced Armaments. All three of us are prototypes, fast-tanked to grow and learn quickly." She looked at me. "How old do you think I am?"

"About my age."

She shook her head. "I'm twenty-six. I went from decanting to adulthood in three years. My younger sister is about nineteen months old."

I swallowed. "What about your other sister?"

She worked her jaw. "She looks about twelve, but she's only eight months old. Or was, I guess."

"What happened to her?"

"The two of us, we tried to bring her with us. We got popped at the anchor on Luminous. You know the planet?"

I nodded. "It's where LiaoCon execs go when they think the Life Corporate isn't indulgent enough, right?"

"That's that one," she said, her voice now a whisper. "I faked a work order to bring them along on an assignment because I thought Luminous would be the perfect place for us to Breach. All those ships coming and going, and Security Services would be so busy making sure the wrong people didn't get in they wouldn't care who tried to get out. We were at a berth, waiting for a fueling crew to finish. We were going in through the main reactor coolant lines, see? Our skin could handle it. Two of us got in before fifty goons showed up. We reached back for Jennifer, but they got her by the legs. We pulled, and they pulled, and..." She shook her head, then let the weight of her skull carry her gaze to the ground. "She made us let go. Raked our wrists, jabbed at nerve points. We couldn't hold on. She let us go. Letty knows how to find her."

"How?"

"She could get the entire Union to look for her. All of it. Through all of Occupied Space. She gets priority spots on the punch probes. She showed us."

"What, your sister?"

"No, how it worked." Her throat caught once. "I believe her. She has the reach. She has the power. I miss our sister. She let us go so we could live free." She looked at me, and I thought my heart would break from the way her perfect face and perfect eyes now looked as weathered and beaten as a hardcore dockworker's. "You can't do that. Not you, not your Union."

"*Our* Union." I nodded at the fist on her face. "You joined. You became one of us."

"Because it was *convenient*." Her sadness turned to a sneer. "There's no solidarity. There's no great big circle looking out for each other. Maybe there's families that do that, but not here. Not anywhere. The Union is worthless."

"It's worth what you put into it," I said. "I put in my work, my time, my life. Lots of others do, too. We all get lost, we all lose focus, but we don't let go of that bond, Jennifer. Five fingers make a fist, and a lot of fists make things happen. You help me get out of this alive, and I will find your sister."

She snorted. "You can't deliver on that."

"I can sure as shit try," I said. "Letty may be the Prez, but I'm the Sky Queen of Justice, remember? People sing my song all over Occupied Space."

"Like a washed-up Ward Chair can do anything."

"I got people to stop beating the crap out of each other and start talking. Has Letty done that?"

The lorry came to quick halt. I skidded toward the front of the cabin, but Jennifer stayed planted, like her shoes were magnetized. The back slid open, and Jennifer's younger twin stepped in. They both picked me up like I was a sack of potatoes and hauled me into the middle of a cane field. It was mid-afternoon, and the air was thick with water and heat. I started to sweat right away, though that may have been from terror when I saw Letty standing in the middle of a small clearing. She held a lit blowtorch.

I fought against the Jennifers as best I could, kicking and thrashing. They just tightened their grip, one of them squeezing my lungs until I gasped for air. They threw me at Letty's feet. "Really?" I yelled at her. "I knew you were bad news, Letty, but I didn't think you were a sadist."

She looked at the torch and laughed. "I'm not going to use this on *you*, Padma."

I allowed myself a small breath.

"No." She shook her head as she adjusted the flame. "That would be too obvious. Someone's going to find your corpse, and someone back in Brushhead will demand an inquest. If it looks like you were tortured, it would make things difficult." She nodded to the younger Jennifer, who tossed something in front of my face. The sun glinted off the bumpy sea-green glass. "But I don't think anyone's going to make a fuss over a drunk, despondent distillery owner wandering into the middle of an unsanctioned cane burn. I mean, Soni will, probably, but she's going to be too busy fighting for her job, what with the tuk-tuk bombings and all."

I lunged for her ankles. I had no real balance or leverage, so I just got a faceful of dirt. "Why?" I spat.

"Because it works," said Letty. "There isn't enough cash to go around. You know that by now, what with your cute presentation and all. Accusing me of running everything like I'm some Big Three CEO, pulling strings and letting people starve just so everything balances out."

"It's true, isn't it?"

She *tsk*ed. "You'll never know." She hopped over me, kicking the bottle as she went. She scooped it up and unscrewed the top, pouring the rum all over me. "You make good stuff. I wonder what kind of prescription Dr Ropata would write for you now? You think he'd tell you to drink two fingers of rum? Light a bigger candle?" She smiled as she held up the torch. "I got that covered."

Letty walked to the edge of the clearing and lit the cane on fire. The stalks began to smolder, then burn like sweet, sticky torches. She walked around me, igniting the cane until we were in the middle of a ring of fire. I got my knees to my chest and rolled on them, my shoulder complaining as I got upright.

"How did you know about Ropata?" I asked. "Give me that, at least."

Letty turned off the torch and tapped her temple. "Remember those Ghosts? The little old ladies? It's amazing the kinds of backdoors they could access."

"Weren't you supposed to close them?"

She shrugged. "I don't like destroying useful tools. If I'd known about it when I was in the FOC, I'd have skipped the bombing vote and pushed for hacking into everyone's heads instead. It's a lot more convenient. Which reminds me."

She reached into her jacket, pulled out a handheld bolt driver, and shot both of the Jennifers in the chest. They crumpled to the ground before they could cry out. I could see the older Jennifer's face curled in pain as she gasped for breath, her eyes locked on Letty as she fell to her knees. Letty wrestled Jennifer's limp arms behind her back and snapped a zip tie around her wrists. She did the same to the other Jennifer.

"What are you doing?" I yelled.

Letty pointed the bolt driver at my head. "I am doing my job, Padma. I am making the hard decisions that no one wants to. I am going to steer us out of this crisis, and if it takes a whole lot of dead people to do it, well. At least none of you were from where I grew up."

"Except Onanefe."

"And he'll get his pretty soon." She shook her head, her aim not wavering. "I always questioned his loyalty to the rest of us. The way he spoke about not bombing the ever-loving shit out of you Inks, you'd think he loved you." She lowered the bolt driver. "But you can't use the master's tools to dismantle the master's house. You've got to make your own, even if it means blowing everything up. We're going to have a better world, Padma, but you won't be there to see it. Not after your tragic demise."

"Fuck you, Letty."

"Absolutely tragic," said Letty, tossing the bolt driver in my direction. "A drunk, despondent distillery owner who took two Union stalwarts hostage and executed them. She started a cane fire to cover her tracks, but, since she had zero actual experience in the fields, she was done in by her own cover-up. When word gets back to town, everything you've said will be discredited. And when your role in the tuk-tuk bombings is revealed..." She gave a mocking moue and covered her mouth with her free hand. "Oops. Said too much."

I held up my bound hands. "Don't you think someone would notice *this*?"

She shrugged and gave the cane one more blast with the blow torch before tossing it toward me. "Details are for conspiracy theorists. Good-bye, Padma. Thanks for the vote."

I didn't watch her get in the lorry; I was too busy struggling to get my hands free. Letty had used a good, local-pressed zip tie, not the crappy Big Three kind that snapped if you looked at them funny. All I got was skin burns from trying to flex my way free. A stand of dried cane exploded as the flames touched it; sparks stung my cheek. I buried my face in my shoulder as the heat grew and grew. I was now in the middle of an ever-encroaching ring of fire, and I was so fucking angry about that I could only lie on my back and kick at the ground.

You're going to die here, whispered The Fear.

I stopped struggling against the zip tie and hissed, "No."

No, I was not going to fucking die here. No, I was not going to give in to The Fear. No, I was not going to let Leticia Arbusto Smythe win, not when I could find a way out so I could march back into town and kick her ass all the way into the ocean. No, I would get out of here and kick Letty's ass all the way past the Red Line.

Of course, that meant escaping a ten-meter-tall ring of fire. The afternoon winds had started, and the flames roared higher with every gust. The smoke grew so thick I could barely see the orange of the fire. For once, being stuck on the ground gave me a small advantage. The air stayed clear down here. That gave me a little bit of time.

If I couldn't break the zip tie, I'd have to cut it. I tried reaching for the multi-tool I always kept in my cargo pocket, but I didn't have the reach, of course. So, I'd have to get some reach. That meant getting my arms in front of me.

I hunched over as far as my spine would allow and scootched my ass through the loop of my arms. My back began to holler as I pushed my chest towards my hips. What kind of horrible yoga move would those freaks at the Mermaid's Kick have called this? Buddha Contemplating Her Navel? Inner Facing Idiot? I pushed my shoulders out, sucked my gut in, willed my body to get through the hoop...

I had my arms just far enough before my back flexed.

My wrists caught on my hamstrings, and I could move no farther. I was stuck on my back, looking like a trussed-up hog. Another cane stalk exploded into fireworks, and a hundred white-hot needle-points stabbed my neck and face. The fire was getting hotter and closer, and I was going to melt like a caneplas bottle…

That was it. I didn't have to break the zip tie. I just had to weaken it.

I rolled side-over-side toward the flames, getting a faceful of dirt with every rotation. Sweat poured down my face as I got closer to the fire, and ash now mixed with the soil, hot and soft. I coughed and spat the whole way, half-blind until I couldn't get any closer to the heat. I held my wrists at the crackling flames, pulling at the zip tie and praying it would move enough.

I strained, and my wrists burned, both from the heat and the bite of the caneplas. My whole body was slick with sweat, and my face felt like a mud mask. I pulled my arms as far apart as I could, hoping for just enough room to slip my legs through. I could tell the zip tie wasn't budging. Hot as it was, it wouldn't melt the caneplas. I had to get closer. *You can't do it*, cackled The Fear. *You can't get out of this, because you're not willing to sacrifice. You'd rather hide in your miserable hole in the sewer, clutching your rum and letting the universe spin on without you. You're nothing, and you're going to die–*

"Fuck *you*," I said and plunged backward into the fire.

It hurt. Sweet Working Christ, I couldn't remember the last time I'd done anything that hurt like the fire. It wasn't like getting punched or stabbed or tased; it was waves of pain flashing over my neck and wrists, cutting through my trousers and deck jacket. I could feel blisters forming on my hands, but I held the zip tie in the fire until I felt it give. I screamed as I brought my arms up past my knees, to my ankles, over my boots. I flopped out of the fire, rolling and rolling until the flames on my jacket and trousers were out.

My hands were tomato red, and the stench of burning hair (Jesus, *my* hair) filled my nose. I got to my feet, only to take in a noseful of smoke. Down I went, flopping over the older Jennifer's legs. She gave a tiny cry, and I gave one back. I scrambled off her, then knelt by her head. "Hold still, okay? Just–"

She coughed blood. Blood dripped from her nostrils and her mouth. The front of her shirt was a red, sodden mess. The bolt, a twenty-centimeter coral steel shank, stuck out her sternum. She swatted at me as I tried to gather her shirt to press into a bandage. "Useless," she hissed, a little more blood dribbling from her lips.

"Shut up. We'll get out of here, and we'll all kick Letty's ass."

She snorted and winced. "So stupid. Believing… stupid." Jennifer gurgled, and I pulled her into my arms. Bleeding out was bad enough, but drowning in her own blood… that was no way to go.

"Is she going to set off more bombs? Jennifer, I need to know."

Her head bobbled, like a newborn's. Her eyes lost focus and closed.

I gripped her hard. "Jennifer, I will find your sister. I will find her. But you have to help me."

She opened her eyes long enough to sneer. "Useless. Too soft." She coughed again, and she died. I set her down and checked on the other Jennifer. She had taken a bolt right through the heart.

I went through their pockets and found my multi-tool in one of their pockets, along with their tiny rebreathers. They also had four packets of CauterIce. My fingers were useless, so I tore at the first with my teeth. My lips went numb as some of the gel spattered out, but I didn't care. I squirted it on my hands and sighed from the orgasmic relief of not hurting. I used up the other packets on my neck and face, even rubbing a little on my scalp.

Now all I had to do was not get roasted alive.

The fire had swollen in the afternoon winds, and the smoke sank lower to the ground. My thin layer of clear air was vanishing fast as it fed the fire from the roots up. I remembered what Marolo had said about slash-and-burn drills: *Dig, cover, hold.* Digging wouldn't be a problem; the soil was loose. But cover? The Jennifers had nothing I could use. Their clothes were just as flammable as mine.

But their skin wasn't.

I worked as fast as I could, kicking dirt with my boots until I had a space big enough for me to curl up. I dragged the Jennifers over, leaving a trail of bloody mud behind. The cane crackled, all those hydrocarbons burning bright and hot, even in their undistilled, unprocessed form. There was a reason cane burns were controlled on Santee; this stuff was meant to power cities and starships. This wasn't going to burn out quick and clean.

I lay down and pulled the Jennifers over me. I bit down on the rebreather and did my best to follow my old EVA training: nice, relaxed breathing was the way to go. I had put the Jennifers on their backs, which made my shelter only slightly less creepy. I closed my eyes and thought about how cool the air was... until I remembered why the air was so cool. Then I just screwed my eyes shut even harder.

The shelter got hot for a moment, and the stench of burning clothing filled my nose. There was no point in blocking out what was happening to me, but that didn't mean I had to embrace the situation. Fuck that. This was a horror show, and even The Fear had the decency to shut up. Some of this was my fault, sure, but I wasn't the one who'd shot these two women. I wasn't the one in charge of a bombing campaign. And I definitely wasn't the one who'd shut off the money spigots. Everyone back in town, hungry, angry, just wanting to get *paid*. Hell, I'd wanted to get paid, too, if only so I could throw my salary into the gaping maw that was my debt. Even if I sold my distillery, it wouldn't make a lick of difference. What would I get? A few million yuan, maybe? What could I do with that?

I could pay everyone for a week with that.

I stopped breathing for a moment. What was the number Letty had thrown at me? I tried blinking my pai back to life, but my eye was still screwed up. I thought about squirting the last of the CauterIce in there, then realized, no, that was an incredibly stupid idea. I'd have to rely on my good ol' inboard memory.

I pictured the scene in my head: there was Letty, there was one of the Jennifers, there was me. Letty was waving the bottle around, saying the Union was broke, that it took... dammit, what was the number? Two million? No, it was *two point eight million yuan to keep everyone paid for a week, bennies and all*.

And how much had Vikram said I was worth? *Two and a half, easily, just from the cane alone. Throw in the actual product, and three is a fair offer.*

I had a way to beat Letty. Holy shit, I could sell the distillery, pay everyone on the planet for a week, and end the strike. Everything that had come screeching to a halt would move again: the inspectors would certify the cane, the cutters would harvest it, everyone would process the cane and send it up the cable, because the cable would be working. I could jump-start Santee's economy, and all I had to do was sell the one thing that kept me sane.

Excellent idea, said The Fear.

Except I had my stashes. I had enough Old Windswept hidden all over for the next thirty years. Forty, if I pushed it. "Ha!" I said. The rebreather fell out of my mouth. I scrambled to shove it back between my teeth. I didn't care that it tasted like dirt; I had a *plan*, and it was *good*, and I was going to *kick Letty's ass*.

I waited until the rebreather beeped, letting me know its air filter was done. How long had that been? Thirty minutes? I popped in the second one, but it started beeping after a few minutes. That must have belonged to the Jennifer who'd helped burn my building.

I pushed the bodies off me and got up. The world around me was ash and cinders, all smoldering in the afternoon sun. The wind had blown the fire northeast. To my southwest was singed cane. I looked back at the dead Jennifers, their clothes burned away and their skin blacked with soot. I pulled them side-by-side and cleaned their faces as best I could before snapping a picture. More evidence. I'd send someone back to collect the bodies.

I started walking into the wind. The scorched cane was still hot as I slipped through the stalks. When I got to a stand of clean, unburnt cane, I spat out the beeping rebreather and started jogging.

By the time the sun had dipped toward the horizon, I had spotted a lone comms tower in the distance. That tower meant a transfer station or a loading depot. I hoped it also meant someone who didn't want to kill me. I pushed through the cane as quietly as I could until I heard people talking. I crawled, the edges of a pourform building looming past the stalks.

It was a small farm house. A cycle tractor sat in the front yard, kids climbing up its three-meter-high wheels. A five year-old girl, her face lit up in the twilight, perched on the saddle, barely reaching the handlebars. "I'll stop you, you corporate parasite!" she yelled. "No one can stop the Sky Queen of Justice!"

I sighed with relief. I had found fans.

I stepped out of the cane, my hands in front of me. One of the kids spotted me and froze. Then they all looked up, their mouths agape. "Hi," I said. "I'm Padma Mehta. Are your parents home?"

"They're working," said the girl in the saddle, her voice blank. Then she started and kicked the kids below her. "See! I *told* you the radio was wrong! She wasn't dead!" She jumped down and ran to me, though she stopped half a meter short. I could only imagine how I looked with my toasted hair and sooty skin and God knew how much blood on my clothes.

"Are you really her?" she asked. Her hair was a mess of curls and braids, and her overalls were covered in anime character patches.

"I am. Am I really supposed to be dead?"

She nodded. "The Prez was on the radio just before dinner. Said you were a..." She screwed up her face to remember.

"A traitor!" yelled one of the boys.

"She is not!" the girl yelled back.

"What's your name?" I said.

She looked at her feet. "Laural," she said, her voice just above a whisper.

I took a knee in front of her. "Well, Laural, I promise you I'm not a traitor. As sure as I'm alive. Do you believe me?"

She looked at me, her ocean-blue eyes as big as stars, and gave me a nod. "But I don't know if anyone else will."

"If you help me, I can show I'm not."

Her mouth bunched up into a barely suppressed smile. "How can I help?"

"First, I need you and your friends to run and tell every adult that you saw me, and that I'm going into the city."

She nodded.

"Second, I'm going to need to borrow *that*." I pointed at

the tractor.

Laural hopped down and swatted at one of the older boys who held on to the wheel. "She needs this ride! Back off!"

I climbed up into the saddle. The tractor was just a tricycle with ridiculously big wheels and a whole lot of gears. I gave the pedals a gentle push, and the tractor crunched forward on the gravel.

"One more thing," I said as I aimed the tractor toward Santee City.

"What?" said Laural.

I grinned. "You gotta give me a head start."

TWENTY

Two hours later, the sun had gone down, and the lights of Santee City came into view. I just kept pedaling.

I had kept the tractor off the road, pushing through the cane at a snail's pace. The tractor was meant for hauling bundles of cut cane, not as personal transport. It was a ridiculous machine, the kind of thing that popped up all over Santee through ingenuity, stolen parts, and sheer pig-headedness. It would have worked just fine on the gravel paths back to the city, but I needed the time to think and plan. A plan might keep me from getting killed for real.

A plan might help you get to Six O'Clock, said The Fear. I just kept pedaling.

The only thing on my side was the fact that Laural and her friends had fast feet and big mouths. Rumors obeyed their own special laws of physics, and those laws got torqued when kids were involved. All the adults in the kampong would certainly know of the unscheduled and unauthorized burn, and having the kids tell them that I had emerged from the embers would get other people talking. Eventually, those people would talk to whomever Letty had told that I was a two-timing, back-stabbing, double-murdering villain, and then the debates would start as both stories started wrestling with each other. Letty may have had access to the Public and all of our pais, but even she couldn't stop the residents of Santee from bullshitting with each other.

Of course, Letty had a whole lot of bombs on her side. I just kept pedaling.

Any other night, and I would have probably loved to ride like this. The evening breeze was cool and strong, straight from the depths of the kampong. All that green from the leaves, all that funk from composting bagasse, all that sweet tang from the cane itself. All those billions of hectares of industrial and heirloom, enough energy to power starships, cities, one-night stands. I'd come out here so many times, but tonight felt different. And not just because I was in peril.

I pulled the brakes. The tractor came to a gentle stop. I stood up in the pedals and looked around.

Behind me, the last of the orange faded from the sky. Above me was a canopy of deep purple, lit by a billion stars. When I was a kid, sitting on my parents' veranda after dinner, I'd look up at those stars and think about visiting all the planets orbiting them. I knew most of them were uninhabitable rocks, but I wanted to go anyway, just to see the sky from a different world. I would hop from one world to the next, spending my days collecting views of constellations that no one else would see or care about.

No one bothered to name the constellations when they landed on Santee. Not even the first Breaches did, and their souls were lit up by the poetry that comes with liberating themselves. There were songs and paintings and shadow puppet plays about everything that happened to the first people to get themselves windswept, but none of them had looked at the stars and made pictures out of the points. I had never understood that. They were so busy creating their own mythology, why wouldn't they keep going all the way past the sky?

I took in a breath, letting the smell of cane fill my head. The sky spun, all those stars upon stars, all those billions upon billions who called Occupied Space their home. Somewhere there were other versions of me: the Indenture fighting her way up the Corporate ladder, the Union stalwart punching that Indenture in the face, the little girl looking up at the night sky. If we could talk, what would I tell them about my life? What would I ask them about the choices I had to make? What would I say to them?

I turned my eyes to the eastern horizon, the city lights flickering in the heat haze. There was none of the blue glow from the streetlamps; all of the light must be coming from people's houses. A few streaks of orange reached for the sky – fires, probably. Whether they were from more tuk-tuk bombs or from people torching each other's neighborhoods, I'd have to find out when I got to the city.

My city. My beautiful, messed-up city. I loved this place when it was in a good mood, hated it when it became sulky and selfish. People didn't always work together. The weeks after signing the Contract always saw an increase in bar fights and street knifings. Some idiots would try to make guns, saying the Ban was a relic of another time; that people had to protect themselves. It took a few arrests and angry block meetings to remind everyone that we had to protect each other from the Big Three, not from ourselves. God, no wonder the Freeborn always scorned joining the Union. A week without pay and the idea of solidarity dissipated like a fart in a hurricane.

I looked back at the kampong. I knew the way to Tanque, but I wouldn't go there. I *couldn't* go there, not when Letty was tearing Santee down just because she couldn't think of another way out. People had been pissed at me for making the hard choice. They could sure as hell do the same for Letty, seeing how making hard choices was her job. Messing with our pais, letting the city slide into chaos – that was the kind of crap we'd expect from the Big Three, not our own. I was going to make her answer for everything she had done to me, to the Jennifers, to all of us. And I was going to do it by showing her how wrong she was.

I turned toward the city, stood up in the pedals, and got cranking. I was exhausted, hurt, and hungry, but spite would get me to Xochimilco Grove. That, and the satisfaction that would come with kicking Letty's ass.

Two hours later, I left the tractor at the edge of the kampong. The Co-Op Building loomed over the cane as I pushed my way through the field. Light streamed from the windows, but it was harsh and green, the kind that came from chemical lamps. Shadows paced the top floor, and I heard bottles smashing inside. What better time to put my distillery up for sale?

Someone had tried to build a barricade at the end of Chung Kuong Street, they but seemed to have quit halfway. Chairs and tables and compost bins were stacked together, but they only came to my shoulders. I climbed up, only to have the whole thing collapse in a heap. Behind it stood Todd, the kid who sat behind the lobby desk at the Co-Op. He brandished a crowbar in front of him, straight end out. "Stop! You can't come in! I'm not afraid to use this!"

I put my hands on my hips. "Really? And what are you going to do with that, Todd?"

The crowbar wavered. "Ms Mehta?"

I snatched the crowbar from his hands and took a fighting stance: one foot in front of the other, the crowbar up and ready. "If you're going to threaten someone with that, you have to use it the right way. Hold it by the straight end, aim the hooked end at whoever you want to scare. That's the part that hurts. Got it?"

He nodded, though the terrified look on his face never left. I handed him the crowbar and gave him a pat on the back. "Work on it, kid. Who's up in the office?"

"Mr Ramaddy. He hasn't left, really, ever since you showed up." He squinted. "What happened to you?"

"You know, a little hostile negotiating with management." I dusted off my trousers, leaving streaks of sweaty mud behind. "Why aren't you hiding, too?"

He swallowed hard. "Someone has to protect the street. There's all kinds of bad things going on."

"True, but all of them are in *here*." I turned him around so he faced the city. "It might be a good idea for you to go home. Keep away from any tuk-tuks."

"But my job is here–"

"And it's not worth you getting killed over," I said. "By the powers invested in me by my distillery, I hereby relieve you."

"You sure?"

I patted his shoulder. "As sure as I can be."

Todd sagged and handed me the crowbar. "Thank you." He looked at the ruined barricade. "I can work on that before I–"

"Go."

He went. I waited until he was out of sight before approaching the Co-Op Building.

All the furniture had been shoved against the windows. The ridiculous couches and uncomfortable office chairs made an even worse barricade than the one Todd had built. Through the gaps I could see someone walking through the lobby. A giant shadow loomed on the lobby wall, made cancerous by the green chemical lights inside. The steel doors were locked tight, so I banged on them as loud as I could with the crowbar. "Vikram!"

The shadow stopped moving. I banged again. "It's Padma! Open up, Vikram! I want to talk business!"

Shuffling feet approached the window. Someone moved a set of chairs aside, and there was Vikram, his beard now devoid of henna. His face looked hollow, and his eyes had sunk even further into his skull. "Business? I know of no such thing."

"I want to sell my distillery."

His eyes drifted toward mine and came into focus. He straightened up. "Padma?"

"That's who I said I was."

"And you want to sell–"

"The Old Windswept distillery, yes."

He blinked. "To me?"

I rapped on the window pane, and he jerked back. "Do you have three million yuan?"

"Well, not *personally*…"

I held up the crowbar. "Seven days ago, you tried to snatch my distillery from under me. Now I'm here to sell it, and I'm not in the mood to dick around. Open up, or I'm opening up for you."

Vikram muttered something about the repairs coming out of my dues, but he moved toward the door. I heard him grunting and furniture scraping for a few minutes. The steel doors unlocked and creaked open. "No power," said Vikram, standing aside. "So the mechanisms don't work."

"They will in a few hours," I said, squeezing into the lobby and wishing I hadn't. Vikram had dropped glow sticks on the floor, making them into a small circle around a smoldering trash can fire. Empty rum bottles formed arcane patterns around the glow sticks. "Have you been in here the whole time?"

Vikram nodded, his face ghoulish in the chemical light. His guyabara was limp, and sweat stains darkened its armpits. "It's not safe out there, Padma. You know what they say about civilization being two meals away from anarchy. Once the shops ran out of food–"

"They didn't," I said. "People just *thought* there was a shortage. There's plenty to eat."

"Huh." He scratched his beard, his hand disappearing into its depths. "Of course, if the Public had been up–"

"It is," I said, stepping over the bottles. "Letty's just yanked our access."

"She do the same with the sun? Because the rooftop PVs don't do anything anymore."

"The inverters are tied into the Public, so she probably did something to them, too. There *is* power."

"And food?"

I nodded. "If you come out with me, I'll show you."

He laughed, though it sounded more like a cackle. "That's a good one. Go outside. No, not when Union and Freeborn are blowing each other up. I saw the explosions. It's a war zone outside."

"It's Letty again."

His smile faded. "Why would she do that? Blow up her own city?"

"Because she's wanted to burn us to the ground for fifteen years. She's just finishing the job."

"That makes no sense."

"None of it does, yet here we are. Doing business. Can we get to it?"

Vikram twirled his beard as he stared at the fire. "You're serious?"

"Like a heart attack. I believe you said the offer was around three million."

He stopped fiddling with his beard. "That was a week ago."

"So? It's not like the yuan's collapsed."

"But the Co-Op has!" Vikram clamped his hands over his mouth. "I'm sorry," he said through his fingers. "I shouldn't shout. Stressful situations are the worst time to shout."

"I'd shout if I were in your shoes," I said, pulling a chair off the window barricades. It looked like one I'd helped steal from Thronehill. A whole week of this bullshit, and I just realized there hadn't been a response from the WalWa compound. How had Letty dealt with them?

Vikram let his hands slip down his face. "All the members of the Co-Op voted to disband, because no one wanted to help look out for each other. People who'd bought shares in the mutual fund wanted to cash in, and the way the fund was structured, the payments had to come out of the pockets of the owners."

"That's insane."

"Well, that's what we get for not reading the fine print."

"Are you fucking kidding me? It's your *job* to read the fine print. You and Elisheba and the rest were supposed to look out for us."

"We did! We were going to make you all so much money! I mean" – he laughed, his eyes growing wet – "it was perfect. We had so much rum to sell, so much cane to distill, and it was all just *sitting there*, not earning any money."

"You know, it's been a while since I took micro-econ, but I'm pretty sure that we earned money by selling the actual rum, not hypothetical future rum."

"But it wasn't *enough*."

"It was enough for me."

"Yeah." He chewed his lower lip. "It was enough for Estella, too. She said the whole idea was nonsense, and she wouldn't have anything to do with it."

I smiled. Once again, Madame Tonggow's wisdom had temporarily won the day. "So, what happened?"

He shrugged. "The owners were furious. They demanded

a vote. They took it. I objected because our by-laws say that a vote to dissolve has to be done by all the owners, and it has to be unanimous."

"It wasn't?"

He made a face. "Well, *you* weren't here."

"And those fuckers voted anyway?"

Vikram held up his hands. "It all came apart so fast I didn't have time to think of a way to stop it."

"What? When did this happen?"

"Two days ago."

I pulled down a second chair. "I didn't hear anything about this."

"That's because we thought you were dead."

I wait a moment before dropping the chair. "What!"

He nodded as he sank into the chair. "You'd been blown up in a bombing. Or cut down by a gang of machete-wielding Freeborn. Or you'd hijacked a freighter and piloted it into the sun."

"And you didn't think to check? Like, have someone run to Terminal Island and call up the anchor and ask, 'Hi, has Padma Mehta stolen a freighter?'"

"No, because everyone wanted you *out*. They never trusted you, Padma, no matter that Estella had vouched for you. 'I've built this distillery with my own hands, and I'm not going to let someone who got their distillery through legal tricks stop me from protecting me and mine.' Crap like that. They voted, then ran off to bar the doors and hide."

I lowered myself into a chair. "God, what a bunch of assholes. The minute they get a bigger piece of the pie, they just don't care." I snorted. "Not that I can point fingers."

"I don't recall you leaving your Slot."

"Because I was stupid," I said. "I should have told the Union to go to hell and stayed in Tanque for the rest of my life."

"That's not you."

"Yeah? And just what do you know about me, Vikram? Have we ever talked outside of Co-Op meetings? Have I ever invited you out for tacos? Have you ever asked me home to meet your family? And why the hell aren't you with them right now?"

"They're safe, with my parents, way out in North Key." He smiled. "The fact that you know I have a family says that, at least, you pay attention."

"That's just good business."

"No, good business is not giving a damn about anything but the bottom line." He tapped his cheek. "That's what I learned at MacDonald Heavy. Keep it in the black. Doesn't matter who gets hurt or killed along the way, as long as you keep the numbers in the black. The third-best decision I ever made was Breaching. Getting to say good riddance to all that bullshit saved my soul."

"Only the third best? What were the other two?"

He laughed. "Second best was asking Ojana out for coffee." He looked at the coral steel band on his left hand. "And the first best was coming here instead of Collai Prime."

"Collai Prime is a beautiful place."

"But it isn't *this* place. The Union has a strong presence there, but it doesn't run the planet. And all they grow is industrial, which means they're completely locked into the whims of the Big Three's evil brains. Rum isn't much to start an industrial base, but it gives us a tiny sliver of independence." He sighed. "Except when it doesn't."

"It could have, if we hadn't gotten tied up with Letty's plans."

Vikram stroked his beard. "She drove a hard bargain. Those two women she sends to do her dirty work… they terrified us. Just sat in the corners and stared, like reef eels daring you to get too close."

"She killed them," I said, and my throat tightened up. "Holy shit, Vikram, she shot the two of them just a few hours ago."

He leaned forward. "What?"

I told him of my adventures over the past few days, making sure to emphasize Letty's problems with fire. By the end of the story, Vikram was the picture of angry sobriety. He stood up.

"You okay?" I asked.

"No," he said. "I am most definitely not." He stepped over the mandala of bottles and made for the stairs.

"What are you doing?"

"I have some important papers for you to sign, so come along please."

I followed him to his office. It was slightly less of a disaster area than the lobby, but not by much. A week's worth of laundry hung from the ceiling, and empty canning jars lay about the floor. The only thing untouched was the filing cabinet. It looked like a monument to bureaucracy, standing proud in the middle of chaos. Vikram spat in the lock and slid a drawer open. He wore a mad grin as his fingers danced through the forms. "Yes!" he cried, holding one aloft. "Eight twenty-six stroke B, 'Abandonment of Co-Operative Membership Prior to Title of Transfer.'" He cleared a space on his desk and started writing on it.

"That sounds downright poetic," I said, reading over his shoulder.

"I'm assuming that you want to get as much money as possible for your distillery while giving the Co-Op the finger, yes?"

"There's a form just for that?"

"There is." His smile grew as he wrote. "This means that you are withdrawing from the Co-Op, and that you are due any moneys owed to you. As you weren't a part of the

Mutual Fund, you're exempt from paying out shares. You're also entitled to certain administrative damages thanks to the other members voting to dissolve without you." He looked up. "Everyone has to work together. If some members want to stick it out, and everyone leaves anyway, they need to pay back whatever the dissenting members have sunk into the Co-Op. Dues help everyone, even if no one takes the help."

I smiled back as what he said sunk in. "In other words, by paying dues but not giving a shit, I'm actually going to come out ahead?"

"Better than that, you can call up another vote about dissolution. In fact, you have to, because it's the only way that the other members can hang onto their money." He tapped the form with his pen. "This was built into the Co-Op's DNA. Work together, or pay separately."

I thought for a moment. "Is there a way to make sure that no one can buy controlling shares of Old Windswept?"

"Indeed there is." Vikram pulled another sheet out of the filing cabinet. "Four sixty-four stroke C, 'Disbursement of Shares Pending Transfer of Title.'" He scribbled on this one. "You can't stop people from buying shares, but you can limit how many each buyer can buy. Of course, the other members might collude, but–"

"Considering how they're so bad at playing together now, I can't see them shaping up any time soon. Where do I sign?"

Vikram pointed at the six spaces on each form that needed my signature. I held the pen over the first line and froze. "Twelve years ago, right after Hurricane Paik, some asshole had looted my shitty little flat in Partridge Hutong. The only important thing I had in there was a bottle of Old Windswept. I didn't want to be caught unawares like that again, so I went to the distillery and bought a case. It ate up all my savings.

"I'd never met Tonggow until I went out there to make the pickup. I'd taken the bus, then walked, 'cause I was so damn broke. It was a hot day, so I was this sweaty, dirty mess when I got to the distillery. Tonggow met me at the front door and gave me a glass of heavy mint tea. She was done up like a society grande dame – pearl earrings, hair permed – but she also wore work boots and a coverall. Didn't say a word about my appearance. Just asked about work and how long I'd been on Santee and how I liked to drink my rum." I laughed. "I just said I took it neat, a little finger at the end of the day. When I started walking down the road with the case, she made her foreman give me a lift back to town."

My hand shook as I stared at the lines. "She texted me the next day to ask how the party went. She'd assumed I had bought all this rum for some kind of bash, and I was too embarrassed to make up a story. I told her about getting ripped off, and then she acted embarrassed, like she'd overstepped some boundary I didn't know about."

"I hid the case with a neighbor I trusted, but she got ripped off, too. Now I was broke, and all I had was the bottle I kept with me at all times. Even if I'd had the money, I couldn't go back and buy another case. How would that have looked? I know it looked bad enough that I always had this bottle of rum with me."

I took a deep breath. "I need to take a drink every night, Vikram. Something happened to my brain when I was in transit. The hibernant damaged my posterior cortex, and if I don't take a sip every night at six o'clock, then I will begin to go crazy. And I don't mean the way that a real rummy gets the shakes. I mean that…"

My left hand hovered over my skull, my fingers wavering. The Fear let out a guttural shriek: *He won't believe you*.

I looked at the form and remembered what it felt like to

read the deed two years ago. *Banks believed me*. I swallowed and looked Vikram right in the eye.

"I call it The Fear. First it eats away at my confidence. Then it takes away my cognitive abilities. I forget how to draw a number three or what color the sky is. There's no real treatment here, not when there are so many other mentally ill people who *really* need the few meds we get. So, a doctor said that I should light a candle, think about my place in the universe, and sip a finger of Old Windswept. It's kept me sane for the last sixteen years, and I never told Estella Tonggow that it was the only reason I wanted to buy her distillery. I should have been honest with her, Vikram. She wouldn't have said boo. That woman had smarts and class and compassion, and she got killed because of me. That Ghost Squad? One of them killed her just to get to me.

"And now Letty's going to try and do the same thing. When she finds out I'm alive, she's going to do everything she can to slander me, to make me look like a basket case, even though *she's* the one who shot two women right in front of me. God knows what else she's done, but she's not going to get one over on me again. She won't be able to. I need that distillery, but it's not worth it if this whole planet burns just 'cause I'm too chickenshit to stop her."

I signed all six lines. Vikram blinked at each one, then handed them back to me. "You might want to make copies for yourself."

I pointed at my right eye. "My pai's a little busted. What now?"

Vikram scooped up the papers and put them inside his jacket. "Now, I'm going to help you make a metric fuckton of money. You ready?"

I smiled. "I like the cut of your jib, mister. Let's go."

TWENTY-ONE

Vikram and I had gotten to the lobby when he stopped and blinked. "Holy cow," he said. "My pai just came on."

"Big surprise. Letty's probably watching all of, ah, OW..."

My right eye burned as hot orange text scrolled past. I clamped both hands over my eye, but the letters and the fire continued. Any screams I might have had were caught in my throat as the text turned into error messages. Angry error messages. The kind that transformed into lightning bolts that ran from my pai straight into my brain. And I couldn't turn them off.

I might have heard Vikram calling my name. I know I felt someone try to pull my hands off my face, but I sent my elbows flying. Moving my hands would mean taking away the pressure that was keeping my eyeball from exploding. It also meant that I couldn't escape the onslaught of messages until they suddenly stopped on their own. I caught my breath. The burning had stopped, too.

After a moment, I looked at Vikram. He rubbed his thigh. "That hurt."

"Sorry," I said, my heart still pounding. "Did you get a bunch of errors?"

He shook his head. "You okay?"

"No, but I'll have to deal with it later." I lifted my hands from my eye. It didn't blow up, which was nice. It still hurt like hell. I opened my eye, and Vikram made a face. "Looks a little bloodshot, but not too bad," he said. "Can you see me?"

I nodded, then tried blinking. Another jolt, followed by more errors. "Guess mine isn't back online. Can you make a recording for me?"

"Of course." He squared his eyes at me but didn't blink. "You want to clean up or anything?"

I looked at my ragged clothes, touched the streaks of dirt on my face. "No," I said. "I want everyone to see me as I am. Hit it."

He blinked and pointed at me: *You're on.*

I took a breath and smiled. "Hi. Believe it or not, I'm Padma Mehta, and I've had a really, really weird forty-eight hours. We can talk about that later, because I want everyone to know now that I'm putting the Old Windswept Distillery up for sale. You can find the particulars on the Public, along with the terms of the sale. If you've ever wanted to roll with the swells in Chino Cove, now's your opportunity. My share price is firm, so don't bother to negotiate."

I was about to say, *I can't get your messages anyway*, when, for once, my brain's better judgment kicked in. Letty may have had a backdoor into my pai, but she might not know that it wasn't working properly. "Seeing how everyone's pai access has been spotty, the best way to reach me will be through any Public terminals that are still operating. I'm in Xochimilco Grove, and I'll be making my way to Brushhead. I hope that some of you have heard or seen the presentation I made this morning in Bakaara Market. If you haven't, start asking around." I leaned toward Vikram and smiled. "It's the one where I accuse Leticia Arbusto Smythe of engineering the strike to cover up her malfeasance. Oh, and she murdered two people in front of me before she tried to burn me alive. So, you know, I wouldn't really put a lot of stock in what she has to say."

I nodded at Vikram, and he stopped recording. "How long until the shares start moving?"

"No idea," he said. "It'll have to filter out across the Public, and that could take–"

He flinched and blanched. "What is it?" I said.

"They're gone. All sold." He laughed. "I think you should check your bank account, Padma. You've just become insanely rich."

We left the Co-Op Building for the nearest Public terminal. It stood on the corner of Chung Kuong Street and Singa-Laut Boulevard, covered in tags. Someone had lit a trash fire next to it, and soot filmed the screen. I wiped it clean and logged in. The number that popped out of my bank account made my heart skip a few beats. I had never seen that many commas in a number that belonged to me. Three million forty-six yuan. Tonggow's asking price had been a whole lot less. My guts twisted. She had built that distillery from nothing, and she was going to hand it to me for a song. I wondered what she would have thought about all this. Maybe she would still appreciate the romance of it, though damned if I could find any right now.

"Is there any way to know who the buyers are?"

Vikram shook his head. "One of the perks of being a member of the Co-Op is that you don't have to tell anyone outside of it who's in."

I narrowed my eyes. "So I'm really out? No longer a part of the Co-Op?"

He shook his head again, and his eyes were actually sad. "You don't have a distillery anymore, Padma. I wish you still did, 'cause getting all these new buyers involved is going to be a massive pain in my ass."

"Well, like they say, when one door closes, an entire house falls on you."

"Are you really going to start spreading that money around?"

"Looks like I have to now."

"Any way I can help?"

I thought for a moment. "Tell everyone you see that I'm making payroll."

He raised his eyebrows. "Everyone?"

"Well, everyone you think *needs* the cash. If you run into anyone from the Executive Committee, for instance, feel free to tell them to go to hell."

He gave me a nod and made his way up Singa-Luat.

I pulled up Public profiles of people who could get things running again. The city had to be fed, cane had to get pushed up the cable, and everyone probably needed a doctor. The closest address was a family of longshore crew two blocks over. It wasn't just any family: the Shavelsons were three generations of Union stalwarts living under one roof. They were the kind of people who showed up to every committee meeting and complained, even for meetings outside of their Ward. Ethylene Shavelson, the matriarch, would spend her allotted two minutes of public speaking to denounce me, the Big Three, the Union, and anyone who was on her ever-growing list of People Who Had Done Her Wrong.

The Shavelsons' house was four stories tall and looked like it had attacked and grafted other houses on to it. Ethylene had buried four husbands, and each one had added a few kids to the brood. Some of them moved out, but most stayed under the ever-expanding family roof. Each Shavelson kid who brought home a spouse added on to the house by cannibalizing bits from other neighborhoods. There were pieces from the striver rowhouses on Cheswell, panels from cargo can hutongs, even some black glass roof tiles from the Union office at Beukes Point.

I banged on the door, and got a gruff "Fuck off" from inside.

"I'm here with payroll," I yelled.

There was a pause. "Bullshit," came the reply.

"There are sixteen of you in here who haven't gotten paid in weeks, and I am prepared to drop nineteen thousand yuan into your accounts. This offer expires in two minutes."

The door swung open, and Ethylene Shavelson, all one and half meters of her, filled the doorway. The streetlights glinted off her face. She had decorated her tattoos with dots of reflective ink so her face looked like stars on black velvet. She had done the same with the tattoos on her massive arms. "That should be nineteen thousand *twenty* yuan," she said, her voice sweet as honey. Behind her, in the shadows, I could see a few grandkids peeking out from the end of the hall.

"Really?" I said. "Well, it's a good thing you're on top of your family's salaries, Ethylene."

She sniffed and wiped her upper lip with her thumb. "What are *you* doing here? You've got nothing to do with payroll or cargo."

"It's a new day, Ethylene, and I am putting myself in charge of both. I want you and your family to get back to work."

She squinted up at me before bursting into laughter. "Oh, that is funnier than the time you tried to punch Diesel at the Union Hall."

"She was prying the ornaments off the clock face," I said.

Ethylene shrugged. "She wanted to make a mobile for her baby. Do you not like kids?"

"I love kids. I just don't like it when their mommies vandalize an important piece of neighborhood art 'cause everyone's too afraid to call them on their shit."

Ethylene tightened her smile into a smirk. "You come here to sour talk my daughter?"

"I came here to get your family and your entire crew to work sending cargo up the cable. That's forty-five seconds. You want to get paid, or you want to hide in your castle for another week?"

She rolled her eyes. "We've been through strikes before."

"They had a *point*. This one doesn't. Or are you going to tell me otherwise?"

Ethylene leaned against the doorjamb and sucked on her teeth. "I'm going along with everyone else. I hear there's a strike, I go on strike."

"I admire your sense of solidarity. Can you eat it for dinner?"

"We got plenty stashed."

"I'm sure. What about your crew? Have you checked on them?"

Her smirk crinkled. "Some of them aren't doing so hot, no. Georgiou Little, he's out of insulin. Lucy Cousins, her little girl's inhalers are out."

"Then help me help them by getting back to work. Make the call. I'm good for the cash."

"We'll get paid when the strike's over."

"Then you can send my condolences to Georgiou and Lucy. 'Cause the strike isn't going to end, Ethylene. Letty's going to drag it out as long as possible because it's the only way she can get the Union to cover its debts. If people are dead, they don't draw payroll. If their families are dead, they don't draw benefits."

"That is highly nihilistic."

"And it's the truth."

She shook her head. "You got video to back that up?"

"We're not talking about that. We're talking about you

getting back to work. And my two minutes are almost up."

"Send me a peek at your bank account."

I shook my head. "You want to get paid, you come with me to the Public terminal on Oshkosh and Bloor."

"You don't trust me?"

"I want people to *see* you with me. I'm good for the money. You good with letting Georgiou go into a diabetic coma?"

"I want to know what your game is."

"There is no game, Ethylene." I stepped back from her front stoop. "There's just people who work because we don't live in a future where we've become beings of pure thought who subsist on light. We live in the future where we've got to work to put food on the table to keep from starving. We chose to Breach and join the Union, and that means a lifetime of looking out for each other, even if we don't *like* each other. Letty may have failed you, but I won't. Twenty seconds, and I'm walking over to Jack Lopez's house. You know he'll take my offer, and *he'll* be the one convinces everyone else to go back to work 'cause people listen to him."

She bristled. "They'll listen to me more."

"Then walk with me to Bloor."

"Gran?" One of the kids appeared behind Ethylene. He struggled to hold up a kit bag bigger than his torso. "You going back to work? You need your gear?"

"Oy, Markel! Didn't I tell you to stay away from that?"

The boy beamed at her. "I like to help."

"Then you can help by doing what I say when I say it. Gimme that."

Ethylene took the bag just as the kid was about to fall over from the weight. She tossed the bag over one shoulder and scooped Markel into a hug. "You run back inside. I need to finish talking with this lady."

He nodded at her and gave me the eyeball. "You here to exploit my Gran?"

"I sure hope not," I said. "Though that's going to depend on what she chooses."

He stuck out his tongue and ran into the house.

Ethylene shifted the bag, keeping a firm grip on the straps. "Nineteen thousand, huh?"

"And twenty."

Ethylene grunted and turned back to the house. She put her fingers in her mouth and blew a whistle that rattled the windows. "It's a work day!" she yelled. "Get a move on!" There was a clatter of feet, and, within minutes, every working Shavelson had assembled in the front hall. A few of them weren't wearing pants, but everyone had their kit bags.

Ethylene jerked a thumb at me and addressed her family. "If what this woman has to say is true, then we're all going back to work. If it isn't true, you can throw her into the ocean off Sou's Reach."

Diesel Shavelson Thompson cracked her knuckles, then cracked her husband's. I just smiled. "If you'll all follow me, we can get started." I hustled down the street, the Shavelsons all muttering amongst themselves. Only Ethylene had a pai; all her kids had to exchange information the old-fashioned way.

When we rounded the corner to Bloor, I saw six other people holding kit bags huddling around the terminal. I stepped back to Ethylene's side. "Send a little message, did we?"

She *harrumph*ed. "It'll take more than the sixteen of us to get things rolling." She smirked. "Besides, if you hadn't mentioned Jack Lopez–"

"He's going to get paid, too," I said. "Everyone is."

"Yeah," she said, hitching her kit bag on her shoulder.

"But we're getting paid *first*."

I sighed. "Rah rah, Solidarity."

I looked into the terminal's retinal scanner and spat on its touchscreen. It unlocked, and I saw that big, beautiful bank account balance stare back at me. There was so much I could buy with three million yuan: the best food, the finest men, the kind of life only meant for the upper echelons of Big Three Shareholders. I could fulfill my every physical need for the rest of my natural life. Hell, I could probably extend my natural life. Lord only knew what weird biomedical kinkiness the Big Three had dreamed up while I'd been on Santee Anchorage. Maybe I could buy myself a brand new brain. That would show The Fear who's boss.

No. There would always be a mess to clean up, and I would rather spend my money cleaning up this mess. Plus, there was the chance to spite the ever-loving hell out of Letty.

I typed on the touchscreen and beckoned to Ethylene. "You're due back wages from before the strike. This amount look right?"

She glanced and nodded. "What about today's wages?"

"You get those when you clock out at the end of your shift. I've got it punched into the Public, and I won't be able to cancel the order."

"You can always cancel an order."

"But not this one. We square?"

She spat on the touchscreen, and the terminal said, "Contract approved. Congratulations!"

We shook hands, and she squeezed extra hard. "What about tomorrow's wages?"

"That depends on how much you dock monkeys can send up the cable."

Ethylene laughed. "You just watch." She nodded at the rest of the longshore crew, and they all stepped up to spit on the dotted line.

By the time I had paid out that first twenty-one people, another twenty had shown up. Six of them were Freeborn. "You can march right back to the kampong," said one of the non-Shavelsons, a guy with a wagon wheel tattoo.

"We heard you're paying back wages," said one of the Freeborn, a woman with freckles and a tightly wound bun. "We're machinists. Did a contract with the Roads Committee that ended before the strike. We never got paid."

"Show me," I said, pointing at the terminal.

"Oh, like she knows how to use one of those," said Wagon Wheel. The rest snickered.

Freckles didn't hesitate. She stepped to Wagon Wheel, keeping a breath away from his face. "You say something?"

Wagon Wheel smiled. "You got hearing problems? Cane in your ears?"

Freckles made a face. "That doesn't even make sense as an insult."

"Go back to the kampong, lady," said Wagon Wheel. "You can mooch off us after we get everything working again."

I took a step toward them, but a powerful hand gripped my shoulder. I looked back, then down: Ethylene held on to me and shook her head.

Henriette Shavelson, the youngest of the clan, marched up to Wagon Wheel. "You got a problem, Nevniz?"

The man shook his head. Henriette was a head shorter, but Nevniz's spine began to invert until he was looking up at Henriette. "Hey, I'm just fooling."

"Fooling. That's funny," said Henriette, with absolutely no mirth in her eyes or voice. "I could have sworn I thought I heard you say something disparaging about someone who says they're due wages. And there's nothing funny about that. Is there?"

Nevniz swallowed hard. "No."

"Damn right," said Henriette. Nevniz took a step back.

Freckles stepped up to the terminal and spat on it. Sure enough, a signed, unpaid contract for five thousand yuan popped up for services rendered to the Roads Committee appeared on her profile. "That should have been a Union job," said Ethylene.

Freckles shrugged. "Steamrollers don't care who fixes them. We were in town, we got offered the gig."

"That doesn't make sense," said Ethylene.

"Of course it does," I said. "What better way to piss off as many people as possible, than by offering a Union job to non-Union people, and then not paying? Ask around. You'll find plenty of contracts like this." I blinked money into Freckles' account, noting that her actual name was Martha. "And I intend on paying as many of them as I can."

"Hey, what about us?" said Henriette. "Your brothers and sisters in Solidarity?"

"Today, there's enough money to go around," I said. "But that also means everyone goes back to work, right?"

The people mumbled to themselves.

"Jesus, I've seen more vitality in a management trainee convention. Are you a bunch of lifeless Big Three drones?"

"Hell, no!" yelled Henriette. A few of her siblings and the Freeborn joined in.

"And are you gonna stand around while the Big Three wait for us to tear each other to pieces?"

"NO." Wagon Wheel and his crew joined in this time.

"Are you ready to remind those Big Three fuckers that they don't own us?"

"YES!"

"Are you ready to get the hell back to work and earn?"

"YES!"

"Then get your asses in gear! Go, go, go!"

They cheered and marched up the street, the Freeborn

swept up with the Union people. Ethylene gave me a wink as she followed her family. I grinned and kept grinning, even as I pulled up my bank account and saw the tiny dent in the balance. Maybe this wouldn't be so bad.

Someone tapped my shoulder. I turned around and saw fifty more people lined up. "You covering benefits, too?" said a middle-aged man with one eye. He had a baby in a sling across his chest.

I took another look at my balance and swiped it aside. "Sign in, and let's see what you're due," I said, doing my best to smile. It didn't work.

By the time that fifty had filed past the terminal, I was down another twenty grand. I was also good and furious after seeing the payments that people hadn't gotten: injuries on the job, pension installments, childcare. All the basics that the Union had been formed to provide, and Letty had let them slide for a week. People hadn't saved because they hadn't needed to. When there were hurricanes or cancelled orders, we came together to get through them. Hell, we had had criminals and lunatics in the Executive Committee before, but even they kept the cash flowing. No one starved. No one got left behind. Seeing these families who'd worked their asses off getting screwed over...

I walked to Shire Square where I found a hundred people standing around the terminal. I didn't say a word. I just marched right to the terminal and logged in. Out went the yuan by the thousands. The words of Romas Landry, the crusty guy who taught contracts negotiation back in B-school, rang in my head: *Any problem you can solve with money isn't a problem at all*. Two years ago, spending this money would have felt like pulling teeth. Now it was the most natural thing in the world. It was going to make everyone's problems go away.

I worked my way southeast, stopping for the ever-growing crowds to spit and swipe. Money flowed like water: it gushed into the accounts of people owed back wages, and it huddled behind dams for release at the end of day's shifts. I left a wake of open storefronts, raucous buyers, and people who were not killing each other. There was also a crowd of a few hundred people who had attached themselves to me. They didn't ask for anything or make any declarations. I got it. They just wanted to come along and see what happened next. So did I.

When we turned onto Asa Randolph Avenue, a group of fifty people waited for us. They carried lit torches and machetes. I saw their shirt fronts glitter in the firelight, and I didn't have to get closer to know they all wore glass Temple pins. I slowed, and my crowd slowed with me.

"We don't want a fight," I called out. "It's time to go back to work."

A woman at the head of the Temple mob shook her head. She was the one who had led us into the murder house. "We're going to cut you all down."

That sent the people behind me into a fury. There were shouts of *Hell, no!* and *You first!* and a whole lot of other babbling bullshit. I turned around and glared until I got silence. It took a while, but the shushes soon overwhelmed the shouts. I looked back at the Temple woman. "No one's getting hurt anymore. I don't know what Letty told you, but it's over. She's going to be done, and you'll likely be going back to Maersk."

She sneered. "We are *never* going back there."

"You're going because you broke the law," I said, loud and clear. Inside, my guts churned. We may have outnumbered the Temple mob, but those machetes could cut down too many too fast. Everyone else would get crushed in a panic. "And you'll go for whatever else you've done this week. We're going to make sure of that."

"You got no evidence," she said. "And you won't have any now." She tapped her temple, and a shout came from behind me: *Dammit, my pai!* It rippled through the crowd. Letty had pulled the plug again.

I took a step forward and blinked hard. "I'm recording you right now. Whatever you do to me, it's going to come back at you. You cut me down, you blow me up, it'll be on the Public for everyone to see. You want to risk that?"

She laughed. "You think we really care about you? About *any* of you? We busted our asses to get here, and how does the Union repay us? You sent us to that fucking rock to rot!"

Well, that probably has something to do with whatever crimes you committed, I made sure not to say. "Then why not come with us?"

She gave me a side-eyes glare. "Where?"

"We're going to the Union Hall to kick Letty's ass."

Now everyone in the street started talking. "We are?" said a man behind me.

"You bet we are," I said. "Because… you know, I've been talking about this bullshit for the past day. You want to know why? Ask around. I'm heading there right now. You want to come with? Come with. You want to cut me down? Do it another day. I got work to do."

I walked up to the woman. She patted the flat of the blade against the palm of her hand. "I'm still going to cut you down," she said. "That's what I got paid for."

"Then I'd rather you find another line of work," I said. "There's not going to be any room for any more thuggery."

She sneered. "Someone always needs to be cut. You're about to do it yourself. You match my price, and I might even–"

I kneed her in the groin. She doubled over, and I managed to slap the machete out of her hand before she caught her breath. She stood up, murder in her eyes. I took a swing, but we both knew it wouldn't do anything but piss her off. I got a fist in the stomach and what little food I'd had that evening splattered on the pavement.

I heard the machete scrape. All I could think of was the taste of bile, the way my body locked up, how this angry, angry woman was going to kill me and start another riot after I had paid so much goddamn money to avoid one. I looked up and saw her smile as she raised the machete...

So I punched her in the groin. Hell, a kick had worked the first time.

This time, she held on to the machete as she took a step back. She hissed something that sounded like "Fuck you," but it was hard to tell from the way she had clamped her lips together. She pointed her blade at the crowd, and they charged in a screaming, roaring mass.

The whole street exploded in a mass of white.

TWENTY-TWO

At first, I thought it was a tuk-tuk bomb. What a lovely way to go: instead of getting chopped to pieces by Letty's thugs, I was blasted to atoms by one of her bombs. It was a great-smelling death, at least. The scent of vanilla hung heavy in the air. Just as well I could only see white fog. This had to have been my brain's way of masking the terror of death: by making everything smell like a milkshake.

Something nudged my side. "Padma? Is that you?" It sounded suspiciously like Soni.

I couldn't move, but I could breathe. The fog cracked in half, and Soni looked down at me. She was in a patrol uniform a size too big, and a streak of grime slashed across her face. "Sorry we took so long. Everyone got so hung up on getting paid that I had to remind them they weren't getting a dime until they went back to work."

"*We*?" I said, reaching for her hand.

Soni pulled me out of a cocoon of hardened riot foam. A hundred cops stood in the streets, all of them in regular patrol outfits. None of them had riot armor, but they were all cradling cans of foam. Behind them were fifty or so white, fluffy lumps, like clouds that had plopped in the middle of the street. "Two precincts' worth of my best people. I've got another two spreading out around the city, opening up station houses, patrolling." She smiled. "You know. Doing the work."

"Is that going to be enough?"

She rubbed her head, now shaved smooth. "Depends if you're really going to try and kick Letty's ass or not."

"Trying is for amateurs," I said. "I'm a goddamn pro."

"Right." She grabbed a cop and told her, "Get me another fifty people, fast as you can."

"What made you come around? Back in Bakaara–"

"I was wrong, okay? I was wrong, and I didn't want to admit I was wrong because I am *also* a goddamn pro." She cleared her throat. "I let you down. I let the *city* down. My gut told me Letty was up to no good, that having everyone stand down was a stupid, bone-headed mistake, and I followed her instructions. I did as I was told." She spat on the ground. "When I Breached, I told myself I was *done* with that."

"You were thinking about your people."

"You're *all* supposed to be my people." She looked away and pulled off her badge. "I don't deserve this."

"Bullshit." I put my hand on her shoulder. To her credit, she didn't snap it off at the wrist. "Put that back on. People need to see *their* police out here. By the way: good move on having everyone wear their street uniforms instead of the riot gear."

She snorted. "Yeah, I didn't think it was good for us to look like an occupying army," she said. "Also, I didn't have enough equipment for everyone. All the assholes who didn't report in apparently raided the precinct houses for supplies, including all our armor. Oh, and *that*" – she pointed at the encrusted convicts – "is the last of our riot foam."

"Well, keep that to yourself. Speaking of which, is your

pai back on?"

She waved her hand from side to side. "Service has been weird."

"Letty has a backdoor."

"Into the Public?"

I tapped my temple.

Soni made a weary face. "So she knows about the foam. And everything else we've talked about."

"I'm working under that assumption. I have to admit, it's kind of liberating to know your nemesis is watching your every move. No need to hide. She can see us coming."

"You realize that gives her an incredible tactical advantage over us, right? A dominating, crushing advantage?"

"I do, but I'm at the stage where I'm past being angry. Now I just want shit fixed. I think everyone else does, too. Speaking of which, you want your people to get paid?"

Soni laughed. "Sure. Who wouldn't? You think Letty can make our payroll?"

I shrugged. "If she wanted to, sure. But I can take care of you guys right now."

Soni narrowed her eyes. "You're serious. That's never a good thing when you're serious. What did you do?"

"I sold the distillery."

Soni's face froze for a good thirty seconds before it curled up in anger. She grabbed me by my shirtfront. "You. Did. WHAT?"

"I had to, Soni! Rallying the people didn't do squat. They wanted to get paid!"

"Oh, so you took it on yourself to become the chair of the Finance Committee? Jesus, here you are *again*, making a big, stupid decision without thinking about the consequences."

"Seeing how doing *nothing* has resulted in fires, bombings, and maniacs with machetes wandering the streets, I figured it was worth the chance. Besides, who's gonna get hurt by this?"

"You, stupid!" Soni let go of me. "As long as I've known you, you've only cared about getting that distillery. Two years later, you're *selling* it? What is *wrong* with you?"

"It wasn't the distillery," I said. "It was the rum."

Soni groaned. "Look, I dig a mojito as much as the next girl, but–"

I took her hand. "WalWa broke my brain, and the only thing that keeps it unbroken is Old Windswept. That's why I wanted to buy the distillery, Soni. Tem Ropata came up with this whole ritual thing, and it *works*. Remember all those times I'd get spacey and weird?"

She smirked. "Show me one person on this rock who isn't like that every now and then."

I wasn't sure whether to hug her or slug her. "The rum has this psychoactive affect, and it keeps me sane. I only take a finger a night. That's it."

The smirk faded. "Hold it. I have seen you ripped to the gills before."

"Sure, on someone else's booze. And has it ever been before six o'clock?"

"Why six o'clock?"

I shrugged. "It's just when Ropata said to do it. That's all. No magic, but it works. And it works because of this place." I laughed. "Holy shit, I finally realized it. Ropata had me figure out my place in the universe, and it always starts here. Wherever I am, I'm always on Santee, in this city, as we're spinning away through space."

"Are you okay?" said Soni.

"No," I replied, "but I know one thing that will make me feel better."

"Does it involve going to the Union Hall?"

"You bet your sweet boots it does. But first, you all gotta get paid."

"You're damned right we do."

The police wages were slightly higher than everyone else's, seeing how they got hazard pay on top of their usual salaries. "Letty declared a state of emergency two weeks ago," said Soni.

"That was a pretty quiet declaration," I said, sending money to the last of her officers. "Great way to spin up dissension in the ranks. Maybe she really is some kind of Ghost agent."

"I have no idea what she is," said Soni. "None of my Freeborn contacts wanted to talk about her."

"Freeborn... oh, God, Onanefe. What happened to him? We need him to rally the Freeborn. Or to stop them from doing something equally as stupid as our people."

"He's okay," said Soni. "Got a detail guarding him."

"A good one?"

"No, Padma, he's being watched by crooks and assassins."

"Hey, at this stage, I have to double-check. Can you get him to meet us at the Hall?"

She waved one of her officers over and passed the message. "He's probably going to bring friends," said the cop.

"Good," I said. "I think that's the only way this will work. Shall we?"

It was a different march from the ones that had happened earlier this week. There were no signs, no slogans chanted. There was none of the giddiness, either. We just walked, picking up people as we went. Soni and the police faded into the midst of the growing mass, breaking up fights and helping people who stumbled. It was six kilometers to Brushhead, and I kept falling behind to pay more people. People broke off as we passed their job sites: network towers, manhole covers, half-finished houses. The tone was somber without being funereal. We were done celebrating and fighting. Now it was time to get back to work, starting with the little job of overthrowing our own government.

Nobody talked, which was good because it let me focus on what little leverage I had. There was plenty in the Union Charter about how to remove a standing president, including processes for times just like this (i.e. the What To Do When The Prez Has Gone Mad With Power subclause). The problem is that they all required a relatively functional city to make them viable. Even if everyone got back to their jobs tonight, it would take weeks for Santee to come out of its coma. That would give Letty plenty of time to regroup as the city bled through its supplies. Plus: she had bombs.

I slowed at every corner to make sure there were no tuk-tuks parked on the street. I shuddered at the *putt-putt* of backyard cane diesel engines. Of course, Letty could have ordered the Jennifers to turn every single object in the city into something explosive. I had no idea how long she'd been cooking up this scheme or how much boom-boom she'd made and stockpiled. With Saarien consulting, she might have carved out a gigantic munitions factory beneath the Union Hall. The first thing I had to get out of her was the locations of all her bombs. Well, the first thing right after I figured out how to get *anything* out of her.

The streetlights flicked on as we turned south onto Solidarność Street. A hundred people stood beneath the pale blue glow, the tired lines on their faces made deeper by the shadows. Onanefe stood in front of them, hands in his pockets.

"The casual look works for you," I said. "Like you just happened to be hanging around with nothing to do."

He shrugged. "I've *always* got something to do. I just choose to look good while doing it."

I embraced him and clapped my hands on his shoulders. "I could really use your help. Yours and every Freeborn you can reach."

He nodded. "You know you got me. You got my crew. Everyone else I've talked to, they're still not sure. There's a lot of talk of just fading into the kampong while the city burns."

"But they're still here."

Onanefe smiled. "People also want to see how this plays out. The wind smells like there could be a new deal in the air."

"There will be," I said. "There has to be. It'll be a lot of boring, unsexy work, but I'm going to make it happen."

"All by yourself, huh?"

"Why not? I already made one big stupid choice today, and it's working out pretty well so far."

He surveyed the crowd. "That is a fine mob you've got for yourself."

"I'll have you know this mob represents a cross-section of Santee society from every trade, demographic, and bar."

"What do you plan to do with this assembly?"

"I have no idea. Maybe we'll sit down and sing songs. I heard that worked on Dead Earth."

"I heard that resulted in people getting blasted with fire hoses and attacked by dogs."

"I like my version better. Besides, whatever we talk about isn't going to be the plan, 'cause Letty can see and hear everything."

He blanched. "It's that damn thing in your eye, isn't it? In all of your eyes?"

"She's got a backdoor into all of our brains. It's not a pleasant feeling."

"She can't control you or anything, right?" His eyes grew wide.

I looked at the crowd. "If she could, she's doing a bad job of it. But she can certainly hear and see all of us. She can access our buffers. I don't think she can get into our Public profiles, but I'm sure she's working on it. The last thing I need is for her to reverse all the payments I made."

"Payments?"

I told him about selling the distillery and his jaw dropped. "That's..."

"Insane?"

"I was going to say 'impressive,' but your word works, too." He cleared his throat. "So, she can see and hear us, which is why you can't talk about the plan. But you got one, right?"

I nodded. "Just come along with me, and you'll see." Right. See how quickly I can pull one out of my ass, that is.

We swept down Solidarność, and everyone got even quieter. All I could hear was the shuffle of feet, like water running down the canals after a hurricane. The clock tower on top of the Hall appeared, its glass face lit from within by an array of multicolored LEDs. Some of the lights were stolen from ships above. Some were made here in town. All of them were of varying quality and hue. Whenever one burned out, the Maintenance Committee just slapped in whatever was on hand, so the clock face became a slow motion light show. The color was mostly blue like the street lights, but, as we got closer, I could make out streaks of red, like angry lightning bolts. I usually loved seeing the clock, because that meant I was going to the Union Hall, and the Hall had always meant home.

We crossed Koothrapalli, and there was the Hall, that simple square of recycled concrete with ironpalm accents. I had gone to this place for more weddings, funerals, debates, sub-committee elections, dances, and hurricanes than I'd lost count. It always felt like sanctuary, the one spot in the city welcome to everyone, no matter their status or trade. Now it was surrounded by a ring of harsh yellow stadium lights, probably boosted from Camp de la Indústria, the football pitch over in Poble Sèc. At the base of each light stood a pair of armored, black-clad, machete-wielding figures. As we got closer, they started clacking the flats of their blades against the light poles. The sound rang across the street and bounced off the face of the Hall. A worried murmur started behind me and, oh God, I didn't blame them. How I wished we were facing WalWa goons. Their clubs hurt, but they didn't cut.

I kept walking. Soni materialized at my side, and Onanefe stepped to the other. I took their hands, and they took the hands of the people next to them. The closer we got, the more the machetes clanged on the light poles. I linked arms with Soni and Onanefe; they did the same with the people next to them. We pulled each other together as the sound of metal-on-metal filled our heads, like we were in the middle of a typhoon made of coral steel.

"If they charge," I said to Soni, "we are all running like hell."

She squeezed my arm. Onanefe grunted.

I slowed in the middle of the street and looked behind me. An ocean of people surged the lengths of Solidarność and Koothrapalli, all facing the hundred with machetes. I unhooked from Soni and Onanefe and walked up to the steps. I focused on the two women in front of me. They had black scarves wrapped across their faces, leaving only their eyes uncovered. I could see a lot of hate in those eyes from the way they narrowed and focused on me. I stopped and yelled above the din, "Would you mind telling your boss we'd like to talk with her about her job performance?"

They just kept clanging their blades.

"We can wait," I said, and I sat down on the sidewalk. Somewhere in the storm of clattering metal, I heard a whoosh of air. I thought someone had thrown something, so I turned and saw everyone else had sat where they were, like we were all at a picnic or a concert. What I wouldn't give to have the Brushhead Memorial Band behind me, tootling out songs while people passed around bottles and plates of tacos.

The women in front of me stiffened and stopped their machetes. Their comrades followed suit. A pregnant silence hung in the air. What would Letty's next move be? What about mine? I know I certainly wanted to throw up just to get rid of the ball of acid churning in my guts, but that would not be a move that inspired confidence.

I took a breath and did the first thing that came to mind: I sang.

"When the union's inspiration through the workers' blood shall run
There can be no power greater anywhere beneath the sun"

– my voice felt thin and wavering, like a candle lit during a stiff breeze. I kept going –

"Yet what force on earth is weaker than the feeble strength of one
For the Union makes us strong?

– it was such an old song, such a *cheesy* song, one that not even the hardest of the hardcore believers in The Struggle could sing without rolling their eyes. It was so bright-eyed and earnest, but I knew it was backed with centuries of *real* struggle, of people who got their heads caved in by crooked cops for the crime of demanding an honest wage for honest work. That's what we all wanted. That's what we all had earned. That's what we were going to get. Not just bread, but our goddamned roses, too. I swallowed the spit out of my mouth, took a great breath and belted out the chorus –

"Solidarity forever, solidarity forever

Solidarity forever
For the Union makes us strong"

I needed this. I needed to hear these words coming out of my mouth, because words were all I had left. I wasn't a fighter or a hero. I was just a woman who'd stupidly signed her life away to a juggernaut that wanted me only as grist for its mill. I was someone who'd walked away from a life that had promised everything even though it valued me for nothing. I was someone who looked at a hundred people with machetes and murder in their eyes and sang the next verse, the cheesiest of the whole song:

"Is there aught we hold in common with the greedy parasite
Who would lash us into serfdom and would crush us with
his might?
Is there anything left to us but to organize and fight?
For the union makes us strong!"

And Soni and a few others joined in with the first *Solidarity forever*, and then another dozen for the next, and then the whole crowd blasted out the words *For the union makes us strong*!

We sang the whole song, all of us, those words from Dead Earth echoing throughout my neighborhood. We got all the way to the last verse, the one written by those first Breaches, the one that started –

"On these shores we built our city, made ourselves a brand
new life;
Indentured slaves no more, free from crushing corporate
strife"

– when the machetes clanged again. Metal clashed, and sparks flew, and those people *howled*, that terrifying sound that had haunted our nights for the past week. I looked the women right in their faces, and I raised my voice as loud as I could to belt out the chorus. So did everyone else. We sang the chorus again and again until we drowned out the sound of the machetes and the howls. My throat burned. My eyes were wet. If I stopped singing, I would die. Our song was the only protection we had, and it couldn't do a damn thing against a coral steel machete.

The blades stopped. They walked up the steps. I didn't move. I could hear the people behind me begin to cheer, begin to surge. I held up a hand: *wait*. I didn't stop singing, though. I wanted to make sure our voices followed those fuckers all the way to Letty's office. If she couldn't hear us through our pais, she could hear us with her own ears. And what better way to drive her out of our heads by singing the song she couldn't?

I didn't expect her to come out of the great coral steel doors, not alone. But she did, her head high and her smile haughty, the look of a queen, not an elected official. I stood up and walked to the first landing. I wasn't going to give her the satisfaction of standing over me, never again.

Her clothes were clean, her green hair in a perfect ponytail, but dark bags dragged her eyes toward the ground. "I fucking hate that song," she said. "Can you ask them to stop?"

"Why don't you order them to?" *Solidarity forever* rolled around and around behind us.

She shook her head. "You know it doesn't work like that."

"I have no idea how things work anymore," I said. "I do know that they'll start with you stepping down and turning yourself over to Chief Baghram."

She laughed. "And then what? You think that's going to keep everything together? You've only put a plaster over a gunshot wound. There's no money. There's no income. We're–"

"We're going to figure that out, and we're going to do it without you," I said. "You'll step down, you'll relinquish all control over every operational aspect of this planet, and you'll get a fair trial for your many, many crimes."

"And how are you going to find an impartial jury? Hell, how will you find a *judge* who isn't connected to me? I'm the President of a Local with three million people. I pay *everyone*. There's no such thing as impartial here."

"Then we get a judge from another planet," I said. "I think everyone can wait four years for that, after what you've done."

Letty crossed the short distance between us. "You can't prove a thing, and you know it," she said, her teeth gritted. "You can talk all you want, but in the end it's just words. Words don't get people fed."

"No, but they get them working."

"Work. What the hell do you know about *work*? You don't understand the first fucking thing about work until you've grown up out *there*." She sneered as she pointed west toward the kampong. "Get up before dawn to cut cane. Spend your childhood watching out for vipers or breaking up cane rat nests. Watch your parents starve because there isn't enough food for everyone, so they give up their dinners so they can grind their lives away growing cane for some parasites a billion light-years away. *Work*? You think because you're down in the muck at that plant you know about work? You and every other Ink on this planet don't know the first thing about *work*."

"So you're going to teach us all, huh? You're going to burn this city down and let people starve?"

"I'm going to balance out this city because no one can say *no*," she said, her face growing dark. "All this bullshit about Slots and seniority just keep us from moving *forward*. I'm going to make that happen, and if people die, well, revolution is messy."

"Are you kidding me? You'll just blow everything up and sift through the wreckage and call it a society?"

"Like you've never wanted to level this city and start over."

"I want it to change on its own, not jab it with a sharp stick. You ever stop to think about what the people right here want?"

"They want to get drunk and screw and forget what a great big mistake they made coming here," said Letty. "They want to pretend they're still living the Life Corporate. They want to fight over the Big Three's scraps instead of *making* their own future."

"Bullshit," I said. "All that time you spent with the FOC and on the Executive Committee, and you *know* that's bullshit. People came here because they didn't want to get screwed by the Big Three. They didn't want to sit back and become consumers. Everyone came to Santee because they knew it was an actual *life*. That's why we have a Union: to work together to make everyone's lives better."

Letty clapped. "That's *adorable*. You sound like you mean it."

"I do," I said. "Every goddamn word."

"Too bad your words can't do anything to fix this. They sure as hell can't make me step down." She crossed her arms and shrugged. "What are you gonna do about it, Padma?"

I looked at her, at that self-righteous smirk, and all I could do was laugh. "All that power you earned, all that you've squandered, and the best you can do is taunt me like some boardroom bully. So, you know what I'm gonna do?

I'm gonna show you how to get shit done."

I walked halfway down the steps and held up my hands. A minute later, the entire crowd was silent. "Pass the word, everyone," I said. "Letty thinks she has all the power. She thinks that we can't do anything without her. We're going to show her otherwise."

The front row turned and spoke to the people behind them, and they did the same, all the way to the ends of the streets. It was like watching a wave breaking and rolling back. When eyes were back on me, I thought, How *do we show her?*

Of course. *We do the work.*

"I'd like you all to go home, eat up, and rest. If you've got food to spare, share it with someone who's hungry. Then, go back to work. Whatever your shift is, go to it. I want this whole planet working, just for twenty-four hours. If you don't have a job, you can help clean up or check on the injured or the shut-in."

This time, the murmuring wave was louder, the faces confused and angry. I could hear *Really?* and *Is she kidding?* "We're going to show Letty and her thugs that we don't need them. This planet works without them. But it can't work without us."

I pointed at the clock, its hands telling me it was half past eight. I froze at the sight and felt The Fear give a solitary hiss in the back of my brain. I would be sure to make tomorrow's Six O'Clock. "Work for twenty-four hours, then come back here at six o'clock. Get home safe."

I walked down the steps. Soni had put on her Cop Face. "Really?" she said. "That's it?"

"That's enough for now," I said. "How many police have you got in the crowd?"

Soni glanced at the worried faces surrounding us and whispered, "Maybe two hundred. You don't want us to try and take the Hall, do you?"

"Hell, no," I whispered back. "We don't know what's inside there. I just want you to make sure everyone gets home safely."

"Define 'safely.'"

"Not getting hacked to pieces."

She nodded. "I can do that. But you've got a plan for tomorrow, right?"

"Of course."

She paused. "Are you going to share it with us?"

I tapped my temple, and she rolled her eyes. "I can't wait to get this shit fixed." She wandered into the crowd toward a knot of cops and shooed them to work.

Onanefe had found his crew. Their funeral whites were now a dingy gray. "We'd ask to crash with you," said Onanefe, "but it looks like you're in the same boat as us."

For a moment, I thought about telling them to hop into their Hanuman and bring us to Tanque, but ugly reality smashed that idea to pieces. I didn't own the distillery any more. The new owners had probably already changed the locks.

"I was going to Big Lily's," I said. "She can probably put us all up."

"She got food?" asked one of the crew.

"Jesus, I hope so." I looked around the emptying streets. A few people still stood around, singing, but the rest walked away, looking at the ground or off in the distance. I pushed my way up Koothrapalli, hoping I hadn't played into Letty's hands again.

TWENTY-THREE

"Padma." A shake.

"Fuggoff."

"Not this morning," said Big Lily. "Come on, you got work, and I gotta open up for the breakfast crowd."

I groaned and opened my eyes. Weak morning light crept through the windows. Big Lily stood above me, offering me a steaming cup and a not-steaming bowl. "Your friends, the cane cutters, they left half an hour ago. Almost cleaned me out, but I saved you some tea and suafa'i."

I sat up, the foil emergency blanket crinkling around me. The floor of her place was made of ironpalm slats, and they had sucked all the heat out of my body. Even with the blanket, I shivered. My back was knotted, my neck was stiff, and I was not a fan of Big Lily's suafa'i. She always used too much sago so the porridge became a gummy mass. I set the bowl next to me and wrapped myself around the cup. I willed all the heat in the tea to enter my body. It would be cold in the mains when I went to work.

I froze. Holy crap. *Work.*

I slurped the tea and inhaled the suafa'i. "Gotta get to the plant," I muttered as I pulled on my boots. I stopped.

"My God, who's been at the plant all week? *Has* anyone been there?"

Big Lily took the bowl. "I think they had a skeleton crew running the place. Service has been spotty, but the water's been clean. Ish."

"Ish?"

Big Lily made a face. "It's been smelling a bit like, um, lard."

I groaned. "Fatbergs. My favorite."

She handed me a cold bacon roll. "Do I want to know?"

"Just imagine all the cooking oil and rendered fat in the city coming together into one great, quivering mass."

She made a face.

"Exactly," I said. "Usually, someone upstream from me monitors filters to keep most of it out, but with everyone gone…" I put the roll in my pocket. "Well, if they show up, we'll fix it. If they don't, then I apologize for this week's water quality."

"They'll show," she said.

I caught myself from saying *I sure hope so* and gave her a wink. "Then make sure you break out the good stuff for tonight. People are going to want to celebrate."

She nodded. "Wish you'd have told me you were going to unload the distillery, though. I'd have put in one last order."

"Good thing I left those two cases here for emergencies."

Big Lily gave me a cock-eyed grin. "What do you think the last week has been?"

A chill crept up my back. "Lily… you *do* have those cases, right? The ones I said not to touch unless the world was ending?"

She put her hands on her hips. "Well, shit, Padma, I'd think this has qualified."

I got to my feet. "Where's the rum?"

"I traded it for food."

"Did you trade *all* of the rum?"

She nodded, a sad look in her eye. "The prices have been *obscene*. You have any idea how much sago was going for?"

I looked at the empty bowl in her hand. One bottle of Old Windswept could last me a year if I were careful, and I was *always*… well, I was usually careful. I was certainly careful with where I'd put my other stashes. I had cases hidden everywhere in the city. Big Lily and Hawa weren't the only ones I'd trusted with my secrets. And I'd always made those deals when we had shut off our pais. I had paid *extra* to make sure that hadn't happened. My rum stashes were safe, right?

Right?

Big Lily kept an ancient wind-up clock above the bar, and it chimed half-past seven. I had to be at work in thirty minutes. It was a five minute walk to the water works. That gave me twenty-five minutes to run like hell over to Mooj Markson's konbini on Handel. I always sold Mooj Old Windswept at a good rate, and he always kept a case in reserve for me. *Just in case*, I'd said. I threw a good-bye over my shoulder as I charged out the door.

The only sounds I heard were my boots pounding on the pavement. Brushhead was graveyard quiet. A work morning like this, there should have been a low-level bustle of tuk-tuks and bikes, but I had the streets to myself. Cafés were still rolled up behind their hurricane curtains, and there were none of the usual breakfast smells of coffee, beignets, and fish sausage. Scorch marks lined storefronts where diesel bombs had flared. A streetlight bent low over the sidewalk, its sides marred by sledgehammer blows.

I rounded Reigert and blew past my old Union office, its windows covered by layers of graffiti, none of it friendly. I turned on Handel and skidded to a halt; a tuk-tuk bomb had gone off in the middle of the street. A blackened crater yawned from the pavement, and all the surrounding buildings were ruins.

One of them was Mooj's konbini.

I walked toward it. The blast had blown the fruit stand aside like it had been made of cardboard. The konbini's front had caved in, bringing part of the two stories above down on the sidewalk. I peered into the darkened ruin and coughed at the stench of burned cane plastic and rotten food.

"Hey!" came a voice behind me. "Get lost! You hoods already took everything!"

An angry Mooj Markson stormed at me, brandishing a rolling pin. "I got nothing left! Go loot someone else!"

I held up my hands. "Mooj!"

He swung. I turned in time to get hit in the shoulder. The same one I'd been stabbed in only a week before. My entire left arm went numb, and I fell to my knees.

"Serves you right!" yelled Mooj, waving the rolling pin. "You blow up my store, you take all my food! What more do you want?"

"My rum?" I panted, holding up my right arm.

Mooj's face softened. "Oh, Padma." He dropped the pin and rushed to my side. "Padma, forgive me, I've had all these people picking over my store's carcass!"

"No, that's okay." My fingers tingled as they regained their sensation. "I should have called you from the sidewalk. You okay?"

"I been better," he said, "but I been worse, too. None of us got hurt in the blast."

"Good. Good." I looked back into the blackened wreckage of the konbini. I'd stuffed the cases into the ceiling crawlspace above the back storeroom. I couldn't see it from here, but if I could just hop in and take a look…

"Come on," he said, helping me to my feet. "We got burned out of our home, so Eleanor's brother has been putting us up. We still got some painkillers in the first aid kit."

"Thank you, no. What I need are those two crates of Old Windswept."

He laughed. "Kind of early, isn't it?"

"I'm thinking ahead. You still got 'em, right?"

"I did." He motioned toward the burned-out shell of the konbini. "I had a lot of other stuff, too. But that bomb did my store in. What the shock wave didn't break, the fire burned. And then the looters took the rest."

"But I *hid* those cases, Mooj, remember? In the storeroom, up in the ceiling."

Mooj shook his head. "Gone, Padma. It's cleaned out."

My heart sank. "Everything?"

"Yeah. But it's okay, 'cause I re-upped my insurance. Special policy."

I groaned. "Let me guess. A young woman with really, really great skin?"

He nodded. "That's her! She said it was backed by a joint venture between the Union and the Co-Op, so I figured..."

I didn't hear the rest of what Mooj said. I didn't have to. I could see the scene: the younger Jennifer knocking on Mooj's door, telling him about a deal that sounded too good to be true. The bomb, parked outside the shop, going off in the middle of the night. The store burning, Mooj's family escaping, finding their policy was backed by bullshit. One more layer of chaos that Letty had sewn. I would have to look on another stash after work...

... unless *that* had been Letty's target.

My blood ran cold as I remembered the bombing in Howlwadaag. The crater had been in the middle of García Avenue, all those shophouses had burned... and one of them had been Patel's Flowers. Where else had those bombs gone off? Where else had Soni and Onanefe said? Only every other neighborhood where I had stashed Old Windswept.

It's not enough to know where you've been, Letty had said yesterday. But it was. Oh, that bitch, it *was*.

It didn't matter if I had shut off my pai when I talked. I could still be tracked by my habits, my trips, my constant goddamn need to make sure no one screwed with the rum I'd stashed. I was as predictable as the tides, given enough data and the spiteful desire to analyze it all. Letty would have made an awesome marketing engineer by the way she could predict where to hit me best.

"I have to go to work," I said. Mooj might have replied, but I just turned and walked toward the plant. There were a few more people in the street, but not enough to make me think that I had done nothing but completely and utterly failed. I hadn't gotten people back to work. I hadn't gotten Letty to resign. And I had probably lost every single bottle of Old Windswept I had hidden.

The waterworks loomed overhead as I trudged down Courtland Lane. The stained clock above the front door told me I was ten minutes late for my shift. I had never been late for a day of work in my life, but there was a first time for everything.

The locker room was dark and dusty. As far as I could tell, no one else had clocked in. I slipped into my ancient environment suit, double-checking its seals and rebreather. It was a size too big, so walking through the mains was always a chore. I had to deal with the suit's bulk as well as the sludge that gathered around my waist. It would probably be even thicker today.

My office for the past eighteen months was a twenty-meter-square pourform pool. Four pipes emptied into one end, and another four slurped in water from the other. My job was to clean out the sediment that settled on the bottom and to ensure none of the pipes got clogged. Even with the giant fans roaring away, the air smelled like a back-flowing toilet. It was an important job, one of the oldest Contract Slots on Santee, but that never translated into anything like pay or prestige. Anyone could do this job, which was why no one wanted it. If the Big Three could ever make proper compliant AIs, this would have been their first task.

But it was mine and mine alone. No one ever came down here unless I reported busted piping. It wasn't a place to socialize. Other places in the waterworks, like the final treatment pools, were downright pleasant. Not here.

The mains were clogged with great, gray, glistening fatbergs, which meant my suit was soon covered in gunk. I slipped and slid my way through work, sweating despite the suit's internal coolers. I didn't bother to break for lunch. I just lost myself in labor, clearing all the crap that the city had flushed into the sewers over the past seven days: engine parts, bones, coconut husks, hair, shit, oil. No bodies, at least. That was a pleasant surprise.

Seven days and people had stopped using their backyard digesters. They had just flushed stuff down their toilets or into the storm drains. They had lost all sense of water discipline, of making sure to keep the aging water system from becoming overloaded. Never mind that we had gotten through thirteen hurricane seasons with minimal injuries and downtime, but one stupid strike and the whole place went to hell.

As I worked, I realized what a perfect spot this would be for Letty to kill me. There was no pai reception, the walls were thick, and the noise from the pipes and the fan could drown any screams. It didn't help that The Fear prickled at my brain, turning shadows into kill squads.

Somewhere around three o'clock, I heard the distinct heavy clack of the room's only door. I froze. Oh, shit. She was going to do it. This was a stupid plan, and now it was going to be the end of me. All I had was the rake. I hunkered down in the pool and backed to its far corner. Only my hands and face were above the murky water.

Four people filed in, all of them in rebreather masks. They held tools: a crowbar, a torque wrench, a pipe saw, a welder. All the things you'd need to kill someone and dispose of their corpse. They fanned out. My hands shook, but I willed myself to wait until they got close enough to strike. There would be no hiding in here, no running. I wasn't going to let Letty take me without a fight.

Torque Wrench made his way toward the outflow pipes and stopped. He looked right at me, and I could see his eyes crinkle in a grin. That was enough for me. I gripped the rake and jumped out of the pool. Torque Wrench's eyes widened as I hit him square in the chest. Momentum carried us all the way to the wall, where the rake's handle snapped. The tines clattered to the floor, and I held the splintered end of the handle to Torque Wrench's neck. "Give me one reason not to drive this in, motherfucker," I hissed. "Just one."

Torque Wrench gurgled, "We brought you lunch."

I didn't take my eyes off his. Sweat ran down the outside of his rebreather. Through the scratched-up glass I saw Somboon Hallorhan, who was in charge of pH levels in the settling tanks. I glanced at the others and recognized them: Danica Thorwald, Li-Han Wai, and Annie Lonon. They were all people I worked with.

I looked back at Somboon. "You didn't take a lunch break, and we got worried," he said. "You're usually up there with us. So we came down to tell you we brought lunch. It's back in the break room."

The door clacked again, and three more people entered.

They were also carrying tools. I pressed the handle into Somboon's neck. "Who the fuck are they?"

"Your relief!"

"Bullshit."

"Padma, I know you've been under a lot of stress–"

"You have no *idea* how true that is."

"– but people have been showing up to work all day," said Danica from behind. "Shifts are getting double- and triple-staffed. These three usually work on the lifter, but they're overstaffed, so they came here looking for anything to do. They want to fill in for you."

I gave them a closer look. They had rakes and shovels and all the implements you'd need to do my job. Of course, they also could have come down here to rush me all together. Seven on one, those were really good odds.

"Padma, please," said Somboon. "I know you don't want to trust anyone, but I'm going to ask you to. Please don't hurt me. Come and eat. It's just like you've been asking everyone to do."

I laughed. "Nothing's gone like I've asked."

"We're here!"

"You weren't this morning," I said. "I was *late*, and none of you had clocked in."

"Because we were late, too! I didn't want to come into work until Danica and Li-Han dragged me here."

I glanced over my shoulder. Li-Han and Danica nodded.

"I fucking hate this job, but I'm here," said Somboon. "I'm here because what you said was right. We can't look to Letty to resolve this. We gotta do it ourselves, and we start by trusting and talking, right?"

You believe this? hissed The Fear. *Your own words, thrown back at you. You can take all of them. Start with this one, then hit the rest. It's a trap. Get out now.*

That was new. The Fear, encouraging me? Granted, it

was encouraging me to stab Somboon in the neck, but it was still cheering me on rather than cutting me down. The Fear had stayed silent all through work, but now it wanted me to do something that was part self-preservation, part homicide.

Fuck The Fear.

I put down the rake handle.

They didn't rush me. They didn't come near me, not even the three replacements. They hopped right into the pool and got to work.

I led the way out the door and up to the locker room. I kept glancing over my shoulder as I peeled off the environment suit and hung it on the cleaning rack. My four co-workers stood there, as I clicked off the seals of my rebreather. Then my heart stopped because I smelled samosas and galbi and freshly cooked rice. The locker room stench tried to fight with the scents of food, and the food won. Christ, I didn't realize how *hungry* I was.

I turned around and saw the entire crew was watching me. They had left their tools behind and removed their rebreathers. I knew these people. I had worked with them, helped them, let them help me. They weren't going to kill me.

"Well, let's wash up and eat, huh?" I said, and everyone sighed with relief.

The spread was even better than I imagined: pickles and chutneys and noodles spread out in an array of open tiffin-boxes. We sat down and passed bowls of bean sprouts and spinach, plates of roasted yams and grilled fish. I attacked my lunch, then went back for seconds. Li-Han made a joke – at least, I figured he did, because everyone cracked up. I was too busy eating to hear it, but I smiled all the same.

"I can't wait to see the look on Letty's face when we all show up," said Danica.

Li-Han choked on his food. "You *campaigned* for her

when she ran!"

"So?" said Danica. "I can change my mind. We shouldn't have let a Freeborn into the Union anyway. They just don't get it."

I paused, noodles halfway to my mouth. "Don't get what?"

"Oh, you know, Padma," said Danica. "They didn't grow up around the Life Corporate like we did. They don't get what it's like to be a part of something *bigger*. To look out for each other."

"Like everyone has this past week?"

There was a deathly silence. Danica put down her bowl. "What I'm saying is that Letty wasn't a good leader. She wasn't looking out for us. We need someone who will."

"Really?" I said. "If anything, I think we need to look out for each other even more. And not just Union people. The Freeborn, too."

"But they don't want that," said Li-Han. "They never have."

"Because we've never offered them anything worthwhile." I threw down my chopsticks. "Holy shit. We're just going to repeat ourselves. We got into this jam because we didn't pay any attention. We let the Executive Committee run out of cash, we let them get in bed with the Co-Op over this stupid Mutual Fund, and we'll get screwed all over again when the cane gets certified."

"But WalWa's holding up the certification," said Somboon. "Aren't they?"

"It doesn't matter, because there's no goddamn reason for us to rely on WalWa. Not for certification, not for Slots, none of that. We work against each other when we should be working together to do one important thing: kick WalWa off this planet."

"What?" said Li-Han.

"But we need them to buy our cane," said Annie. "And we need all the stuff they make."

"Because we aren't making it ourselves, and we're not doing that because we don't have the right people. We don't have the right people because we're waiting for them to come shimmying down the cable. And that doesn't happen because the Big Three limit the traffic we get. And doesn't that piss you off? You came all the way to be free from them, but we still depend on them. We still need them because we say we do."

Danica scratched her nose. "So... we don't?"

"Not the way they think we do." My brain itched, but in that good way, the way it always did when I was lost in work and didn't care about anything else. I had a few of those moments when I was still with WalWa, but they were so infrequent they didn't really count. Keeping track of logistics for sports stadiums was nothing compared to taking apart the old brush factory or pulling Breaches from the ocean or just going down a list of people's complaints and resolving them, one by one. No matter the problem's size, I fixed it, and that mattered. I did the work. We all did the work.

"We all do the work," I muttered. That was it.

I looked at the clock: five-thirty. I tamped down the panic about not having any Old Windswept and stood up. "Come on. We need to get to the Hall. All of us. Tell everyone you see to get there. Freeborn, too."

Annie groaned. "But they won't come."

"They will, because we're going to listen to what they want, and they're going to get it. We're all going to get it, and we're not going to take Letty's bullshit. We're not just going to ask her to step down. We're undoing everything and starting over."

They all looked at each other. "Padma, what are you going on about?"

I took a deep breath so I could focus on this tiny bubble of an idea. "We need to dissolve the Union and start over. We need to get rid of these barriers between us and the Freeborn because we are all so much stronger together. We have the one thing the Big Three need: cane. And not just us on Santee. I'm talking every world in Occupied Space that grows the stuff. The Big Three are completely dependent on us for fuel. That means *we* have the power, and we are going to bloody well seize it. Together."

I walked out of the break room, not waiting for them to follow me. I knew they would. Whether they would go along with what I was proposing was another matter. Dissolve the Union and start over? That would be an insane amount of work. It would be decades of work, and the Contract was up for renegotiation in, what, four months? Wouldn't that just plunge us into more trouble?

I passed the back of Lam's Butcher Shop. Two skinny dogs snarled and fought over a rib bone, each taking turns snatching it from each other's mouth. The back door to Lam's was wide open, and I saw a freshly butchered hog hanging on a hook. Its snout almost touched the floor. Lam must have been feeling pretty good about business to have a whole hog ready for sale.

That was us. Freeborn and Union, bickering over who got more of the scraps while the Big Three had a whole feast within reach. We would keep up this idiotic cycle until we started working together. The first Union people got that, but they got caught up in protecting the institution itself. That the Union was worthless without a constant stream of new members wasn't lost on the Big Three. No wonder they had shunted traffic from Santee. We didn't just lose them money. We were an actual threat.

I hadn't seen that when I was a recruiter. I thought the work would be easy because who didn't want out of their horrible Indentures? Who wouldn't want cane from Santee Anchorage? There would always be ships coming by until there weren't. The Big Three would seed another planet with cane, let it fester for a while, then move on. The Union might get a foothold, but it wouldn't be enough. Not unless we all worked together.

Ten blocks away from the Hall, and the crowds were already thick. I nudged my way through, and people gave me smiles or pats on the back as I worked toward the Hall. *We're with you*, they said. I sure hoped they would be after what I had to say.

Soni and a hundred police officers stood at the front of the crowd. They formed a perimeter around the Hall. I stopped long enough to give Soni a hug before climbing the steps. Letty stood at the top, surrounded by fifty of her machete thugs. She smiled as I approached, then held up something.

It was a triangular bottle made of bumpy, sea-green glass. She held it label-out, but I didn't have to see it. I knew what it was. She knew what it was. She unscrewed the cap, and the seal cracked, a sound like a gunshot.

"Buy you a drink?" she said. She held the bottle at her side, at arm's length.

The clock tower behind her chimed six.

TWENTY-FOUR

I looked at the bottle. It was perfect, like it had just been filled and capped this morning. Lots of other distillers liked aging their rum in the bottle, but Estella Tonggow never did, so I never did. It wasn't just a matter of the pharmacology; I thought it tasted better. I wanted to taste it again. And again. And again.

The six chimes of the clock echoed off the buildings. I took a step toward Letty, and she spilled a little rum on the pavement. "Oops," she said. I backed off.

"If you want it, you'll tell everyone to go home," she said. "You'll go back to your job. You'll quit talking about having me sent up or dissolving the Union or whatever it is you've done over the past day."

"Or?"

She splashed more rum on the pavement. "This is the last bottle. I checked and double-checked. All of your stashes are blown up, and every bar in the city that sells it has found their inventories reduced. Maybe if you run back to work, you can smell the last of it getting flushed down the toilet."

I couldn't take my eyes off the bottle. "The distillery can

always make more."

"But not the way you did," she said. "The new owners are going to mess with the process, trim out all those inefficiencies that Tonggow baked in. They'll buy cheaper cane, use different barrels. You need things to stay just the way they are, Padma. You and I know it." She cocked her head. "Or maybe everyone else needs to know it, too. I wonder, how will it look when everyone finds out that you're nothing but a functional alcoholic?"

I swallowed. "I'm sure I wouldn't be the first."

"No, you certainly wouldn't." Letty swirled the bottle around, the rum forming a dark vortex. "I learned a lot about the people who had my job, and they were just as corrupt and clueless as you'd expect. Some of them were good, but the rest..." She shrugged. "They were content to do less. Just let things slide."

"Not like you, though."

She shook her head. "I could see the way things were going back when I was in the FOC. The Big Three would kill as much traffic as they could, and they'd extract as much cane as they could, and then they'd be done with us." She brought the bottle to her side. "You know what's going to happen, come Contract Time? There won't be any Slots. WalWa is going to withdraw from Santee Anchorage. They're going to shut down Thronehill, go into orbit, and pull the lifter up behind them. We're too much trouble."

"You're sure?"

She nodded. "It's all in their preliminaries. There's a lot of talk about traffic forecasts and cutbacks on staff. I can read between the lines. They're done with Santee."

"So why do all this? Why the bombings and the strike?"

"To shake everyone out of their comas," she said. "We have to prepare. We have to get used to a different life. One that's going to be hard."

"Then you don't do it by blowing up the city!"

"That was being efficient. I got people scared *and* I knocked out your stashes."

"Why the hell are you picking me out of the crowd, Letty? What have I ever done to you?"

"Nothing. It's what you *could* do that worries me."

"What?" I said. "What could I possibly do to hurt you?"

She nodded at the street. I turned, and my breath caught in my throat. I saw nothing but people for ten blocks in every direction. I allowed myself a smile.

"You talk, and you believe," said Letty. "What's more, you also know how to temper that belief with reality. Someone like Saarien, he believes, but he doesn't question. He sees opportunity, he works within the system to get his way, but he will never question The Struggle." She pointed at me. "You do. You have. And you convince people to come along with your way of thinking. It's easy to scare people, but to inspire them? To get them to think of more than themselves? That's hard. I can't do it. You can. And that's why you have to step aside. Or else." She shook the bottle.

I think she means it, said The Fear. I looked at her, looked at the bottle. I could make that last a year. In that year, I could round up enough of Old Windswept's new shareholders to make sure the place didn't change. Hell, I could find new investors, enough to have a stake in the process. In that year, I could scour every single building on this planet and find any bottles that had been squirreled away. There was no way Letty had found all of them.

She took a swig from the bottle, and all I could think about was leaping on her and pounding that smirk off her face. The crowd would love that. They would tear the machete thugs to pieces to protect me. They would make me their fucking queen, and I would *command* them to make me an endless supply of Old Windswept rum. And if WalWa left and shut down the lifter, well, I'd live out my days presiding over a sybaritic paradise. To hell with the future. We would live in the now. It would be glorious, the kind of life only available to the people at the highest level of the Life Corporate. Just the thing I'd signed up for when I became an Indenture.

Except that I knew that was bullshit. I looked at the faces below, all those people from my neighborhood, my city, my planet. Soni and her beat cops held hands as they formed a black-and-yellow line around the crowd. Big Lily and her staff passed around cups of water to everyone nearby. Khamala al-Jones and members of her congregation held their hands to their faces, breathing their prayers out and up. So did people clustered around Archbishop Yoon and Rabbi Žvaigždė and everyone from every church and temple and coven in the city. The Freeborn hung together, but I could see them holding hands with Union people. Onanefe was out there, and KajSiab, and Sirikit, and all those kids who'd been swept up in Saarien's church because they knew they needed to be a part of *something* bigger that was willing to fight for their future. Hell, even Saarien himself was there, his arm in a sling made from the ruins of his suit jacket. I gave him a nod, and he nodded back.

I looked at the bottle, I looked at Letty, and I walked down the steps until I was within shouting distance of the crowd. "If your pai is working," I called out, "please turn it on and start streaming. Ask people to turn on Public terminals. Repeat it for anyone without a pai. I need to talk with everyone, and I want to make sure you all hear me."

There was a furious wave of blinking and whispering. After a minute, Soni tapped her temple and gave me a nod: *You're on*. I took a breath, feeling my face grow numb at what I was about to say, so I said it.

"When I was in transit to Santee, WalWa used a new batch of hibernant. That was part of being an Indenture – we were all test subjects, whether we liked it or not. We weren't people. We were just units, and damaged units are a part of business.

"The hibernant damaged my brain. I don't dream. I know I've used that line in fundraisers, but it's true. And it's not the only thing."

You wouldn't, hissed The Fear.

Fuck you, I hissed back.

"I started to lose focus, and then I started to hear a voice in my head. A single voice, and all it did was cut me down and make me question everything I did, whether it was tying my boots or breathing. I call it The Fear, and it ran my life until I went to see Dr Ropata. He told me my brain was waiting, that it had been on hold during transit."

The crowd tittered.

"I know, I told him that sounded like bullshit. He agreed, but it was the best he could do with the medical tech we have. He gave me a treatment, and it has kept The Fear at bay for the past thirteen years." I smiled. "I go home at six o'clock, I light a candle, I think about my place in the universe, and I have a sip of Old Windswept. And that's why I worked so hard to buy the distillery, because I wanted to make sure the supply never ran out."

That got the crowd going. People talked to each other, pointed at me. A few of them made *drinky-drinky* motions with their hands.

I pointed back at Letty. "She has, as far as I can tell, the last bottle of Old Windswept on the planet. She blew up every place I'd stashed rum, and she's cleaned out every other bottle around. If you ever bought rum from me or Estella Tonggow, tell me I'm wrong. Tell me your Old Windswept is still safe and sound."

The hubbub died down. Holy shit, Letty really had done it.

"She wants me to tell you all to go home, just so I can get my hands on that last bottle. She wants us all to go back to our lives, to pretend that none of this happened. She wants all this because there's some seriously bad shit coming our way, and she doesn't have what it takes to lead us."

That got their attention. I turned back to Letty, whose haughty grin had turned to terror. She shook her head. *You wouldn't.* I gave her the finger and turned to the crowd. "There isn't going to be another Contract. WalWa is leaving Santee Anchorage, and they're going to pull the lifter up with them as they go. They're cutting us off from the rest of Occupied Space."

Letty yelled something, and the machete thugs started scraping their blades on the steps. The police tensed, and the crowd behind them stepped through their line to link arms. Soni started yelling for people to stay where they were, and the machetes clacked on the pavement.

No, not today. "IT DOESN'T HAVE TO BE LIKE THIS!" I yelled. I yelled it again and again until my throat hurt. When my voice gave out, I fell to one knee. I was so fucking tired. I just wanted another bowl full of curried noodles, some head, and a nap. Was that too much to ask for?

The crowd had stilled again, and I got back to my feet. "It doesn't have to end like that. Not if we all work together. And I mean *all* of us, Union and Freeborn alike. The Union can't fix it as is, so we dissolve the Union and start over. We sit down, we talk, we work it out, and we make sure that we keep the lifter open and running until the end of time! Unless you want to be cut off from the rest of Occupied Space. Do you?"

I got a smattering of *No*s. That wouldn't be enough. I needed a tsunami. "I know we all want independent lives. We want to make our own stuff and not have to rely on the

Big Three for meds or parts. We *should* live like that. And we *will*. But first we gotta dig ourselves out of this hole we're in. If the lifter goes, it's going to get bad here, and fast. That's why we need to start over *now*. It will be a whole lot of work, but it will be a lot less painful than sticking with Letty or letting WalWa pull the lifter up behind them.

"I know you're willing to work. You did it today. You came *here*, hoping to see Letty get her ass kicked." I looked up at her. "We're not going to do that. We're going to vote. Any member of the Union can call for a vote if there are enough of us assembled. It looks like we're all here.

"So, here's the question: do we stick with the way things are? Or do we start over?" I took a breath. "If we keep to the status quo, go ahead and go home. If we dissolve the Union and start over, sit down, right where you are."

I sat down on the steps and tucked my feet under my legs.

Letty cleared her throat. "If I may interject?"

I sighed. "Enough of your bullshit, Letty."

"Oh, this is no bullshit. I just want to know what you're going to do with the fifty thousand yuan you got from the Union Treasury?"

I blinked. "What?"

She nodded, her smile growing. "In the middle of this crisis, when people are in desperate needs of funds, you just got a fifty thousand yuan payment."

I blinked out of reflex and got a stab in the back of my eye. But I didn't have to check my balance. Of course that money was there, right on time, like Letty said it would be. My head reeled. "You *authorized* that payment. A week ago."

"Can you prove that?"

"No, because you had a goddamn scrambler!"

"Did I? You sure you didn't make that up?"

"Jennifer, your bodyguard, was there."

"And where is she now?"

I narrowed my eyes. "You know where she is. Out in the middle of that cane field where you shot her and her sister."

The crowd stirred, but Letty's smile didn't fade. "That's a nice move, shifting suspicion on me to cover up your own crimes. It's the kind of thing we should expect from someone as mentally unstable as you."

From my spot on the base of the steps, I could see a few people let go of the police and melt back into the crowd. I heard feet shuffling and saw ripples in the ocean of torsos and legs in front of me.

I stood up. "What do you want me to say, Letty? You wanted me to help stop this strike. You came to me and *begged* me to help you, and you said you'd knock fifty K off my debt. Do you think I'm so proud I wouldn't take a lifeline? 'Cause I'm not. None of us are, not when we've been shit on for so long. And I don't think anyone out there is going to hold that against me, especially when you haven't offered them anything but misery and heartache."

"And what are you offering? Hope? You can't eat hope."

"No, but hope can get us back to work. And that's more than you've done."

We stared at each other for a few minutes. Letty finally flinched, and, when she looked away, her face broke out into a mad grin. "Look what hope's got you."

The streets were clear, save for a few hundred who had sat down. I looked at them and realized they were old or sick. They'd sat down because they had no energy to leave.

"Well, shit," I said.

Letty laughed, high and clear. There was no malice in it. She just laughed and laughed until her machete thugs joined in. "I'm sorry, Padma," she called down to me. "I really thought more people would stick around, but…" She laughed again. "Oh, God, I overestimated you. If I'd known *this* would be the result, I wouldn't have gone through all the trouble."

I took a breath and put my palms on the ground. "I'm not leaving, Letty," I yelled over my shoulder. "I got nothing left you can take from me, so I'm hanging on to this."

"Oh, for God's sake, let it go!" She came down the steps until she was a meter above me. "You *lost*. You and the Union and Solidarity and all that crap. There's just fear and hunger out there, and that's all we've got. Maybe we'll get some freakishly smart babies getting born to keep us aloft, but–"

A stream of silver shot into the sky, bursting into a blazing rainbow chrysanthemum. Four more followed, then a dozen, until the sky above Santee City glowed bright with fireworks. I looked back at Letty. "You really know how to rub it in."

"This isn't me," she said, her face blank. She turned to run up the steps, but she vanished in a sudden puff of smoke. That got me to my feet, just in time for a riot cop to charge up the steps shouting, "GET DOWN, IDIOT!" She bowled me over, and I lost my footing and tumbled down the steps. In the blur, I heard popping and shouting. When I hit the sidewalk, my head and shoulder ached, and the air stank of rotting vanilla.

I looked up at the Union Hall. It was now surrounded by a wall of expanding riot foam. Armored police were running up the steps of the Hall and lobbing grenades or wrestling machete thugs to the ground. The fireworks kept exploding overhead as black-and-yellow bumblecars drove to the bottom of the steps.

And then the tuk-tuks roared up the street, a multicolored parade that *putt-putted* its way the length of Koothrapalli. One of them screeched to a halt in front of me, and Sirikit climbed out. "You okay?" she said as she helped me up. "I would have gotten here earlier, but we were clearing the last of the bombs out of our rides."

"Did you get them all?"

"I hope so," said Soni, walking down the steps. She had her face shield up and a giant slash across her armor's chest plate. "They had about a hundred tuk-tuks wired to blow with these little fertilizer packages. It was sloppy work, but we had to check all of them. You have any idea how many tuk-tuks there are in this city?"

"I thought you were out of riot foam."

"No, I *told* you we were out. I had no idea how much Letty knew, so there was no need for you to know."

"Anything else I don't need to know?"

"Only that you might be about to get what you wanted," said Soni. "Look."

The tuk-tuks had all cut their motors and their sound systems. The drivers got out and sat down next to their rides. And they started *singing*:

> *"Sit down, just keep your seat*
> *Sit down and rest your feet*
> *Sit down, you got 'em beat*
> *Sit down, sit down!"*

A chorus of voices rose from the side streets and joined the drivers for the next verse:

> *"When the boss won't talk go and take a walk – sit down,*
> *sit down!*
> *When the boss sees that she'll want a chat – sit down, sit*
> *down!"*

People streamed out of nowhere. They filled the streets right up to the edge of the Union Hall, and they sat down.

Row after row of people, Union and Freeborn, all sitting down, all singing:

> *"When they make a deal that'll let them steal – sit down, sit down!*
> *When they tell you lies and blind your eyes – sit down, sit down!"*

I pulled away from Sirikit and sat back down. Waves of people went back as far as I could see, all of them sitting down and singing. That song from Dead Earth had been inspired by a bunch of auto workers who had staged simultaneous sit-down strikes against their employer, some company whose corpse had been rolled into the Big Three centuries ago. They had held out against police and the state security agencies and the thugs their bosses had hired to break the strike. They kept their plants clean and organized, and they dealt with spies and dissension and all the other petty bullshit that happened when people got tired and hungry. In the end, they won, and their union organized every other auto plant in the country. Granted, that union got smashed to pieces forty years later, thanks to the rise of borderless corporatism, but what the hell. It was a good song.

I didn't bother to count how many people showed up. It was more of a vote than I had hoped for. I looked back at the pile of foam where Letty had been. Three police had pulled her out and cuffed her. A fourth waved a red light stick in front of her face. Letty just sneered at them and yelled, "That won't do any good. I already did it!"

I saw a flash and felt a *boom*, the low kind you get from a powerful explosion a long way away. Some of the crowd got to their feet and pointed northwest. I stood up and saw a thin line of black smoke rise above the rooftops.

"Shit," said Sirikit. "We missed one. Where is that?"

I ran up the steps, my head swimming the whole way. At the top, I saw the smoke column curl, its underbelly lit by flashes of orange and red. The explosion had triggered a fire. What the hell was in that part of town? There weren't any refineries, any machine shops, anything with a lot of fuel.

Or a lot of hydrocarbons.

Or a lot of *cane*.

I looked back at Letty, and my guts turned to ice. I ran down the steps and grabbed Sirikit's arm. "We need to go," I said. "Right now."

"Where?"

"Tanque. The distillery."

"But you don't own it–"

"I don't care! We need to go! Now!"

Sirikit didn't hesitate. She walked to her tuk-tuk and shouted "MOVE!" The crowd parted like a well-lubed door, leaving us with a clear path up Solidarność. I jumped in behind Sirikit, and she floored it.

The seated crowd didn't end as we tore away from the Hall. It branched off on every cross street we passed, all of these people sitting on the sidewalk or the street or their stoops or in front of their businesses. The workers who spun cable, the stevedores who unloaded canal boats, the drivers and cooks and strippers and priestesses, they were all outside, sitting down. I saw Freeborn faces next to Union faces, some of them angry, some of them weeping, all of them sitting.

"I know you're not in the mood to hear this," said Sirikit, "but it was really brave of you to say that in front of everyone. About the reason why you held on to the distillery."

"There was nothing brave about it," I said. "Letty wanted to use it as leverage, and the only way I could take away her power was to admit it myself. Everyone's going to think I'm a drunk or a nutcase or both."

"They'll know you're one of us," said Sirikit. "You're trying to get your shit together the best you can. We all are."

"My best is a finger of rum and a candle."

She shrugged. "Nobody's perfect."

A horn blatted behind us. I looked over my shoulder and saw a white Hanuman with ten people standing in the back. They waved and cheered. In the cab, Onanefe had his fingers wrapped around the steering wheel, and he gave me a curt nod. I nodded back.

More joined us: delivery lorries and tankers and a lumbering fire truck. By the time we left the city, we were at the head of a column of fifty vehicles. As we passed the goat farm, I saw nothing ahead but smoke and flame. Some of the windbeasts were on their sides, knocked over by the blast. The dust flew thick, mixing with the stench of burning metal. My right hand ached, and I realized it was because I had curled it into a fist so tight my nails had cut into my palm.

We slowed in front of the distillery. The air was full of the stench of ash and burnt caramel. A giant smoldering hole sat in front of the press house, and a slightly smaller hole had been blown through the wall. The curing house was nothing but a roaring fire. I had Sirikit make a circle around the place, but we were stopped by the flaming wreckage of the press. The giant cylinders had been blasted through the press house wall, and all the cane juice embedded in them had caught fire. They glowed a dull red.

Onanefe and his crew got to work, as did everyone else with firefighting experience. There wasn't any risk to my neighbors, as the grasslands that surrounded the distillery were too green to catch fire. I just sat in Sirikit's tuk-tuk and watched them work. As much as I wanted to run in and grab everything I could, I would only get in the way.

Within thirty minutes, the fire was out. Onanefe walked over, his clothes streaked black. "Not much left," he said.

I sighed. "Fortunately, I now have that fifty thousand you say I owe you."

He shrugged. "Don't worry about that."

"No, I pay my debts, even when I'm not sure they're really mine." I looked at the ruins. "The new owners are gonna be pissed. Whoever they are."

He wiped his brow. "This is gonna take lawyers, isn't it? Man, I hate dealing with them."

"Me, too," I said. "But if you find someone good, keep 'em. A good lawyer can save your life."

I got out of the tuk-tuk and walked around, Sirikit and Onanefe trailing behind me. The buildings were gutted, and any machinery had turned to slag. Broken bottles crunched under our boots, and the ashes from labels floated in the air. "What the hell am I going to do now?" I said to no one in particular.

Onanefe held out a hand. "Come on. Come on out of this place. Come back to town. We have a lot of work to do, and people are going to count on you to show them the way."

"That's going to be a neat trick once my brain seizes up." The Fear hissed in assent. *I can't wait.*

"You talked to *one* doctor," said Sirikit. "And you kept your treatment a secret. There are lots of other people to talk with, and you know they'll all want to help. It's what we do, right?"

"So you believed my bullshit, too?"

She shook her head. "It wasn't bullshit. It was the truth. We're all here on this rock, and we either help each other out or cut each other down. I'd rather help."

"Us, too," said Onanefe. "It's going to be a hell of a lot of work, like you said, but it's the best way forward."

Sirikit held her hand out to me, and I reached for it. "Okay," I said. "But first, I'm going to need a very, very stiff drink."

TWENTY-FIVE

In my time as an organizer, I'd gone to plenty of meetings in the Prez's office. It was on the fourth floor of the Hall, in a coral steel atrium in the middle of an ocean of desks and tables. The office's positioning was symbolic and practical: the Prez had to be at the center of everything to make sense of what was going on. Someone had called it the Hurricane's Eye fifty years ago, and the name stuck.

Glass art covered the walls of the Eye, collages of driftglass and hand-blown chimes and stuff that looked like it had staggered home from a really good party at a foundry. The head of the staffers, a loping man named Moritz Nguy⬛n, told me that it had all come from Letty's predecessor, and that Letty hadn't really done any decorating. "If you want to change anything, though," said Moritz, holding his hands in front of his stomach. "Just say the word."

"How about the desk?" I said.

The desk was a rickety thing, nothing more than an unfinished door perched on top of two sawhorses. The surface was sanded smooth but for two discolored indentations about half a meter apart, probably where past Prezes had rested their elbows. Two rusted wire baskets labeled IN and OUT sat on either end of the desk. The IN basket held a stack of yellowed paper ten centimeters high. The OUT basket was empty.

Moritz cleared his throat, which stretched his long face and made the quill inked on his cheek look like a mutant chicken leg. "You're welcome to something else, of course, but it's considered tradition to keep this desk here. The first Prez used it when the Union was formed, so…"

I picked up the top sheet of paper. It was a crop report from five years ago. I rooted to the bottom of the pile and found a request for reimbursement dated the day my grandfather had been born. "Why is this still here?" I said. "Hasn't it been scanned and filed?"

Moritz nodded. "It's meant to be a reminder of the responsibilities of the office, and how the Prez is supposed to consult with the past to point the way to the future."

I dropped the paper. "You're kidding, right?"

He made a face like he'd just swallowed a bug. "It's, ah, tradition. Passed down with the office."

"We're going to burn it," I said. "Please help me take all this out in the middle of the street so we can set fire to it."

"Are you sure, Madame Presi–?"

"And please, do not call me that," I said, giving Moritz the warmest smile I could muster. "I know it's my job to make the decisions, but it's a job, not a title. I'd like you to call me Padma. What would you like me to call you?"

He cleared his throat. "I suppose 'Moritz' will be fine. I'll be sure to tell everyone else. Some of the older staffers might grumble, but…" He sighed. "What the hell. Those guys are assholes anyway."

I nodded. "I think we're going to get along just fine."

It took two trips, one for the door and the second for the sawhorses and baskets. A dozen curious staffers followed onto the sidewalk at Koothrapalli to watch as Moritz and

I took turns putting our boots through the door. It cracked and splintered nicely. People asked if they could help ball up paper for firestarters, and I was all too happy to let them. "Is there any more crap like this?" I said. "Useless stuff that we're hanging on to because we're supposed to? And I don't mean art or history or anything like that. I'm talking receipts and broken shit."

The staffers ran back into the Hall and reappeared within minutes holding busted machinery, moldy books, and stacks of paperwork. After Moritz assured me their contents were all accounted for on the Public, I helped people throw it on the pile. I pulled a lighter out of my pocket and set the pile ablaze.

Within fifteen minutes, it was all embers. We stomped on them until there was nothing but ash. A few squirts from fire extinguishers, and a hundred years of dead weight were flushed into the gutter. I blinked up the time: quarter to six. "Perfect way to wrap up a first day," I said.

"Do you want a new desk?" said Moritz.

"No, I'm not going to be spending much time at the office," I said. "We'll host the initial meetings at the Hall, 'cause we've got enough room for everyone. But the next sessions are going to be out in the city and the kampong."

"Really? Do they have the facilities?"

"We'll have to string up some signal boosters for pai reception, but we need to do that anyway. Make sure you get permission from the landowners and pay them the same rate you would in town, got it?"

He nodded. "We have the funds, but it'll take some lead-up time to get the equipment out there. Most of our line crews are busy doing firmware updates by hand." He grunted. "There are a lot of backdoors to close."

"Get as many people as you can spare, working in the kampong," I said. "We've got a couple of weeks, but I'd rather not cut it too close. Take it out of the emergency overtime fund if you have to."

He blanched. "There isn't a lot left in there."

"We'll deal," I said. "It's not like we have much choice." I held out my hand, and he shook it. "See you tomorrow. I got an appointment to keep."

As I walked up Koothrapalli, I stretched and twisted. My back ached from sitting on the floor. For the past week, I'd been hosting the first sessions of what we simply called The Convention, and all of our meetings had been in the Hall. I had come up with the bright idea of having us all sit on cushions so we would all be on a truly level field. No one could sit next to someone they knew or were allied with, which made for an interesting game of Musical Cushions every time we convened. The plan had worked for the most part. We were all equally sore and grumpy, but we'd hammered out a hell of a lot of details. Plus, it had helped me avoid going up to the Hurricane's Eye after everyone elected me President of the Convention.

I didn't want the job. After Onanefe nominated me, I told him I didn't want the job. After everyone there elected me, unanimously, I shouted I didn't want the fucking job, to give it to anyone else. They pointed out that my not wanting the job made me perfect for it, and I told them all to go to hell. They just clapped and applauded themselves for sound democratic judgment, the bastards.

I turned down Kripner Lane, a neighborhood of pourform flats. This was one of the older neighborhoods, built around the time of the first Contract. The building materials were part of that bargain, the housing a step up from the cargo can hutongs. The flats had seen better days, and their water-stained façades looked like a bunch of sweaty old people huddling together after a long day's work. Kids played in the street, drawing on the sidewalk or jumping in and out of the bomb crater. Some of them climbed up on the pile of rubble that had once been a building. Jeanine Doughtey, an airship engineer, had lived here, and she had held a stash for me. She and her family hadn't been in their flat when the bomb went off, but some of their neighbors had. It would be months before Letty went to trial, and finding an impartial jury would probably be next to impossible. There was talk about doing the whole thing in the kampong since the people out there were the least affected, but that just set off a fresh round of arguing on the Public.

A giant sat on the steps of one of the buildings. He took up most of the stoop, his brows furrowed deep in thought. "You get those supplements?" I called up to Kazys.

He looked down at me. "They taste like chalk."

"That's because they are," I said from the sidewalk. "Well, diatoms, mostly. But they're supposed to be easier on your stomach."

He grumbled. "They are, actually. Thanks."

"Anything else you need right now?"

He grunted. "A flat where we both fit would be a nice start."

"That's gonna mean new construction."

He grumbled.

I cleared my throat. "New construction means *jobs*, Kazys. Like for Class Two Mechanists."

He cocked his head, then nodded. "I hear you."

"Then make sure Gwendolyn hears you so everyone can hear her." I walked up the steps and held out my hand. He took it and most of my forearm. "You working on anything new?"

He laughed. "An oral history of the strike. I'm going to be fifty characters in fifty minutes."

"I'd pay to see that."

"You're in there, of course."

"Oh, God, why?"

"Because I need a musical interlude." He cleared his throat and belted out the chorus to "Solidarity Forever." I rolled my eyes. It was better than hearing "Sky Queen of Justice." With any luck, I'd never hear that again. I hurried down the street.

Off Kripner, tucked behind a pocket park, there was a small, green rowhouse with a ground floor garage. The garage door was open, and the bright red tuk-tuk parked inside looked like an apple hiding inside a leafy tree. The tuk-tuk was up on blocks, and Sirikit was underneath, swearing at the transmission. "That doesn't work," I said from the doorway. "Abuse just begats more abuse."

Sirikit sighed as she crawled out from underneath. She wore a filthy coverall, and lube streaked her face. "Can't you get us all to switch to bicycles? They're a lot easier to work on than these damn things."

"And then I'd have every tuk-tuk driver in the city screaming for my head."

"To hell with 'em," she said, wiping her hands on a rag. "All they do is sit around, anyway. The exercise would be good for them."

"That's a hell of a way to talk about your fellow tradespeople."

"Feel free to report me to my slavedriving boss. That kid's gonna be the death of us, anyway, the way she makes everyone actually work for a living." She set down the rag. "How are you doing?"

"Are you just being social, or are we starting early?"

She shrugged. "What do you think?"

I sighed. "This is the reason I avoided actual therapy all these years. The bottle never made me question what I was doing."

"Until it did."

"Ah, so we *are* starting early."

"Not until I've gotten out of *this*." She motioned to her work clothes. "Tough to focus when everything itches."

I followed her inside her flat. It looked a lot like my old one; they were both built around the same time, during the Union's heyday when people were coming down the cable faster than they could find housing. Anyone who brought bags of pourform or other building materials with them became immediate best friends with architects and builders. Both of our places had probably come off the same drafting table.

There was a kitchen and a parlor and a single bedroom off to the left. The bay window looked out over a tiny garden. Rows of tomatoes and cucumbers lined the yard, and ricewheat stalks surrounded a single peach tree. It was bright pink with blossoms. It would be months before it bore fruit, but Sirikit said the peaches were worth the wait. The air from below smelled fresh and green.

On the circular table in front of the window was a single hurricane candle, two rocks glasses, and a triangular bottle made from bumpy, sea-green glass. On the label was a cartoon of a woman's foot propped up on a lanai railing. Tied to her big toe was a string, the anchor to a box kite flying high near the label's top. Some shirtless, brawny men sat on a cartoon cloud, great puffs of air coming from their straining cheeks as they kept the kite aloft.

Sirikit sat down and glanced at the clock. "Almost six. Shall I pour?"

I nodded.

She unscrewed the bottle, and poured water into the glasses. Letty had indeed held on to the last bottle, and she'd turned it upside down when the riot foam consumed her. The bottle, though, had escaped unbroken. Soni's last act before resigning as Chief of Police was to release it to me from evidence. The crime lab had gotten all the prints and chemical analysis it needed. It wouldn't figure into the trial, anyway.

Sirikit pulled the blinds closed and lit the candle. We clinked glasses and took a sip. The water was cool and clear and absolutely nothing like Old Windswept rum. But The Fear had kept silent since Sirikit laid out this course of treatment, and I would have to trust in that for the time being. I could feel The Fear lurking in the back of my brain, like a weight inside my skull. Maybe I wouldn't need to buy from the rebuilt distillery. Maybe I would. We'd see.

We put down our glasses. "Okay," she said. "Let's begin. Where are you?"

I closed my eyes and saw her tidy home. "In your house."

"Where's that?"

I pulled back in my mind's eye to see the little blue house with the red tuk-tuk in the garage. "Off Kripner Lane."

"Where's that?"

I smiled as I floated above the neighborhood. There was the minaret of the Emerald Masjid, there was the bell tower of Our Lady of the Big Shoulders. There was the lot where my old flat had been, now swept clear of wreckage and ready to be rebuilt. "In Brushhead."

"Where's that?"

There were the BBQ joints, the tiny theaters, the music conservatory. There were the strip clubs, the machinist shops, the rowhouses. "In the southwest part of Santee City."

"Where's that?"

There was our city, huddled between the kampong and the ocean. The green cane swayed in the evening breeze, and the crews and farmers made their way home, stacks of cane on their tractors and lorries. There was Thronehill, surrounded by a small army of students and kids. They had turned back everyone who tried to sneak out, even holding down the struts of their patrol craft. WalWa wasn't going anywhere, and neither were we. "On the eastern edge of the Big Island."

"Where's that?"

Off shore was Terminal Island, the mess of cargo cans clustered around the ground end of the lifter. The giant black ribbon soared into the sky, and I knew I was going to follow it up into orbit. "Twenty klicks away from the lifter."

"Where is it anchored?"

Up and up and up I went, shooting into the sky until we were at the anchor. WalWa may have paid to move the asteroid into orbit, but they hadn't done the work. Those first people who dropped the cable had shimmied their way to the ground and breathed that fresh air, gotten themselves windswept. I had started there, screaming my way out of a hibernant bag. Somewhere in my skull, I still might have been screaming. Maybe that's all The Fear was: my outraged brain demanding to know what I had done to it. "Thirty-six thousand kilometers above the surface."

"And what are you above?"

Oh, Santee Anchorage, you beautiful, messed-up dirtball. All those islands covered in cane, all the sea water pumped into the fuel cans for fusion drives, all us people clinging to the edge of Occupied Space. Soni and Onanefe and Meiumi Greene with an "e." They were all there, living and working and loving and dying. I never thought I would end up here. I never thought I'd want to stay here. But here I was. Here I would stay. "Santee Anchorage."

"And where is that?"

Back and back we went, away from the sun, away from our stellar cluster, away from our galaxy, out and out until I looked down on the whole of the universe. All those stars, all those worlds, all those hopes and dreams and deaths and dramas. One day, it would all come to an end, long after I was dust myself, long after the Big Three had consumed itself. Maybe they would figure out a way to cheat entropy and crack reality, opening the frontiers of a new market. I hoped not. But I also knew it was something I didn't have to deal with right now. All I had to do was remember my place in the universe, small as it was. I had to remind myself of how I fit into the whole, in my tiny way.

I opened my eyes. "Here. I'm right here."

Sirikit nodded. "Let's start."

I blew out the candle.

I still haven't dreamed yet. Maybe I never would. But, as I breathed in the air from the garden, I figured, hell, this would do.

AUTHOR'S NOTE

The song lyrics quoted in Chapter Twenty-Two are from "Solidarity Forever," written by Ralph Chaplin in 1915. It is sung to the tune of "John Brown's Body."

The song lyrics quoted in chapter twenty-four are from "Sit Down," written by Maurice Sugar in 1937. The author would like to thank Professor Sam Gindin of York University, who said to check with Kathy Bennett at UNIFOR, who said to check with the Walter P Reuther Library at Wayne State University, whence reference archivist Kristin Chinery appeared and wrote back to say that the song probably wasn't under copyright and that it would be okay to quote it. You can find the tune on YouTube or whatever video archive exists in your time period.

THE GOOD STUFF
AT THE END

This is the fastest draft I've ever written. It's also the first time I got paid for writing a book *before* I actually wrote it, so that probably figured into the speed. According to the plugin I use to keep track of how much work I do (because the world is ruled by metrics), I started on December 12, 2014 and finished on June 9, 2015. A lot happened between those two dates: the murders of Freddie Gray and Walter Scott at the hands of the police, Greece's struggle with the EU's moneyed class, the fight for a $15 an hour minimum wage in the United States. They're baked into this book. How can they not be? I have probably done an incredibly terrible job at incorporating them into *Like a Boss*, so all the fault is mine. You can yell at me on Twitter @rakdaddy.

Right now, as I write this little afterthought, it's July 20, 2015. I'm in my wee apartment in Santa Monica, and it feels like we're at the equator. It's hot and muggy. Hurricane Dolores has just dumped enough water over the Southwest to wash away a bridge on the 10, and the air feels like it has another foot of rain ready to unload. It's a slightly better disaster than the one that hit a few days ago, when a brush fire swept across the 15, forcing people to abandon their cars and run for their lives. Rain and freeways are the things that allow for the ridiculous lifestyle we have in our corner of the continent, and they're not getting along well. I would argue we don't have enough rain because we have too many freeways (and we also have too many fires because we have too many freeways), but it's an argument that means engaging with the kind of people who would be all too happy to sign their lives away to the likes of the Big Three.

Of course, I might, too. Comfort beats the hell out of starvation, but that comfort comes at a monstrous price (environmental degradation, workers living in near-slavery conditions, and the continuing presence of the chattering classes that populate our current political discourse). I would prefer that our generation pay that price as quickly as possible so my daughter and my nieces and nephews don't have to, and God knows I spend too much time thinking about it. I haven't come up with a solution. If there's a third book in this series, I'll probably have to address all the joy that is the post-capitalist (or pseudo-post-capitalist, or the Oh-God-We're-All-Screwed) era, though it's going to need a few jokes to make the whole thing palatable. Laughing at entropy might be the best way to cope with the inevitable. It certainly beats punching each other in the face.

Some people to thank:

– Joshua Bilmes, Sam Morgan, and everyone at JABberwocky Literary who continue to cheerlead, give good advice, and get me to sing when I'm on speakerphone.

– Mike Underwood, Phil Jourdan, Penny Reeve, and Marc Gascoigne at Angry Robot. Top bants and a cheeky Nandos all round, what?

– Myke Cole, Wes Chu, Greg van Eekhout, Jenn Reese,

and John Berlyne, who all provided invaluable career and writing advice in the last year but I didn't mention them in the first book so here you go.

– Molly Crabapple, Teju Cole, Kelly Sue DeConnick, Daniel José Older, G Willow Wilson, Ta-Nehisi Coates, Jamelle Bouie, Dahlia Lithwick, and Warren Ellis, none of whom I've ever met but whose essays, books, drawings, and Tweets are really, really important for fermenting my brain juices. You should buy everything they have ever written.

– Sofia Samatar, Kameron Hurley, Ramez Naam, Brenda Cooper, and Madeline Ashby, whom I *have* met and are also really important in the brain juice fermentation department. You should also buy everything they have ever written.

– The Freeway Dragons, for their continued awesomeness.

– Daryl Gregory, even though he hasn't read this book, but I keep thanking him so why break with tradition?

– Yuki Saeki, whose name I misspelled in the acknowledgements for *Windswept*. Sorry about that, Yuki. I am a terrible slef-editor.

– The staff at La Monarca, who never asked me to leave despite my hogging table space all morning. Thank you for the pineapple danishes and Café Oaxaca.

– My parents, especially my mom, who got Texas Instruments kicked off the campus of UCLA because they wouldn't interview her because she was a woman. Take *that*, TI!

– My brother, his wife, and my niece. Hi, kid! I hope you read this book when it's age appropriate, because I want to keep getting invited to Thanksgiving.

– My amazing wife, Anne, who has made this all possible. I hope I can pay you back one day, love.

– Our daughter, Grace, who's in this book and was impressed when I told her that. I hope she remains impressed.

– You, because you liked the first book enough to buy the second. Writing books is the only job I ever wanted, and every book is a new job interview. Thank you for hiring me for this job. Go get yourself a taco. You earned it.

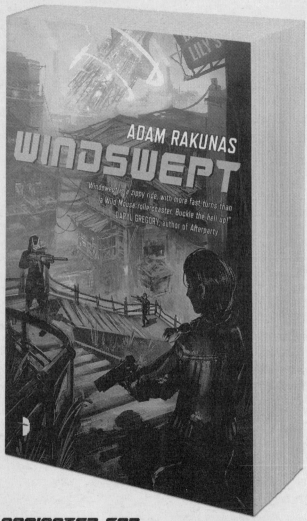